The Salvation of Poetry

A Novel

SUE MAGRATH

Tracy —
Your spiritual
companionship
has been a blessing
to me. Love,
Sue

"Fog" from THE COMPLETE POEMS OF CARL
SANDBURG. Copyright © 1969, 1970 by Lillian Steichen
Sandburg. Reprinted by permission of HarperCollins Publishers.
All rights reserved.

THE POEMS OF EMILY DICKINSON, edited by Thomas H.
Johnson, Cambridge, Mass.: The Belknap Press of Harvard
University Press, Copyright © 1951, 1955 by the President and
Fellows of Harvard College. Copyright © renewed 1979, 1983 by
the President and Fellows of Harvard College. Copyright © 1914,
1918, 1919, 1924, 1929, 1930, 1932, 1935, 1937, 1942, by Martha
Dickinson Bianchi. Copyright © 1952, 1957, 1958, 1963, 1965, by
Mary L. Hampson.

"Do Not Go Gentle Into That Good Night" (one-line excerpt)
By Dylan Thomas, from THE POEMS OF DYLAN THOMAS,
copyright ©1952 by Dylan Thomas. Reprinted by permission of
New Directions Publishing Corp.

Prayer from Contemporary Worship 5 copyright © 1972 Augsburg
Fortress. Used by permission.

Cover photo: Denise McGuiness

Author photo: Shauna Magrath

DEDICATION

To my mother, who quoted poetry to me from the time I was a young child. This book would never have happened without her. I miss her more than words can say.

"When I was drowning, poetry saved me."

-Seher Kaur

PART I

SPOKANE

1944—1959

Chapter 1

Deep fog descends
Dark miasma of despair
Blotting sight
Smothering hope
Feeding my dis-ease.
　　　　—Emily

1944

The telegram fluttered to the floor, already stained with tears. In a nearby wingback chair, Madeline Snow clutched her daughter in her lap, Emily's tiny frame wracked by inconsolable sobs. The father she had loved was gone, cut down by the savagery of war on the beaches of Normandy and lost to them both forever. Madeline felt engulfed by her grief. It seemed as though she was grieving for Emily too, for all the things it would mean to grow up without a father's love. Daniel, like many others, had joined the army in the aftermath of Pearl Harbor, when Emily was almost five. Now seven, she had few clear memories of her father, and the telegram had put an end to any hope of more.

I should have prayed more, or differently, Madeline thought. She had never felt comfortable asking God to protect her husband when so many women were losing theirs. How could she put Daniel's life above all the others? Instead, she had prayed for strength and courage for them all, the soldiers and the families they had left behind, and for a swift end to the war. Would it have made a difference, she wondered, if I had asked God to save him? But she knew that God was powerless against the brutality of those who would make war, instead offering solace to the people who turned to Him in their darkest hour. "I need that solace now, God," she prayed, "and guidance to help me navigate a future without Daniel. Help me love Emily enough for two."

Gradually, Emily's sobs subsided, and she raised her head. "What are we going to do, Mama," she asked plaintively.

"We're going to live, Emily, and we're going to laugh again, but not today. Today, we're just going to hold onto each other." Madeline bent down and gently kissed her daughter on the forehead, tears glistening in a ray of sun that slanted through the living room window.

1958

Emily awoke to a familiar raw ache in her loins. The familiarity, the frequency of it, made it no less painful. Even so, the physical pain was a mere shadow compared to the mystifying darkness and sense of foreboding that descended each time her husband came to her for the satisfaction of his manly urges—four nights a week, week in and week out. The only variance in this routine had occurred once when a stomach ailment had rendered George incapable of anything other than reclining weakly in bed clutching a basin in which to wretch with astonishing frequency. Despite the demands of tending him in his illness, it had been the most peaceful week of Emily's married life.

Eyes falling on the bedside clock, Emily gave a start and quickly rose from her bed. She dressed hurriedly and began drawing George's bath. As soon as she turned off the taps, she heard his alarm sound. Satisfied that the water was the perfect temperature, Emily returned to the bedroom, murmured, "Good morning, darling," and continued on into the kitchen.

She carefully measured the coffee, leveling the cup with precision before pouring it into the basket to perk. Two slices of bread went into the toaster, two eggs slid gently into boiling water for poaching, the same breakfast every morning. As Emily prepared the eggs, still caught in the dark tunnel of dread that had awakened her, a wave of nausea passed over her such that she had to sit suddenly and put her head to her knees. Seconds ticked away, a minute, maybe more, before she became aware of the sounds of George dressing in the other room. Quickly, she poured his coffee and laid his plate of food on the table just as he entered the kitchen. Never one for morning conversation, George sat down and took a sip of his coffee. A small nod communicated his approval. He cut into his eggs, then paused. "Emily darling, did you set a timer for the eggs?"

"Oh, dear! I forgot. I'm so sorry. I felt faint for a moment and had to sit down. It must have been longer than I thought."

"Well, it's too late for sorry now. You've ruined these eggs, and I don't have time to wait for you to make more. We can ill afford to waste food, Emily, or did you think we had money to burn?" George stood and dumped his eggs into the waste bin, glaring at his wife. "Enjoy *your* breakfast, Emily," he said as he thrust the empty plate at her and slammed the door behind him.

Emily's knees buckled, and she sank to the floor. The tears that had been lurking could be contained no longer, and Emily gave in to them, sobs clawing at her throat as they burst from deep within.

After a day of cleaning and ironing, Emily glanced through the kitchen window, anxiously awaiting George's arrival. She hoped he would be pleased by her efforts so they could have a pleasant evening without the tensions that had started the day. Though exhausted, she had bathed and paid special attention to her appearance. The table was set with the good china, dinner warming in the oven, a lovely piece of Dover sole for this Friday meal along with scalloped potatoes, George's favorite. When she saw George pulling into the driveway, Emily checked her reflection in the glass, tucking back a stray strand of her hair and smoothing her skirt. Then, with a deep breath, she went to greet her husband at the kitchen door.

It became immediately apparent that George had made some preparations of his own. He carried a small posy of flowers, which he handed to Emily as he kissed her cheek. "How are you feeling, my dear? I fear I was rather abrupt with you this morning and failed to inquire about your fainting spell. Are you alright?"

"Thank you, darling! I'm fine, just a little tired is all. Here, let me take your coat. Dinner is ready, and I think you'll be pleased."

Emily brought their meal to the table, and George bowed his head to offer the blessing. "Bless us, O Lord, and these Thy gifts, which we are about to receive from Thy bounty. Through Christ our Lord, Amen." They crossed themselves and began to eat. George exhaled a sigh of pleasure at his first bite of the sole, and Emily began to hope that they would enjoy an evening without tension. That hope was short-lived.

"What time do you want to go to confession tomorrow, Emily?"

Emily immediately felt bile rise in her throat. "Oh, George. I was hoping to skip confession this week. I still don't feel very well, and I thought a nice lie-in would help immensely. I guess I overdid it with the cleaning today, but I wanted you to come home to a spic and span house after your busy week."

A frown appeared on George's forehead. "Since when has it been acceptable to *skip* confession? I thought we had talked about this, and that you and I agreed that it was important for us to receive absolution on a weekly basis. Yet I constantly feel that if I didn't push the issue, you would stop going to confession altogether! I guess you think you don't have anything to confess. Is that it?"

"Of course not, darling. I just . . . sometimes I'm not in the right frame of mind. I'm sure God wants me to come to confession with the appropriate attitude of penitence, don't you?"

"Well, I suggest that you *get* in the right frame of mind. Unless you think you are without sin—do you think you're the Blessed Mother herself?"

"That's ridiculous! I would never presume that."

"I should think not! With as many faults as you have to confess—your laziness and wastefulness for starters—I should think you would make more of an effort to do penance. And that starts tomorrow, bright and early. I refuse to share my bed with a wife who is not in a state of grace."

Body slumped, eyes downcast, Emily barely whispered, "Yes, dear." Her appetite was gone, but she forced herself to swallow every bite for fear of further comments on her wastefulness. When dinner was over, she picked up the table and filled the sink with soapy water, choking back the tears that threatened to fall.

The rest of the evening was uneventful. Now that George had gotten what he wanted—her capitulation—he acted as though his earlier pique had never happened. When they went to bed, he fell asleep quickly, slipping into the deep breathing that signaled his demands for the day were over. But Emily lay next to him, wide awake, still troubled by her thoughts and overwhelmed by her unrelenting melancholy. She slipped out of bed and walked quietly to the window, looking out at the wintry streets. The sky was clear and cold, stars gleaming brightly as they often do in winter. There was something about the night sky that allowed Emily to breathe just a little easier and lifted some of the weight from her heart. She leaned toward the window until her forehead rested on the cold pane and wondered, will I ever feel warm again?

> The moon, barely conceived,
> Cries a feeble light,
> A dark pine knifes the sky.
> Still world, now void of day's occupation,
> has room for Pain and me.
> I uncurl and watch
> Pain expand and soar;
> I feel the rush of wings
> as it leaves the nest.
> Alone,
> I breathe my own breath
> 'til dawn,
> when Pain returns to roost
> and I must breathe for two.
> —Emily

Immediately after breakfast the next morning, George and Emily drove to their parish church. Emily knelt, shivering in the chilly sanctuary, praying for release from the overwhelming anxiety that hounded her each time she came to confession. She knew she was supposed to be seeking a state of repentance, but her sense of shame wasn't about anything she had actually done so much as about who she *was*, an inexplicable sense that she was innately bad. She found it strange that George actually seemed to enjoy confession, although what he might possibly confess to, she couldn't imagine. He seemed to believe that everything he did was perfect, and everything she did was deeply flawed. But it wasn't just her sin and shame that made her want to avoid confession, there was something about the confession booth itself that filled her with dread. It was as if a dark chasm opened up inside her and began pulling her inexorably toward it. No matter that Father McCaffrey was a genuinely nice man and rarely made her do any penance beyond a recitation of the rosary and a few "Our Fathers," every time Emily stepped into that tiny closet, her entire body felt paralyzed with fear.

This morning was no different. Giving up on any hope that prayer would help her, she got up from the kneeler and joined the line of penitents awaiting their turn. The closer she got to the front of the line, the greater her anxiety and dread until she could hardly breathe. Then suddenly, it was her turn. What would people think if she turned and ran? Would George come after her? Would they think she was crazy? Undoubtedly so, and truth be told, Emily was beginning to wonder herself. The narrow door yawned open, and somehow, she managed to put one foot in front of the other until she was inside. And then there was Father's pleasant voice and caring manner. Emily stuttered the litany of George's grievances with her, and the priest gave her the usual penance, reassuring her of God's forgiveness. As she left, full of relief, she berated herself as she did every time for her irrational thoughts, yet she knew that each week would be a repeat of the last. I really must be crazy, she thought.

1944

"Good morning, sleepy head! Time to rise and shine. We're going on an adventure today," Maddy said as Emily rubbed the sleep from her eyes.

"Where are we going, Mama?"

"Well, ladybug, we need to find another place to live. This house is too expensive for us now without Daddy's pay, and I need someplace close to bus routes so that I can sell the car. I've made a list of potential apartments, and we are going to take the bus to all of them."

Emily squealed and clapped her hands. "Yay! I love to ride the bus!"

"I thought that would make you happy. So let's get moving. Get dressed while I fix our breakfast, and then off we go!"

It didn't take long for Emily to pull on her clothes and wolf down a bowl of oatmeal. Then, the two of them walked to the bus stop hand in hand. Maddy tried to smile and be hopeful for Emily's sake, but inside she felt worried that they might not find a place that met their needs and sad that they would have to leave the home whose threshold Daniel had carried her over on their wedding night. After three bus rides and three apartments that were dirty and run-down, mother and daughter sat on a park bench to eat the sandwiches Maddy had made that morning. Emily's energy was flagging, and she looked as discouraged as her mother felt.

"I didn't like any of those places, Mama. What are we going to do? Do we really have to leave our house? Will we get to take our things with us?"

"Of course, we can take our belongings, Emily! That means your Raggedy Ann doll and your books and clothes and everything else that is ours. And yes, we really do need to move. We're going to have less money now, and I'm going to have to work more to make up for the money the Army paid Daddy. That means that I probably won't always be home when you get home from school, so I'd like to find a place where there are close neighbors who could check in on you from time to time. I know the places we looked at this morning weren't very nice, but I'm sure we will find something that is just right." Maddy flashed Emily a big smile and hoped that her daughter wouldn't see the doubts behind it.

After another two shabby apartments, the bus had lost its allure, and Emily's feet were dragging as they walked down the street to the last address on the list. The neighborhood looked nice enough, with neatly kept front lawns and paint that wasn't peeling off the exteriors of the homes. Finding the correct house number, they turned up the front walk and knocked on the door. A plump, gray-haired woman opened the door and smiled. "How can I help you, dears?"

"We've come about your advertisement for an attic apartment. Is it still available?"

"Why, yes dear! It certainly is. Would you like to see it?"

Daring to hope, Emily's mother nodded her head. "Yes, we'd love to see it. We haven't had much luck today."

Expecting to be invited in, she was surprised when the woman stepped out her door and led them around the side of the house toward the garage. "It's just around here, dear. I hope you don't mind stairs. It's up here over the garage."

Mother and daughter followed the woman up a set of steep stairs and into a cozy apartment. "Here it is. It's small, but clean, and the coal stove keeps it nice and warm in the winter. Oh! Where are my manners? I haven't introduced myself. I'm Mrs. McGill. I live here alone. My husband passed away two years ago, and my children live on the other side of town, so I like having someone living up here to keep me company."

"And I'm Maddy Snow, and this is my daughter Emily. My husband was killed in Normandy, and we can't afford to stay in the house we'd been renting. We're having to make a lot of adjustments right now, so finding someplace homey would certainly ease some of our worries."

"Oh, you poor dears! I'm so sorry to hear that you've lost your husband and daddy. He must have been very special."

Emily had been gazing around the room as the women talked, but she turned to look at the nice lady when she heard her father mentioned. She nodded at Mrs. McGill and said, "Yes, ma'am. He was the best daddy ever. I miss him a lot." Her lip trembled.

Maddy knelt down beside her and gave her a hug. "What do you think of this place, Ladybug?"

"I like it. It feels really cozy, and there's no holes in the floor like that other one we looked at."

"Yes, I like it too." Maddy rose to address Mrs. McGill. "I know this is a lot to ask, but if we take this apartment, would you be willing to keep an eye on Emily from time to time? I'm a nurse, and I'm going to have to be working longer hours at the hospital now and won't always be home when she gets home from school. She's very independent and capable, but I would worry about her being alone."

"Oh, lovie! Of course, I'd be delighted to watch over her for you! I miss the days when my own children were laughing and playing in the house. And you losing your husband to the war and all, it'd be my way of giving back for the sacrifice he made for our country."

A stray tear slipped down Maddy's cheek. "Thank you! I'm more grateful than I can say. Just having one thing less to worry about is such a relief! We love the apartment, and we'd love to live here. I think your ad said you were asking $75 a month. Is that correct?"

"Yes, dear. And that includes the coal for the stove. You'll just have to haul it up from the coal bin in my basement. I'm sure that won't be a problem for someone as young and vigorous as you."

The two women discussed terms of the agreement while Emily wandered around the single large room that combined kitchen and living room and the small bedroom and water closet under the eaves. Then they went back down the stairs and into the woman's house to sign a piece of paper. Soon Maddy and Emily were retracing their steps to the bus stop swinging their clasped hands, grateful to have found a new home. But the gratitude and excitement were dampened somewhat by the sadness at having to leave the only home Emily had ever known and the memories it held of a beloved husband and father.

Chapter 2

Oh the Earth was made for lovers, for damsel, and hopeless swain,
For sighing, and gentle whispering, and unity made of twain.
All things do go a courting, in earth, or sea, or air,
God hath made nothing single but thee in His world so fair!
—Emily Dickinson

1944

Emily and her mother were lying on the soft green grass, heads touching, hands intertwined, eyes focused on the brilliant blue expanse above them. This was one of their favorite pastimes, whether skies were blue, cloudy, or filled with stars. Despite the long hours that Maddy worked at the hospital and the myriad chores and errands that needed doing on her days off, she always made time for sky-gazing with her daughter. These were occasions for sharing deep thoughts or fanciful ones, for imagination and dreaming, for gossiping about the neighbors or expressing frustration with multiplication tables. And sometimes they would go for long periods of time without saying anything at all. It was into one of these prolonged silences that Emily spoke. "Mama, why do Grandma and Grandpa Hobbs hate us?"

Maddy hesitated a moment before responding. "Why do you think they hate us, Ladybug?"

"Well, I know that you write them letters, but they never write any back, not even when Daddy died. And they never come to visit us. Patty's grandparents come to see her all the time."

"I guess it could seem like they hate us when you put it that way. But I don't think they do. They just don't approve of the choices I've made. My parents are Catholic, and they were terribly upset when I married your father, because he was Lutheran. A lot of Catholics believe that theirs is the only true religion and that anyone who belongs to another religion is not going to go to heaven."

Emily sat up abruptly. "Does that mean that Daddy's not in heaven?"

"No, Ladybug. I am absolutely positive that your Daddy is up in heaven smiling down on us right now. Just because that is what Catholics believe about heaven doesn't make it so."

"But I still don't get why they won't talk to us or visit us at all. Doesn't Jesus teach us to treat people like we would want to be treated? Or don't Catholics believe in Jesus?"

Maddy smiled. "Of course Catholics believe in Jesus, Emily. But your grandparents are the kind of people who put following rules above loving people, and they refuse to associate with anyone who doesn't follow the same rules they do."

Emily pondered that for a minute. "But Patty is Catholic, and she doesn't do that. We play together at school all the time."

"Yes, I know you do. Patty is a lovely girl and a good friend. There are lots of Catholics who are loving and kind and follow the Golden Rule, but I think my parents are just very unhappy people who believe God is always waiting to catch us breaking the rules so he can punish us. That just never made any sense to me. I think God loves us all the time, even when we make mistakes. And I think God wants us to be happy. Your father made me happy, so I married him. And that's why Grandma and Grandpa Hobbs shut us out of their lives."

Finally satisfied, Emily lay back down and returned her gaze to the heavens, while Maddy's memories wandered back in time to the moment she met Daniel.

1935

Madeline Hobbs nervously smoothed her crisp white nursing uniform as she waited with the other nurses to walk rounds. She studied the positioning of their caps, fearing that hers was not on straight enough to satisfy the head nurse, who was known to be a stickler about such matters. Madeline had just completed three years of nursing school and was lucky enough to have been hired by Sacred Heart Hospital despite the challenges of finding a job during the Depression. There were plenty of her former classmates who were still looking for work, and she didn't want to join them by offending her supervisor on the first day. Taking a deep, calming breath, she glanced around the large ward. Hospital beds lined the long hall on both sides, and tall windows made the space feel light and airy. The linoleum floor was polished to a high sheen, and the smell of antiseptic filled the air. Madeline felt as though she might lift right off the floor. Nursing had been her dream since she was a little girl, and now she was finally here. She couldn't wait for the day to begin.

Just then, Nurse Connor strode up to the group of waiting nurses and cleared her throat. "Alright, ladies. I trust you're ready for rounds. We have a number of new patients today, so be on your toes. Nurse Hobbs, welcome to the staff. Pay close attention, and if you have questions, ask one of the other nurses. I'm afraid we'll all be running our feet off today." With that, she turned abruptly and walked to the first bed, where she picked up the patient's chart and rattled off his diagnosis, vital signs, and most recent doctor's notes. Turning to the young nurse standing next to Madeline, the head nurse asked, "Nurse Green, what will you need to do for this patient today?" As the nurse launched into a recitation of medications to be administered and symptoms of infection to watch for, Madeline's nerves increased at the thought of being put on the spot when her turn came.

The next two patients were assigned to Nurse Green as well, Nurse Wells got the next three, and so it went down the row of beds. Madeline began to relax and let her eyes wander. In the next bed lay a young, blond man with his left arm swathed in bandages and supported in a sling. Catching her eye, he winked at her. Madeline gave him a polite smile, which was cut short by the sound of Nurse Connor's voice saying her name, "Nurse Hobbs! Are you so sure of yourself that you don't need to listen to this patient's information? Even though he is not assigned to you, you may need to provide care if his nurse is occupied with another patient."

"No, ma'am! Uh, I mean, yes, ma'am. I'm sorry, Nurse Connor. It won't happen again," Madeline stammered, her face flushing bright red. And out of the corner of her eye, she could swear she saw the gentleman in the next bed grinning ear to ear.

Soon, the group of nurses was moving to this man's bedside, where Nurse Connor addressed Madeline again. "Nurse Hobbs,

Daniel Snow will be your patient. Please give us the run-down on his treatment."

If anything, the young man's grin got wider as Madeline picked up his chart and scanned it. Trying to pull herself together, she cleared her throat and began to speak in a manner which she hoped sounded cool and professional. "Mr. Snow is a 24-year-old white male with a dislocated left shoulder, a deep laceration to the forearm, and severe abrasions to his left side from an accident at the rail yard. He is currently on 25 milligrams of morphine every two hours for pain, given intravenously. His laceration will need to be bathed with antiseptic and the bandages changed regularly. The abrasions will also need to be debrided and irrigated with antiseptic. His most recent vital signs appear normal." Nurse Connor received her report with a nod and moved the group along down the room, but Madeline snuck a quick glance back at Daniel Snow, who dared to wink again. Madeline decided that he was an incorrigible flirt and resolved not to allow his charm to sway her from a professional reserve.

1945

As though reading Maddy's thoughts, Emily turned on her side, head on her hand, and said, "Mama, tell me again about when you met Daddy."

Maddy smiled. "Emily, you already know this story by heart. You could probably tell it yourself."

"I know, Mama, but I like hearing you tell it. You always look so happy."

"OK, then. I guess I could give you the short version." Maddy sat up and curled her legs under her. "I met your daddy on the first day I went to work at the hospital. He had had a bad accident at the rail yard. His hand got caught in the coupling of a car that was being moved to a side rail, and it dragged him and dislocated his shoulder. He was in a lot of pain, but that didn't stop him from flirting with me non-stop! I tried very hard to be professional, but I couldn't help but admire his positive attitude and his fun-loving approach to life. It was so different from the way I had been raised.

"And he had a serious side, too. While I was cleaning his wounds, we would talk about our hopes and dreams as a way of distracting him from the pain. Pretty soon we figured out that our dreams were the same. He kept asking me for a date, and I kept telling him that I couldn't date a patient, but that didn't stop him for long. About a week after he was discharged, he walked right up to me as I was leaving the hospital after work and said, 'I figure that I'm not your patient anymore, so how 'bout I take you to dinner?' He looked so handsome, and he smiled that irresistible grin of his and winked that wink, and well, I just couldn't say no. After that night, there were a lot more dinners, and long walks in the park, just talking and laughing, and six months later we were married. Your dad was the one who started calling me Maddy. He was a good man, Ladybug, and I've never for a moment regretted marrying him, even when my parents disowned me. I didn't get near enough time with him, but my memories of him will keep me company until the day I die. And we had you, and you are a blessing to me every single day." With that, Maddy's eyes welled up with tears.

Emily jumped up and threw her arms around her mother. "I'm sorry, Mama. I didn't mean to make you cry."

Maddy squeezed her daughter and laughed. "Oh sweetie, these are happy tears! I'm glad you made me tell the story again. It reminds me how lucky I am."

Relieved, Emily snuggled into her mother's embrace. "I love you, Mama. I'm lucky, too."

1957

Emily stood outside the bank, checking her reflection in the front window. She anxiously smoothed her skirt and ran a hand over her blond waves to make sure there was no hair out of place. It wasn't that she'd never been in the bank before, but today she was actually opening a savings account, something that felt very foreign and grown up. She had just gotten a raise from her job at the phone company after two years in their employ, and she was determined to start saving money for her future. She didn't exactly know yet what that future would be, but being alone in the world meant she had to be careful with her money. She wasn't sure that poor houses still existed, but her foster father had certainly instilled a fear of them with his frequent lectures about the consequences of extravagance.

Suddenly Emily was startled by the annoyed "Harumph" of a gentleman standing behind her. "Are you going in or not?" he said impatiently. She jumped and looked around, realizing that she was blocking the door.

"S-so sorry, sir!" she stammered. "I'll get out of your way." After he swept past her, Emily took a deep breath, straightened her jacket, squared her shoulders and pushed open the polished front door of the bank. Standing uncertainly in the center of the lobby, she looked around, unsure of where to go. She looked to her right, where a number men in suits and ties were working at imposing desks. Shining brass signs sat on each desk, indicating the name and position of its occupant. Emily stepped closer and scanned the signs, hoping for a clue as to who would be able to help her. At that moment, one of the men looked up from his work and met her eyes. Perhaps sensing her hesitancy, he rose and walked toward her with a smile.

"How can I help you, ma'am?" Something in his voice made Emily feel a sense of relief, that here was someone who would take care of her.

"Um, I was hoping to open a savings account."

"Excellent! I'm George Edwards, one of the account managers here, and I would be happy to help you. Come right this way." Mr. Edwards guided Emily to his desk with a solicitous hand on her elbow and pulled out a chair for her. "Please be seated. Now, let me find the necessary forms, and we'll get started."

Emily tried not to stare as he bent to pull several sheets of paper from his desk drawer. He wasn't the best-looking man in the world, but he obviously took great pains with his appearance. His brown hair was neatly combed with a precise part exactly in the center of his head. Emily didn't think she had ever seen a shirt so white in her life, and there were no creases to be seen. Even his tie was knotted perfectly. Papers in hand, Mr. Edwards tapped them on his desk to straighten the edges, then placed them carefully in the center of his desk. He looked at Emily and smiled. "Now, what is your name, young lady?"

As Emily provided answers to his questions—name, address, employer, marital status—he wrote them neatly on the forms. She was starting to relax when the next question floored her. "And who can we put down as a reference?"

"I, uh, what do you mean?"

"We need a reference, someone who can vouch for you. Someone we can contact if we are unable to reach you for any reason. The most logical choice for a young, single woman like yourself would be your parents."

Emily felt herself go cold. "My parents are both deceased," she replied, and to her horror, her eyes began to fill with tears. She hadn't had to say those words out loud for a long time, and the force of them hit her like a hammer.

"Oh, my dear! I'm so sorry. Please forgive my thoughtlessness. I should have known when you gave your address as a boarding house. And so young, too! Here, take my handkerchief. Can I get you a drink of water?" When Emily nodded her head, Mr. Edwards rushed off. Grateful for the moment to not have anyone looking at her, she dabbed at her tears and tried to pull herself together. It's not like her parents had died yesterday, for heaven's sake, she thought. Her father had died in the war, and her mother in an accident when Emily was just ten. Why this sudden spate of tears? Perhaps she was more aware of their loss now that she was no longer in foster care or school where there had been familiar adults who were shaping and guiding her. Now she was faced with the realities of making her way in the world without a family to support and care for her.

"Here you are, Miss Snow. Are you feeling better? I can't imagine the prospect of a young woman like yourself facing the future alone. Do you have any brothers or sisters? Is there a young man in your life?" Emily merely shook her head, still not trusting herself to speak. "How difficult for you!" Mr. Edwards suddenly looked around and became aware of eyes turned their way, alerted perhaps by his raised voice. Lowering his tone, he said, "Now let's figure out who we can put down as a reference. How about your landlady?" They made their way through the last of the details, and Emily gave him the twenty-five dollars she had put aside as a first deposit to her new account. Finally, he asked her to sign at the bottom of the form. Then, before she could withdraw her hand, Mr. Edwards reached over and laid his hand on hers. Lowering his voice still further, he said, "Now, Miss Snow, I know this might sound presumptuous, but if there is ever anything I can do for you, anything at all, please let me know. I'd like to think that I could be someone you could trust to come to for advice or a helping hand. I want you to know that there is someone who is watching out for you."

Emily rose, shook his hand, and thanked him for his kindness before exiting the bank. She walked a few steps before stopping to lean her back against the brick façade. She was aware of a strange mix of feelings—the grief and anxiety that had overwhelmed her in the bank alongside a rare sense of being cared for by Mr. Edwards' surprising offer. Emily looked down and noticed that she still clutched his handkerchief in her left hand. Given his immaculate appearance, there was no way she could return it to him in its current soggy and crumpled state. She would have to wash and iron it first, which would occasion an opportunity to see him again. A small smile turned up the corners of her mouth.

Three days later, Emily was again standing in front of the bank, this time with a strange flutter in her chest that she'd never felt before. Carefully folded inside her purse was a freshly laundered and ironed handkerchief. With a deep breath and a lift of her chin, Emily entered the lobby and turned her gaze toward George Edwards' desk. He was busy with another client, so she had an opportunity to observe him for a moment. Even though she couldn't hear his words, his manner was clearly friendly and polite. He listened carefully to the person in front of him before responding with a smile. There was an air of confidence about him that attracted Emily, a sense that here was a man of the world, one who could manage every situation with ease. He might not be the wittiest or most fun-loving person, but a girl could feel safe with a man like this.

At that moment, George looked up from his desk and caught her gaze. His face lit up with a smile, which just as quickly was suppressed as he turned back to his client, but he continued to sneak glances at Emily periodically as if to reassure himself that she was still standing there. Eventually, both men rose from their seats and shook hands, indicating an end to their business dealings. George followed his client across the lobby and stopped in front of Emily. "Miss Snow! How good to see you again! Is there something I can help you with?"

Emily found herself blushing under his attentive gaze. "No business today, Mr. Edwards. I've come to return the handkerchief you so graciously lent to me the other day." She withdrew the smooth linen square from her purse and handed it to him. His fingers inadvertently brushed hers as he took it, protesting that she needn't have bothered.

"That's very thoughtful of you. And since you're here," he said, "I wonder if you would consider it too forward of me to invite you to dinner on Saturday night?"

"I, um, why, no, I mean, yes, I mean . . ." Emily stammered. She took a breath and started again. "No, it's not too forward, and yes, I would be delighted to have dinner with you." She found herself smiling widely and wondered if she looked like a silly school girl swooning over a matinee idol.

But George's smile seemed equally as bright. "Lovely! I already have your address in your bank file, so shall I pick you up around seven?"

"Seven would be fine, Mr. Edwards. I look forward to it."

George's eyes suddenly flickered to a gentleman standing nearby, and his demeanor changed immediately. "Well then, Miss Snow, I'm glad I was able to resolve this issue for you. And now I really must let you get on with your day. Thank you for your business." He quickly returned to his desk and straightened the papers that still lay there from his previous customer. Emily watched as the other gentleman, who she presumed was the bank manager, abruptly turned heel and walked purposefully toward a large office at the rear of the bank. Without risking another glance at George, Emily left the bank.

She didn't walk home so much as she floated. "My first date!" she thought. The idea of being on the receiving end of a man's attention was utterly foreign and exciting to her. A professional man like George Edwards could have his pick of women, and yet he had chosen to focus his attentions on her! She wondered where he might take her, imagining a posh restaurant with candles on the tables. Then suddenly it struck her—what on earth would she wear?

At precisely ten minutes of seven on Saturday, Emily was standing in the downstairs drawing room, trying desperately not to chew on her lips, which would ruin the effect of her carefully applied makeup. She had a feeling that George would be punctual, and she didn't want to keep him waiting in the clean but shabby room. She checked her reflection for the tenth time in the ornately gilded mirror, hoping that her borrowed dress of blue silk was nice enough for the evening ahead. When she had come home from the bank that day, bemoaning her paltry wardrobe, Kathleen, who lived down the hall, had insisted Emily wear this dress she had bought for her own engagement party. Sadly, the engagement had ended only a few days later. "I've only worn it the once, Emily, and probably never will again at this rate, so somebody might as well get some use out of it!" The dress fit her perfectly and brought out the blue of her eyes. Taking a deep breath, Emily turned away from the mirror just in time to see George approaching the rooming house door.

Opening the front door, Emily watched the pleasure rise in George's face as he took in her appearance. "Emily, you look lovely! Every man in the Davenport will have his eyes on you tonight. Are you ready?" She nodded, and George offered her his arm and escorted her to his car. It was an older model Plymouth, but its shining exterior spoke of an owner who took excellent care of it. George appeared to be just as careful with his driving as he was everything else and spoke little on the short trip to the Davenport Hotel. Emily stared out the window, her anxiety growing as she contemplated eating dinner at the fanciest place in town. She hoped against hope that she wouldn't commit any faux pas in her ignorance of etiquette.

As they walked through the entrance to the Davenport lobby, Emily gasped with delight. "It's beautiful!" Crystal chandeliers hung from the vaulted ceiling, and the tables were set with snowy white linen and fine silver. The waiters all wore tuxedos as they brought food to the tables on gleaming silver trays.

"I thought you would like it," George responded, smiling at her obvious pleasure. They walked up to the maître d, who gave a slight bow to Emily before escorting them to their table. Once seated, Emily gazed around at her opulent surroundings, filled with wonder that she was actually here with such an attentive gentleman seated across from her. Then she opened her menu and suffered a shock when she saw the prices.

"George, it's so expensive!" She feared that his bank salary was not adequate to pay for this meal.

George smiled knowingly, and said, "Nothing but the best for you, my dear. I suspected that you had never been anywhere this sophisticated before, and I wanted you to have the experience. Please feel free to order whatever you like." Once they had ordered, George leaned back in his chair. "Now, Emily, please tell me more about you. I want to know everything!"

Emily told him haltingly about her parents' deaths, about her foster family, and her schooling. When she mentioned St. Ignatius Academy, he sat up a little straighter and said, "Oh, good, you're Catholic. That's all right, then."

Puzzled, Emily asked, "What do you mean?"

George smiled, "Well, I'm Catholic, too, and as you know, Catholics are not allowed to marry outside their faith. I wouldn't want to invest in a relationship that had no chance of going anywhere."

As the meaning of his remark sunk in, Emily was first startled and then flattered that someone like George would consider her marriage material. She began to feel a glow that started somewhere deep inside and slowly expanded until it emerged as a breathless smile. In truth, she had never seriously considered marriage. For some inexplicable reason, she had not believed that any man would want her. She had always been quiet and shy and tended to avoid situations that would focus attention on her. And now, here she sat across the table from a man who was clearly interested in more than just a casual date.

Emily's thoughts were interrupted by the waiter arriving with their food. With a flourish, he placed her plate in front of her. She looked at it in bewilderment. She had ordered prime rib, medium well. The meat on her plate was blood red. Noticing her reaction, George asks, "Is there something wrong, Emily?"

Not wanting to make a scene, she shook her head. "No, nothing. It's fine. Really."

"No, it's not fine. I remember, you ordered medium well." As he spoke, the color in his face rose, and he turned to the waiter with obvious irritation. "This is outrageous! The meat on her plate is practically still bleeding! It's unacceptable! Take it back immediately."

Clearly flustered, the waiter apologized profusely as he removed Emily's plate and promised to correct the problem. Emily was mortified to have caused such a scene. "That really wasn't necessary, George."

"Nonsense," he exclaimed. "Emily, you are young and unschooled in the ways of the world. You need to learn to stand up for yourself, or people will walk all over you. But you don't have to worry about any of that, because I'm here to take care of you now." Still flushed from embarrassment, Emily lowered her eyes, not knowing how to respond. For a moment, there was silence before George realized her discomfiture and reached across the table to take her hand. "Oh dear! I upset you. I'm so sorry, Emily. I didn't mean to make such a scene, but I wanted everything to be perfect for you tonight. I've been thinking about this all week, and I guess I was a little too anxious. I took it out on the waiter, and it wasn't called for. Can you forgive me?"

Emily smiled at him tremulously and squeezed his hand. "Of course I forgive you, George. Let's not give this another thought." As if on cue, her plate arrived, this time cooked to perfection, and they began to eat. The rest of the meal passed uneventfully with George telling her about his job and his ambitions. Emily remembered the look the bank manager had given him the other day, and said, "I hope I didn't get you into trouble for talking to me at the bank on Wednesday."

"Oh, no, it was nothing. Just a little reminder to be more attentive to people who might be waiting for help. I have a good enough service record that I have nothing to worry about."

All too soon, the evening was over, and George was walking Emily to the door of her boarding house. Sudden anxiety fluttered inside her as she realized that she had no idea how first dates are supposed to end. Should I let him kiss me? Should I just extend my hand for him to shake? Say "good night" and walk through the door before he has a chance to do anything? Too late! George had stopped and turned her to face him. "Thank you for a wonderful evening, Emily. I hope you enjoyed it as much as I did."

Emily managed to stammer, "Yes, yes I did," just as he began to lean in. His lips met hers softly, gently, not insistent, but inviting. She felt herself responding, returning the pressure, inexplicably feeling a flush grow in the core of her. Then he backed away and smiled. He said goodnight and turned to walk to his car as Emily continued to stand there, breathless. What was this strange stirring inside her, she wondered. Excitement and desire wrestled with shame in a confusing cocktail, and somewhere hidden within, something dark and dangerous began to awaken.

Strangely, as she fell asleep, it was not their date or the kiss that was on her mind, but her mother and father, whose love story transcended all the artificial divisions and conventions that human beings could devise.

1944

Maddy was home on a rare day off from the hospital, enjoying the quiet as she ironed her uniform and waited for Emily to get home from school. She was hoping she could finish her chores in time for them to take a walk to the park before dinner. It was a fine autumn day, and nothing would be better than she and her daughter walking hand in hand, smelling the scent of red and gold leaves that fluttered and fell along the streets of Spokane. Life without Daniel was hard, and working long hours as a nurse meant there was too little time to spend with her precious Emily. Nonetheless, Maddy was grateful for a decent place to live, a helpful neighbor who watched over Emily when Maddy was at work, and the ability to earn a living wage when so many others were struggling to put food on the table.

Breathing a prayer of thanks, Maddy picked up the pile of folded sheets to put in the linen closet, when suddenly Emily threw open the door. Her face was flushed and damp with tears, sobs bursting from her chest. "Emily! What is it?" Maddy cried as she dropped the sheets and enfolded Emily in her arms. Emily continued to cry inconsolably for some time, until the strength and comfort of her mother's embrace gradually seeped into her, and the sobs subsided into hiccup-y breaths.

"They called me a baby, Mama. They were so mean! I'm

never going to school again!"

"Goodness, Emily! What on earth happened to make you say that? You love school! Now, take a deep breath, and tell me all about it. Who hurt your feelings like this?"

"It was that nasty Jimmy Gates. He always teases me, but today was even worse. And he got his friends to make fun of me, too."

"But what were they teasing you about? Start at the beginning."

"Well, Mrs. Van Patton was giving out our English assignment for this week. She wanted us to write a theme on 'What My Father Does for a Living,' and I started to write it down in my notebook, but then I started to cry, because I don't have a daddy anymore." Emily's eyes filled with tears again as she remembered the difficult moment.

"Oh, Ladybug, I'm so sorry. Didn't Mrs. Van Patton remember that you lost Daddy in the war?"

Emily nodded. "She did when she saw me crying. Then she apologized and gave me a different topic. She yelled at the kids who were snickering, but it didn't do any good. Jimmy and Bobby and Stewart chased me after school and called me a crybaby. They blocked the sidewalk so I couldn't get past them, and pretended to cry like babies, and then just laughed when I told them to stop and let me go home. They made me so mad! Am I a crybaby, Mama? "

"Absolutely not! You are tough and strong, and don't ever let anyone tell you otherwise! I bet those kids don't know how hard it is to lose a father. You are Mama's little helper, and you never complain about the chores you have to do to help me. I know you get sad sometimes and cry about how much you miss your daddy, but that's normal. It's really hard to lose someone you love so much, and crying is an important part of letting those feelings out. But when you're done, you pick yourself up and get back to doing everything you can to help me out and do your school work and be the kind and loving girl that you are. Your smile is what gives me the strength to wake up every morning and go to work and soldier on without your dad!"

Emily's eyes had grown wider and wider as Maddy grew more and more emphatic. "You sound mad, Mama."

Maddy smiled and let out her breath, suddenly aware that her indignation at her daughter's tormenters could be misperceived. "Well, I am mad at those boys for what they did to you. It was very cruel of them to make fun of you when they have no idea what it's like to lose their own fathers. But what I really want you to know is that there are going to be a lot of people in this world who call you names and accuse you of being something you are not. And you can't let their words make you doubt yourself. You are a very special little girl, and I never want you to forget that. No matter what anybody says about you, you must always stay true to who you are. You are smart and independent and strong, and I love you more than you could possibly imagine. Now, how about a walk in the park?"

Emily's face brightened, and she threw her arms around her mother's neck. "Yes, Mama! And maybe an ice cream cone, too?"

1957

Emily and George sat on a blanket in Manito Park in late May, having just enjoyed a picnic dinner Emily had prepared. They had been stepping out together for several weeks now and were increasingly more comfortable in each other's company. Emily had just finished telling George about the time her mother had brought her to this same park to distract her from a bad day at school. They had brought breadcrumbs to feed the ducks at the pond, and both of them had somehow tripped over each other and fallen in the water. Mother and daughter had laughed so hard, it took several minutes to pull themselves together and regain their footing on the slippery bottom so they could climb out. George chuckled as Emily told the story and said, "I wish I could have met your mother. She sounds like a wonderful woman. But I don't think I would have been able to go get an ice cream afterwards with all that slimy algae all over me. Yuck!"

"She *was* a wonderful woman, and a loving mother," Emily replied, "but George, you've told me nothing about your parents. What were they like?"

George's face darkened. "Well, my dad was in the war, too, and sometimes I wish he hadn't come home at all. But he did. He had always been particular about things and had a hot temper, but it got much worse after the war. If I didn't do something exactly the way he wanted, he would yell and scream at me and wallop me with his belt. And then he started drinking, too. He would be drunk half the day and then go out at night and drink more with his old army buddies. He and Mom fought all the time, and he would threaten to leave, but she would always give in and beg him to stay. She just couldn't tolerate the thought of being without him. Even when he wasn't drunk, it was like being around a powder keg. There were plenty of times when I went to school with bruises, but the nuns never said a word."

"Oh, George! I'm so sorry. That sounds awful. Are your parents still alive? Whatever happened to them?"

"Mom is still alive. She moved to Portland to live with her sister when I moved away from home. She couldn't stand being alone, and truthfully, I was glad to have someone else looking after her for a change. I don't know where my dad is or even if he's still alive. He left when I was fourteen. Woke me up in the middle of the night to say he couldn't take it anymore. He was stone cold sober for the first time in ages, and he told me he was leaving and not coming back. He said I was the man in the family now and probably had been for longer than he cared to admit. He told me to take care of my mom. Then he shook my hand, said 'I love you, son' and walked out the door. I never saw him again."

Emily took George's hand in hers. "How sad for you! I can't imagine what it must have been like to shoulder all that responsibility from such a young age. No wonder you are so mature and so successful! You've really had to be."

George smiled slightly and said, "Let's change the subject. What about you? I've never been able to figure out why you were living in the boarding house even before you finished high school. What happened to your foster parents?"

Emily sighed. "Well, my foster parents had so many medical bills, what with Mother's illness, that when I turned eighteen and social services stopped paying for my care, they decided they couldn't afford to support me anymore. Their own kids were older by then and didn't need me to watch them as much, which is the only reason they fostered me in the first place. So on my eighteenth birthday, they gave me two weeks' notice to find another place to live and get out of their house."

"They threw you out into the cold, cruel world just like that? It's appalling! I don't know how you managed to find a room and a job and still finish high school at the same time. I mean, thank goodness you did, but you must have felt so scared and alone. Emily, I don't ever want you to be alone in this world again. I want to be the one to take care of you and protect you for the rest of your life." He stopped for a moment and took a deep breath. "Will you marry me?"

Emily gasped. "George! This is so sudden! I mean . . . I don't know what to say. I . . . but . . . well, of *course* I'll marry you. Oh, George!" She fell into his arms as he gave her an ardent kiss.

"I love you, Emily, and I promise I will make you happy. Let's go and look at engagement rings over lunch hour on Monday, shall we?" Both smiling broadly, they began to plan their life together.

Later, they took a final stroll through the park's renowned rose garden as evening fell. Emily had always loved being surrounded by these amazing red, pink, and yellow roses, their fragrance wafting through the air and perfuming every breath. She let out a huge sigh of contentment. George stopped and pulled Emily into the shadows of a weeping willow. He took her into his arms and bent his head to kiss her. His kiss was urgent, more passionate than ever before, and Emily responded eagerly, clinging to him with matching passion. Breathlessly, almost frantically, George pulled her more tightly into his embrace. Emily was giddy, overwhelmed by the intensity of the moment, when she felt something hard and unyielding pushing against her belly. Confused, she broke off the kiss, and George pushed her from him and turned away.

Voice breaking, he said, "I'm sorry, Emily. Forgive me. That was shameful. I shouldn't have forced myself on you like that. You're just so beautiful, and I love you so much. Can you forgive me?"

"I forgive you. How could I not? I love you, too, and I didn't exactly push you away. Please look at me, George. There's no need for you to feel ashamed."

George turned back to face her and gave her a twisted smile. "Well, I think there is, but thank you for your graciousness. But then, that's who you are, isn't it? Our wedding cannot possibly happen soon enough for me. I can't wait to start spending the rest of my life with you." He gave her a gentle kiss on the cheek and said, "Let's get you home. It's starting to get chilly."

During the drive back, Emily began to feel slightly queasy and unsettled. As soon as George walked her to the door, she ran upstairs to her room, puzzled by this unexpected feeling. It had been a wonderful day, topped off by George's sudden proposal of marriage, yet her happiness felt dampened in the same way that gathering clouds took away the brightness of a lovely summer's day. Suddenly a knock at the door interrupted her thoughts. Emily shook her head as if to clear her mind of confusion and opened the door. Kathleen burst in, eager for news of the date. Ever since their first date, she had been living vicariously through Emily's experience of first love. Kathleen threw herself on the bed, gushing, "Well? Tell me all about it. Where did he take you? You look positively glowing. C'mon, spill the beans."

Emily broke into a brilliant smile, and said, "You'll never guess. George proposed!!"

"What?! He didn't! Oh, Emily, that's wonderful! Sit down. I want to hear every word."

Laughing, Emily flopped down next to Kathleen and related her entire day, from beginning to end, especially the part where George told her he wanted to take care of her for the rest of her life. Their happy conversation moved from the proposal to wedding plans and back again before another of the residents stuck her head in the door. "Hush, you two, before Mrs. Olsen comes up here and reads you the riot act!" Reluctantly, the girls hugged each other good night, and Kathleen tiptoed back to her room.

Sitting in front of the mirror to brush her hair before getting into bed, Emily realized that she was still smiling. Sharing her good news with Kathleen had banished the dark thoughts from her mind. *And that's as it should be,* thought Emily. *This has been the best day of my life. Now I'll never be alone again.*

Nonetheless, sleep did not come easily. Excitement kept her mind spinning, while a slender thread of foreboding lurked unseen in the shadows.

Likewise, George was far from sleep as he lay in the dark. Their passionate kiss had created in him an agonizing state of arousal and shame. He groaned in his misery, praying for a release that would not come. His Catholic upbringing prevented him from pleasuring himself, and even the fact that he wanted it so much felt like a sin. In his desperation, he began reciting the Hail Mary over and over until finally the feelings began to wane, but as he gradually slipped into slumber, he could swear he heard his mother's voice calling out for him, pleading as she had done so many times, "Georgie, please come and sleep with me. I'm so lonely. I just need you near me. Please, Georgie."

Chapter 3

I never lost as much but twice,
And that was in the sod.
Twice have I stood a beggar
Before the door of God!
—Emily Dickinson

1947

Snow was falling heavily, as it had all afternoon, when Emily, now ten, climbed the outdoor staircase of their attic apartment. She loved the little apartment with its interesting nooks and crannies, its sloping ceilings and dormer windows. While others might have thought it cramped, Emily considered it a cozy nest for their family of two. The main room housed both the kitchen in one corner and a small living area with a couch and rocking chair in front of the coal stove that was their source of heat. There was a small bathroom and a bedroom under the eaves that Emily shared with her mother. The side by side twin beds always made her feel safe and content when she snuggled under the covers at night. What else could one possibly need?

Kicking the compact snow from her boots, Emily opened the door, dropped her schoolbooks on the floor, and shrugged off her winter coat, leaning out to brush off as much of the white powder as possible onto the stoop. During the winter, mopping up melted snow was almost a daily chore, and she was attempting to save herself the extra work. It was the week before Christmas, and Emily and her mother had plans to decorate their tree tonight. Tingling with anticipation, Emily got out a big pot and a bag of popcorn kernels. Stringing popcorn into long garlands was one of her favorite holiday traditions, and she wanted everything to be ready when her mother got home. A glance at the clock told her that she still had an hour in which to do her homework. Retrieving the books from the floor where she had left them, Emily spread her work out on the kitchen table and began tackling the vexing math problems Mrs. Butler had assigned at the closing bell.

Maddy glanced out the hospital window at the curtain of snow blotting out any view of the buildings across the street. She still had another hour on her shift, and the buses would be running extra slow on a day like this. She worried about Emily being home alone for too long on the best of days, and it looked like this storm was going to make Maddy late for their special evening. Just then, Nurse Connor joined Maddy at the window.

"Thinking about Emily at home by herself in this blizzard, aren't you?" she said. Then, before Maddy could respond, she added, "It's slow here. Why don't you clock out early and go home?"

Maddy turned in disbelief. Normally Nurse Connor was all business, following hospital policy to the letter. "Are you sure, ma'am? Won't the other nurses be upset?"

"Don't you worry about them, Nurse Snow. You work rings around them most of the time anyway. They can pick up your slack for once. Now get out of here!"

"Thank you. Oh, thank you! If I hurry, maybe I can catch the 3:15 bus and get home before the conditions get any worse. Good night, Nurse Connor. Be safe tonight."

Maddy hurried to get into her coat and boots, wrapping a bright red scarf around her neck as she ran down the stairs and made her way out into the storm. She was in such a rush that she almost ran into an elderly woman who was standing on the sidewalk outside the hospital shivering in the cold. Her coat was threadbare, and the woman was whimpering as her body shuddered.

"Oh, my goodness! What are you doing standing here in this miserable weather? You'll freeze to death!" Maddy shouted over the wind.

In a barely audible voice, the woman replied, "My doctor just released me from the hospital, and I'm waiting for my son to pick me up, but it's taking so long."

"Well, let's get you inside where it's warm. Someone in the hospital can keep an eye out for your son, while you have a cup of hot tea." Maddy put an arm around the woman and steered her back inside the hospital, settling her in a chair away from the door where she wouldn't be exposed to the draft as people entered and exited. Then Maddy went over to the discharge desk and fixed her gaze on the clerk sitting there. "What on earth were you thinking?" she hissed. "That woman has been standing out in this weather for who knows how long, and you just LET her! She's barely able to stand up, for heaven's sake!"

The young clerk's cheeks reddened. "I'm sorry, Nurse Snow, but she said her son would be here any minute. How was I to know?"

"Well, if you'd look outside, you'd know that nobody is getting anywhere in just a few minutes! Get her a cup of tea to warm her up, and then keep your eye on the sidewalk for her son. Find out what kind of car he drives, and when he gets here, I want you to personally walk her out there and not leave her until she is safely in the car. Do you hear me?"

"Yes, Nurse Snow. I'll take care of it. I'm sorry."

Damnation! Maddy thought as she hustled back out the door. *Now I'll never make the bus.* Lowering her head against the wind, she walked as quickly as she could through the snow toward the bus stop a block away. When she arrived, she saw a large crowd of people standing there. "Oh, good! I didn't miss it," she said to no one in particular.

A tall man in a navy great-coat turned and looked at her. "All of the buses are running at least fifteen minutes late today. The streets are a nightmare."

"Well, just as long as I get on this bus and don't have to wait for another one, I'll be alright," Maddy replied. She huddled close to the rest of the group for warmth, using their bodies as a shield from the wind. Still, it was a relief to see the bus coming down the street and sliding to a stop in front of them. Relief turned to dismay as she saw that the seats were already full.

The bus driver opened the door, shouting, "Standing room only, folks! Standing room only!" People began filing on, gradually crowding the aisle, until the only place left was right next to the bus driver. Maddy was the last to get on the bus, and all she was thinking was that she couldn't wait to get home to the warmth of her apartment and the embrace of her daughter.

The bus driver peered through the small area of windshield that wasn't fogged up, trying to navigate the deep snow that had been piling up all day. The snow plows couldn't keep up with the onslaught, and most streets were at least six inches deep in wet, sticky snow. The bus tires slipped and slid, then grabbed and lurched, while the bus driver held onto the steering wheel for dear life. The standing passengers swayed, sometimes falling into the laps of people sitting on the aisles. Signaling a left turn on Tenth Avenue, the driver slowed to negotiate the sharp turn. Midway through the intersection, the bus began to slide, and then there was a sudden impact at the right rear, altering the bus's course. Out of control, the bus driver could only watch in horror as shoppers in the corner grocery looked up to see the bus looming closer and closer. Then the world exploded into screams and shattering glass.

Emily was almost done with a short essay for English class when the phone rang. She got up from the kitchen table and lifted the receiver from its cradle. "Hello, Snow residence."

"Oh, Emily dear, I'm glad you're home safe! This is Mrs. McGill. Is your mother home yet?" Mrs. McGill kept an eye on Emily when her mother was working, and she was a bit of a busybody, but pleasant and kind.

Glancing at the clock, which read four o'clock, Emily replied, "No, Mrs. McGill. She's just now getting off work. She won't be home for another half hour or so."

"Oh, good! I was so worried. There's been a horrible accident down at the corner. A bus drove right into the front of Anderson's Grocery, and there are ambulances and police cars everywhere! I couldn't get close enough to see anything, but a lot of the bystanders were crying. Who knows how many people were killed or injured! Well, let me know when your mother gets home, Emily. And it might be a good idea for you to shovel the steps so she doesn't slip in the snow when she does arrive."

"Okay, Mrs. McGill. I'm almost done with my homework, so I'll take care of it. Thanks for calling."

"You're such a good girl, Emily. Your mother is lucky to have you. Have a good evening, dear!" With that, she hung up, no doubt bustling off to her next task, always in motion.

Emily placed the phone onto the cradle and put the finishing touches on her assignment. Then she stacked her books neatly on the table, bundled up in her boots and coat, and braved the wind and cold to shovel the deepening snow off the stairs. By the time her task was done, she had completely forgotten about the accident Mrs. McGill had described. Having some time to spare, Emily curled up on the couch with a warm blanket and her new favorite book, *Pippi Longstocking*. Absorbed in the engaging tale, time passed without notice. Finally, at the end of a chapter, Emily checked the clock and frowned. It was now 5:15. Mama should have been home thirty minutes ago. *The buses must be really slow,* Emily thought. She wondered if she should start re-heating the leftover stew from the night before so that it was hot and ready when her mother walked in the door. She decided to give it a few more minutes and returned to her book, but was more conscious of time passing. At six o'clock, she stood up, anxious, but not quite knowing what to do. She went to the window, hoping to see her mother walking down the street, but her view was obliterated by the continued onslaught of snow.

Emily began restlessly pacing the floor, watching the clock almost constantly. Time slowed to a crawl, each minute an eternity, as she waited to hear footsteps on the stairs or the ring of the phone. Six thirty came and went. Then six forty-five. Finally, Emily couldn't wait any longer. She called Mrs. McGill.

"Mrs. McGill, my mom's not home yet, and I don't know what to do. Even if the buses are running late, she should have been here by now. Do you think she decided not to wait for the bus and got lost in the snow?"

"Oh, dear! I'm sure she's fine, Emily, but maybe I'll just call the hospital to see when she left. She might have had to work late if other nurses couldn't make it through the snow in time for their shift. I'll find out and let you know as soon as I can."

Emily flopped down on a kitchen chair in relief. *That must be it,* she thought. *She just had to work late. But usually she calls me if that happens. Maybe the phones at the hospital are out. Maybe they're snowed in!* Emily's thoughts spiraled downward in ever more fearful circles. Time passed. The ticking of the clock became almost deafening.

Emily's stomach was gnawing in hunger and twisted with alarm. At long last, she heard footsteps on the stairway.

Racing to the door, she peered out to see if it was her mother. But the feeble light at the bottom of the stairs revealed a shorter, rounder silhouette than that of Maddy. It was Mrs. McGill, followed by a much taller figure with broad shoulders. Trembling, Emily opened the door.

It was indeed their landlady, and when the man with her entered the room, Emily saw that he was a policeman. Paralyzed with fright, speechless, Emily allowed Mrs. McGill to steer her into the living room and seat her on the couch. The policeman sat on a chair opposite Emily and removed his hat.

"You're Emily Snow, daughter of Madeline Snow?" he asked gently.

Numbly, Emily nodded her head.

"I'm Officer Flynn from the Spokane Police Department. Emily, I'm so sorry to have to tell you that your mother was killed in a bus accident this afternoon. She was sent home early from the hospital, and she was on the bus that crashed into the grocery store down the street. In the confusion, it took us a long time to identify her, and even longer to free someone up from all the other emergencies to come and tell you what happened. I'm sure you've been worried out of your mind waiting for her to come home. I'm terribly sorry, Emily. I know this is the worst possible news for you."

Emily felt as though the walls were closing in around her. The policeman and Mrs. McGill continued to talk, but their voices were muffled as though she had cotton balls in her ears. Mama was dead! She was never coming back. The darkness that had been looming finally overtook her, and she slid to the floor in a faint.

When Emily came to a few minutes later, she heard the raised voices of Mrs. McGill and Officer Flynn. By the sound of it, Mrs. McGill was winning the argument. "She is NOT going to some children's home tonight! That would only traumatize her more. I raised four children of my own, so I think I know a thing or two about taking care of a child who needs someone familiar to give her comfort and affection. Policies be damned! You can have the social worker come over tomorrow and see for herself. We'll let her decide what Emily needs, but you, sir, are not taking her any further than my front door tonight. Is that clear?"

The police officer threw up his hands in defeat, saying, "Alright, alright! I can see that you are determined to keep Emily here with you, and God knows I have more than enough to do tonight dealing with this storm. But don't be fooled into thinking this is the end of the issue, because it's not. The state has policies that must be followed in situations like this. We are the ones who decide what is best for Emily, not you."

Emily sat up from where they had laid her on the couch, and both the adults turned to look at her. Mrs. McGill rushed over immediately. "Now Emily, you're going to come and stay with me for a while until we can get things figured out. I'll go gather up a few things to take downstairs for tonight, and this nice officer will help you down the stairs." Mrs. McGill scurried into Emily's bedroom, leaving Emily with Officer Flynn. Emily still hadn't said a word, but silent tears streamed down her face. Taking a long look at her, Flynn questioned her ability to manage the stairs in her dazed condition, so he wrapped her up in a warm quilt taken from her bed, swept her up in his arms and carried her out the door and down to Mrs. McGill's front door. Right behind them, the determined woman opened the door and directed him to her guest room, where he placed Emily on the bed.

Seeing no more need for his presence, Mrs. McGill ushered the policeman out the door and shut it firmly behind him. She returned to Emily's side to find the girl lying with her face to the wall, still having not uttered a word.

"Oh, you poor, sweet child!" Mrs. McGill fussed. "This is just so awful! I'm sure you are petrified about what is going to happen to you now, but things will look better after you get some rest. You must be starving! You haven't had any dinner. I'll just run into the kitchen and rustle you up something to eat."

Still lying with her back to her landlady, Emily finally found her voice. "I'm not hungry. And nothing will be better in the morning. Nothing will ever be better."

"Oh. Well, I don't suppose you do feel like eating right now, dear. Let's just get your nightgown on and get you to bed." Pliable again, Emily allowed herself to be undressed and have her nightgown pulled on over her head. Mrs. McGill pulled down the covers and helped Emily climb in. She gave the heartbroken girl a warm hug, placed Emily's own comforter over her small body, and then tucked a familiar doll in next to her. It was Emily's Raggedy Ann doll, retrieved by the older woman when she had searched Emily's room for anything that might give her comfort. Emily silently pulled Raggedy Ann into the crook of her arm and closed her eyes.

"Good night, dear. I'm so sorry about your mother. I know you will miss her very much. Try to sleep now." Mrs. McGill crept out of the room and closed the door softly. It wasn't long before she heard the sobs of a motherless child keening through the night as the silent snow continued to fall.

1957

Emily walked slowly up the aisle, holding a small nosegay of white daisies and pink roses. Having no father to walk beside her, she took these steps alone, eyes fixed on the man who would soon be her husband and protector for life. George's eyes met hers, and she smiled tremulously, still feeling such wonderment at the whirlwind courtship that had led to this day. Also waiting at the front of the church was Lottie, her childhood friend, serving as matron of honor. Beside the groom stood George's best man, one of his colleagues from the bank. In the pews sat Kathleen and a few of the other girls from the boarding house, George's mother and aunt, a handful of bank employees, Sister Mary Francis, and Mrs. McGill. Seeing these two women's familiar faces somehow eased Emily's tension, and she stepped more confidently to join George at the front of the church. He offered her his arm, and she slipped her hand into the crook of his elbow, turning to face the priest.

"Dearly beloved, we are gathered here today in the sight of God and these witnesses to celebrate the marriage of George Walter Edwards and Emily Irene Snow." The words flowed over Emily like a warm summer rain, words she had never believed would be said for her. "And who gives this woman to be married to this man?"

A strong voice from the pews spoke up. "I do, Father," said Mrs. McGill, smiling and giving Emily a wink. Then the words flowed on, circling around her and wrapping her in a cocoon of love and safety, magic words that signaled belonging, something rare and precious that Emily had never allowed herself to hope for. And then the best words of all, "I now pronounce you man and wife." George's kiss was short and chaste, nothing like the passionate kisses of their courtship, but Emily understood his shyness about kissing her in front of the priest.

Then the bride and groom made their triumphal walk back down the aisle and received the warm wishes of the guests who had gathered to celebrate with them. Emily's cheeks hurt from smiling so much as she received pecks on the cheek from the men and tight hugs from all the girls from the boarding house that she would miss so much. Finally there was no one left but George's mother and aunt with whom they would eat dinner before going home. Home! Such a wonderful word! George had refused to let Emily see the house that he had bought before they met, wanting it to be a surprise for her on their wedding night. He had taken all of her things from the boarding house to their home the day before so they would be waiting for her when George carried her over the threshold.

Dinner with George's family was a bit awkward, with his mother gushing on about how lovely the wedding was and what a handsome man George had become and how much she was going to miss being the number one woman in his life. Meanwhile, the aunt said almost nothing, staring stolidly at her plate as the conversation rolled right over her. Emily said very little as well, but listened and smiled, trying and failing to answer the rather pointed questions that George's mother posed to her without giving her the space in which to respond. "How did you learn to cook, dear? I mean, losing your mother at such a young age must have been so hard for you. I hope you know how to clean thoroughly. The good Lord knows that Georgie likes an immaculate house. You'll give up your job, of course. Didn't you just hate working for the phone company? I know I would."

At one point, seeing a certain look in Emily's eye, George reached under the table to take her hand and give it a gentle squeeze. Luckily, he had warned her that Mrs. Edwards could be a little overbearing, but Emily now thought that had been an understatement. Eventually, the meal was concluded, and they dropped the two women off at their hotel. They would be taking the train back to Portland in the morning.

Finally, George and his bride were alone. Emily became aware of a certain anxiety that began in the pit of her stomach. Until now, she hadn't had a moment to think about the wedding night. As they drove towards George's home, her nerves started to build as she wondered what it would be like. Neither her mother nor her foster mother had ever talked to her about sex, although Mrs. Hutton did occasionally hint that she considered the physical aspect of marriage a not-so-pleasant duty. The romance novels Emily had read usually glossed over the details with vague innuendo and flowery hyperbole, leaving a lot to the imagination. Now, as Emily remembered some of the feelings that had been stirred in her by George's urgent kisses, she thought perhaps sex might not be so bad. But still . . .

An hour later, Emily lay in the marital bed, staring at the ceiling. George was sound asleep beside her. The consummation of their marriage had been surprisingly abrupt and impersonal. And painful. After carrying her over the threshold and giving her a brief tour of her new home, George had helped Emily out of her wedding dress and immediately taken her to bed. The negligee she had bought for this moment remained folded neatly in the suitcase on the floor. He had given her one deeply urgent kiss, then thrown off his clothes and climbed on top of her. The next thing she knew was a searing pain as he penetrated her, causing her to cry out. "Oh my God, I've waited so long for this," George groaned, thrusting vigorously in his arousal. Emily had the strange sense that he hadn't even been talking to her. Fortunately, the pain was over as quickly as it had begun, with a loud moan and a final thrust. If Emily had expected loving pillow talk, she was sadly mistaken. George had kissed her briefly and said, "What a day! I'm exhausted. Good night, Mrs. Edwards." With that, he had rolled over and fallen immediately asleep.

Feeling a sticky substance between her legs, Emily slipped out of bed and went to the bathroom to clean up. The pain was beginning to subside, but the sight of George's discharge on a tissue was surprisingly unsettling, and its sour yeasty smell turned her stomach. Unexpectedly, she shuddered. *Well, they sure don't talk about this in my romance novels,* she thought. She tried to reassure herself that George was just tired from all the stress of planning the wedding and getting the house ready to receive her. She sighed and told herself everything would be fine once they had both gotten some rest.

Having finished cleaning herself up, Emily slid back into bed and closed her eyes, but sleep wouldn't come. She felt strangely disturbed without knowing why. Even after she slipped into a light slumber, shadowy images populated her dreams, stalking her and calling her name. Emily tossed and turned until she felt George's arm drape around her and pull her close. At long last, she fell into a deep and dreamless sleep.

1947

When Emily awoke in the morning, she was disoriented to find herself in a bedroom that was not her own. Then the events of the previous night came flooding back along with the overwhelming grief and uncertainty. The sadness she had felt when her father died was nothing compared to this gaping hole in her life where her mother had been just yesterday morning. What would happen to her now? Where would she go? Who would take care of her? Because of her father's death, Emily knew how to do a lot of things that other ten-year-olds did not and was certainly much more independent, but that did not prepare her in the least for having to make her own way in the world.

There was a gentle knock at the door, and Mrs. McGill inched the door open until she could enter the room with a tray in her hands. "Good morning, dear. I hope you had a bit of a rest. I brought you some breakfast if you want it."

Emily was surprised to find that she was indeed hungry, and nodded to Mrs. McGill as she scooted up to a seated position in the bed. The older woman placed the tray on Emily's lap and plumped up the bed pillows to support her. "It's just some scrambled eggs and toast and orange juice to drink. Do you want me to leave you alone?" Clearly Mrs. McGill had recognized Emily's need for space after her outburst last night.

Emily considered, then shook her head. "Please stay." She paused before adding, "What's going to happen to me, Mrs. McGill?"

"Well, as you probably heard last night, they want to take you to an orphanage . . ." Seeing Emily's eyes widen, she quickly continued, ". . . just temporarily, until they can find you a foster family to live with. A woman from social services will be coming sometime today to talk to the both of us. I'm hoping I can persuade her to let you stay with me for a while. I used to work as a cleaning lady in a children's home before Mr. McGill came along and changed my life, and I wouldn't want any little one to have to live there for very long. All dark and dingy, and the food was horrible."

Emily's lip trembled as her eyes welled up with tears. "What if nobody wants me?"

"Oh, what utter nonsense, dear! Of course, someone will want you! Wasn't I just telling you yesterday what a good child you are? You're so helpful and well-behaved. Any family would be happy to take you in. Now, don't you worry. Let's wait and see what the social worker has to say. I'll call them up right now and find out when we can expect her."

Mrs. McGill hurried out of the room, leaving Emily to finish her breakfast and change into the clothes she had worn the day before, the day that changed everything. In the bathroom, she glanced in the mirror at her reflection as she splashed water on her face and wondered how she could still look the same when she didn't feel at all like the same person she had been just yesterday. She studied her unruly blond hair and the smattering of freckles across her nose and cheeks, wondering if there were prettier girls also hoping for a new family right now. The thought of having to compete with an orphanage full of other children felt daunting, bringing with it a sense of inadequacy and anxiety. Everything that Emily could count on was gone, and this new world was full of uncertainty and fear.

Due to the still snow-clogged streets, school was closed, and the social worker was not expected to arrive until mid-afternoon. The long hours of waiting stretched out before Emily like an endless day. Too anxious and distracted to focus on reading, too grief-stricken to help Mrs. McGill bake Christmas cookies, she spent the morning on a chair staring out the window with Raggedy Ann held tightly to her chest. The storm had passed during the night, and a bright winter sun shone on the piles of pristine snow outside. Brilliant light sparkled off the icicles hanging from every roof. Blanketed in snow, the world seemed clean and new. Emily saw none of this. Instead, she saw a bleak future where nothing lovely or good would ever happen again. Thinking about life without her mother was too painful, so she resolved to not think about anything at all. Numb and defeated, she waited.

Emily was startled by a knock at the door. Having no idea how much time had passed, she was surprised to see that it was three o'clock. Mrs. McGill opened the door, and a pleasant-looking woman with shoulder-length brown hair and glasses entered the room. She introduced herself as Mrs. Kinney before turning towards Emily with a gentle smile. "Hello, Emily. I'm so sorry to hear you've lost your mother. Would you like to tell me about her?"

Emily had not been expecting this question, but considered her response nonetheless. "She was perfect. She was funny and smart, and she always knew how to make me feel better when I was upset or sad. One of our favorite things to do was lie on the grass and look up at the sky. If it was daytime, we would watch the clouds to see if we could find shapes of animals and things. At night, we would look at the stars and try to count them or think about God looking down on us at that very moment. We pretended that the stars were all the people who had ever died and tried to figure out which one was my daddy." Emily began to cry, and through her tears, she managed to say one more thing, "She called me Ladybug."

"Well, Emily, your mother sounds every bit as perfect as you say. And now it seems that there is a new star in heaven, and I know she is looking down on you right now. Let's see if we can figure out how to best take care of you. The first thing we need to know is if there are any family members who could take you in. Do you have any aunts and uncles or grandparents we could contact?"

"I don't think so. Both Mama and Daddy were only children, and Daddy's parents died before I was born. I think my mom's parents are still alive, but they shut her out of their lives when she married Daddy. I don't think they would want me."

"Well, Emily, you never know how family is going to respond in a situation like this, so let's give them an opportunity to prove you wrong before we start looking farther afield. Do you have their address?"

"Um, I think it's in Mama's address book in the kitchen. I can show you. Mama used to send them letters even though they never answered."

Mrs. McGill volunteered to take Mrs. Kinney upstairs to retrieve the address book and then ushered her to her car. She re-entered the front door, stomping the snow off her shoes. "Well, I'm certainly glad Mrs. Kinney thought to ask about family. I had clean forgotten that your mother's parents are still alive. Now, that gives you something to hope for, doesn't it?"

Emily nodded, but she had grave doubts that her grandparents would have changed their feelings enough to welcome her into their household. And she wasn't entirely sure she would want to live with them even if they did.

Two days later, Mrs. Kinney returned. "I'm sorry, Emily, but your grandparents are unable to take you in. Apparently, your grandfather is very ill and requires a great deal of care. Your grandmother said she couldn't possibly care for him and a child at the same time. She said to tell you she's sorry."

The way she said it made Emily think her grandmother probably wasn't all that sorry. While she had long ago resigned herself to not having grandparents like other kids, it still hurt to know that she wasn't wanted. And at the same time, there was relief at not having to go live with the stern, uncaring people her mother had described.

Mrs. Kinney interrupted Emily's thoughts. "Well, now we just need to roll up our sleeves and find you a nice family to live with. Families that are looking for a foster child usually want to know more than just a child's age or whether they are a boy or girl. They want to see if they have something in common with you, something that would help you relate to each other. So I'm going to ask you some questions to help us with that. For example, what are your favorite subjects in school?"

"Oh, I love school!" Emily replied. "Well, maybe not math. I suppose my favorites are English and Social Studies, but I like learning all kinds of things."

"And what do you like to do when you're not in school?"

"Um . . . I like to read and skip rope and play in the park. Sometimes on rainy days, I play pretend school with my dolls. I'm the teacher," she explained, just in case there was any question.

Mrs. Kinney smiled in delight. "Well, I guess you really do

love school. I'm sure any family would be happy to have you come and live with them. In the meantime, we're going to let you stay here with Mrs. McGill. She's perfectly capable of caring for you, and it will be good for you to be somewhere that's comfortable and familiar. You can still be around your neighborhood friends, too. That way there's not too much change for you all at once, while you get used to life without your mother. I don't know how long this will take, Emily, but I'll stop by every once in a while to let you know how things are going. How does that sound?"

Emily nodded and clutched Mrs. McGill's sweater, filled with relief. She watched the social worker walk out the door, then turned into Mrs. McGill's arms and cried her heart out.

1957

An insistent buzzing sound drew Emily out of a sound sleep. She rolled over and opened her eyes to find George gazing at her with a smile. "You're really here. I thought I must be dreaming, but here you are next to me. I feel like the luckiest guy in the world." He leaned over and kissed her gently. Emily returned his smile and stretched lazily.

"What's that sound, George? Did you set the alarm clock?"

"Of course, darling. We need to get going or we'll be late for Mass. I'll go start your bath."

"We just celebrated Mass at our wedding yesterday, George. Doesn't that count? I was hoping for a lazy day to just enjoy being a married couple."

George frowned slightly. "Sunday is the Lord's day, Emily, and we honor the Sabbath like all good Catholics. We can rest this afternoon, so out of bed, lazy bones!"

He whisked into the bathroom, and the next sound Emily heard was that of water pouring into the bathtub. Slowly, she extricated herself from the covers and stood to pull on her robe. She opened the closet door, hoping George had thought to hang up her clothes so they wouldn't be wrinkled. She didn't particularly feel up to ironing anything, since her husband clearly had a timetable for the morning. She needn't have worried, for there hung her few dresses, lined up neatly with shoes carefully placed beneath them. *It's a wonder they're not color-coded,* Emily thought, immediately feeling guilty for the unbidden sarcasm. She hurriedly grabbed a dress off the rod and scurried into the bathroom just as the faucet was turned off.

After her quick bath, Emily refilled the tub for George while she dressed. It suddenly occurred to her that she would need to cook breakfast as part of her new wifely duties. She smiled at the thought. "George, darling! What would you like for breakfast?"

"Two poached eggs and two slices of toast, dear, if you don't mind."

"Of course, I don't mind! I'm your wife now, George. I've been looking forward to our cozy domestic life since the day you proposed. Two poached eggs coming right up!"

"And not overdone. I like the yolks runny. Butter on the toast, no jam. Oh, and coffee. Strong and black."

Emily looked around the kitchen with dismay, realizing she didn't know where anything was. Searching through cupboards, she found most of what she needed, but no apron. She had never needed one, as meals were provided at the boarding house, and obviously George wouldn't own one. His housekeeper had always left dinner in the oven for him daily, except on weekends when he went out to eat. Well, she would just have to do without for today. She would have to buy one on Monday at the local five and dime. She quickly prepared the simple meal of eggs and toast and set the table.

George walked in tightening his tie. "You look lovely, Mrs. Edwards! Might I be permitted to kiss the cook?" Emily walked into his arms for a warm embrace and a long kiss which ended as George pushed her away. He cleared his throat. "Mustn't get too carried away, or we'll be late for church!"

Sitting at the kitchen table together felt so comfortable and homey that Emily felt that she was radiating joy. She picked up her fork to take a bite of egg when George said, "Aren't we forgetting something, dear?" Emily looked confused. "Grace. We haven't said grace yet." She quickly put down her fork as George bowed his head. "Almighty God, this meal is a sign of Thy love for us. Bless us and bless our food, and may we always seek to be worthy of Thy gifts, through Jesus Christ our Lord. Amen."

When her husband took his first bite of egg, Emily noticed a slight crinkling between his brows. "Is something wrong, George? Did I use too much salt?"

"No, the seasoning is fine, but the yolks are a little more done than I like. Not to worry. I'm sure you'll soon figure out how to make the perfect poached egg. And the toast is just right. The coffee could be a little stronger, though. Tomorrow I'll show you the exact measurement for perfect coffee. I hope you're not disappointed that I have to go right back to work tomorrow. Things are just too busy at the bank right now for me to take time off, and I couldn't have afforded a honeymoon anyway. If we're thrifty, maybe we can save up and take a trip to Seattle next year."

"I understand, darling. Seattle sounds lovely."

After the newlyweds returned home from Mass, flushed from the many congratulations they had received, Emily prepared a simple lunch, then asked George, "Would you like to take a walk in the park this afternoon?"

"Actually, darling, I was hoping to show you the ropes in regards to keeping the house clean. As you know, I let my housekeeper go on Friday, since I won't need her anymore. I have a beautiful wife to take her place now. Let's start here in the kitchen."

The house was small, but it was well-kept and adequate for two. The kitchen was on the back of the house, with a door that opened to the back yard and a carport that was accessed from the alley. Just off the kitchen was a small pantry that included a wringer washing machine and shelves for foodstuffs and pots and pans. The kitchen opened onto the front room that held an elegant but well-worn crushed velvet sofa and a rocking chair that turned toward the fireplace on the side wall, lending a cozy atmosphere. In the corner stood a walnut occasional table which held a lovely wood-encased radio, George's pride and joy. To the left of the front door was a hallway that led to the two bedrooms and the bathroom.

For two hours, George walked Emily from room to room, explaining what he expected her to do and how often, in great detail. Emily felt as though she should be taking notes and hoped she wouldn't forget everything by the next day. "I think that Mrs. Morris left a roast thawing in the refrigerator yesterday morning before she left. I imagine you'll want to get that in the oven before long, dear. I hope you don't mind, but I want to sit and read the paper for a while." He gave her shoulder a quick squeeze and kissed her on the forehead. "I love married life already!"

Emily stood in the middle of the kitchen. She hadn't spent this much time in the kitchen since the day she left the Hutton's home, evicted so suddenly that she barely had time to pack. She had forgotten the grind of preparing three meals a day plus cleaning house and caring for their two children on top of her schoolwork, all starting at the age of eleven. Her co-workers at the phone company had marveled at how she was able to complete her senior year of high school while working swing shift as a telephone operator. She didn't tell them that it felt like a piece of cake compared to what had been expected of her in the Hutton household. *Well, I'm not going to accomplish anything just standing here reminiscing,* she thought and began to assemble everything she needed for a pot roast dinner. At least this was something she knew how to fix.

1948

Emily was relieved when the Christmas holidays were over and she could go back to school. The winter break had given her way too much time to think about how things would have been if her mother were there. The pain of missing her was an actual ache in her chest that nearly doubled her over at times. She spent hours trying to fix in her mind the way her mother looked, how she talked, how she laughed, even how she smelled. Fearing that she might forget, that her memories might fade, Emily was determined to hold onto them, knowing that her recollections of the past, of her life with her mother, were all that she had left.

Mrs. McGill tried hard to give her a nice Christmas, but it just wasn't the same. Perhaps she tried *too* hard. Even when Mrs. McGill wasn't fussing over Emily, she was watching her like a hawk, all the while pretending she wasn't. It was suffocating.

The weather had remained gray and gloomy, matching Emily's mood, but on the first day back to school, the skies lightened a bit, and she felt almost normal as she walked into her classroom. This feeling was short-lived however, when every child in the class stopped talking to stare at her. Mrs. Butler rushed over to her side and gave Emily a hug. "I'm so sorry about your mother, Emily. We're glad to have you back with us, though, aren't we children?"

"Yes, Mrs. Butler," the class chanted in unison, then quickly looked down at their desks or resumed their conversations. Emily walked to her desk and slid into her seat, avoiding the gaze of the children who dared to sneak quick glances her way. She was not prepared for this awkwardness, had thought that everything at school would just go back to normal. Emily swallowed hard against the lump in her throat, determined not to let her classmates see her cry. Just when she was about to lose that battle, Mrs. Butler instructed them all to take out their math books, and the school day began.

Things improved at lunch, when Emily's best friend, Patty, sidled up to her in the cafeteria and squeezed her hand. "Can I sit with you?"

"Sure," responded Emily. "There's a spot over there."

The girls carried their sack lunches to a table and sat down. Then, instead of the condolences that Emily feared, Patty asked, "Did you understand that math this morning? I swear, I've forgotten all about fractions over the break!" Emily breathed a sigh of relief, and they spent the lunch hour chatting away just like they used to.

Gradually, this new life settled into a routine of school, homework, and helping Mrs. McGill around the house. Emily brought some things downstairs from the apartment and squirreled them away in her room to take out when she needed to feel close to her mother. One of her favorites was the sweater Maddy used to wear on chilly evenings. Even though it was miles too big for Emily, sometimes she would put it on and wrap it around herself so that she could pretend she was in her mother's embrace just for a moment. The sweater carried the faint scent of Maddy's cologne, and she would breathe in the smell and be transported to a time when life was good, and the future was not something to fear. Bedtimes were the hardest, when Emily felt her mother's loss most deeply. This was when she noticed the heartache the most, and Raggedy Ann's hair of red yarn was often moistened with tears as Emily clutched her to her chest as she fell asleep.

January passed, and then it was February. One morning, as Emily walked into Mrs. McGill's kitchen, she noticed the calendar on the wall and realized that it was almost her birthday. Mrs. McGill was mixing up some pancake batter at the counter. Hesitant, Emily asked, "Mrs. McGill, did you know that I'm having a birthday next week?"

"Why, no dear! That's lovely. What should we do to celebrate?"

"I don't know. I don't want to be any trouble."

"Nonsense! We need a celebration around here. How did your mother celebrate your birthday?"

"Well, she baked me a chocolate cake and allowed me to invite one of my school friends over to play and have cake and ice cream. Then later, Mama would give me my present once my friend had gone home."

"Well, I can certainly manage that. Who would you like to invite? And what sort of gifts did your mother give you?"

"Oh, when I was younger, it was a toy or doll. My Raggedy Ann doll was a birthday present when I was six or seven, I think. Then she started giving me books, because I love reading so much. Last year it was a book of poetry. There was one poem in there that she started reciting to me every night at bedtime. It goes, 'Good night! Good night! Far flies the light; but still God's love from far above, will make it bright. Good night! Good night!'"

"Oh, goodness, Emily. That just tugs at my heart strings! You must miss her so much." The woman surreptitiously dabbed the corners of her eyes with a handkerchief. "But you haven't told me who you want to come to your little party."

"Oh! Definitely my friend Patty. We haven't gotten to play together since . . . well, you know."

"Alright then. That's decided. Let's see. Your birthday is the 17th, which is a Friday. Shall we do it on that Saturday?"

"Yes! I'll talk to Patty at school today. I hope she can come. Thank you, Mrs. McGill. You're a peach!"

When the day arrived, the sun made a surprise appearance, glittering on the snow. Emily bounced out of bed with anticipation, looking forward to a day of play with her friend. She was pretty excited about the cake, too. She dressed quickly and raced to the kitchen for breakfast. Something smelled wonderful. Sure enough, when she walked in, Mrs. McGill was pouring batter into the waffle maker.

"Happy birthday, Emily dear! I know how you love my waffles, so I'm making some special for you. I opened a jar of my canned peaches and made a lovely compote to spoon over the top. How does that sound?"

"Delicious! Thank you so much!" Emily threw her arms around Mrs. McGill's waist and squeezed.

"Oh, my! What brought that on?"

"I'm just excited about the day, I guess. You're being so good to me."

"Well, I'm glad to do it, but enough of this gushy stuff. Now wash your hands and sit at the table. These waffles will be ready in a jiffy."

After breakfast, Emily brushed her teeth and tidied her room, looking forward to Patty's arrival. Before long, right on the dot of ten, there was a knock at the door. Emily got to the door before Mrs. McGill and opened it wide. The two girls squealed and embraced as if they hadn't seen each other for a month instead of just yesterday. Since Patty was already bundled up, Emily put on her parka, snow boots and mittens so they could go outside in the sun and build a snowman. When they got too cold, they came inside and played with their dolls. Time passed quickly, and soon it was time for lunch. Mrs. McGill had fixed tomato soup and toasted cheese sandwiches. When they had eaten their fill, she brought the cake to the table, eleven candles burning brightly on top.

Emily paused to make a wish—that Mrs. Kinney would soon find a family for her—and blew out the candles. The girls scarfed down the cake and played for a bit longer before Patty's mother came to pick her up. Once she was gone, Mrs. McGill brought out a gift wrapped in the Sunday comics, just like Emily's mother used to do. Eagerly ripping the paper away, Emily found a small, framed piece of embroidery. There were small purple flowers in the corners, and in the middle was the poem Emily had recited just days earlier—"Good night! Good night! Far flies the light . . .."

Emily stared at it for long moments, overcome by emotion. Then she looked up at Mrs. McGill, eyes shimmering. "Thank you," she whispered. "Oh, thank you!"

Mrs. Kinney made it a habit to call on a weekly basis to let

Mrs. McGill know about any progress in finding a home for Emily. Each time, the report had been "not yet." Despite how long it was taking, she seemed content to let Emily stay with Mrs. McGill, because she never mentioned taking her to an orphanage. This was reassuring, but Emily knew that Mrs. McGill couldn't keep her forever. As much as she liked being in familiar surroundings with someone who was kind and generous, she wondered how long she would have to wait to know what her future held.

Then one afternoon, Mrs. Kinney was waiting in the living room when Emily got home from school. She looked up and smiled as Emily walked through the door. "Good news, Emily! I may have a family that would be willing to take you on. The only concern is that they are looking for a child with a Catholic upbringing, and Mrs. McGill seems to think that you are Lutheran. Is that right?"

"No! I'm Catholic," Emily blurted out. "My daddy was Lutheran, but Mama was Catholic. Her parents raised her Catholic, and even though we went to the Lutheran church, Mama was teaching me some Catholic stuff."

Mrs. Kinney looked dubious, but Mrs. McGill chimed in, "You know, I seem to recall that Maddy did tell me one time that her parents were Catholic. They had a royal fit when she married outside the faith, but she kept hoping they'd come around some day. I didn't realize she'd been tutoring you in the catechism though."

Emily nodded vigorously. "She had. Really! I know how to say the Hail Mary and why we don't eat meat on Fridays and stuff like that." Behind her back, Emily's fingers were crossed, grateful that she had learned enough about growing up Catholic from her friend Patty to say the right things. She did not want to miss out on this chance at a normal family life.

"Well, I'm sure the Huttons will be glad to hear that, Emily. Mrs. Hutton is ill, and they have two small children she needs help with. Mrs. McGill tells me you are quite handy around the house, so that should impress them as well. I'll go talk with them again tomorrow, and I'll let you know as soon as they decide." Mrs. Kinney rose from the couch and gave Emily a hug. "I sure hope this works out for you, dear. I know how much you want a family, and as wonderful as Mrs. McGill has been, we always meant for this to be a temporary situation. Be sure to say a prayer when you go to bed tonight, and crossing your fingers wouldn't hurt either!" At that, Emily brought her hand from behind her back and held up her fingers, eliciting a laugh from Mrs. Kinney. "I should have known you would be way ahead of me. Good evening, Emily." She nodded to Mrs. McGill and swept out the door.

Two days later, the phone rang, and Mrs. McGill answered. "Oh, hello, Mrs. Kinney, how are you doing, dear? Do you have good news for us? . . . Wonderful! I'm sure Emily will be thrilled to hear it. . . .. Certainly. Saturday should be fine. I'll have her ready. You'll pick her up at ten? . . . Lovely! See you then. Good-bye."

By the end of the conversation, Emily was nearly jumping out of her skin. "Do they want me? Are the Huttons going to take me? Are they?"

"Now slow down just a bit, my girl. Things never go quite that fast with social services. They want to meet you. Then, if they like what they see, there will be paperwork and legal matters to be considered. But this is certainly a good sign. Mrs. Kinney will come and get you Saturday morning and take you to the Hutton's home to introduce you to the family. Mrs. Hutton is still bed-ridden, otherwise they would come here. But this will allow you to meet their children and see how you would get along together. You'll have to be on your best behavior, so they can see what a good girl you are."

"Oh, I will, Mrs. McGill! I promise I will. Just wait and see."

Saturday morning arrived early for Emily, wide awake at six AM and so nervous she couldn't get back to sleep. She knew this day could be a turning point for the rest of her life, and she hoped and prayed it would mean the end of the uncertainty she had been living with for the past three months. She slipped out of bed and was bathed and dressed by the time Mrs. McGill shuffled into the kitchen in her bathrobe and slippers.

"Goodness, Emily! What are you doing up so early? But my, don't you look sweet! That dress is perfect on you."

"Do you really think so?" Emily twirled around in the new dress Mrs. McGill had bought her the day before. It was made of pale blue poplin with a close-fitting bodice, white Peter Pan collar, and a flared skirt that billowed out when she spun in a circle. Emily thought it might be her favorite dress ever, and she hoped it would be her luckiest.

"Of course, I do! Now let's get you some breakfast. How about some nice hot oatmeal?"

Emily wasn't very hungry, but she forced herself to eat, knowing that if she didn't, she could end up famished and shaky right in the middle of her visit with the Huttons. It was also a way to pass the time until Mrs. Kinney arrived to pick her up. Even when breakfast was over and the dishes were done and put away, it was only eight o'clock. Two hours to wait, and the clock moved at the pace of a snail inching its way along the sidewalk in summertime. Emily tried to do some homework but just couldn't concentrate. After what seemed like a century, the doorbell finally rang, and she jumped up from the sofa and ran to open the door.

"My, don't you look pretty," said Mrs. Kinney. "I sure don't need to ask if you're ready to go," she laughed. "And here's Mrs. McGill with your coat." She bent down to look Emily in the eyes. "Just be yourself, sweetheart, and you'll be fine. Any family would be lucky to have you. Okay?" Emily nodded. "Then let's go meet the Huttons."

Minutes later, they pulled up in front of a two-story brick home on a street that was lined with large oak trees, branches still bare in the last days of winter. Piles of melting snow were heaped along the sides of the front walk, but Emily hardly noticed. Her hands were shaking, and she could barely breathe. The front door opened suddenly, and a tall man wearing a gray sweater vest over a white shirt and tie stepped out to greet them. His dark hair was combed back from a broad forehead. "You must be Emily," he said as she and Mrs. Kinney approached. He patted her awkwardly on the head and nodded to the social worker. "I'm Mr. Hutton. Please come in."

Chapter 4

The trap is set!
Innocence takes the bait.
To be alone and lone again
makes attention seem so sweet,
unaware how bitter
the poison will become.
Too late,
too late.

—Emily

1957

After a month of married life, in which she had fallen into a rhythm of housework according to George's exacting expectations, Emily discovered that she was bored. Even with all the cleaning, laundry, ironing, and cooking, she still had hours of the day left over and nothing to fill them. She was always glad when it was time for George to come home so they could enjoy the evening together in conversation or companionable silence as they listened to the radio, especially on Wednesday evenings when one of the stations played opera. Even though opera wasn't Emily's favorite, George loved it, and she loved George. Often, they would sit together on the sofa with his arm around her, her head leaning on his shoulder until it was time for bed. Bedtime was Emily's least favorite time of day. Their physical relations hadn't improved at all since the wedding night. George was still rough and impersonal and unconcerned with Emily's own pleasure, but the worst part was that it was still quite painful. She wondered how long it would be this way or if it was normal, but had no one to ask. The only good part was that it didn't last long, and after a perfunctory kiss good night, George would soon be fast asleep, oblivious to his wife's discomfort.

In her desire to fill the lonely hours, Emily decided to revive her love of reading. During her life at the Huttons and after, when she worked at the telephone company, she had had little time for the luxury of reading, and now she realized how much she missed delving into the world of intriguing characters and faraway places. Finishing the dusting early one afternoon in August, Emily walked to the library and spent an hour there browsing the shelves, reminiscing about stories read long ago and inhaling the heavenly scent of old books. Ultimately, she decided on an old favorite, *Jane Eyre,* and a collection of poetry by Emily Dickinson. She had a fondness for the poet who shared her name, an interest encouraged by Sister Mary Francis, her favorite teacher at St. Ignatius Academy. Humming as she strolled homeward, Emily felt the sweet anticipation of diving into the pages of the treasured books she carried.

Emily walked in the kitchen door just as the clock struck five. She gasped, realizing that George would be home soon, and she hadn't yet started dinner. Dropping her books on the kitchen table, she quickly put potatoes on to boil and pulled a package of pork chops out of the refrigerator. Yet despite her fevered preparations, dinner was not ready when George walked in the door.

"Mmm. What smells so good?" George asked just before he noticed that the table wasn't yet set. His tone changed immediately to something more stern and disapproving. "Emily, why isn't dinner on the table yet? And what are these books doing here?"

"I'm so sorry, George. I went to the library this afternoon and just lost track of time. Dinner is almost ready. Why don't you go ahead and get out of your work clothes, and I'll have it on the table before you know it."

In a steely voice, George began to interrogate her. "What on earth possessed you to go to the library? Don't you have better things to do? And this!" gesturing to *Jane Eyre*, "What were you thinking bringing this trash into my home?"

"I . . . I was bored, darling. I used to read all the time as a little girl, and I miss it. I often finish my daily tasks long before you get home, and I was looking for a way to pass the time. And *Jane Eyre* is a classic! Why would you call it trash?"

"Because it's immoral! It's about an adulterer who seduces a young woman despite being married. And then, once his wife is dead and buried after having been driven mad by his infidelity, that girl agrees to marry him despite his sinfulness! I won't have you reading this. You will take it back first thing in the morning, and the poetry, too. Surely you can find more worthy ways to occupy your time." With that, George stormed out of the kitchen and down the hall, slamming the bedroom door after him.

Stunned and hurt, Emily hastily put the finishing touches on dinner and set the table. George had never yelled at her like that before, and for the first time, she sensed a gulf between them that she didn't know how to bridge. Holding back tears, Emily pulled off her apron just as George returned to the kitchen. He immediately walked over to her and enfolded her in a tight embrace.

"I'm so sorry, my dear. It was a long, busy day at the bank, and I'm too tired to be able to hold my temper. I shouldn't have yelled at you like that. Will you forgive me?"

"Oh, George! You're forgiven. I hated having you be angry with me. I couldn't bear the thought of upsetting you so! And I'm sorry, too. I should have paid better attention to the time. I know how much you count on having your dinner ready the minute you get home. It's ready now. Please come and sit down."

After George blessed their meal, Emily asked about his day, and they fell into the usual rhythm of conversation to Emily's relief. Then, as she served their dessert, a peach cobbler she had baked in the morning, George asked, "So help me understand how you can be so bored, Emily. Surely there's plenty for you to do around here without resorting to idle pursuits."

"Well, when I was living with the Huttons, between caring for the children, cooking, cleaning, and homework, I had to learn how to work quickly and efficiently. Thankfully, they sent their laundry out, but even with doing your laundry, I still have extra time on my hands. I actually miss my job at the telephone company, to be honest."

"Now, Emily, we've talked about this before, and it just wouldn't be fitting for the wife of a bank executive to be working in such a lowly job. It might give the impression that I can't support you on my salary, and I don't think that would please my boss at all. I'm sure we can find more productive ways of filling your days. You know, my mother used to embroider. Why couldn't you do that? In fact, I think there's a sewing circle in the parish. That might be a more appropriate activity for you. And while we're on the subject of sewing, I have some socks that need darning."

"Yes, dear. I'll take care of it tomorrow. And I'll call the parish and find out more about the sewing circle, too." The rest of the evening passed as though nothing had happened, but inside, Emily felt diminished in a way that she couldn't put into words. At least George didn't seem in the mood for marital relations that night. And in the morning, she took the books back to the library. She didn't feel like humming this time.

Not long after, Emily heard the mailman dropping mail into their box outside the front door. She went out to retrieve it and noticed a small white envelope that was addressed to her. Since she rarely got mail of any kind, she couldn't imagine who it could be from. Inside, she hastily slit it open with George's letter opener to find a white card with neat printing inviting her to a bridal shower in honor of Kathleen Dempsey's upcoming wedding. Delighted, she smiled in anticipation. Kathleen had been a good friend during the time she had been living at Mrs. Olson's boarding house. After a broken engagement, it was good to know that she had now found someone new to share her life with. It would be lovely to attend her shower and celebrate such a happy event. With work yet to do before George arrived home, she left the card on the counter and got out the ironing board.

When her husband walked in the back door later that afternoon, he walked straight to the counter to peruse the mail as was his custom. Emily greeted George cheerily as she stirred something on the stove. When she turned to look at him, he was holding the invitation in his hand. "What's this?" he asked with a frown.

"It's an invitation to a bridal shower. My friend Kathleen is getting married. Isn't that wonderful?"

"I'm sure it's wonderful for her that she's landed a husband, but I don't want you going to her shower."

"What do you mean, George? Why on earth not?"

"I've explained to you before, Emily, that I don't want you associating with those girls from your past. You need to put all of that behind you. You're starting a new life with me, and that's what matters. Besides, I'm not sure that your friends from the boarding house are the caliber of people you ought to be spending time with."

Emily started to bristle. "Exactly what caliber of people are you talking about, George?"

"You know, people whose circumstances force them to live in such lowly conditions."

"You mean, people like me? What are you implying?"

"Don't use that tone with me, Emily. You know that's not what I mean. Your circumstances were not of your own making. You had no other options."

"Well, dear, you don't know what options Kathleen had either. You know nothing about her from which to judge on your high and mighty judgment seat."

George slammed his palm down on the counter. "That's enough! I will not tolerate your insolence. You are not going to this shower, and that's final. Just put that thought out of your head, and serve me my dinner." With that, he took the invitation and tossed it in the trash.

1948

The day of going to live with the Huttons was finally here. Although Emily was looking forward to being part of a family, she was also more than a little nervous. Suddenly she was aware that she was going to be living with people she barely knew in a strange house in a completely different part of the city. And she was sadder than she'd expected about leaving Mrs. McGill and her familiar neighborhood. And then there was her beloved school and all her friends there. Would she ever find a friend as good as Patty? Most of all, so many memories of her mother were here in the little upstairs apartment.

As though reading her mind, Mrs. McGill walked up behind her and placed her hands on Emily's shoulders. Emily turned and buried her face in the woman's ample bosom. "I don't want to go! Why can't I just stay here with you? Just call Mrs. Kinney and tell her I've changed my mind."

Mrs. McGill chuckled. "Oh, Emily, you're just suffering from a case of nerves is all. You know I'm too old to be raising a child, no matter how well-behaved and helpful you are. My own daughter needs me to be helping with her wee one, and even a couple of hours of that wears me out! And the state has only been letting me keep you temporarily so you didn't have to be in the orphanage while they found you a proper placement. It will be alright, Emily, I promise. I'll still be here, and you can come to visit me anytime you want. And your Ma will always be with you, no matter where you go. Never forget that, my dear." Emily nodded, but quiet sobs still racked her small body. "There, there, now child. You don't want tear stains on your clothes when you go to live with your new mom and dad, do you? Chin up, my girl."

Mrs. McGill knelt down to look at Emily eye to eye. "I know life has been hard for you, dear, but today is a new day. It's a new beginning for you. You've just got to be brave and do the best you can to be the person your parents raised you to be. You are a fine, fine lass, and the Huttons are very lucky to have you come live with them. You hear me?"

Emily wiped her tears and nodded, taking a deep breath as she did so. "I'll be brave, Mrs. McGill. I will. Thank you for everything. You've been so good to me."

"Oh, now don't you think nothin' of it. Anybody would have done the same. You just don't forget to come visit this old woman from time to time!"

The sound of a car door interrupted their good-byes, and they looked out the window to see Mrs. Kinney making her way up the front walk. As Mrs. McGill opened the door, Emily put on her coat and gave her former landlady one last fierce hug, before turning to face the social worker and her future.

"Well, Emily," said Mrs. Kinney, "this is the big day, and it looks like you're all ready to go. This is one of the favorite parts of my job, seeing children matched up with families that will take good care of them. I'm sure this is going to work out just fine." She picked up one suitcase, Emily the other, both waving a last good-bye to Mrs. McGill as they walked to the car. And as it pulled away from the curb, Emily glanced up at the second-floor apartment where she had lived with her mother. It was still empty, just like the hollowed-out place in Emily's heart. She watched until the house was out of sight, vowing never to forget the love that had turned a small walk-up apartment into a home.

Compared to the relative calm of Emily's first visit to the Hutton home, the scene that greeted her upon arrival this day was one of hubbub and chaos. A young woman with bright red hair and a pale complexion flung the door open and promptly ran off, chasing after a squealing toddler who was laughing and waving a dripping soup ladle in his hand.

Mr. Hutton appeared in the hallway. "Blast it all, Fannie! You were supposed to keep these kids under control this morning. We wanted to give Emily a more dignified introduction to the family than this."

"Sorry, sir! I was helping Meg with her shoes, and Joey gave me the slip. How he got all the way to the kitchen so fast, I'll never know!"

Just then the little imp circled around and made for the door. Anticipating his getaway, Emily quickly grabbed him under the arms and swung him up in the air. Joey laughed delightedly and allowed this newcomer to settle him on her hip. Fanny skidded to a halt in front of her, breathless. "Oh, bless you, child! You've got quick reflexes; I'll grant you that. Welcome to the household. You're sorely needed." The two girls grinned at each other, recognizing kindred spirits.

"That'll do, Fannie. Now, take the children upstairs and keep them occupied while I help Emily get settled in." Dismissed, Fannie took Joey from Emily's grasp, and left the room. Mr. Hutton turned to Emily with a tight smile. "Welcome to our home, young lady. Come in. Just leave your bags right there, and I'll take them up to your room later. Thank you, Mrs. Kinney. I expect we'll see you for regular visits to check in on Emily. In the meantime, don't you worry. I'm sure we will all get along famously."

Emily experienced a moment of panic as Mrs. Kinney walked back to her car but suppressed the impulse to chase after her. Instead, she smiled shyly at Mr. Hutton and followed along as he showed her around her new home. The living room was situated to the right of the front door and had a brick fireplace on the side wall. A large finely-woven rug occupied the center of the room with a sofa, Mrs. Hutton's chaise lounge, and chairs covered in floral chintz surrounding it on polished wooden floors. Opposite the living room and to the left of the door was the dining room with a mahogany table and crystal chandelier. Toward the back of the house was the kitchen. Emily smiled with delight at the bright white cabinets and gleaming turquoise tile. From there, a back hallway led to a stairway, a bathroom, and the master bedroom, where Mrs. Hutton lay resting in bed.

She reached her arm out to take Emily's hand. "Welcome to our home, Emily. I had hoped to be able to greet you at the door, but this is not one of my better days. Have you met the children yet? I know they are very excited to have a big sister. What was that ruckus I heard?"

"That was Joey leading Fannie on a wild goose chase through the house," huffed Mr. Hutton. "I don't know why she can't keep better track of him."

"Oh, Charles, you know what a handful he is. Now that Emily is here to lend a hand, I'm sure Fannie will have an easier time of it. Now, Emily, where were we?"

"I love your house, Mrs. Hutton, especially the kitchen. The turquoise is really pretty!" Emily smiled tentatively at this woman who would be her new mother.

"Now, dear, enough of this Mrs. Hutton business! You must call me Mother. And Mr. Hutton will be Father, just as he is to our own children."

"Yes, Mother," Emily replied, feeling a little traitorous as she did so, but her desire to please was stronger.

"Charles, take Emily upstairs now. My heart is fluttering a bit, and I need to rest. And Emily, I'm so glad you're finally here." As Emily left the room with Mr. Hutton, she turned back to see Mrs. Hutton taking a pill from a small silver pillbox next to her bed.

Her new father led her up the stairs and into one of the two bedrooms. "This will be your room. I hope you don't mind sharing with Fannie. We just don't have enough space for you to have your own room right now. Fannie is our live-in maid and nanny. She's been with us for about six months now, ever since, well . . . since Vivian became ill."

"Oh, no, Mr. . . . I mean, Father. I don't mind sharing at all. I think it will be fun." Emily gazed around the room that was to be hers. There was a small dormer window that looked down on the street below, with a huge oak tree in front that would provide wonderful shade once its newly forming buds unfurled into full leaf. The room contained two twin beds on either side of a study table under a larger window on the side wall, and a dresser tucked into the corner by the door. Embroidered white coverlets adorned the beds, and gauzy white curtains hung at the windows. Small, braided rugs in pinks and blues were placed beside each bed, providing a warm place to step when crawling out of bed on cold mornings. It was such a lovely room, Emily felt like she should pinch herself to make sure she wasn't dreaming. She turned and smiled at Mr. Hutton, "It's beautiful, Father. I can't wait to unpack my things."

"Well, first things first. Let's introduce you to the children, and then you can get settled in. They're just across the hall." He led her into the nursery, where Fannie was attempting to read a book to the little boy Emily had encountered earlier and a small girl with golden ringlets and a quiet demeanor. While the girl sat calmly in Fannie's lap, the boy squirmed to get away. Sensing that intervention was needed, Mr. Hutton walked over and scooped up Joey in his arms. "You've already met our little Joey who's two, and this beautiful girl is our daughter, Margaret, but we call her Meg. She's five and very anxious to start school next fall."

Emily knelt down next to Meg. "Hello, Meg. I'm Emily. I see you've been reading a book. I love to read, too. What's your favorite book?"

Meg smiled shyly and said, "All of them."

Emily laughed. "Me, too! I've never met a book I didn't like. Perhaps we could read a book together this afternoon." Meg nodded her head vigorously.

Mr. Hutton cleared his throat, impatient to move things along. "Fannie, hold onto Joey for a minute while I bring up Emily's bags. Then you can take Meg to the kitchen with you while you finish preparing lunch. I'll keep Joey out of your hair, and Emily can unpack."

"Sure thing, Mr. H. Lunch should be ready in half an hour. I just need to add rice to the vegetable soup."

The rest of the day passed in a blur, and it wasn't until bedtime that Emily had a chance to talk with Fannie. Whispering so

69

as not to wake the children, they were both eager to learn more about the person they were sharing a room with. Emily shared her story first, then said, "OK. Now it's your turn."

"Well," Fannie began, "I came to the Huttons just six months ago when they lost the baby, and Mrs. H. couldn't take care of the bairns anymore."

"What? What happened?"

"Mr. H. told me that the missus was terribly anxious during this pregnancy, not like the other times, and her blood pressure was up, but the doctor didn't suspect anything more serious than nerves. Then, two weeks before she was due, she had a seizure right in the middle of the kitchen. When they got her to the hospital, they had to deliver the baby right away to save the missus' life, but the baby was already dead. They call it toxemia or something like that, and sometimes it happens after you've had a couple of babes already. Of course, Mrs. H. was devastated, and she has heart damage and other stuff now. She has to take nerve pills all the time to stay calm and to sleep. She was in a pretty good mood today, but don't be surprised if it's not always that way. Sometimes she can have a foul temper, if you know what I mean."

"Gosh, that's awful. Losing my mom and dad was a terrible thing, but a baby! I just can't imagine it. I feel really sorry for her."

"It's horrible, alright, but after you've been around a while, you might not be so sympathetic. Anyway, I love takin' care of these wee ones, and it's a nice place to live, I'll give you that. A far sight better than my folks' tumble-down shack, I'll tell ya."

"How old are you, Fannie? You look too young to be living away from home."

"I'm sixteen, old enough. My pa kicked me out on my sixteenth birthday, said he left home at that age, and it was the best thing for 'im. They couldn't afford to keep me around anyway, with five other mouths to feed. So, I got this job with the Huttons, and it's hard work, but I got a fancy roof over my head and food in my belly and the little ones to look after. I do miss school, though."

"You had to quit school?! How can you stand it? I absolutely love school!"

"Well, you're lucky then. You'll get to go to that nice Catholic school down the road a bit. And maybe you could pass along some of the stuff you're learnin' after the bairns are in bed at night."

"I'd be glad to. Well, I guess we'd better get to sleep now. Sounds like we'll be up bright and early to get ready for church."

"Yes, and Mr. H. runs a tight ship, so you'll want to look lively in the mornin'. I'm glad you're here, Emily. I think we're goin' to be fast friends."

1957

By late summer, Emily had begun to realize that George's tantrum over the library books wasn't an isolated incident but part of a pattern. She had become accustomed to regular angry outbursts whenever anything she did failed to live up to his exacting standards. He never hesitated to berate her if her housekeeping or cooking didn't meet his expectations or if she spent time doing anything he didn't feel was useful or worthwhile. He was especially critical of Emily's behavior in church. To him, Catholicism was the center of existence, and he expected his wife to be just as devout as he was. If she performed the rituals of the church by rote and without appropriate devotion, she would be chastised when they got home. If she mumbled the words of the liturgy or winced at the hardness of the kneeling benches or allowed her mind to wander during long homilies, Emily could expect to hear about it at great length. Emily had never known anyone who used their religion like a weapon before. Even though the Huttons had been devout Catholics, as long as Emily was quiet and still during mass, they didn't care about anything else. Mr. Hutton had been far too busy tending to his law practice and his invalid wife, and Mrs. Hutton was rarely lucid long enough to pay attention to her own children, much less whether Emily was Catholic enough. It seemed to Emily that George was so intent upon following the letter of Catholic doctrine that he often missed out on the spirit of the law altogether. The God that her mother talked about and the joy Emily experienced from attending the church of her childhood seemed long ago and far away from this rule-bound and punitive practice of religion.

Emily had taken up needlework as George suggested and attended the church sewing circle weekly with the other wives of the parish. She did enjoy the conversations with the women, but she was all thumbs the moment she picked up a needle. She was just plain bad at it. No matter how much the women tried to help her, Emily couldn't learn anything more than the most basic stitches. Her projects often sported blood stains from the numerous times she had pricked herself while embroidering. Night after night, she sat next to George on the sofa practicing while they listened to the radio and George read the paper. The music was often punctuated by Emily's exclamations whenever the needle pierced her tender fingertips. It gave her an almost perverse pleasure to interrupt George's quiet evening in this way. She knew he couldn't complain about it, since this "womanly pursuit" had been his idea in the first place.

One lovely summer morning, Emily left the house with sewing bag in hand on her way to the weekly circle gathering. The sun warmed her face, and birds were singing as they flitted from tree to tree. It felt like there was a golden haze over the neighborhood that filled Emily with delight. At that moment, she knew that she couldn't tolerate a morning spent indoors engaged in the tedious and fruitless effort to produce yet another ugly dish towel. Without even forming the intention, Emily turned right instead of left at the next corner and headed toward the park. Suddenly it occurred to her that she would be walking right past the library. She glanced down at her bag, and a traitorous idea began forming in her mind. Almost laughing out loud, Emily promptly walked in the door of the library, emerging a short time later with a single book carefully hidden underneath her sewing.

When she arrived at Comstock Park, Emily found an empty bench in the shade. This park was only about a mile away from Manito Park, where she had spent so much time in her childhood, but it had an entirely different feel. Tall ponderosa pines towered over the grassy terrain, and the slightest breeze turned their branches into instruments, playing nature's song. There was a playground nearby, and she could hear the shouts and laughter of children playing. Setting her bag on the bench beside her, she took a deep breath of the clean, fresh air and let it out slowly, savoring the moment of solitude and freedom. She thought of her mother and the many days they had spent together in the outdoors, enjoying the earth and sky and each other. In the years since Maddy had died,

Emily's life had been too full of school and work to find many opportunities for outings like this, and she realized now how much she had missed it. She felt her body and mind relax for the first time in a very long while. Then she pulled out her book and began to read.

1948

Emily awoke to the sound of Fannie's voice, "Up and at 'em, girlie. It's time to get ready for school. You have to get there early to meet with the principal, and Mr. H is already chompin' at the bit."

Jumping up quickly, Emily felt a momentary panic at the thought of a new school where she knew no one. However, excitement won the day, and she quickly threw on the school uniform Mr. Hutton had laid out for her the night before. She ran downstairs for breakfast, and sure enough, there was Father, fully dressed and sitting at the table, sipping his coffee and waiting for Fannie to place a plate of eggs and toast in front of him.

After a week of practice, Emily was starting to get used to calling the Huttons "Mother" and "Father." It had been a week of playing with the children, helping Fannie with household chores, and observing the family's routines. Father worked long hours at the law office and spent his evenings reading the paper or talking quietly with Mother in their bedroom. The extent of his interaction with Meg and Joey was a pat on the head when he came home and a perfunctory hug and kiss when Fannie brought them downstairs to say good night. Mother spent most of her days in bed, ringing a bell for Fannie or Emily when she needed something. She was very sensitive about noise disturbing her sleep, and when that happened, she didn't hesitate to direct a sharp rebuke to the guilty party, most often Fannie for failing to properly control the children.

Mr. Hutton looked up and greeted Emily with a smile. "Good morning, Emily. Are you excited about your first day in your new school?"

Emily nodded. "I guess so. I'm a little nervous though. Everybody always stares at the new kid. And I bet that nobody sits with me at lunch. At least I'll be wearing the same thing as everyone else, so they won't have my clothes to tease me about."

"Now, Emily, I'm sure everything will be just fine. The nuns expect their students to be more well-mannered than that. You'll make new friends in no time. Now, eat quickly. We need to leave in about ten minutes."

Emily gobbled her breakfast and scurried back upstairs to gather her pencil box and notebook. She checked her appearance in the mirror over the dresser, tweaking the collar of her white blouse and admiring the blue and green plaid of her jumper. Blue and green were her favorite colors, so she couldn't have been happier with the thought of getting to wear this outfit every day. Downstairs, Father was waiting by the front door. From the Hutton's bedroom, Emily heard Mother calling, "Have a wonderful day at school, Emily." Emily shouted her thanks and waved to Fannie in the kitchen just as Father opened the door, and then they were off.

Emily had already seen the school, which was next door to the church, when they had attended Mass the day before. It was a solid brick building and looked very similar to her old school, which gave her a sense of familiarity that eased her anxiety a tiny bit. When they walked in the big double doors, Emily inhaled the magical scent of chalk dust and floor wax, a smell that was like heaven to her. The school secretary, Mrs. Wisener, had been expecting them and led them to a closed door marked "Principal" in gold letters on the dark walnut wood. She knocked lightly, and a voice within called, "Come!"

As they entered, a large woman in full nun's habit stood and came out from behind her cluttered desk to greet Emily and Mr. Hutton. "Hello, Mr. Hutton, Emily. I'm Sister Mary Gregory. Welcome to Saint Ignatius Academy. Please have a seat." Emily stared at this woman who was almost as tall as her foster father and had a formidable figure. Emily had the sense that her new principal would brook no nonsense from her students.

Father nudged Emily. "Stop staring and say hello."

Emily extended her hand to shake as she was taught. "Pleased to meet you Sister Mary Gregory." She sat on the proffered chair and crossed her ankles.

"Now then, Mr. Hutton, tell me about Emily and how she came to live with you?"

"Well, my wife has been ill for some time, and we decided to take on a foster child to help out around the house and keep tabs on

our two young children. The child services agency introduced us to
Emily, who had just recently lost her mother and whose father had
previously died in the war. We were immediately taken with her and
saddened by her plight, so we said yes, and here she is. Of course, we
want her to have a Catholic education. Her mother was Catholic, but
their financial circumstances didn't allow for private schooling, so
Emily had been attending public school. Apparently, she did well
there, but we are concerned that she might be a bit behind the
standards of a Catholic school."

"Well, Mr. Hutton, we shall do our best to help her catch up.
Emily, are you prepared to work hard to measure up to our high
academic standards?"

"Oh yes, Sister. I love school, and I've always gotten good
grades. I promise not to disappoint you."

"Excellent! Now, I'm sure you need to be getting to work,
Mr. Hutton. I'll take Emily to her classroom, so you can be on your
way."

Mr. Hutton stood and put his hand on Emily's shoulder.
"Have a good day, Emily. Pay attention to your teacher. Are you sure
you remember the way home?"

Emily nodded. "I'll be fine, Father."

"Okay, then. I'll be off. Thank you, Sister." He turned and
left, and Emily suddenly felt very alone and scared.

"Come along, Emily. Don't dilly-dally." The school matron
sailed out of the room like a ship leaving port, with Emily trailing
along in her wake. They walked down a corridor to the right of the
main office until they came to a door which still sported the bright
decorations created by the other fifth grade students for Easter.
Inside, a nun was writing math problems on the chalk board. When
she heard the door open, she turned and broke into a delighted smile
that lit up her entire face. Short and rather plump, her rosy cheeks
dimpled when she smiled, so that Emily couldn't help but to smile
back. "You must be Emily! I'm so excited to have you in my class. I
already told the other children you would be coming after Easter
vacation, so they will be looking forward to meeting you this
morning. New students are always quite exciting! Oh! And my name
is Sister Mary Francis. You'll see on the blackboard the schedule of
classes and special events, but if you have any questions, please don't

hesitate to let me know. Now let me show you your desk." The principal bade teacher and student good-bye and swept out of the room.

Other students began filing in, and in order to avoid their stares, Emily looked at the schedule her teacher had pointed out to see what she might expect in the coming days and weeks. Two words jumped out at her as if written in neon—catechism and confession. She gulped, wondering how on earth she was going to sustain her claim to be Catholic when she knew nothing of what would be expected of her in either of those situations. This charade was going to be harder than she thought. She suddenly wished she hadn't lied to Mrs. Kinney. If she'd kept her mouth shut when the social worker asked if she was Catholic, Emily might still be living with Mrs. McGill and going to her old school and her comfortable routine. Then the bell rang, and Sister Mary Francis began calling roll.

That first day of school passed in a blur of meeting her fellow students, frantically trying to keep up with a slightly different curriculum, and finding her way around the school. One of her classmates had been assigned to be her special friend for the day, which relieved Emily's fears about getting lost or making mistakes out of ignorance of school policies. Charlotte immediately asked Emily to call her Lottie, claiming distaste for the name her parents had given her. "Mother was a big fan of Jane Eyre," she said. She was a chatty girl with an impish smile and a propensity for trouble. Her auburn hair was barely contained in a braid that hung down her back, and she had even more freckles than Emily's light sprinkle across her nose. Best of all, she claimed to live just down the block from the Huttons and promised to show Emily all the great places to play in the neighborhood. Walking home with her new friend, Emily decided that Catholic school wouldn't be so bad after all.

The next morning, as Emily waited for Lottie to show up at their agreed-upon meeting place, she remembered that her class would be having catechism that afternoon. Instinctively, she knew she was going to need an ally to help her navigate the ins and outs of being Catholic. Given that her knowledge of Catholicism was limited entirely by what little she had picked up from Patty, Emily wasn't sure she would be able to fake it enough to be convincing. She'd only known Lottie for one day, but she seemed trustworthy, and she really didn't have anyone else to turn to. She saw Lottie approaching and took a deep breath. The girls greeted each other and began walking.

"Lottie, I need to tell you a secret, and you can't tell anyone else, not even your parents." Lottie looked surprised, but nodded her assent. Emily continued, "I'm not really Catholic. My mom was raised Catholic but left the church when she married Daddy. We always went to the Lutheran church. But after Mama died, I was staying with our landlady while the state looked for a home for me, and she said I might have to go to an orphanage if they couldn't find a foster family to take me in. When the social worker told me the Huttons were looking for a Catholic girl to come live with them, I lied and told her I was Catholic. I just blurted it out, and then I couldn't take it back. I know a little bit about what it means to be Catholic, but there's a lot I don't know, and I'm afraid that people will figure out that I lied if I goof up too much on stuff I'm supposed to know. So can you help me? Because we've got catechism today and confession on Friday, and I have no idea what to expect or what I need to do."

Lottie was staring at Emily with wide eyes. "Golly, Emily! That must have been so scary to think about going to an orphanage. Of course, I'll help you. And I promise I won't tell a soul. Catechism is taught by the parish priest, and Father Devlin is a real stickler for getting it right. He reads us the riot act if we make a mistake or aren't paying attention. Basically, he asks different students to recite all the stuff we're supposed to know by the time we get confirmed, which isn't until next year, but there's a lot of memorization to learn between now and then. He wouldn't be surprised by a mistake here or there, but since you probably don't know any of it, we're going to have to come up with a good excuse for why.

"But at least confession is no big deal. It happens every other week, and we get called to go to the chapel by classes, starting with the first graders. We sit in the pews by row and then go in order. Given where you're sitting in class, there will be lots of kids in front of you so you can see where to go when it's your turn. Father Devlin will be sitting on the other side of a black curtain, because he's not supposed to be able to see you. Confession is supposed to be private, but of course, he'll eventually be able to recognize your voice. I know, because sometimes in catechism, he'll say something that he

77

wouldn't know if he hadn't heard someone's confession. Anyway, you go in and kneel on the kneeler. Then you say, 'Forgive me, Father, for I have sinned. It's been two weeks since my last confession.' Then just tell him some little thing you did, like sassing your parents or forgetting to pray before bed, or that your mind wandered during church. Then he'll give you a penance, like saying ten Hail Mary's or apologizing or doing something nice for your parents. And then you're done. It's really no big deal. You'll get the hang of it really quick."

The girls plotted possible explanations for Emily's lack of knowledge of the catechism for the remainder of their walk to school, so when two o'clock came around, Emily was as prepared as she could be. The classroom door opened on the dot of two, and in strode a tall, gaunt man with salt and pepper hair and ice blue eyes. Seeing him close up as opposed to way up in the sanctuary of the church, he was more forbidding than he had seemed on Sunday. Even if she hadn't been warned, this man's appearance would have put her on notice that he would brook no nonsense and tolerate no mistakes. She dared a glance over at Lottie and grimaced. Lottie winked back and then turned to face forward, hands clasped demurely on her desk. Emily followed her lead and waited anxiously to see what this catechism thing was about.

"Good afternoon, class. I hope you've been working hard at your lessons despite the Easter holiday, because last time I was here was not your best effort. My drills are not going to be in any particular order today, so be prepared. And I'll be calling on you randomly. Steven, you're first, since you failed so miserably two weeks ago. Recite the Act of Contrition for me."

Steven, a gangly boy in the second row, gulped hard and opened his mouth. "Uh, yes Father, uh . . . I think it's 'O my God, I am heartily sorry for having offended Thee, and I detest all my sins, um, because I . . . dread the loss of Heaven and the pains of Hell . . ..'" The boy continued falteringly as Emily's anxiety increased. This prayer was something she had never heard before, and if this was how all of the questions were going to be, she was in serious trouble. If she didn't pull off her story about why she didn't know these things, she feared the priest would take it upon himself to inform the Huttons of her lie. She began praying fervently that Father Devlin wouldn't call on her today.

The clock ticked by second by excruciating second, and Emily began to think she might escape the questioning when the priest's eyes fell directly on her. "Well, who do we have here, Sister Mary Francis? Is this a new student I see?"

The plump teacher replied, "Yes, Father. This is Emily Snow. She has recently come to live with the Hutton family, and this is her first week at St. Ignatius."

The priest turned to face Emily. "Welcome, young lady. Since you're new, I'll give you an easy one. What are the seven sacraments?"

Emily felt her face flushing as her mind raced in an effort to come up with any answer at all. She knew a couple of the Lutheran sacraments, but surely Father Devlin was expecting more. "Well, I think one of them is baptism, and maybe . . . confirmation? I, uh, I guess I don't know about the others."

Father Devlin's eyebrows raised, displeasure emanating from him. "Where did you go to school before? Have you not had *any* catechism? These other children could have answered that question when they were in second grade!" He turned to Sister Mary Francis. "What is this girl's history, Sister? How can she not answer such a basic question as this?"

Flustered, the teacher spoke in a low voice that the children strained to hear. "Perhaps that is a conversation to have after class, Father. Privately?"

Annoyed by her challenge, but catching sight of the clock, he turned to the students, saying, "Well, perhaps time is getting on. The bell will be ringing any minute now. For the most part, you all did better today than last time I was here, but you still have a lot of studying to do to stay on course for your confirmation next year. I want to see a marked improvement next week."

Emily rose with the other students and hoped to escape unnoticed, but the priest stopped her. "Emily, is it? I'd like you to stay behind. Alright, Sister. Tell me about this girl's background."

"Well, Father, Emily was recently orphaned, and the Huttons have taken her on as a foster child. Apparently, Emily's mother was Catholic, but the parents couldn't afford private school. Is that right, Emily?"

Emily nodded. The priest looked indignant. "Well, why didn't they just take her to the catechism class at their parish after school? Really, poverty is no excuse for a Catholic child to be so ignorant of basic Catholic precepts." Turning to face Emily, he continued, "Well, speak up, girl! I need an explanation."

"I, uh, m-my father was killed in the war, so it was just me and my mom. She was a nurse at Sacred Heart and, uh, she couldn't get off to take me to catechism. I had to take the bus home after school." Head down, she waited for him to poke holes in her story.

Instead, surprisingly, he put a hand on her shoulder. Emily wanted to pull away but forced herself to stay still. "Well, I can see that must have made life difficult. Still, I'm sure she could have found a way to get you a proper Catholic education if she had just tried harder. Nonetheless, we must find a remedy for your lack. Sister, I think the only solution is for me to pull Emily out of class once a week to come to the rectory so I can tutor her in an attempt to have her ready for confirmation next year."

"As you wish, Father. Emily, what do you think of Father Devlin's generous offer?"

Emily thought it sounded awful. To be the sole focus of his fierce attention on a regular basis made her cringe, but clearly there was no saying no to the priest. "That's very kind of you, Father. Thank you."

He gave her a thin-lipped smiled and patted her on her head. "It's settled then. Go along home, and I'll work out the details with Sister Mary Francis."

Emily walked out the door as quickly as possible without breaking into a run and found Lottie waiting for her just down the hall. "What was that all about?" Lottie asked.

"You're not going to believe this!" Emily responded. Once they were away from the school grounds, Emily related Father Devlin's suggestion of weekly tutoring at the rectory. Lottie was aghast at the very thought. "Oh, you poor thing! Father Devil is so mean! A full hour of him picking apart every little mistake would be torture." She sighed. "I'm sorry Emily. I don't mean to make you feel bad. Maybe it won't be as awful as all that."

Emily responded, "Well, at least I don't have to pretend I know stuff that I don't. I guess our story worked. And it really wasn't a lie."

Emily trudged toward the rectory, each step slower than the one before as she approached the time of her remedial lessons in catechism with Father Devlin. Given Lottie's assessment of his personality and her own experience in class the other day, she was definitely not looking forward to being alone with him for a full hour. She paused on the doorstep, taking a deep breath before she opened the door and entered the reception area. A middle-aged woman with graying blond hair pulled up in a bun was seated at a desk facing the entry, behind her a row of filing cabinets, a mimeograph machine, and a table in the center with rows and rows of envelopes laid out neatly. She smiled and said, "You must be Emily. Welcome to St. Ignatius. I'm Mrs. Northrup, the parish secretary. Father Devlin told me to expect you, so I'll just go let him know you're here." She walked down a long hall to Emily's right and disappeared from sight. Returning moments later, she nodded. "He'll see you now. Take this hall and turn left at the end. You'll pass a conference room and a couple of other doors before you come to his office on the right. The door is open, but he likes people to knock anyway in case he's working on something and doesn't see you standing there. Have a good lesson, Emily."

The hallway had three tall windows facing the front of the building, and Emily looked longingly at the green lawn and flower border, wishing she could be anywhere but here. Then she pulled herself together, lifted her chin and turned down the other hallway that led to the priest's office. Standing in the doorway, she knocked, and Father Devlin lifted his head from some papers on his desk. "Ah! Emily. Come in," he said briskly. He rose and gestured her to a straight-backed wooden chair facing his desk as he closed the door behind her. "Sit. I hope you are prepared to work hard. You have a lot to learn. I'm going to lend you a beginning catechism book, so you can study from home, but for today, I am going to lecture you on the basics of Catholic doctrine. I'm glad to see you brought a notebook, as you will definitely need to be taking notes."

"Yes, Father. Thank you again for helping me catch up with the other students. I'm looking forward to learning the catechism finally."

And so the priest began. He droned on and on, Emily frantically trying to keep up with her note-taking. At times, he would veer off topic to tell stories that highlighted his knowledge and expertise. Emily wondered who he was trying to impress, her or himself? But she did her best to feign interest. Finally, he looked at the clock on the wall behind Emily's head and said, "I see our time is up. For next week, I want you to write the Hail Mary ten times and bring that to me. You will also need to be able to recite it from memory, since this is the foundation of most of the penances you will have to do after confession. Any questions?"

Emily shook her head. "No, sir. Ten Hail Mary's and commit it to memory." She stood and walked toward the door. He followed and put his hand on her shoulder, giving it a squeeze, then letting it linger.

"Good job today, Emily. I think we are going to get along just fine." Emily was pleased by the compliment, but something about his touch left her uneasy, though she couldn't say why. At least the hour was over, and it hadn't been as horrible as Lottie had predicted, just boring.

Chapter 5

The fog comes
on little cat feet.
It sits looking
over harbor and city
on silent haunches
and then moves on.
     —Carl Sandburg

1957

  Initially, Emily had thought that her morning escapade at the park would be a one-time thing, but once begun, it was difficult to deny herself the freedom the experience had given her. She didn't go there every week, for fear that one of the ladies at her sewing circle would mention Emily's absences in front of George on a Sunday morning. Instead, she would slip away every few weeks, usually on sewing circle days, but occasionally on a day when she knew George would be far too busy at work to telephone her.

  One particular fall morning, after days of rain and high winds, Emily couldn't bear to be cooped up inside the house a moment longer. Gathering her sewing bag and a small towel in case the park benches were still drenched, she left the house and turned her steps toward the park. It was still a raw day, windy and cool, but the wildness of it felt exhilarating. She drew in deep breaths of the brisk air, laden with the smell of autumn, of chimney smoke and decaying leaves. When she arrived at the park, she was stunned by the number of branches that had broken off in the storms, even more so when she reached her usual resting place and saw that a large Ponderosa pine that had towered over most of the other trees in the park was now lying lifeless on the ground, its massive trunk broken and diminished. Saddened, Emily sank down on her bench without even thinking to wipe off the puddled rain drops. Unbidden memories poured into her mind, other parks on other days, other trees soaring to unimaginable heights for a small girl who loved to dream of another world, unreachable for her but touched by branches far above.

Emily sat in silent reverie for many minutes until she felt a drop on her hand and realized that she was crying. She was taken aback by her deep feelings of loss over the toppling of this beautiful giant. And then she realized that so many of those memories had contained magical moments with her mother, moments that had slipped away with her death. Feeling a deep need to record this moment and these feelings of grief, she began rummaging in her sewing bag for something to write on. She usually carried a pencil with her to scrawl notes on her patterns, and there it was, at the bottom of the canvas tote along with a pattern that only took up one side of a piece of paper. The book of poetry that was also nestled there gave Emily an idea, and soon she was scribbling away on the crinkled page.

Requiem for a Ponderosa

The fallen giant lies shattered now,
its mighty trunk,
which once stood tall and proud,
now broken and silent upon the ground.
'Twas oft my muse,
this grand old tree,
whose lofty limbs once pierced
the changing sky—
shades of brilliant blue, and steely
gray and inky dark brushed
by deep green splendor.
Heavenly stars once adorned
its graceful boughs,
and passing winds once stirred them
into stately dance.
This same wind proved its end
in one fierce and violent gust,
and these same branches now spread

lifeless
over the welcoming earth,
returning as all created things must do.
Dust to dust
and so to death,
and I can only watch and weep
at a life once elegant and green,
and catch my breath,
still glittering with tears,
as underneath the mulch of dying
is revealed a fragile seedling –
fresh from God's own womb –
waiting to make its own march into the sky.
In glad sacrifice, the ancient sentinel
suckles its young,
the fragrance of its passing
rising like incense.

When she finally looked up from her writing, Emily realized that she had been at the park far longer than she intended. She still had ironing and other tasks to do, so she gathered her things and rushed home. As usual, she placed her sewing on the floor next to the couch, but pulled the poem out first, wanting to rewrite it on nicer paper when she had a chance. Instinctively, she knew that writing poetry would not be an activity that George would approve of. She took it into the bedroom, intending to hide it in a drawer underneath her nightgowns, when the phone rang. Hastily, she set the poem on top of the dresser and ran to answer the call.

It was George, asking her if she had remembered to pick up his black dress shoes from the repair shop on her way back from church. Inwardly uttering a curse, Emily crossed her fingers and told a lie. "Of course I did, George. You need them for your big meeting tomorrow. How could I forget that?" Hanging up, she threw on her coat, grabbed her purse, and raced out the door.

Now hurried by the interruption, Emily was hard pressed to complete her other afternoon chores and get dinner ready in time for George's arrival. She had just finished setting the table when he walked in the door. "Hello darling, how was your day?" she said as she walked into his arms for a quick embrace.

"Extremely aggravating, to tell you the truth. I had a run-in with Caruthers again over bank policy. He seems to think that regulations are meant for everyone but him. It's maddening to the extreme!"

"I'm so sorry, George. Hopefully a quiet evening by the fire will help calm you down. Dinner is ready as soon as you are."

"The man is in direct violation of bank policy, Emily! The only thing that will fix that is for him to recognize the error of his ways or get fired. I don't think a cozy fire is going to remedy my situation!" With a harrumph of annoyance, he left the kitchen to hang up his suit jacket and tie.

Emily busied herself putting steaming dishes of food on the table. When she straightened up and turned, she was startled to find George standing right behind her with a familiar piece of paper crushed in his fist. Her heart sank like a stone. "What in God's name is this, Emily?" George's voice vibrated with quiet fury.

"I . . . uh . . . it's a poem . . . I wrote. I was going to show it to you. D-did you read it?" Emily stammered. She realized that she was shaking.

"A poem. About a fallen tree. Where did you see this tree, dear?" The sneered endearment increased Emily's anxiety.

"Um . . . at the park down the street."

"And exactly when were you at the park?"

Looking down at her hands, Emily mumbled, "This morning."

There was silence as George absorbed this information, did the calculations in his head. "This is the day you usually attend sewing circle. Are you saying that you skipped your commitment in order to take a jaunt to the park? Were you planning to tell me about this?"

"I . . . it's been so stormy the last few days, I haven't been able to be outside at all, and I just didn't feel like sitting in a room with all those gossipy ladies this morning. So I went to the park. And the tree was down, and it made me sad. I'm sorry, darling, truly sorry."

"So you ducked your responsibilities in order to write a silly *poem*?! It doesn't even rhyme! It's trash!" And to punctuate his words,

George suddenly ripped the paper into confetti and threw in into the garbage bin. "How many other times have you skipped out on sewing circle in order to go fritter away your time at the park? How many times have you *lied* to me?" Without warning, he raised his hand and slapped her hard across the cheek. Emily gasped and reeled backwards, eyes wide with disbelief. "You're just like Caruthers. Tell people what they want to hear and then do whatever you want behind their backs. You disgust me! I can't even bear to be in the same room with you right now." He quickly slopped some food onto a plate and took it into the bedroom, slamming the door behind him. Emily collapsed onto a chair, body convulsing as sobs burst from her chest and echoed through the house.

1948

Emily awoke to a world encased in fog. This was unusual for spring, but it had been raining for days, and all the moisture had coalesced into a ground mist that wrapped around the houses like a blanket of cotton batting. The huge elm in the Hutton's front yard loomed like a faint shadow out of nothingness. None of the other homes on the block were visible, and the silence made Emily feel as though she were alone on an island in a vast sea. She wrapped her arms around herself to hug the solitude to her. As much as she had wanted to be part of a family, she had been very accustomed to being alone when her mother was at work. A household with two adults, a nanny, and two small children besides herself was not the quiet refuge that home used to be. In the room next door, Meg squealed in protest to Fannie's attempts to get her dressed, and the magic spell was broken.

Emily and Lottie walked to school in the fog, chatting happily about a Social Studies project they were working on together. In the short time Emily had been living with the Huttons, she and Lottie had become great friends, sitting together at lunch and playing hopscotch at recess with some of the other girls. Lottie was not allowed to come to Emily's house because of Mother's health, but occasionally, when all her chores were done, Emily would get permission to go down the block to Lottie's.

As the girls entered the classroom that day, Emily's eyes alit on short poem written on the blackboard, entitled "Fog." A spark of recognition swept through Emily and brought a smile to her face. She immediately ran up to her teacher's desk. "I know that poem, Sister! My mother used to recite it to me on foggy days. She recited other poems, too, but this was one of my favorites."

Sister Mary Francis returned her smile. "How wonderful, Emily. I'm not accustomed to children your age being that excited about poetry. Perhaps you could help me talk about this poem today. Would you like that?" Emily nodded eagerly and took her seat. Despite her usual shyness, she was pleased to discover that reciting poetry was less scary than giving a book report, and she even managed to talk about her mother a bit. Then Sister gave a lesson on poetry, the different types and some of the famous poets. She taught them about haiku and asked the children to write one for their English homework that night. Emily was so engrossed that she was surprised when the bell rang for morning recess.

On the playground, Lottie and Emily ran to the swings. The girls had discovered that this was the place to go when they wanted to talk without being bothered.

"How is your tutoring going with Father Devil?" Lottie asked.

Emily shrugged. "Okay, I guess. It's not as bad as I expected, but he's so creepy. He doesn't really yell at me all that much. He just looks at me funny, and then he always touches my hair or rubs my back when I leave. It's weird."

"Ewww! I wouldn't want him touching me. But at least he's not cutting you down all the time like he does in class."

Changing the subject, Emily asked, "Didn't you love the poem we learned this morning?"

"I don't know. I thought poetry was supposed to rhyme. English isn't exactly my favorite subject anyway. I'd rather do word problems in Math!"

"You're crazy! *Nobody* likes word problems." The two girls giggled, but Emily was aware that her excitement was sharing space with a little bit of sadness in her heart, missing her mother with whom she had shared this love of poetry.

1957

Fog crept into the neighborhood during the night, dampening sound and obliterating sight. As Emily prepared George's breakfast, she felt the gloom of the morning creeping into her soul, sapping her of her normally cheerful disposition. Even George seemed quieter than usual as he went about his morning routine. After breakfast, he gave Emily a perfunctory kiss on the cheek and closed the kitchen door behind him on his way to work. It had been almost a month since his outrage over what he considered to be Emily's betrayal by sneaking to the park behind his back, and she hadn't been there since. Nor would she be going today. The fog was too dense, too enervating, too depressing for her to brave the chill and the chance of discovery.

Leaving the dishes to congeal on the table, Emily slumped into a chair and stared out the window at the bleak landscape. This fog wasn't the mysterious and fleeting mist of the Sandberg poem she remembered from childhood, but a suffocating miasma of despondence. Rather than bringing to mind happy memories of her mother, the gloom pressed in upon Emily, reminding her of what she had lost. This grief felt like a physical weight pressing in on her.

The day passed slowly as Emily went listlessly about her household tasks, alternately missing her mother intensely and reflecting on the prison that her marriage had become. Without friends, without books, without meaningful work, she felt lonelier than she ever had, even in the aftermath of her mother's death. At least then she had Mrs. McGill, her friends at school, her books, and after moving in with the Huttons, she had Fannie and Lottie and the children. And Sister Mary Francis, who had encouraged her not only to read poetry, but to try her hand at writing it. The poetry had been a means to explore her feelings of loss and fears of the future as well as her attempts to make meaning of the troubles life had dealt her. And now, all that had been taken from her.

There were no maternal figures in her life from whom she could seek advice, no friends to commiserate with. She still had some contact with Lottie, but only quick phone calls when George wasn't around. Lottie already had one child and another on the way, so she had precious little time to spend on phone calls or outings. George hadn't explicitly told her she couldn't have friends, but his response to Kathleen's shower invitation made it quite clear that he didn't want her maintaining relationships with the friends from her past.

And there were very few activities he deemed acceptable enough for her to take time away from the job of caring for him and his household. He was no longer even allowing her to go to the sewing circle, since she had used it as a means to steal moments of freedom from under his watchful eye. So she had no job to go to, no friends to confide in, no reading or recreational activities that gave her enjoyment, no poetry.

Worst of all, the George she thought she was marrying—the kind, thoughtful, protective man who had promised to cherish her until death parted them—had turned into an exacting, controlling man with a trigger temper and a perverse desire to punish. Emily remembered little of her father before he had left for the war, but what she did remember was how he and her mother had laughed together and hugged and cuddled with obvious love and affection. George's embraces had gotten fewer and farther between, and this morning's peck on the cheek was becoming a regular statement about the quality of their marriage. But this did not stop the routine of their intimate relations. Frequent intercourse continued uninterrupted by arguments or George's frequent criticism of Emily's failure to live up to his expectations of cleanliness and thrift. But their love-making was just as devoid of tenderness and love as the rest of their lives. It was a rough and painful act that never varied.

By dinnertime, the fog had not lifted either in Emily's heart or in the world outside. She and George sat eating in a silence only occasionally broken by a reminder from George about something Emily needed to do the next day or an incident at work he thought she would be interested in. Eventually, he realized that she was barely even looking up when he spoke. "Emily dear, is there something wrong? You seem so quiet tonight."

"Oh, it's this thick fog that's getting me down. It reminds me of my mother, and I'm just missing her so much it hurts. I've felt off all day."

George immediately got up and went over to Emily, pulling her up from her chair and into his arms. "I'm so sorry, darling. Sometimes I forget what a horrible loss you've suffered. It's natural for you to be sad sometimes. But I'm here for you now, and all you have to do is tell me whenever you're feeling low, and I'll offer you all the comfort I can."

It felt so good to be held tenderly and hear such kind words that Emily leaned into George's chest and let out a deep sigh. They spent the evening quietly listening to the radio with George's arm around her shoulder, as they had in the first two months of their marriage. Nonetheless, when bedtime came, and Emily realized that it was a Wednesday, she just couldn't face having sex with her husband. "George," she said hesitantly, "I know it's Wednesday, but I am still really down, and I'm just not in the mood for sex tonight. Would you mind if we put it off to tomorrow?"

"Oh, come now, Emily! Don't you think you're being a bit melodramatic? Offer it up to the cross, dear. Surely you don't think your suffering compares to the suffering Christ, do you? It is a wife's obligation to submit to her husband, or have you conveniently forgotten that part of Scripture? There will be no postponing of your wifely duty."

Perhaps it was only her imagination, colored by her dark mood, but it seemed that George gained extra pleasure from the roughness with which he took her that night. And in the silent darkness of the aftermath, Emily felt a chill that had nothing to do with the weather.

1948

Emily was seated at Father Devlin's desk, copying the Ten Commandments from the book he had given her. Repetition was one of the chief ways he thought children learned, and copying things down was his favorite tool to achieve it. The one time she had failed to complete a copying assignment, he had had a fit. When Emily had explained her many duties at home in helping with the children and the housework, he had taken to making her finish any uncompleted assignments in his office under his supervision. He often stood behind her as he did so, making her feel self-conscious and uncomfortable.

Assignment complete, Emily put down her pencil. Father

Devlin put his hands on both shoulders and rubbed them down her arms. He leaned over her and murmured, "You're such a good girl, Emily. And so lovely. You're going to make a man very happy one day." He lifted one hand to her head and began to stroke her hair. "Come over and sit with me on the davenport, and let's talk." There was a small, upholstered sofa in green velvet along the side wall of the office, where he pulled her onto his lap, putting his arms around her. Emily cringed inside, feeling the awkwardness of an eleven-year-old sitting on a grownup's lap. And his legs were bony and uncomfortable.

"I'm sure it must be hard for you having lost both of your parents. And I don't imagine you get much affection from Mr. and Mrs. Hutton in between his work and her illness. It sounds like they just took you in as cheap labor. But I want you to know that I see how special you are. I want you to feel that you can tell me anything."

Emily could feel something hard in his lap pressing against her legs, and his hand continued to stroke her arm. She felt a confusing mix of pleasure at this positive attention alongside a feeling of discomfort and confusion. "Thank you, Father, I will. I really should get back to class, though, if we're finished for the day."

"Of course! I lost track of time. Continue to study the Ten Commandments and copy down the principal effects of Confirmation ten times for next week. Now, off you go."

Emily walked back to her classroom wondering what had just happened. Was it possible that Lottie had been wrong about Father Devlin? It *was* nice to have someone say nice things about her and sympathize with her, but then why did she feel so strange?

Chapter 6

Adrift! A little boat adrift!
And night is coming down!
Will no one guide a little boat
Unto the nearest town?
　　　　　—Emily Dickinson

1948

Fannie and Emily whispered and giggled by the dim light of a desk lamp in their upstairs room. Emily was diagramming sentences while trying to teach Fannie the difference between an adjective and an adverb. This was their nightly ritual—Emily sharing what she was learning in school and Fannie telling funny stories about what the children had gotten up to that day. "So in the sentence 'The little boy ran quickly with his mother's hairbrush,' what is the adverb?" Emily asked impishly, turning Joey's latest escapade into an English lesson.

Fannie grinned. "Let's see . . . the verb is a word that shows action, so that would be 'ran,' and an adverb describes the verb, so I'm going to guess 'quickly,' but that wasn't the half of it! More like lightning, I'd say. Lord, that boy can run!"

"Except lightning is a noun," Emily teased.

"Oh, now you're really trying to get me confused! Isn't it time for bed by now?"

Emily agreed and stacked up her books on the desk ready to grab when she left for school in the morning. Over the past two months the two girls had become firm friends despite their age difference. They found that they worked well together as Emily took on more responsibility for housework, childcare, and tending to Mrs. H's needs. Just the previous week, the Huttons had informed Emily that Fannie would be dismissed for the summer, and Emily would take over her duties as soon as school was out. Alarmed, Emily had sought out Fannie to apologize.

93

"I'm so sorry, Fannie! I had no idea they would do this. What will you do? You need this job!"

"Don't fret yourself, lassie. It will be alright. The Huttons said I could still live here for a small amount of rent, and I've arranged with my uncle to work in his laundry doing the ironing. It will be hot and miserable, but I won't mind having a break from the missus' demands. Mind you, I'll miss the little ones. I'm sure I could come and give you a break on my half-day off, so I can play with them a bit. You'll be needin' it, for sure!"

Emily was already beginning to learn what Fannie meant about Mother's temper. She could be sweet as pie some days, and then she would have days where she did nothing but mope and cry. But the bad days were when she would snap at both the older girls for the slightest thing—if her tea wasn't the perfect temperature, if the children were too noisy, or the room was too dark, too light, too hot, too cold.

The next day, Fannie met Emily as she came in the front door after school. "I'm off to start learnin' how to use the big pressin' machine at Uncle Seamus's. Watch how you go, now. Mrs. H is in a spittin' temper today, I tell ya! The wee ones are coloring quietly upstairs for now, but that's not gonna last for long, I'm guessin'. You know how Joey is. Won't sit still for five minutes! I've left a roast in the oven for dinner, but you'll want to boil potatoes for mashing later. You remember how I taught you to make the gravy, right?" Emily assured her that she did and rushed upstairs to dump her books on the desk and poke her head into the children's room. Surprisingly, they barely looked up from their coloring, seemingly intent on a shared project that was holding their attention.

Emily ran lightly down the stairs and entered her parents' bedroom. Mrs. Hutton was propped up on pillows in the bed, fussing fitfully with her covers. "Hello, Mother. How are you feeling today?"

"How do you think I'm feeling, you stupid girl! How would you feel if you were confined to this bed all day every day? I'm sick of it! Everyone tiptoes around me like I'm some fragile flower, and when they're not fussing at me, they're ignoring me completely. I need a drink! Bring me some crème de menthe in one of the cordial glasses in the hutch, and be quick about it."

Emily did an abrupt about face and hurried into the kitchen.

She had to use a chair to reach the liquor cabinet, and as she dragged it over to the counter, Mother hollered, "Quit making such a racket out there!" *Fannie was right,* Emily thought, *Mother is truly in a temper today.* She carefully extracted the crème de menthe from the other bottles and then hefted the chair with her arms to keep it from scraping across the floor as she returned it to the dining room. Not entirely sure what a cordial glass looked like, she chose a small, fluted crystal glass from the array of stemware in the hutch. She then filled it halfway with the creamy green liquid and placed it on a tray. Mother insisted that all food or drink brought to her in the bedroom be served on a tray. She said it was how civilized people did things, but Emily couldn't help remembering with longing the more casual way in which she and her Mama had dined in their cozy apartment.

Carefully balancing the tray as she re-entered the bedroom, Emily was almost to the bed, when a thud of footsteps came from the stairway, and a small body suddenly hurled itself at her legs. Thrown off balance, she stumbled, and the tray went flying. A spray of green liquid arced across Mother's bedspread, and the glass hit the corner of her bedside table, shattering into pieces. Mother let out a screech, and cried, "Look what you've done! Look what you've done, you clumsy child! Can't you even control a two-year-old? What on earth good are you, anyway?! Well, don't just stand there staring. Do something!"

Holding onto Joey to keep him from cutting himself on slivers of broken glass, Emily stammered, "I'm so, so sorry, Mother. I thought he was in his room. Don't move! I'll take care of it. Let me take Joey back upstairs, and then I'll pick up the glass and get you cleaned off." In the meantime, Meg had come down to see what all the commotion was, and Emily grabbed her as well, before she could get too far into the room. As Mrs. Hutton continued to shriek, Meg began to cry. "Come children, let's go back upstairs. Everything's alright. We just had a little accident, and your mother is startled, that's all. Don't cry, Meg." Emily and the children trooped upstairs where she settled them down and got out a puzzle for them to put together. "Now, Joey, you stay here! I have to clean up that mess downstairs, and I can't have you running all over the house. You could get hurt if you touch the broken glass. Do you understand?"

The toddler, looking suitably repentant, nodded solemnly and

sat down on the floor. "I'll be good, Emmy, I really, really will."
Heart melting, Emily gave him a quick squeeze and a kiss on the head
before scurrying back down the stairs.

She grabbed the trash bin from the kitchen and rushed into
the bedroom. As she carefully picked up the larger pieces of glass,
Mrs. Hutton continued her tirade. "Look at this spill all over my
bedspread! You'd better hope that stain comes out, or you'll be
paying for it out of your allowance! And that glass was part of a
complete set that belonged to my grandmother. It's irreplaceable!
How are you going to make up for that?"

Flushed and angry at the unfairness of this tongue-lashing,
Emily was silent as she worked, fetching a broom in order to sweep
up the smaller particles. When she was finally able to approach her
mother's bed to remove the soiled spread, Mrs. Hutton swatted at
her weakly, then started to cry. "I'm just so useless. Do you know
what it's like to have to rely on others to do everything for you?"

"I'm sorry, Mother. It must be just awful. Let me get this
quilt off of you and help you change your nightgown. I'll get another
blanket too, so you don't get cold. Then I'll check on the kids to
make sure they're occupied before I bring you another drink."

Mother took in a deep, shaky breath. "Thank you, Emily. I
must seem like a complete lunatic to you, but I just get so
discouraged being in this bed all day long. Now hurry along—I'm
starting to feel chilled."

Eventually, Emily got her foster mother cleaned up and
tucked into bed. Another glass of crème de menthe had been
delivered without incident, and Mother was calmer, even giving
Emily a trace of a smile as she left the room.

After dinner that night, Father left the table to go speak to his
wife, but a short while later he tapped gently at Emily's bedroom
door and poked his head in. Emily lifted her gaze from her
homework. "Can I come in?" he asked. Emily nodded. "I hear you
had a rough afternoon today. Do you want to tell me about it?"

As Emily shared her side of the story, he nodded
sympathetically. "Well, Mother is much calmer now, and she is very
sorry for having yelled at you like she did. Fannie told me she thinks
her uncle can get the stain out of the bedspread, so you needn't
worry about that. As for the broken glass, we certainly don't entertain

anymore, so I don't think not having a full set is going to be all that great a tragedy. Thank you for being patient and understanding. Nonetheless, I think the lesson to be learned from this is that when Fannie isn't here, you will have to keep a much closer eye on the children, especially Joey. Understood?"

Emily nodded again, and Father leaned down to give her an awkward hug, then told her good night and left the room. Emily breathed a sigh of relief, glad that the difficult episode was over, but also aware that it would be a long, hard summer without Fannie. Having pretended to be asleep while Mr. H was there, Fanny whispered, "Are you alright, my sweet?" Emily nodded as she climbed into bed. She lay awake for a long time, listening to the sound of Fannie's regular breathing and becoming suddenly aware of a longing for her own mother. It was a long while before she fell asleep.

1958

Winter passed—long, cold days of dreary weather that sapped Emily's normal cheerfulness. Even the advent of spring, the greening of grass and the budding of trees, didn't do much to lift her spirits. She did enjoy the tulips in their neighbor's yard, but she longed to have that lovely riot of color in her own yard. She had asked George once about planting bulbs and lilacs, but George preferred the uniformity of a fastidiously mowed lawn and precisely trimmed shrubs. Emily gradually learned to adjust her expectations of marriage to George and settled into the daily grind of cleaning, laundry, and cooking. To fill the long and isolated hours when boredom threatened to swamp her, Emily wrote voluminous journal entries and poetry, taking care to burn it all in the fireplace before George returned home. She used the backs of envelopes, scrap paper, anything she could find to write on so that George wouldn't question her wasteful use of stationery. She was determined not to be so careless as to get caught again as she had in the innocent days before she fully understood George's controlling nature. But neither was she willing to give up the one activity that gave her some solace and helped her make meaning of the losses and trials that life had thrown at her.

When the weather permitted, Emily had to satisfy her longing for the outdoors by walking to the store for groceries or running other errands in the neighborhood. She studiously avoided the library, knowing that the temptation to bring home a book would be too strong. Then one day, Emily looked at the calendar and was startled to realize that it was July already, and their first anniversary was right around the corner. That night at dinner, it appeared that George had also noticed the upcoming anniversary. "Darling," he said, wiping his mouth after a bite of potatoes and gravy, "How should we celebrate our wedding anniversary? It's been some time since we went out on the town. I was thinking it might be nice to have dinner at the scene of our first date. What do you say?"

"That would be lovely, George. But are you sure we can afford it?"

"Well, you only have a first anniversary once, dear. I think we can scrape together enough for a nice dinner just as long as you don't order the chateaubriand. And I've been hinting to Mr. Matthews that I'm long overdue for a raise, so our financial situation may improve before too long."

"You certainly deserve it, darling, as hard as you work. And dinner at the Davenport will be the perfect way to celebrate. Thank you for thinking of it."

Two weeks later, Emily and George were seated at a table in the grand dining room that had been the setting for their first date. Emily was certainly more familiar with the ways of the world than she had been a year ago, but she was still awed by the grandeur of the setting, the waiters in their black tuxes, snowy white cuffs at the wrists fastened by gleaming gold cuff links. It felt like a different world from the street she grew up on. She wondered if the other patrons in their finest attire had any idea of her own humble roots. But she also realized that appearances could hide all kinds of dark realities and well-kept secrets.

In an expansive mood, George ordered a bottle of wine, and after the waiter had filled their glasses, George lifted his for a toast. "To my beautiful wife and the life we share. May we always be as happy as we are today." Emily forced a smile and touched her glass to his, all the while wondering how he could be so unaware of her discontent. Soon their food arrived, and they began to eat the lavish meal. Out of the blue, George cleared his throat and took a deep breath as if to speak.

"What is it, darling?" Emily asked.

"Well, dear, I had really hoped you would be pregnant by now. We both want lots of children, right? I'm just concerned that something is wrong."

"I'm disappointed about that too. It's getting to the point that every time my 'monthly' comes, I feel downcast for days. I don't have any idea why it is taking so long for me to get pregnant. And it's not for lack of trying!"

George gave the slightest of frowns. "I don't know about that. I've been thinking, and I'm not sure that's true. I really think we need to try increasing the frequency of our conjugal activities."

Emily looked at him, dumbfounded. "You don't think four times a week is enough?"

"No, I don't. Unless we're making love daily, we could be missing the window when you're most likely to conceive. I think we need to step it up to every day except Sundays. And it's hardly a sacrifice, is it?" George actually winked.

Realizing that protest would be futile, Emily managed a tight smile, and said, "You're right, dear. If it results in a baby, I'm all for it." Inside, however, the old darkness long held at bay reared its ugly head. Emily found that she had suddenly lost her appetite.

1948

As soon as the alarm clock sounded, Emily flung her legs out of bed and threw on some clothes before Meg and Joey woke up. School had been out for a week, and she was learning that getting a jump on the children was imperative to a peaceful beginning to the day. If they got out of bed and ran downstairs before Emily could get to them, they might wake up Mother, which would make her cranky and tired the rest of the day. Having complete responsibility for them and Mrs. H as well as the cooking and cleaning took every bit of energy she had. Keeping Mother's upsets to a minimum was essential. Thankfully, Mother usually didn't wake up until 9 AM, so

Emily had time to get the children fed, dressed and engaged in quiet activity before she had to attend to the needs of her invalid foster mother.

After Meg and Joey had breakfasted, Emily hustled them upstairs and brought out some blocks for them to play with. She watched for a moment as Joey began building towers which he would knock down as soon as they got high enough, and Meg started on a house that would soon hold her dolls. Satisfied that they were engaged for the moment, Emily went downstairs to awaken Mrs. H. She pulled the drapes to let in light and paused for a moment to look out at the sunny morning. When she heard the sounds of Mother stirring, she turned. "Good morning, Mother. Did you sleep well? Do you need some help getting to the bathroom?"

"I'm feeling a little weak today, but not bad. If you could just help me up, I think I can manage from there." Emily pulled her into a sitting position before putting her arm around her mother's back and boosting her to her feet. She watched the woman shuffle to the bathroom, then turned to straighten the covers on the bed and stack extra pillows to allow for a semi-seated position. Soon Mother returned and was helped back into bed.

"What would you like for breakfast? There's still some oatmeal that I fixed for the children, but I can fix you an egg and toast if you'd prefer."

"Oatmeal would be fine, dear, with brown sugar, please. And hot tea with milk and sugar. But before you go, hand me my date book. It's over there on the dresser."

When Emily returned with the breakfast tray, Mother reminded her, "Dr. Gunderson is coming today at one o'clock for my monthly check-up. You'll have to make sure the children are kept occupied so that there are no interruptions."

"Yes, Mother. I'll make sure they're quiet. Do you want me to bring them down after you've eaten, so you can read them a story?"

"That would be lovely, Emily. Bring the one about Ferdinand the Bull. That seems to be their favorite."

Emily left the room with a smile. It was going to be a good day. She spent the morning dusting furniture and mopping the kitchen floor. After lunch, Meg and Joey were ready for a nap, so she took them to their room and tucked them in. Hopefully, they would sleep right through Mother's appointment and give Emily a few moments of peace. The doorbell rang at precisely one o'clock, and she went to let Dr. Gunderson in, escorting him to the master bedroom. She closed the door and went into the living room to enjoy a few quiet moments of reading, all the while keeping an ear out for the children.

A few minutes later, Emily heard Mother raising her voice. Curious, she went quietly to the door to hear what was being said. The lower voice of Dr. Gunderson was saying, "I know you're upset, Vivian, but you just can't keep taking these pills as frequently as you are. I've told you how addictive they can be, and I fear that you are very close to that now. I must cut back your dosage and frequency."

"Please, doctor, you just don't know what it's like! When I try to cut back on the pills, I get so anxious and upset. I can't stop thinking about losing the baby, and I can barely stand to be pleasant to anyone. I can't imagine what my own children think of me when I get that way. Please don't take my pills away!"

"Vivian, I'm not telling you to stop them entirely, but if you don't cut back, there could be dire consequences. And you won't be much good to your children if you are in a stupor all day long. You have to focus on the children you have, not the one you lost. It's a great tragedy, I know, but you can't just withdraw from life altogether."

Mother's voice turned from wheedling to angry in a flash. "Fine, doctor, do what you have to do. I'll just find another doctor. I always thought you were a quack anyway, and now I know. Get out of here before I get out of my bed and throw you out!"

Emily dove into the bathroom before she could be caught eaves-dropping just as the doctor barged out the door. From behind him came a bottle of pills whizzing past his ear. So much for the good day she had been hoping for! The front door slammed, quickly followed by Mother's voice calling her name. "*Emily!* Get in here!"

"Yes, Mother, I'm right here. What's wrong?"

"*Everything* is wrong! That dunce of a doctor doesn't know what he's talking about. Wait until I tell Charles! He'll take that charlatan down a peg or two! I'm just so distraught I don't know what to do. Now retrieve my pills from the hall and bring me some water."

Emily ran for the water and pill bottle, hoping the children were able to sleep through all the shrieking. She returned to Mother's room with the water and watched as she took not one, but two of the pills Dr. Gunderson had left behind. Still agitated, Vivian fussed with her covers, crying and moaning. Emily wanted desperately to be able to help, but didn't know what to do. She began stroking Mother's hair and talking in a low and reassuring voice, "Hush now, Mother, it's going to be alright. I'm here, and Father will be home soon. Shhh." This seemed to have some effect, but Emily didn't know how long she could stand leaning over the bed in this uncomfortable position. Looking around, she spotted a book of Robert Burns' poetry on Mother's nightstand. Maybe that would help. Pulling over the ottoman, Emily sat, opened the book, and began to read, "Flow gently, sweet Afton among thy green braes/ flow gently, I'll sing thee a song in thy praise . . ." Gradually, Mother's breathing slowed, her hands became still, and her tears subsided. When she closed her eyes, Emily paused to see if she was asleep.

"Don't stop, Emily. Don't stop. Your voice is so comforting." And so Emily continued until Mother's breathing deepened into a regular rhythm and her head sagged to one side in sleep. Quietly, Emily closed the book, replaced it on the table, and tiptoed out of the room.

That night when Father arrived home, Emily told him over dinner what had happened. He sighed and rested his head in his hands. "Father, what's wrong with Mother? Why does she have to stay in bed all the time? She walks back and forth to the bathroom, so why can't she come out of her room?"

Father raised his head to look at her as he spoke, "I can see why it might be confusing for you, Emily. She looks perfectly fine, but when she lost the baby, it caused some complications that make it dangerous for her to over-exert herself. The toxemia caused damage to her heart and worsened her high blood pressure, both of which are very dangerous. And her condition also makes her very anxious. Don't forget that she's grieving too. I hope you will never know the pain of losing a child, Emily. It breaks your heart, and it can just about destroy your faith in God. I'm really proud of you for thinking to read poetry to your mother today. I'm sure that was a great comfort to her."

"Is it going to make things worse if she can't get enough of the pills she takes?"

"It might make her moodier for a while until she adjusts. Those pills are for her anxiety, but she takes other pills for her heart and blood pressure. Dr. Gunderson wasn't trying to cut back on those."

"I see. But what does addictive mean?"

"It means that people can start to depend on certain medicines if they take too much, and then they need more and more of them to have the same effect."

"So I guess I'm going to need to read to her a lot until she gets used to not taking so many pills. Does she have more poetry than that one book?"

Father smiled and patted her cheek. "I'm not sure, but I'll found out. And if not, I'll make sure to buy more. You're a good girl, Emily."

1958

Two months into the implementation of George's plan to conceive a child, Emily felt herself spiraling into a perpetual melancholy. It wasn't just the increased frequency of the act that troubled her, but also a deepening darkness inside her that she couldn't explain. She felt her energy leaving her through invisible cracks in her very being. Even the simplest household chores made her feel as though she were walking around in cement overshoes. She had quit writing altogether, feeling she had no thoughts worth committing to paper. She found it difficult to focus on tasks or conversations due to the swirling thoughts in her head. The nights were long and restless, and even when she did manage to fall asleep, her sleep was troubled by feverish dreams. Snippets of incidents long past floated up from the dark morass and disappeared again. Disembodied faces taunted her—Mrs. H., Father Devlin, the boys who had teased her at school after her father died, the hateful woman from church who had told her God had taken her daddy from her.

Possibly worse than these things was George's intense preoccupation with Emily's failure to get pregnant. He continually asked her how she was feeling, watching her for signs of nausea or weight gain. He questioned her about when her period was due, and about a week prior he would begin asking "Has your period started yet?" on a daily basis.

One Saturday in September, Emily finally reached her limit. When he asked the same question yet again, she snapped, "George, will you please stop pestering me? If my period starts, I will tell you! All your questions just increase my anxiety, and I'm sure that isn't an ideal condition for conceiving a child."

George went silent, but anger emanated from him in waves. "I will not have you speak to me in that manner, Emily! What is the matter with you? You act like you don't even want a baby. Is that it? Are you doing something to prevent a pregnancy? Are you?"

"No, George, of course not! I want a baby just as much as you do, but you're putting so much pressure on me, I can't relax. You heard Mrs. Harrington the other day at church. She said that we need to relax and try not to think about it, and it will happen. Well, there's apparently no chance of that in this house!"

"I'm only doing it because I love you, and I'm eager to be a father. I chose you to be the mother of my child, but your attitude lately is starting to make me wonder. What's wrong with you? You mope around the house like you'd lost your best friend. It takes you twice as long to get things done as it used to, and you barely even speak. You are not the girl I married anymore."

"I don't know, George. I feel dejected all the time, and I don't know why. I'm not sleeping well, and I just don't have any energy."

"Well you know what they say about chronic melancholy, don't you? It's caused by separation from God, and that separation is caused by sinfulness. Perhaps you need to examine your conscience and truly repent of your sins. Confession doesn't do any good if you don't come before God with a contrite heart."

"Trust me—repentance is not going to fix this. I don't know what I need, but it's not that."

"And how would you know? Now that I think about it, maybe your sinfulness has been the problem all along. All the bad things that have happened to you in your life, maybe God has been punishing you, and you just aren't getting the message. If you were as sweet and pure as you pretend to be, surely God would have blessed you rather than cursed you."

Emily reeled from the blow of his words, just as if he had slapped her. She felt as though the breath had been knocked out of her. Mouth gaping open, no words would come. Her only thought was of escape. She pushed back from the table, knocking her chair down as she stood and ran out the door. Stumbling down the walkway, she reached the alley and began to run, no destination in mind but *away*.

1944

"Mama, I'm mad at God!" Emily and her mother were walking home from church, hand in hand on a summer morning about a month after her father had been killed.

"What on earth would make you say that, Ladybug?"

"Because God took my Daddy away. Mrs. Richards said so."

Maddy was quiet for a moment, then said, "What else did Mrs. Richards tell you?"

Mimicking the older woman's squeaky voice, Emily replied, "She said, 'Oh, Emily, you poor dear. I'm sure you miss your daddy, but everything happens for a reason. God just needed him more than you do. But don't you worry, if you're very, very good, maybe God will bring you a new daddy someday.'"

They were nearing a bus stop, and Maddy guided Emily over to the bench. "Let's sit down here for a minute and talk about Mrs. Richards. First of all, she's an old biddy who doesn't know what she's talking about. This is just between you and me, because I don't want anyone thinking I was talking disrespectfully about her, but she was very, very wrong to tell you that. 'Everything happens for a reason' is just something people say when they don't know what else to say. They think it will make you feel better, as though God has some sort of grand plan, but it doesn't make anyone feel better. Ever. God didn't take your daddy away, Emily. God doesn't go around deciding who to take and who to leave behind. God doesn't cause the bad things that happen to us on earth. You didn't deserve to lose your father; in fact, no one deserves such a thing. Never forget that. War is what killed your father, and war is an entirely human invention. God doesn't wage war, people do. A lot of the bad things that happen on earth are because of the choices people make or the tragedies that just happen, no matter who you are or how hard you pray. People make war, people do bad things to other people, accidents happen because they're *accidents*, and people get sick and die. God is not the cause, but God is there in the aftermath, loving people, comforting them, and giving them strength to face such awful things. And God is with us, Ladybug, right here and right now. God is giving us this beautiful sunny day to remind us that God is as present as the sun, even on days we can't see it. God is all around us in the people who care for us and help us, like Mrs. McGill and Reverend Truitt. Do you understand what I'm saying, Emily?"

"I think so. The Germans killed Daddy, and God didn't have anything to do with it. God's job is to help us remember that He loves us so we don't feel so alone. Is that right?"

"Yes, little one, that's exactly right. See? You are already much wiser than Mrs. Richards! So instead of being mad at God, we need to be grateful for all the ways He is taking care of us and comforting us when we're sad."

"I'm grateful that God gave me you, Mama."

Maddy smiled and wrapped her daughter in an embrace, holding her tight so Emily wouldn't see the tears that had sprung to her eyes. "Me too, Ladybug. Me too."

1948

The summer dragged on, day after day of endless work. At night, Emily fell exhausted into bed and could barely stay awake long enough to chat with Fannie a bit before falling fast asleep. Her only respite was the two hours she was allowed to play with Lottie on Saturday afternoons while Father watched the children and cared for Mother's needs. The girls crammed as much fun and chatter as they could in the time allotted. Then it was back to work for Emily, fixing dinner and putting the children to bed. Sometimes, Father would take over the nighttime routine, so that she could at least read for a while until she couldn't keep her eyes open any longer. On an occasional

Sunday afternoon, Fannie would come for a bit to play with the children, allowing Emily to work uninterrupted in the kitchen, preparing the family's Sunday dinner, always a more elaborate meal than the other days of the week.

Mother had not yet adjusted to the change in medication, continuing to be anxious and argumentative. When it got really bad, Emily would drop everything else and read poetry to her as she had the day of the broken glass. This usually helped to calm Mother down, but it took valuable time away from Emily's other duties. Mother was also asking Emily to prepare her a drink more frequently. One evening, when Father came home from work, he headed toward the liquor cabinet and took out a bottle of gin. He had a puzzled look when he noticed that it was almost empty. "Emily, do you have any idea why so much gin is missing from this bottle? Last time I saw it, it was nearly full. I can't imagine that it's you, but how else could this happen?"

"Oh, it's OK, Father. I've just been making gin and tonics for Mother. She likes one in the afternoon before you get home. And sometimes more than one. I was just about to tell her that we're almost out." As she spoke, Father's features settled into a frown. Now anxious, Emily asked, "Have I done something wrong?"

"No. Um . . . No, Emily, it's fine. I'll just go have a little talk with your mother before dinner." He went into their bedroom and closed the door firmly behind him. Emily could hear their voices, quiet at first and then Mother's raised in anger, followed by Father's voice, firm and insistent. By the time he came back into the kitchen, Emily had Mother's dinner tray ready.

"Shall I take this in to Mother now?"

"I don't think she's in the mood to eat at this moment, Emily. I'll try taking it to her in a little bit. Why don't you call the children down to dinner so we can get them fed and ready for bed?"

Mother never did eat dinner, and Father took over the task of getting her settled for the night, almost as if he didn't want to expose Emily to the mood Mother was in.

The next afternoon, just after Emily had put the children down for a nap, Mother called her into the bedroom. "Yes, Mother? What can I do for you?"

"Come over here, girl. I need you to walk down to the market and pick something up for me. Talk to Mr. Price behind the counter and no one else. He will hand you a package, and you're not to look in it for any reason. Bring it home to me, and make sure you don't drop it."

"Yes, Mother, but won't I need to pay for it?"

"Don't worry about that. I've spoken to him, and he'll just put it on our account. And don't say a word about this to anyone, not even your father. *Especially* your father! Do you understand?"

Uneasy, Emily nodded. "I understand, Mother. Mr. Price only. And don't drop it."

"Now go on. You need to get back here before Meg and Joey wake up."

As Emily walked to the store, she wondered what this was all about. She'd never been asked to run an errand like this before, and she felt uncomfortable with the secrecy that was being asked of her. Nonetheless, she carried out her instructions and delivered the package to Mother, who gave her a big smile and a pat on the arm. "Good girl, Emily. You're a life saver." Just then Joey hollered from upstairs, and Emily ran to help him out of his crib before he climbed out by himself. Plunged back into her regular duties, she promptly forgot about the unusual incident.

However, the request was repeated the following week and every week after that, sometimes more than once a week. Occasionally, when Emily entered Mother's bedroom, she would catch her taking a sip of a clear liquid out of a bottle, then quickly hiding it. Emily noticed that Mother's tantrums became less frequent, but she often seemed groggy and slurred her words.

One Saturday afternoon, when Emily was over at Lottie's house, they went into the back yard to play with their dolls on the patio. Lottie's parents' bedroom window was open, and unbeknownst to them, their conversation was audible to the girls.

"I can't believe how that woman works that child to death! It's a disgrace! I wish we could do something about it, but since he's a lawyer, I don't think we'd get very far. I doubt he even knows what's happening in his own household. Do you know that Millie saw Emily at the market the other day receiving what looked like a bottle in a brown paper bag from Mr. Price? She's making that poor girl buy her booze! I can't imagine what she's thinking. And as for Mr. Price, I'd like to give him a piece of my mind!"

"Now, Betty, calm down! Believe me, I understand your frustration. It is truly an outrageous situation, but we can't interfere. The only thing we can do is extend our kindness to Emily and make sure that she sees what a real, loving family can be."

"I know you're right, John, but it just breaks my heart. I wish we could take her in, but God knows we're bursting at the seams as it is."

The voices trailed off as the adults left the room, leaving Lottie and Emily staring at each other with the mouths hanging open. "Is it true?" Lottie asked.

"I guess so," Emily responded. "I haven't ever looked in the bag, but I kind of suspected. I just try not to think about it. I feel so guilty for not telling Father, but he's just happy that she's not nagging him about getting more pills from the doctor anymore."

"Jeepers, Emily! That's awful! I mean, I knew it wasn't good for you over there, but I had no idea how bad. I just thought they were strict, not that they were working you so hard."

"It's alright, Lottie. It's better than being in a children's home, I guess. I'll be okay."

The girls continued to play and chatter, wondering what sixth grade would be like and who their teacher would be. Lottie was excited about an upcoming family day at Natatorium Park, a big park near the river with a carousel and carnival rides. Their time together passed too quickly, as usual, and soon it was time for Emily to go home.

Just as she was about to leave, Lottie's mother called for her to wait. "Oh, Emily, I'm glad I caught you. I was wondering if you'd like to join us next Saturday for a day at the park. You've been working so hard all summer that I'm sure Mr. Hutton would give you permission to have some fun with us. Tell him to call me about it, and I'll give him all the details."

The two girls looked at each other and began jumping with excitement. "Oh, Mrs. Fisher, thank you! I would love to go! I'll ask Father as soon as I get home." She crossed her fingers. "I hope he says yes." She hugged Lottie and ran down the sidewalk, wondering if she dared hope that Father would let her go.

Before walking in the front door, Emily stopped and took a

deep breath. She knew that racing in the house and disrupting whatever might be happening would not be a good way to start this conversation. She opened the door and entered quietly, taking the temperature of the household. No loud noises and no yelling. So far, so good. She poked her head into the master bedroom where Mother appeared to be napping. She then went upstairs to check the children's room. There she found Father playing hide and seek with them. His eyes were tight shut as he counted to ten, while Joey hid under his crib in plain sight and Meg giggled from the closet. As soon as Joey saw her, he shouted "Emmy!" and ran to hug her knees. This brought Meg out of the closet, and Father opened his eyes.

"Aha!" he exclaimed, "I've found all of you in one shot. Welcome home, Emily. Did you have fun at Lottie's?"

"Yes, Father! And I have something I need to talk to you about."

"Alright. Children, please play quietly in here for a few minutes while I go talk to Emily in her room. Then we'll be back to finish the game. We should make Emily be 'it' for interrupting us, don't you think?" Meg smiled and clapped her hands before turning to her pile of stuffed animals while Joey climbed on the rocking horse in the corner.

Once in her room with the door shut, Emily told Father about the Fisher's invitation. "Can I go, Father, please? Just this once?"

"Well, that's a really nice gesture. Are you sure you girls didn't pester Mrs. Fisher about this?"

"No, Father! Honest. She just asked me out of the blue as I was leaving."

"Well, you have been working awfully hard and saving us money by taking over for Fannie. Let me call Mrs. Fisher for the details, then I'll ask your mother and see what she thinks. If she agrees, I think I could probably manage to keep the children corralled for the day. Now get in there and entertain Meg and Joey before they start a revolt!"

Emily waited on pins and needles, wanting this opportunity with all her being. She thought Father would be willing, but it all depended on the mood Mother was in. Emily thought back over the morning to see if there was anything that Mother might be upset about. Nothing came to mind, in fact, she remembered that Mother had actually said "Thank you," when she had brought in her morning tea. That was a good sign. But then, anything could have happened between then and now to sour her mood. All Emily could do was wait and hope.

After finishing the game of hide and seek, Emily went downstairs to start dinner. She heard voices in the master bedroom, and the door was closed. At least it didn't sound as if they were arguing. Finally, Father emerged and came into the kitchen. "Well, Emily, we've decided to let you go. Mother was concerned that you wouldn't complete your chores, but I assured her that you would work hard to finish anything that was needed on the following day. You will need some extra money for the rides and maybe some treats, but I think we can find some spare cash. You can consider it a bonus. Just don't expect this to be a regular event."

Emily ran over and hugged him around the waist, which was as high as she could reach. "Thank you, Father! Thank you so much. I *will* work hard and get all my chores done, and I won't expect this all the time. I think the Fishers only go to Nat Park once a year anyway."

Father harrumphed and awkwardly broke free of Emily's embrace. "Okay, okay. No need to get mushy about it. Let's get dinner on the table, shall we?"

The following Saturday dawned bright and clear. Emily jumped out of bed and was dressed and ready to go an hour before they were expecting to leave. She quickly prepared breakfast, got the children dressed and made their beds so that would be one less thing Father would have to do. When the time came, she waved goodbye to her family and ran down the street. The Fisher's station wagon was waiting in the driveway, and their four children were clambering into the back. Lottie was the oldest, so she and Emily got to sit in the space behind the back seat, while the little ones sat on the bench seat, fighting over who had to sit in the middle. Mrs. Fisher, pregnant with their fifth child, tossed a bag in the back with Emily and Lottie filled with all the accoutrements she would need for the smaller ones for a day at the park.

As they neared the park, Emily gawked at the brightly colored rides. Her mother had never been able to afford to bring her here, so it was a new and exciting experience. When they parked and got out of the car, she could hear the carnival music, bright and jangling. Hawkers yelled, "Step right up!" seeking to draw customers to their stalls filled with a cornucopia of prizes. There were so many things to see, she could scarcely take it in. It was decided that once they purchased ride tickets, Emily and Lottie would be on their own, while Mr. and Mrs. Fisher rode herd on the younger children. All the children were vibrating with anticipation, and it was all they could do to walk, not run, to the ticket booth. And then they were free! Emily and her best friend held hands as they walked around, taking it all in and plotting which ride they would go on first. Then Emily saw the carousel. The brightly colored horses, gleaming in the summer sun, the calliope music, the blur as it whirled round and round. She was transfixed.

"We have to ride the carousel first," she said. "It's so beautiful! Oh, Lottie! Can we?"

Lottie smiled with delight. "I was hoping you'd say that. It's my favorite, too." The girls got in line, dancing on tiptoe as they watched the riders fly by them. After what seemed like forever, it was their turn. Emily chose a deep blue horse with a flowing silver mane, and Lottie sat next to her on a red one with a golden saddle. Climbing aboard, they felt the carousel slowly begin to turn, then faster and faster. Emily laughed and leaned her head back, feeling the breeze blowing through her hair. She abandoned herself to the sensation, to her own delight, forgetting about everything but this moment, feeling like a child again for the first time in what felt like forever. It was a perfect day.

1958

Since their argument in September, George and Emily barely spoke. Emily's spontaneous rebellion had hardened into resolve, and she refused to go to confession. George became even more critical and spiteful, pointing out every slightest failure to meet his exacting expectations. They still went to Mass together on Sundays, but George would shame her before and after, telling her he couldn't believe she dared darken the door of the church in such a sinful condition. Emily's dejection grew worse, and she began to fear that George was right. The shame he had planted in her burgeoned into self-disgust. Maybe he *was* right. Maybe she was innately bad. Perhaps all the tragedies she had suffered had been brought on by her own sin. She wracked her brain trying to discover this secret flaw and came up with a hundred of them. Lazy, disrespectful, rebellious, selfish, slovenly, worthless. She wallowed in shame and misery and began to question whether she deserved to bear a child at all.

None of this stopped George from his nightly attempts to impregnate her. It could not be called love-making by any stretch of the imagination. Indeed, it was more like punishment. Even in what was supposed to be an expression of intimacy, George was brutish, even angry, and Emily sometimes wondered if she was the target of his anger or if he was in some way punishing someone else entirely as he rutted at her.

One night, after another excruciatingly painful episode, Emily laid awake, tossing and turning. Despite her feverish thoughts, sleep eventually claimed her and drew her into dark dreams of dimly lit tunnels, winding into ominous depths. In this dream, she wandered a demonic labyrinth, seeking to escape the terrible monster who was stalking its passageways, lurking everywhere and nowhere. She wondered if perhaps she had already been devoured and was lost in the belly of the beast itself. Dread was her companion, terror rising with each turning, until without warning, she stepped into nothingness, falling into a black abyss. Emily awoke suddenly, gasping in terror. She glanced around at the familiar walls of her room, at her bed, and the sleeping form of George lying next to her, but these things brought her no comfort. She was still falling, and she knew that her fear was not the landing but that she would never land at all.

Chapter 7

Beware the Jabberwock, my son!
The jaws that bite, the claws that catch!
　　　　　　　　　　　—Lewis Carroll

1948

At long last, the first day of sixth grade arrived. Emily was so excited she could hardly contain herself. Sitting in a classroom and learning about fractions, grammar, and American history would feel like a luxury when compared to the grueling labor that had been expected of her over the summer. It would also be wonderful to see Lottie every day. Fannie had returned to her role as maid, cook and caregiver, and Emily looked forward to evenings of homework and laughter. She wolfed down breakfast despite Father's disapproving frown. He would be driving Meg to school, as she had turned six over the summer and would be starting first grade, but Emily had insisted on walking with Lottie. She grabbed her lunch pail and gave the children a quick hug before bolting for the door. "Don't run!" Father admonished, but added, "Have a good day at school." Emily's answer was cut off by the slamming of the door. She waited at the corner for Lottie, who was typically late given the chaos of the Fisher household. When Lottie finally arrived, the girls turned their steps toward the school, walking quickly in their eagerness, speculating again about whose class they would be in and what new knowledge they might gain this year.

When they arrived at the school, they encountered a long line of first grade children on the sidewalk clutching their parents' hands as they waited to get their class assignments. Emily noticed that Father and Meg hadn't arrived yet. Lottie grabbed her hand and pulled her past the line and into the school. "C'mon, we don't have to wait. There will be class lists posted on the wall in the front hallway. We just have to look for our names and the room number we're assigned to. See, here they are."

The girls quickly found the sixth-grade list, but neither of their names were on it. Then Emily noticed that the sheet next to it was for a fifth and sixth combination class. She scanned the list of names and found Lottie's name first and then her own further down. Both girls let out a squeal that was hushed almost immediately by a hall monitor. Clasping their hands over their mouths with a giggle, they took a quick glance at the room number and walked as fast as they could down the hall. At Room 108, they crossed their fingers in hopes of a nice teacher and opened the door. A nun in full habit sat at the teacher's desk with her head bent looking at the attendance book on her desk. When she looked up to see who was entering her classroom, the girls saw that it was Sister Mary Francis.

Emily ran to the teacher's desk and flung her arms around the nun. "I thought you'd be teaching fifth grade again! I'm so glad to see you! Why is there a combination class?"

Sister Mary Francis chuckled and returned Emily's hug. "I'm glad to see you, too, Emily, and you as well, Lottie. The school had an increase in enrollment for both fifth and sixth grades, so they created this special combination class for the more advanced students. I think you'll be excited about the things we're going to be studying this year. It will be challenging, but hopefully fun as well. So find your seats, girls, while I greet the other students." Lottie and Emily automatically chose the desks that were front and center of the classroom, eager to be close to the action of what promised to be a great school year.

Emily almost floated home at the end of the school day, head full of the world of ideas Sister Mary Francis had promised they would explore this year. She was most excited by the section on poetry that would begin the next day with a trip to the school library. There the class would page through books of poetry and find one piece of verse that they found particularly enjoyable or meaningful to write a theme about.

At home, Emily slipped back into the familiar rhythm of the household, anxious for the children's bedtime so she could start on her homework and have time to share the day with Fannie. Seeking to relieve the boredom of being confined to her bed day after day,

Mrs. H had taken up embroidery. When Emily went into the bedroom to check on her, she found Mother sucking on her left index finger, then noticed a small bloodstain on the fine linen pillowcase she'd been working on. "Oh dear, Mother! Are you okay? Can I get you a bandage?"

Mother narrowed her eyes at Emily, almost as though she didn't recognize her. Then, words slow and slurred, she responded, "Iss allrigh'. Jus' take this blasted needle away. I can't find my th-thimble. . .. Where's my bottle? I jus' need a lil' sippy." Emily sighed as she removed the offending needle and the stained linen, uncovering the thimble in the process. She set them carefully on the bedside table then reached under the bed to find the bottle of gin at her fingertips. She handed it to her foster mother and watched as she took a large gulp. Emily had to grab it back before Mrs. H's attempts to screw on the cap could cause her to spill gin all over the bed. "Thass good. Thass a good girl, my Emily. You take good care of me. I dunno what I'd do without you."

Leaving the room to look in on the children, Emily chewed on her lip. Mother's drinking had grown steadily worse, and Father either didn't see it or was choosing to ignore it. At any rate, he wasn't talking to her about it. Where did he think Mother was getting the alcohol? Did he know that Emily was making the trip to Mr. Price's store twice a week? She felt guilty for contributing to Mother's drinking problem, but she also knew that her foster mother could make life miserable for her if she didn't do as she was told. She wished she could talk to Father about it, but feared disrupting the fragile peace that had settled over the household lately. For a moment, Emily thought of her own mother, imagining what life would be like if she were still alive. She missed Mama fiercely. Then, pushing those thoughts aside, Emily went about her appointed tasks.

The next day, Sister Mary Francis escorted Emily's class to the library, where the librarian had laid out many books of poetry for the children to page through in search of a poem for their assignment. Lottie was less than excited about this, but Emily was eager to peruse the treasure trove of poems the books contained. She walked around all the tables first, looking over the shoulders of her classmates, scanning titles and authors. So many intriguing titles to choose from! Names like Walt Whitman, Robert Frost, and Elizabeth

Barrett Browning sounded mysterious and exotic. Robert Burns and William Yeats were familiar to her from the well-worn book of poetry her mother had read to her on cozy evenings in their apartment. Then her eyes were captured by her own name—Emily. Emily Dickinson. Delighted, she snatched up the book before another classmate could claim it. Quickly, she sat down at one of the other tables and began turning pages, skimming the poetry within to see if she could find the perfect poem for this project. Then one particular poem caused her to slow her reading, to forget about her assignment completely and opened the door to the grief she had shoved aside the day before.

> "If recollecting were forgetting,
> Then I remember not.
> And if forgetting, recollecting,
> How near I had forgot.
> And if to miss, were merry,
> And to mourn, were gay,
> How very blithe the fingers
> That gathered this, Today!"

Emily became very still, the chattering students around her fading away as she allowed her sorrow to well up within her. Here in the noisy library, she felt all alone and awash in the pain of loss. This was the poem she needed to write about. The poet who shared her name shared something else as well. She could feel it.

1959

After the holidays, winter closed in around Emily like a cold, wet blanket. As a child, she had loved winter, loved the snow and the cozy feeling of sitting next to a crackling fire on a wintry night. But that was before her mother had died, before life got so much harder, before George had revealed his true colors, before her infertility became the only thing she could think about, before shame and darkness had become her constant companions. After eighteen months of marriage, she and George had still not conceived a child, and even the women at church were beginning to make comments. "Gosh, Emily, we thought you would be pregnant by now." "Emily, when are you and George going to start a family?" But the worst were the ones who didn't speak to her at all, but looked upon her judgmentally, clearly believing that she and George must be using some form of birth control in violation of church teachings.

One evening during supper, George cleared his throat and announced, "Emily, I think it's time for us to go to the doctor and see why you're not getting pregnant. It's been over six months since we started trying harder to conceive, and nothing is happening."

Alarmed, Emily responded, "Are you sure that's necessary, George? Lots of couples have a hard time conceiving, and nothing is really wrong. I don't feel comfortable going to a doctor about this. Let's just give it more time."

"Nonsense, Emily! I think a year and a half of marriage with no pregnancy is more than enough time. If we don't do everything we can to bring a child into this world, we're not fulfilling our Christian responsibility. Besides, I've already made the appointment. I've asked Mr. Matthews to give me Thursday afternoon off so I can take you to your appointment."

Emily put down her fork, suddenly no longer hungry. "Why didn't you talk to me first? I think I have a right to be consulted about seeing a doctor who is probably going to want to do something more invasive than taking my temperature and listening to my heart and lungs! How would you like it if the situation were reversed?"

"Emily, you're being ridiculous! You're going, and that's final."

Emily stood up abruptly, threw her napkin onto the table, and stormed out of the room. Moments later, George heard her slam their bedroom door. Determined not to let his meal go cold, he calmly speared another piece of pork chop and placed it in his mouth.

That night, Emily tossed and turned, unable to escape her sense of panic. It had never occurred to her that their situation would lead to this. She remembered a discussion that had occurred some months ago at the sewing circle about going to see the doctor about "female" problems. One of the women had described the examination in such horrifying detail that Emily had needed to excuse herself. The thought of enduring the embarrassment and invasion of a strange man poking and prodding at her was more than she could bear. She tried to think of a way to get George to cancel the appointment, but she knew that once her husband set his mind on something, there was no persuading him otherwise. She even considered leaving the house on the day of the appointment before George came to get her, but quailed at the thought of his rage at her defiance. Ultimately, her frantic thoughts were replaced by resignation and hopelessness. Worst of all, she knew that there was nothing the doctor could do to help her. Over the long months of trying, Emily had come to believe that her infertility was truly a punishment from God.

1948

Even though it wasn't required, Emily felt that she wanted to know more about Emily Dickinson for her report. While her fellow students were still paging through the books of poetry, she went to the shelf where the World Book Encyclopedias were kept and pulled out the "D" edition. When she found the entry for Emily Dickinson, she scanned it quickly, looking for a specific piece of information. And there it was. When Dickinson was only thirteen, her close friend and cousin, Sophia, had died of typhus. This explained the tone of the poem and Emily's instinctive sense of connection with the poet. She quickly scribbled down the details she needed and returned the encyclopedia to its place. She then went to Sister Mary Constance's desk and checked out the book of Dickinson's poetry. She couldn't wait to get started on her assignment.

A week later, Sister Mary Francis had finished grading her students' papers and was passing them back. Always careful to avoid allowing the children to see their fellow classmates' grades, she placed the papers face down on their desks. She avoided the red pens and large handwriting that other teachers used so that grades were not readable by students sitting nearby. Emily received her paper and sat still for a moment, heart pounding. For some reason, this grade meant more to her than usual. She could virtually recall what she had written word for word. Finally, she slowly turned over the paper, seeing first the poem, printed neatly, followed by her report:

> My paper is about a poem written by Emily
> Dickinson. I think it is a poem about losing someone
> you love. One of Emily's best friends died when she
> was thirteen. I think that must have been really hard.
> My mother died last year, and this poem is exactly
> how I feel when I think about her. Sometimes I am
> afraid I will forget her completely, and that scares me
> and makes me sad. But I get sad when I remember,
> too, because I miss her so much. And sometimes the
> memories make me smile, because she was such a
> great mother, and we had fun together. It's really
> confusing to have memories make me feel sad and
> happy at the same time. I really like this poem,
> because it makes me feel like this is normal. It's really
> hard to be around other children who have both of
> their parents still living. I don't think they know how
> lucky they are. This poem helps me feel less lonely,
> because someone else understands what it's like to
> lose the person who is your whole life. Even though
> she lived a hundred years ago, I feel like Emily
> Dickinson is my friend. I am going to keep this poem
> by my bedside so I can read it whenever I feel sad.

At the bottom of the page, in Sister Mary Francis'
handwriting, was an A+. She had written, "This is a very thoughtful
paper, Emily. You did a great job of discovering the meaning of the
poem and describing how it applies to your life. Perhaps you yourself
will become a great poet some day!" Emily felt a warm glow suffuse
her body, and a smile spread across her face. When she looked up,
she saw that Sister Mary Francis was smiling back at her.

When the bell rang at the end of the day, the students
gathered their things and began filing out of the classroom. Then
Emily heard her teacher calling her name. "Emily, can you stay
behind for a minute?"

Emily tapped Lottie on the shoulder and said, "Wait for me.
I'll catch up with you in a jiffy." Sister Mary Francis gestured toward

a desk and sat down across from her. Emily had a moment of anxiety, wondering if she was in trouble, but was soon reassured.

"Emily, I was very impressed with your paper. If I'm remembering correctly from last year, you really love poetry. Is that right?" Emily nodded. "So I was thinking, if you'd like, I could lend you some of my own poetry books to read. We'll be studying poetry in class and writing some, too, but I have a feeling that you are going to be miles ahead of the other students. I don't want you to get bored with doing the same things they are, so how about if I give you assignments that are a little different and more advanced than theirs? I don't want to waste your potential."

Emily felt like she was floating above her chair. "Yes, Sister, I'd like that very much. I'll work really hard, I promise!"

"Oh, I have no doubt about that, Emily. You are an excellent student. I also want you to know how sorry I am that you lost your parents. I can't imagine how hard that has been for you. You must miss them both very much."

Hearing the genuine sympathy in Sister's voice brought tears to Emily's eyes. Looking down at the floor in hopes that her teacher wouldn't notice, Emily nodded. "I don't remember my daddy very much, but my mama was really special. I just don't understand why they both had to die."

"Oh, Emily, nobody understands why people have to die when they're so young. Everybody goes through hard things, even if it doesn't show on the outside. But I can tell you that Jesus understands how you feel and cries with you when you're sad. I think that one of the reasons Jesus died on the cross was not just to atone for our sins, but to fully identify with human suffering. Jesus' heart can hold your pain, Emily. And maybe, if you look close enough, you'll see the ways in which he's with you every day."

Emily thought for a moment. "I guess you're right. At least I'm not completely alone. I have a foster family and a good friend in Lottie. Lots of kids like me have to live in an orphanage. That would be awful."

"Indeed it would. You are a fortunate girl in that regard. But Emily, I know that Mrs. Hutton is ill and Mr. Hutton is a busy man, so I don't imagine they are always available to talk to you about how you're feeling. So if you ever need someone to share your loneliness and grief with, I would be glad to listen."

"Thank you, Sister. That means a lot. It really does."

The nun reached over and patted Emily's hand. "Anytime, Emily," she said. "Any time at all."

As she was walking down the hall to meet Lottie, Emily wondered why the Sister's offer of a listening ear felt so much more comforting than Father Devlin's similar invitation last spring.

1959

Thursday dawned, cold and dreary. Emily awoke to a sinking feeling in the pit of her stomach. This was the day of her appointment with the doctor. In contrast to Emily's apprehension, George seemed positively cheerful. He was whistling as he entered the kitchen for his breakfast. "Good morning, darling! How are you feeling today?" When his inquiry was met with a dour stare, he shrugged and sat down at the table. "Cheer up, Emily. You act like you're heading to the executioner! I'm sure it will be just fine. And if the doctor is able to help us have a baby, then it will be well worth it. The appointment is at two, so I'll pick you up at one thirty. Be ready. I don't want to be late."

Emily mumbled something unintelligible, which George chose to ignore. Nothing was going to ruin his optimism this morning. He finished his eggs and toast quickly and rose to pull on his coat and gloves. He was whistling again as he walked out the door.

Agitated and afraid, Emily tried everything she could think of to quell her panic. In desperation, she decided to give the house a thorough cleaning, which she had been neglecting for ages. For three hours, she vacuumed, dusted, mopped and ironed, to no avail. Not even hard physical labor could stop her mind from going around in circles and imagining the worst. She had never undressed in front of another man before, except for George, and even then it was done in the dark. The thought of the doctor putting his hands on her and probing her private parts made her skin crawl. Suddenly, stomach heaving, she dropped the mop handle and scrambled into the bathroom to vomit into the toilet. Hands clutching the porcelain, she gasped and gagged until nothing was left. She laid her head on her forearms and took a deep breath, and then another. A memory of her mother holding back her hair during a childhood bout of the stomach flu came to mind, filling Emily with a longing so powerful it threatened to swamp her. And yet, the thought of her mother also calmed her and made the coming ordeal seem a little less daunting. After a few minutes, she pulled herself up from the floor, splashed cold water on her face and returned to the kitchen to finish mopping. By the time George came to get her, she had bathed and dressed and was ready to go. She walked out to the car with steely determination to endure the examination and whatever lay beyond.

George looked at her in surprise, expecting more resistance and getting none. He nodded once, put the car into gear and drove out of the alley and down the street toward the doctor's office. A receptionist greeted them cheerfully and asked them to be seated while she let the doctor know they had arrived. George reached over and took Emily's hand in his, giving it a comforting squeeze. Emily barely noticed, mind fixed on a single purpose, to endure the next hour without making a fool of herself. Fortunately, they didn't have to wait long before a nurse came and escorted them to an examining room. She had Emily sit up on the examining table and took her pulse and blood pressure while George looked on. She then asked several questions about Emily's periods, how long they had been trying to have a baby, how frequently they were having relations, and such. Telling such personal details to a perfect stranger was embarrassing, but at least Emily still had her clothes on. Then the nurse handed Emily a hospital gown and instructed her to disrobe. "Mr. Edwards, follow me. You can wait in Dr. Merritt's office while he performs the exam." Turning back to Emily, she said, "The doctor will be in shortly."

Just the act of removing her clothes in a brightly lit office was highly intimidating. Emily put on the gown as quickly as she could. She held the edges together in the front while she climbed back up on the table, but she still felt horribly exposed. Not only that, but the room wasn't very warm, and she found herself shivering. Hearing footsteps in the hall, her heart began to beat faster. A tall, stern-looking older man entered the room. "Good afternoon, Mrs. Edwards. I'm Dr. Merritt. I understand you have concerns about not being able to conceive. I assure you, it is very common for couples to have a hard time conceiving initially. And there are many things we can do to help nature along. Now let's have a look." The doctor pulled two metal footrests into place at the end of the table. "Place your heels in these stirrups and scoot forward until your bottom is at the edge of the table." Emily did as she was asked and closed her eyes, steeling herself for what was to come.

She felt something cold and hard being pushed into her, then pried apart. Emily gasped in pain and tried desperately to think of something other than what was happening. Strangely, the first thing that came to mind was Father Devlin's office, the high, white ceiling and the glaring fluorescent light that emitted an occasional buzzing sound that set her teeth on edge. Emily was overcome by panic and a deep desire to escape. Suddenly, the metal object was removed, and then the doctor's hand was inside her. His probing was far from gentle, pushing and poking until Emily whimpered from the discomfort. "Now, Mrs. Edwards, it's not that bad. Please lie still. I'll be done in just a moment. " Soon he removed his hand and began pushing on her abdomen with the tips of his fingers. She flinched once, and Dr. Merritt gave a grunt of annoyance, then finally it was over. Abruptly, he said, "You can get dressed now. Wait here, and your husband will come and get you in a few minutes." He was out the door before she had a chance to ask if he had found anything significant. Too relieved to be annoyed, Emily dressed quickly and sat on a chair in the corner to wait.

Meanwhile, George also waited anxiously in the doctor's office. He looked around at the ornate walnut desk, the shelves of medical texts, and the medical school diploma on the wall. He was glad that Emily had come without further histrionics, and he was hopeful that the doctor would be able to help them conceive. When he heard the door open behind him, George stood and turned to shake the doctor's hand. The doctor gestured to him to be seated and walked around the desk, sinking into his own leather chair. What the doctor said next was the last thing George expected to hear. "Mr. Edwards, are you sure that your wife was a virgin when you married her?"

George gaped at Dr. Merritt. "I-uh, she said she was. It never occurred to me to think otherwise. Why are you asking me this?"

"I'll get to that in a minute. Are you particularly rough in your love-making?"

George bristled at that, offended that the doctor would even ask such a question. "Of course not! What do you take me for, a sadist?"

"Then how would you explain the tremendous amount of scarring on your wife's vaginal walls?"

"I'm sure I have no idea! You're the doctor. What is the meaning of all these questions?"

"Well, as I said, there are numerous scars on the vaginal walls, and from the looks of them, they are not recent. The scarring has thickened the walls, which makes it likely that even if she could get pregnant, that pregnancy would not be viable."

George could barely take this in. "I don't understand. How could this happen?"

"I think you will have to face up to the idea that your wife is not what she claimed to be. The degree of scarring indicates that she has been sexually active for a long period of time and that the sex was most likely quite rough. To be blunt, Mr. Edwards, I would guess that your wife was a prostitute."

1948

On a late fall afternoon, Lottie and Emily were walking home from school. Lottie was worried about the letter they were bringing home about an outbreak of head lice. "Did you read the instructions for checking us all for head lice? Every child in the home will have to be checked! There's five of us! My mom is going to flip her wig!"

Emily nodded. "I bet! And I have no idea what will happen at our house. Mother is in no condition to do it, and Father is always working. I guess I can check Meg and Joey, but Fannie might have to do me. And then, if I have the lice, there's even more work. Stinky shampoo and washing everybody's sheets and stuff. It's gross! Mother will have a fit!"

"I guess it would be worse at your house than mine. At least my mom isn't sick, and I can help her with the little ones. I just hope the baby doesn't get them. I don't think it would be a good thing for a two-month-old. On the other hand, he doesn't have much hair, so we could see them pretty easily." On that note, the girls parted ways, and Emily walked in her front door just as Joey raced by with a mixing spoon in his hand trying to escape Fannie's attempts to catch him before batter got all over the rugs and furniture.

Joining the chase, Emily attempted to ward him off at the pass, barely catching hold of his shirt as he ran by. They collapsed on the floor together as Emily grabbed the hand with the spoon and held it aloft. "Good catch," Fannie cried as she pried Joey's fingers from the spoon. "Do you have time to keep him occupied so I can finish this cake?"

"Sure. I can always do my homework later." It wasn't until later that night that Emily retrieved her school bag from the living room floor where it had landed and saw the instructions for lice checks inside. Not wanting to disturb Mr. and Mrs. Hutton this late in the evening, she decided it could wait until morning.

When she came down to breakfast, Father had already left for an early meeting, and Mother was still asleep. Emily shrugged. Surely another day wouldn't matter.

Regardless of the progress she had made in her catechism studies, Father Devlin had insisted she still wasn't caught up with her classmates, and so the weekly tutoring sessions had resumed. When Emily walked into Father Devlin's office that afternoon, he stood and motioned to her usual chair. Then he went and closed the door behind her. "How are you today, Emily? I'm sure you've read about the lice infestation the school is having. I've been thinking that your foster parents have enough to deal with without the lice checks, so I've decided to perform the checks for them. Now, bend your head down a bit, so I can get a close look at your scalp."

Suddenly uncomfortable, Emily responded, "No, Father. You don't need to! The hired girl can do it. Really. She's going to have to do the little ones anyway."

"Don't be ridiculous, Emily. Why burden your help any more than necessary? This won't hurt a bit."

Realizing it was useless to argue, Emily subsided, and sat still while he went over her head painstakingly with a comb, looking at every strand of hair, or so it seemed. Sometimes, when he would move her head into a different position, his hands would linger on her cheek or chin or shoulder, almost caressing her. Emily noticed his breath growing more rapid and shallow, like it often did during confession. Quite uncomfortable, she breathed a sigh of relief when he straightened up thinking he was done. But he wasn't. "Alright, Emily. I'm going to need you to take off your clothes."

Emily looked at him with alarm. "What for?"

"Emily, dear, just because they're called head lice doesn't mean that's the only place they can lay their eggs. So I need to check everywhere, even under your clothing. You'll have to disrobe."

"But that's not what the instructions said!"

"I'm sure you just didn't read them thoroughly enough, Emily. It was in there. I wrote the letter myself."

Quailing under his insistence, Emily stuttered, "C-can't I get Fannie to do this part? Please, Father, let her do it instead."

"Now, Emily, there's no need to get so upset. This is purely professional. I promise I won't hurt you. Now, do as I say. There's a good girl."

Hands shaking, Emily did as instructed, slowly removing her jumper and blouse while the priest looked on, his eyes taking on a glazed look that made Emily's skin crawl. He bent over and began running his hands over her bare skin as he scanned her body. She shrank from his touch, but he persisted, speaking in a strange, breathless voice, "Just hold still, now."

As Emily walked back to class, she pulled out the letter on the lice outbreak that she had purposefully withheld from her parents. She read it through carefully, line by line. There was no reference to checking any part of the body other than the scalp. Slipping into her assigned seat in the classroom, she was still pale and shaking. Sister Mary Francis looked up from her desk, noticing Emily's discomfiture, and wondered.

1959

Emily glanced at the clock on the wall and wondered what was taking so long. She was anxious to hear what the doctor thought about why she wasn't conceiving. And why hadn't George come back to wait with her? At that moment, the door opened, and George walked in. "Let's go," he said abruptly. The look on his face was ominous.

"Now? Isn't the doctor going to tell us what he found?"

"He told *me*. Now, get your coat and let's go."

"Well, what did he say?"

"Emily, we are not going to talk about this now. Come on!" He grabbed her by the arm and pulled her out of the exam room and through the outer office. He was walking so fast, Emily could barely keep up. Alarmed, she tried to imagine what the doctor had told her husband to get him this upset. When they got to the car, George didn't even hold the door open for her, just walked around to the driver's side and started the car before she had a chance to shut her door. Driving too fast for the snowy conditions, hands gripping the wheel tightly, George's jaw was clenched, lips pressed in a tight line.

"George, please! What's wrong? What did the doctor say to you?"

He nearly spat his reply to her. "I said, we'll discuss this at home. Until then, keep your mouth shut! Do you understand?"

Stunned at his vehemence, Emily blinked back tears and looked straight ahead, terrified of what George's behavior could possibly mean. Even during their worst fights, he had never told her to shut up before. He looked angrier than she had ever seen him. She clasped her hands together in her lap, squeezing tightly in an attempt to keep her rising panic at bay.

Finally, they pulled into their driveway. George got out and stomped into the house. When Emily walked in after him, George turned suddenly and back-handed her across the face. Stunned, Emily gasped and raised her hand to her cheek, face burning. "George! What is it? What on earth is the matter with you?"

"He said that you're a whore! That your insides are all torn up because you like it rough! He says your scars are what's keeping you from getting pregnant. And to think I fell for your innocent orphan bullshit! Here I felt so sorry for you, and you were just looking for a gravy train to get yourself off the streets! All this time, I thought we just weren't trying hard enough. Did you ever even *want* children? No! I bet you didn't! Because you're too selfish. You just wanted a nice house and nice things and to hell with me and what I wanted. And when I was agonizing over my sexual desires before we were married, were you just laughing at me? All my life, I've tried to do the right thing, to save myself for marriage. And it's been torture! Night after night of sleeping next to my mother, fighting my urges, and for what?! I never so much as touched a woman before I met you. Only a few chaste kisses, waiting for the right woman, waiting for holy matrimony. Holy! That's a laugh. And now I find out that I've been sleeping with a prostitute! Well, fuck it! I'm *done* being the good boy!"

George grabbed Emily roughly and turned her around, pushing her upper body down onto the kitchen table. With his left hand, he held her down as she struggled against him. She felt him yank her skirt up to her waist and pull down her panties, heard his belt buckle being undone, and suddenly a sharp, searing pain like nothing she'd felt before. Her roar of pain was a guttural sound that tore from her throat like the scream of a wild animal. And suddenly, the world spun around, and she was no longer in her own kitchen but in Father Devlin's office. The table became his desk, and the smell of his cigars filled her nostrils. It was his voice she heard whispering in her ear, "Hush, Emily, we don't want Mrs. Northrup to hear what we're up to in here."

Memories flooded Emily's mind like hammer blows, one image after another, the office, the confessional, the "games," the thousand violations of her body and soul. There was a voice screaming, "No! No! No!" through the chaos of her mind, until she realized that the voice was her own.

With one final, violent thrust, George stopped. Pulling up his pants and gasping for breath, he sneered at his wife. "Don't worry, I'll never touch you again. And I'll *never* divorce you. You can sleep in the baby's room and think about what you took away from me." He turned his back on her and left the house, slamming the door behind him.

Chapter 8

An awful Tempest mashed the air—
The clouds were gaunt, and few—
A Black—as of a Spectre's Cloak
Hid Heaven and Earth from view.
          —Emily Dickinson

1959

Emily startled awake, cold and stiff. She was still lying on the kitchen floor where she had collapsed hours ago. At first, she couldn't figure out what on earth she was doing there, and then it all came back to her in a torrent—George's violation of her, the memories of Father Devlin that had been repressed for so long. Images waged war in her mind, and her body reeled from the sensation of his hands touching, probing, holding her down. She felt pain invading her most private places, so real that she turned her head in sharp jerks, looking for the offender she was convinced was somehow present in her kitchen. Feet scrambling, she pushed herself back into a corner behind the dining table, gasping in terror, wrapping her arms around her knees in desperate self-protection from a predator who wasn't really there. Whimpering, she began to rock back and forth, back and forth, back and forth. Gradually, her breath slowed, and her body grew still. Her all-consuming fear transformed into a cold numbness that pervaded her entire being. Time passed. Daylight came. And still she sat.

All awareness of time was gone. Eventually, George emerged from the bedroom. He took notice of Emily curled up in the corner, threw her a look of disgust and picked up the phone, dialing a number he knew by heart. "Yes, Maxine? This is George Edwards. I'm afraid I'm a bit under the weather this morning. Can you let Mr. Matthews know that I won't be in today? . . . Yes, I'm sure I'll be right as rain by tomorrow. Thank you, Maxine. Good-bye." Without another glance, George hung up the phone and returned to the bedroom, closing the door firmly behind him.

An urgent need to use the toilet finally penetrated Emily's stupor, and she grasped the countertop to pull herself up to stand. For a moment, it felt as though her knees would buckle and take her tumbling to the floor again, but she held on until some semblance of strength and balance returned. She walked toward the bathroom in a body that felt suddenly foreign to her, disoriented by the flashbacks that had rolled through it like tidal waves. When she sat on the commode, Emily discovered that her undergarments were stained with blood from George's assault. Her stomach turned with revulsion and pain, and she grabbed the nearby wastebasket into which she retched violently. She sat, gasping for breath, until the nausea passed.

Feeling lost, Emily didn't know what to do next. Her life had changed in the blink of an eye, and nothing would be the same again. George had relegated her to the second bedroom that currently held nothing but a few boxes. There was no bed. Everything that Emily needed was in the bedroom the couple had shared, but George was in there, apparently sleeping off the effects of his rage. Emily didn't know when he had returned home during the night, but she felt that he had been gone for several hours, doing what, she did not know. Craving some semblance of normalcy, although the idea of it seemed laughable, she went to the tub and drew herself a bath. The hot water stung from the abrasions George had inflicted as Emily lowered herself into the water. Disturbed by the sight of her naked body now that she was aware of the ways in which it had been violated, she washed herself quickly, rose, and wrapped herself in a towel. With another towel, she dried her hair and reached for her comb.

Suddenly, all she could see was the comb, while all else around her faded. The swirling feeling returned; fear and shame washed over her. *The damned comb! The lice checks. Oh, my God, those horrible lice checks!* Trembling, Emily dropped the comb and slumped to the floor, overcome by memory and pain.

Father Devlin had called her into his office for yet another lice check. She detested this process, but the priest insisted they must continue until they were absolutely sure the epidemic had been eradicated. As he went over her head with the comb, Emily's dread grew. She knew what was coming, what always happened next, the stripping down, the instruction to lie naked on Father's desk. As expected, it wasn't long before he was telling her to disrobe, to climb up on the desk. And then the touching began. Emily squirmed, trying so hard to avoid his touch, but he would have none of it. "Lie still, Emily! The more you wiggle, the worse it will be. Do you think I enjoy this? And for God's sake, stop that whining. You would think I am torturing you." She concentrated on staring at the fluorescent lights on the ceiling, trying to blot out the look on the priest's face, trying not to think about what was happening to her. Focus on the light, let the world disappear, think of nothing but the light . . .

Gradually, Emily became aware of the cold, hard floor beneath her, the damp towel next to her, and the sounds of water dripping from the tub faucet. She didn't understand how she could have forgotten about those long-ago lice checks or the horrible things Father Devlin had done to her. Nor did she fathom how remembering could make her body feel as though the experience was happening to her all over again. She somehow knew that this was just the beginning, and at that thought, she buried her face in the towel and wept.

1948

Long past her earlier anxieties, confession had become routine for Emily, although she never felt truly comfortable around Father Devlin, despite the anonymity of the confession booth. He'd never given any indication that he knew who she was when she was stumbled through her list of transgressions. On this particular Friday, the class lined up to walk down the hall and into the chapel. They filed into the pews according to their rows in the classroom. The back row started first, so Emily, who loved to be in the front row close to her teacher ended up last. As the students took turns entering the confessional, Sister Mary Francis read from Scripture and then instructed the children to pray the rosary as they waited. When it was Emily's turn, her teacher called the class to attention and began ushering them back to the classroom. She told Emily, "We're going to start back so I can get everyone started on our next lesson. You can join us when you're done, since I know you won't have any problem catching up."

Emily nodded her assent and entered the small wooden booth where she knelt. "Forgive me, Father, for I have sinned," she began. "It's been . . .."

The priest interrupted her. "Is that you, Emily? I knew I recognized your voice." Suddenly, he pulled back the curtain. "Come over here, and sit on my lap. We don't need to be so formal, do we?"

Hesitantly, Emily did as she was asked. Sitting on Father Devlin's lap in such a small space was awkward and uncomfortable, nonetheless she launched into the list of sins she had prepared. And then he stopped her. "Tell you what, Emily. Let's play a little game as your penance. Here's what you have to do . . .."

1959

The young Emily looked at the priest and saw the strange look she'd seen before in his eyes. Her anxiety grew as he pushed her off his lap and stood up, filling the tiny space and giving her little room to breathe. "Relax, Emily," he said. "Your penance will be painless." He took her hand and placed it on his crotch. "Feel that," he said. "Now, rub it really hard, and see what happens."

Emily shook her head. "I don't want to play this game, Father."

"Don't be ridiculous, my girl. This is your penance! Now, do as I say. You'll like it; it's magic." And so she rubbed, and the thing inside his pants grew and turned hard as his eyes rolled back and his breath came in shorts gasps. "That's a good girl, Emily. Keep rubbing. Don't stop." Terrified to disobey his orders, she continued to rub. Father began to moan, an ominous sound that made her feel more scared than she had in her entire life. She wanted nothing more than to escape to the safety and calm of her classroom. The moans were increasing in intensity, and Emily herself was whimpering. Then suddenly the priest let out a muffled cry, and his body jerked uncontrollably. After a moment, he took a deep breath, opened his eyes and smiled at her. "See? What did I tell you? Magic! And now you are absolved of your sins."

Emily startled awake, terrified. Eyes searching for the devilish figure of her dreams, she whimpered, breath rapid and shallow. *Oh, my God,* she thought, *the confession booth!* Memories came back, biweekly confession always a game, always an increasing nightmare as he drew her into his twisted desires. Never a time when he didn't bring her onto his side of the booth; never a confession when he didn't force her to do unspeakable things. Shame engulfed her. She felt vile, contaminated, filthy. Perhaps she had deserved it. Perhaps her sin was so great that God had taken her parents, and then, when that was not enough, God placed her in the hands of the devil himself to torture her, to punish her for the great and unforgivable sin of being Emily.

The kitchen door slammed, and Emily heard George stumbling through the house. It had been two weeks since their trip to the doctor and all that had happened after. George had taken to going out after dinner every night and returning in the wee hours, drunk and angry. Sometimes, he would come into the room Emily now occupied and rail at her, ranting about the pain she had caused him, about how she had tricked him, defiled him and used him. The drinking was something new. In the past, he had limited himself to one gin and tonic on rare occasions. It almost seemed that the old strictures he had put on himself had gone by the wayside. His rigid following of church teaching had been tossed aside in one fell swoop, and suddenly, all his moral constraints were gone. And this, too, was Emily's fault. Emily closed her eyes and heaved a great sigh. This was her life now. There would be no escape.

Her days had become a waking nightmare. Emily was assailed by memories at any time of the day or night, vivid images of horrifying abuse that invaded her mind and body as though they were happening in the present. No matter what she did to keep them at bay, they would pounce at unexpected moments, while she was ironing, dusting, or cooking a meal. Often, Emily would find herself rocking in a corner, not knowing how long she had been there or what had triggered this retreat from reality. The flashbacks kept her from performing her household duties in a timely fashion or in a way that met George's standards. As a consequence, he berated her constantly for things undone or mistakes made. Any opportunity to punish her was seized upon. When Emily had asked George about getting a bed for the second bedroom, he had laughed cruelly. "You're a whore; I'm sure you're used to sleeping on almost anything. I'm not spending a penny on making your life more comfortable. You'll just have to make do."

And so, Emily had pushed the boxes together to make a platform and piled as many blankets and old towels on it as she could to make a bed. It wasn't comfortable, but it was better than sleeping on the floor. She had moved her clothes and other belongings out of the bedroom she had shared with George and tried to make this room feel like hers. But no matter how much she tried, there was no longer any place that felt safe, no room that was hers alone, no place that kept out the horrors that stalked her incessantly.

One night, as she was lying on her bed of boxes, she heard George come in through the front door. This was unusual, as he normally entered the house through the kitchen. He stumbled and laughed, and then Emily heard the sound of a woman's voice. *What on earth,* she wondered. Footsteps passed her door and went down the hall to the master bedroom, staggering and occasionally falling against a wall, which led to female giggles. Finally, the door shut and there was momentary silence. Then the creaking of bed springs. A muffled rhythmic sound, barely audible at first, then louder and louder. Emily could feel a black hole opening up inside her even before she realized what was happening, and then it hit her. The sounds of moaning, the slap of flesh, the cries of pleasure. George was having sex with another woman in the next room and not making any effort to hide it! Emily's body convulsed as yet another memory of abuse invaded her, and she curled up into a fetal position with her hands covering her ears. Her mouth formed the words, "Stop it. Stop it. Stop it," over and over again, and whether she was saying them out loud or not, she didn't know.

Eventually, the sounds stopped, and Emily's body ceased its rocking. She heard the woman leave, heard George say, "I'm sure you'll be seeing me again. You can consider me a regular," before closing the door after her.

Impelled by outrage and fury, Emily burst from her room to confront her husband. "What the hell do you think you're doing, George? I can't believe you brought a woman here for sex! Have you no shame?"

George laughed. "You're one to talk about shame! And I'll do whatever I want in my own house. You're just the live-in help now. Apparently, I'd already been sleeping with a whore, so I figure I might as well do it with one who acts like she enjoys it. Get used to it!" With that, he turned and went into his bedroom, slamming the door behind him.

1949

Emily awoke to the sound of the phone ringing at 6 AM. She heard Father's voice rumbling downstairs as he answered the unusual call. Pulling on her bathrobe, she ran down to see if there was an emergency. "What's the matter, Father?" she asked as he hung up the receiver.

"Well, Emily, we're in a bit of a pickle today. Fannie is sick. She stayed at her uncle's laundry last night, because she had to work late, and now she seems to have come down with a bug of some kind. Obviously, we don't want her to expose the children to whatever it is, but that leaves Joey untended for the day. I don't know what we're going to do."

"Oh, dear! That is a problem! I have an important test today, so I really can't miss school. Do you suppose we could take Joey over to the Fisher's house for the day?"

"Well, that's a thought. Let me go talk to your mother and see what she thinks about the situation." Father strode down the hall and entered the bedroom, closing the door behind him. Emily, anxious to know what would be decided, crept after him and put her ear against the door in hopes of hearing their conversation. Father had lowered his voice, but Emily could hear bits and pieces of Mother's words as her voice rose and fell.

"Why can't Emily stay home . . . I don't want Joey over there; they let their children ride roughshod over the whole house! . . . Nonsense! You can't stay home from work. . . . I'm not completely helpless, you know . . . I'm his mother!" There were a few more muffled words before Emily decided to scurry back to the kitchen before Father caught her eavesdropping.

Father looked perplexed as he entered the kitchen. "What is it, Father? What did Mother say?"

"Well, she said that she would watch Joey herself. She says that if you will bring some of his toys and books down to our bedroom, she can keep him entertained for the day. And maybe you could fix some sandwiches before you and Meg leave for school, so they have something to eat for lunch. He can just curl up on the bed with her for his nap. That way, Mother won't have to go upstairs at all. She's confident that she and Joey will have a grand time together."

Emily became aware that her mouth was gaping open. Her mind was racing over all the ways in which this plan could go horribly wrong, but she knew that expressing a contrary opinion would not be welcomed. Besides, this meant that she could still go to school. Not only did she have that test, but the class was working on a special poetry project that she didn't want to miss. They were creating posters of their favorite poems to hang in the halls of the school. Her poster was a poem by Emily Dickinson, of course.

"OK, Father. I'll get busy right now, so that Mother has everything she needs before Meg and I have to leave."

Father smiled and ruffled her hair. "I don't know what we would do without you, Emily."

Emily muttered a quick, "Thank you," and raced up the stairs, flooded with happiness at Father's words of praise. She quickly dressed for school, then went to wake the children. As she dressed them, she filled them in on the change in plans for the day.

"I don't want to stay in Mother's room," pouted Joey. "I want to play with Fannie!"

"Oh, Joey, wait and see. It'll be fun. I promise." Joey didn't look convinced, but he did as he was told and chose some toys to take downstairs. Emily grabbed his favorite books, a couple of games, and some coloring books and crayons to add to the pile. The children helped her shuttle everything downstairs and into their parents' bedroom. Emily smiled and said, "Good morning, Mother. Joey is very excited to be spending the day with you. Here are some of his favorite things to keep him occupied. And now, I'll get breakfast going. I'll be in with your tray shortly."

"Thank you, dear. I'm sure Joey and I will manage just fine."

Finally, all were fed, teeth brushed, hair combed, and ready for the day ahead. Joey was ensconced in Mother's bedroom, surrounded by his toys. Emily gave him some ground rules before she and Meg had to rush off to school. "Be a good boy today, Joey. Mind your mother, and don't leave the room except for going to the potty and right back again. Do you understand?" Joey nodded solemnly, and Mother assured Emily again that they would have a lovely day together. Reluctantly, Emily closed the bedroom door, took Meg's hand, and off they went. She said a silent prayer that everything would be okay.

Even though the day was full of all the things Emily loved about school, it felt like it went on forever. She couldn't stop worrying about Joey being home alone with his mother. She felt guilty that she hadn't volunteered to stay home and wondered if Joey was bored beyond words. Worse yet, what if he were getting into all kinds of mischief and driving Mother into a rage that would fall on Emily's shoulders the moment she got home. When the final bell rang, she rushed down the hall to collect Meg and get home. She was walking so fast that Meg nearly had to run to keep up. "Slow down, Emily! I'm tired." Emily would slow for a bit and then find herself rushing again in her anxiety over what would greet her at home. At last, they arrived. Emily unlocked the door and stepped inside.

She was met by complete silence, which in itself was alarming. She walked quickly to Mother's room and found the door ajar. Mother appeared to be sleeping, and Joey was nowhere to be seen. Emily raced up the stairs, taking them two at a time. Joey wasn't there, either. She looked in the closet, under the bed, inside the big toy chest, then went into her own room, checking every possible hiding place. Panicked now, she searched the first floor, under every piece of furniture, inside every cupboard and closet, to no avail. Returning to the master bedroom, she shook her mother. "Mother! Mother! Wake up! Where's Joey? I can't find him. Where did he go?"

"Wha...? What 'er you shaying? He was righ' here jus' a minute ago. We were having a lil' nappy-poo." Mrs. Hutton struggled to sit up, shaking her head as if to clear her head.

"Are you *drunk*?" Emily was incredulous. "Joey is *not* right here! He is gone! Now get up and help me look for him. I'm going to check the back yard." She ran to the back door, noticing that it was slightly ajar despite the winter chill. Meg suddenly appeared and grabbed Emily's legs, frightened by Emily's urgency.

"What's happening, Emily? Where's Joey?" Tears welled in her eyes as she spoke.

"Oh, Meg. I don't know. Don't cry. I'm sure he will be alright. He can't have gotten far. Do you know if he has any favorite hiding places? Maybe you could help look in the house. I'm going to walk down the block and see if I can find him."

But first, Emily decided she should check the garage. She

turned the handle as she'd seen Father do and lifted as hard as she could. Slowly, the large door creaked slowly upwards on its track until Emily was able to get inside and look around. Nothing was disturbed. Father kept the garage very neat, and everything appeared to be in its place. Emily checked a couple of boxes that Joey might have been able to crawl into, but they were full of old clothes and towels. Frantic, she ran down the alley, slipping and sliding in the sloppy mud and melting snow, looking into the neighbors' back yards. She started calling Joey's name over and over again. There was no answer. Reaching the end of the alley, she turned toward the street and ran up and down the block, then another block, yelling. Finally out of breath, Emily stopped, gasping. She bent over, hands on knees, pulling great gulps of oxygen into her lungs. In her desperation, she prayed, "Dear God, please let Joey be okay. Please help me find him before he gets hurt." In the silence that followed, she thought she heard a small voice. "Joey? Is that you?"

"Emily, I'm stuck!"

Emily's legs turned to jelly in her relief. "Where are you, Joey? I can't see you. Keep talking."

"I'm over here. In Mrs. Palmer's bushes. They're poking me, and I can't get out. And I'm getting chilly!" Emily ran toward his voice until she saw a patch of blue in the middle of a bare-branched rose bush in the corner of Mrs. Palmer's yard. She let herself in through the front gate and rushed over to the offending shrub.

"Oh, Joey! I'm so glad I found you! Didn't I tell you to stay in the house? How did you get in here? You are in such big trouble, buster boy!"

As she began to extricate the boy from the thorns that held him, he told her about his adventure. "I woke up from my nap before Mother did, and I couldn't wake her up. I was thirsty, so I went into the kitchen to get a drink of water. And then I just really wanted to go outside. An' I walked an' I walked until I heard Sparky barking. I like Sparky, so I came here. I couldn't get the gate open, so I climbed the fence. Aren't I a big boy? But I fell in the bush and it poked me! It hurts, too, really bad. Am I bleeding?"

Emily hugged Joey to her tightly as relief overwhelmed her. Then she held him at arm's length to look him over. "A little bit, but not bad. I think you'll be alright. Now let's get you home and cleaned up from your adventure." She picked up the small boy and carried him home. She went to the door of Mother's room, but the woman appeared to be asleep again, so she took Joey upstairs, changed him out of his damp clothing and tended to his scratches. She settled the children down with a puzzle and went downstairs to start dinner. She was greeted by Mother standing unsteadily in the hall.

"Where have you been? Where's Joey?" she shrieked.

"I was looking for Joey, and now he's home, no thanks to you!"

"How dare you speak to me like that! And I would have thought you would have told me he was home the minute you walked in the door. I'm his mother, for God's sake!"

"Yes, his mother who was so worried, she was fast asleep while I was looking for her son! 'We'll be fine,' you said. 'It'll be fun,' you said! But could you bother to stay sober for a few hours to take care of your son? No! He could have been hit by a car! Did you think about that? You're a sorry excuse for a mother! Now, if you'll excuse me, I have to go cook dinner."

Emily made it to the kitchen before her knees buckled. She gripped the counter to keep herself from falling to the floor. *What have I done,* she thought, *she's going to have my head for speaking to her like that!* She felt sick to her stomach at the thought of whatever punishment might await her. She had no idea what possessed her to be so disrespectful. Yet, deep inside, she knew that Mother had deserved the sharp rebuke and was secretly proud of herself for standing up to Mother's bullying.

As soon as Father came home, he went in to speak to his wife. Upon emerging from the bedroom, he went straight upstairs to check in on Joey and give him a stern talking-to about wandering off. Then he came into the kitchen and addressed Emily. "I'm very disappointed in you, Emily. I understand that you were very upset about Joey, but I can't condone the way you spoke to your mother today. No matter how her condition may have contributed to what happened, you still owe her your respect. You can consider yourself grounded until further notice. That means no playing at Lottie's house, and no trips to the public library unless it's for a school assignment."

"Yes, Father. I'm really sorry. I was just so scared that Joey could be seriously hurt or even lost forever. It won't happen again. I promise."

"I appreciate that, but it's your mother you owe the apology to. Go up to your room as soon as you finish the dishes and think about what you've done."

Emily trudged up the steps with a heavy heart. To hear that Father was disappointed in her upset her more than any punishment he could devise. She sat in her room composing an apology letter to Mother, then went to bed early. She tossed and turned for a long time before she finally fell into a troubled sleep.

Fannie woke her up bright and early. "Wake up, sleepy head! I'm feeling right as rain now, so you don't have to worry about a repeat of yesterday's adventure. Fannie's on the job, so go, have a good day at school, and don't worry about Joey."

1959

Emily lay in her makeshift bed, curled up in a fetal position, listening to the sounds of George and another of his trollops having sex in the next room. She pressed her hands over her ears as hard as she could, but couldn't drown out their cries of pleasure. It seemed to her that George was purposefully being as loud as he could to spite her. And no matter how hard she tried to think about something else, she couldn't. No matter how loudly she hummed to drown out their moans, the auditory triggers drew her closer and closer to the edge of the cliff of memory. It was as if she was clawing to maintain a purchase on sanity, but the sounds pulled her down and down until she fell headlong into the horrors of the past.

Emily approached Father Devlin's door with the dread that had become a constant companion. What had started with the caresses that accompanied lice checks had become even greater violations—fingers invading private places, forced touch of his own privates—all while he whispered how much he loved her and how beautiful she was. The look in his eye on this day was even more hungry than usual. He took her hand and pulled her to his side of the desk. "It's time to take our relationship to the next level. I've been wanting this for so long." Suddenly, he lifted her onto his desk, pushed up her jumper and yanked down her panties. She heard the jingle of his belt buckle and almost immediately felt a sudden sharp pain that she thought might rip her apart. This was worse than anything he'd done before, and without volition, she cried out, despite all his previous warnings to not make a sound. He immediately put his hand over her mouth, whispering fiercely, "Shut up, you bitch! Someone will hear! You don't want us to get caught, do you? People would never understand how much we love each other. This is our secret, remember?" All the while, he continued thrusting inside her until the world dissolved around her, and nothing else existed but the pain.

Gradually, Emily became aware of someone whimpering and then realized the sound was coming from her own throat. She felt an intense pain in her groin that she knew wasn't real. Father Devlin was not present in this small room where she lay on her pallet of boxes. And yet, he might as well have been, for the fear and horror were just as real as they had been all those years ago. George and his prostitute were still going at it in the next room, and suddenly she couldn't stand it anymore. She had to get away, away from their debauchery, away from the sound of it, away from her memories. She ran into the kitchen, pulled boots onto her bare feet, grabbed a coat from the coat rack and ran headlong into the cold and snowy night.

Emily had no sense of where she was going, but ran mindlessly through the streets, her only thought to get as far away from the horrors in her mind as possible. She felt as though she was being chased, pursued by what or who she didn't know. Flight was all that mattered. She imagined predators everywhere, prowling the alleyways and shadowed places between houses. Her head turned right and left as though on a swivel, looking for a danger that wasn't there. She was looking over her shoulder when she bumped into something and fell into a heap. She heard a voice say, "Oh dear, I'm so sorry," and looked up to see a dark figure looming over her. The only detail she could see was a white collar—all else was in shadow. The piercing scream that burst from her throat split the quiet night. She scrambled with elbows and heels to try to get away, but the figure followed her, attempting to pick her up. She batted his hands away as she continued to scream, but her efforts were futile. He grasped her upper arms and pulled her upright. Then the streetlight fell on her face, and the man gasped. "Emily? Is that you? It's me, Father McCaffrey! Don't be afraid, I won't hurt you. Goodness, that was quite the spill you took! I guess I should have watched where I was going before I came out of the alley. Are you hurt? Come into

the rectory where it's warm. I want to make sure you're okay."

Emily looked around and realized they were right next to the church. The priest's chatter broke through her frantic thoughts, but she was still trembling as she allowed herself to be steered into the rectory kitchen. Father pulled out a chair for her just before her knees gave way. Realizing that she was wearing a nightgown under her coat, she clutched the coat closer around herself. "How about a nice cup of tea?" Without waiting for an answer, Father McCaffrey busied himself pouring water into a battered teapot and putting it on the stove to boil. As he bustled around the kitchen, he noticed Emily watching him warily, hunched and still clearly frightened. This was a far different Emily than the woman he had come to know. While she had always been quiet and reserved, she had never seemed nervy or hysterical. There was clearly something very wrong in her world. Wanting to give comfort, he patted her arm as he placed a cup of tea in front of her, but she flinched and yanked it away. He pretended not to notice but straightened up and sat across the table from her, hoping that something solid between them would ease her fears. "Now then, Emily, care to tell me what compelled you to be wandering the streets in the cold at this hour of the night?" His kind eyes offered no judgment, but waited patiently for an answer.

Emily paused, considering what she could possibly tell Father McCaffrey about the nightmare that her life had become. So many options, none of them acceptable from the Church's point of view. Finally, she spoke a partial truth, "I had a nightmare."

"Well, that must have been one helluva nightmare for you to run out of the house in your bed clothes. Myself, I was just coming back from the Tate's house. Ruth has taken a turn for the worse, and Wilbur wanted me to give her last rites in case she didn't make it through the night."

Emily looked down at her lap and started picking at a loose thread on her coat. "I'm sorry to hear that. I haven't been to Mass in a while. I didn't know Ruth was ill."

"Yes, I've noticed your absence. George's, too." He paused for a moment, reflecting on Emily's disheveled look, her obvious deception, and the couple's prolonged absence from parish activities. Then comprehension dawned. "Is your marriage in trouble, Emily?"

Emily froze, wondering what he knew. She didn't think

George had been to Mass since the doctor's appointment, so maybe Father didn't know that George thought she was a prostitute. Perhaps this was the safest information with which to explain her behavior. Silently, she nodded, but even that minor acknowledgement of her troubles forced a sob from her throat. Her hand flew to her mouth to suppress the pent-up pain that suddenly wanted nothing more than to come out.

"Ah, I wondered what was going on. It's not like George to miss Mass for weeks. Do you want to talk about it?"

Alarmed, Emily shook her head. There was a part of her that wanted to trust this kindly man, but the collar he wore reminded her that he wasn't safe no matter how caring he seemed to be.

"I understand, dear. Not everybody feels comfortable talking with their priest about such intimate things. But I can tell by how you look that whatever it is, it's bad. Do you have a friend you can talk to, someone you can trust?"

Emily started to shake her head, but paused as the face of the one person in her life she could rely on came into her mind. She nodded.

"Well then, that's a good place to start. Do you think you could call that person tomorrow?" Another nod. "Good. It always helps to have a plan. Now, finish up your tea, and I'll walk you home. But remember, if you ever change your mind and want to talk to me, my door is always open."

As the pair trudged up the snowy street, Emily felt a glimmer of inner strength returning. Now, in the midst of feeling as though she were drowning, a lifeline had been thrown to her. Tomorrow morning she would call Lottie.

Chapter 9

Dying! Dying in the night!
Won't somebody bring the light
So I can see which way to go
Into the everlasting snow?
　　　　—Emily Dickinson

1949

When Emily and Meg got home from school the next day, Father was already there. She could hear his voice in the bedroom talking with Mother. Fannie was in the kitchen with Joey and rolled her eyes when she saw Emily's confusion. "Hi, Meg, how was school today? Joey was just about to have a little snack. Why don't you join him, and when you're done, I think he is eager for a game of Chutes and Ladders. I'm just going to run upstairs with Emily for a moment, and I'll be right back down. Can you keep your eye on Joey for me?" Fannie gave the little girl a quick hug, and then gestured urgently to Emily to follow her up to their shared room.

As soon as the door was shut, Emily blurted out, "What's going on? Why is Father home so early?"

Fannie responded, "He never went to work at all! All bloody hell has broken loose, I'll tell you that! He found Mrs. H's bottle under the bed, and she had to confess she'd been drinking most of the day yesterday. They've been yelling at each other off and on all day. He told her he was cutting her off from the booze cold turkey, and then he called Dr. Gunderson and told *him* about her drinking. Well, Dr. G. was so concerned that he came right over to check her out and talk to her about what she's doing to her health. Fat lot of good that did! She's only now stopped shouting at the top of her lungs. Mr. H. told her he was going to have a stern talk with Mr. Price about supplying her with her booze, not to mention putting it into the hands of a minor for delivery! I think he's going over there tonight, and if I was Mr. Price, I would be very afraid. He'll be lucky if Mr. H. doesn't sic the police on him!"

Emily mouth was agape in consternation. "Oh, no! This is horrible! Mother is going to have a conniption, and it's going to end up being all my fault. I should have kept my big mouth shut and not said a word about what happened yesterday. I am going to suffer for this, wait and see."

Just then, Father shouted from the bottom of the stairs, "Emily, are you up there? I need to talk to you."

"Yes, Father. I'll be right down." Emily gave Fannie a panicked look and ran down the stairs, Fannie at her heels to check on the children.

"Let's go talk in the living room, shall we?" Father said. Emily followed him and sat down on the sofa. Father took the chair opposite, leaning forward with his elbows on his knees. "Emily, I wish you had told me about Mother's drinking long before it got this far. I had no idea that she was having you bring her alcohol from the store. Why didn't you tell me?"

Emily looked down at her lap, ashamed and afraid. "I didn't want to get Mother into trouble, and . . . well, she gets so upset if she can't have a drink every now and then."

"Emily, it seems to me like it had gotten a long way past 'every now and then.' Dr. Gunderson is very worried about what this has done to Mother's health. And she's going to have a very difficult time withdrawing from the alcohol. When people get dependent on something like that and then have to quit, their body still craves it, and a person can have nausea, headaches, tremors and heart palpitations. They also don't sleep very well, and you know how hard it is for Mother to sleep already. I'm afraid we're all in for a pretty rough time until her body adjusts to the absence of liquor."

"I'm sorry, Father. I'm so sorry. I didn't think the drinking was good for her, but I didn't want to disobey either. I just didn't know what to do."

"I understand, Emily. Your mother put you in an impossible situation. And I know that she can be difficult at times, so I understand why you wouldn't want to upset her. I just wish you had come to me about it. I'm going to talk to Mr. Price tonight and make it very clear that if he ever sells a bottle of alcohol to you or Mrs.

Hutton again, I will have the law down on him before he can turn around. And I absolutely forbid you to bring alcohol to your mother from Mr. Price or anyone else ever again. If she even asks you to get some for her, I want you to tell me immediately. This is her life we're talking about here, and I don't want the children to grow up without a mother. Do you hear me?"

Emily nodded. "Yes, Father. I understand. I promise I won't let this happen again. And I'll do whatever I can to help with the withdrawals, even if it means reading to her all night long to help her sleep."

Father gave a small chuckle. "Well, Emily, I don't think that will be necessary, but we are all in for some hard times ahead. But it's certainly worth me buying you another volume of poetry to vary the routine. Now, go on and get started on your homework. Fannie agreed to stay a little longer tonight since things are in such an uproar. I'll be the one to take Mother her supper before I go over to the Price's. Then you can do the dishes and get the children to bed after Fannie leaves for the laundry. That's all, Emily. And you can consider yourself ungrounded."

The rest of the evening went fairly smoothly with not a peep coming from the master bedroom. Apparently, Dr. Gunderson had renewed Mother's prescription for sleeping pills to help with the insomnia until her withdrawals had abated. Still, Emily was anxious about how Mother was going to treat her now that the alcohol had been taken away. Would she blame Emily for being denied her liquor? Experience told her that Mother didn't respond well when things didn't go her way, and this was about to make things even worse. It took Emily a long time to fall asleep that night.

After school the next day, Fannie had to rush out the door the moment that Emily and Meg walked in. "Gotta run! I have to make up for the hours I missed yesterday at my uncle's place with all this hullabaloo. I probably won't get back until you're already in dream land. Good luck with the missus. See you tomorrow!" And with that, she was gone. Emily went upstairs to check on Joey and get Meg settled with her homework before starting dinner. A few minutes later, she heard Mother calling for her. Her heart jumped in her chest as she walked down the hall. "Yes, Mother? What do you need?"

"I need a drink! What do you think I need?" she snapped.

"I'm sorry, Mother. Father poured it all out last night. Is there anything else I can do? Do you want me to read to you?"

"A little poetry isn't going to make me feel better! Never mind. Just leave me alone!" She turned her back on Emily and pressed her face into her pillow. As Emily left the room, she felt a heavy weight settle in her chest, pity for Mrs. H and dread of the coming days mingling in equal measure.

At Emily's next tutoring session, Father Devlin motioned her to the couch right away, putting his arm around her and pulling her close. "Emily, I've been hearing some disturbing rumors about your mother lately. They say that she's turned into quite a lush. I never would have thought it, but I guess some people just don't have enough faith in God to help them through their trials. Anyway, I know this must be very hard for you, especially when you have no one to turn to. I just want you to know that I am here for you any time you need to talk. You are very special to me. I hope you know that." He gave her another squeeze and kissed her cheek. "Now, let's get on with your lesson."

1959

Emily splashed cold water on her face, hoping it would shock her out of the daze she was in after another night haunted by nightmares. Despite her encounter with Father McCaffrey the previous night and the small frisson of hope that had come from thinking about talking to Lottie, she had experienced terrifying dreams populated by a multitude of priests in white collars. Over and over, they descended on her with their hands grasping, mouths twisted in maniacal laughter as she screamed and writhed in her bed. At one point, George had even thumped on her wall and yelled at her to stop the racket and go to sleep. As if sleep would be the answer to her torment!

Emily looked at herself in the mirror and took in the dark circles under her eyes, the gaunt cheeks from days of not eating, the straggly hair, the vacant look of hopelessness. Determined to do something to improve her visage, she grabbed the comb in an attempt to detangle her hair. And yet again, the sight of the comb drew her into memories of Father Devlin and the lice checks he manipulated to begin his campaign of sexual violation. Anger rising in her, Emily gave a guttural yell and threw the comb against the wall. It bounced as it fell to the floor and landed at her feet. Emily sank to the floor, grabbed the comb, and suddenly raked it across her forearm with all the force she could muster. Grunting and frenzied, she did it again and again, raising deep red welts up and down her arm. Finally, she dropped the comb and fell back against the wall, gasping for breath. Her arm burned, yet Emily felt a curious euphoria. There was a strange satisfaction at being the one in control of her pain for once.

An hour later, Emily suddenly awoke, shivering on the cold floor. It took a moment to orient herself and to remember what had happened. The red lines on her arm burned painfully, so she ran cold water over them until the stinging eased. In need of coffee, she made her way down the hall and through the living room on her way to the kitchen. Looking down, she noticed something peeking out from underneath the sofa and bent down to pick it up. It was an open pack of cigarettes with a book of matches tucked into the cellophane wrapper. She turned it over in her hands, pondering its presence in her house. As far as she knew, despite the drinking and carousing, George hadn't taken up smoking. Then again, one of his call girls could have dropped the cigarettes while leaving in the wee hours of the morning. Suddenly, the thought of lighting up a cigarette seemed like a good idea. Hands trembling, she pulled out a cigarette and placed it between her lips. It took a couple of tries to light it, and the first hit of smoke to her lungs made her cough, but something about the acrid burning sensation in her throat made her inhale again. Carrying the cigarettes to the kitchen with her, she made herself a cup of coffee and sat at the table staring out the window into the snow-laden yard.

She thought about calling Lottie and telling her everything. Part of her felt such shame about revealing the ugly truth. How do you tell your best friend that their childhood priest had done such embarrassing and disgusting things to her? People just don't talk about things like that. And then the fact that George had raped her, accused her of being a whore. Would Lottie even believe her? Would she be ashamed to associate with someone whose life had fallen so far from what it used to be? Emily lit another cigarette and inhaled deeply, somehow steadied by it. Then she remembered the hope, the infinitesimal lifting of her spirits when she thought of Lottie last night. How good it would feel to have someone to talk to, to share the truth with. Somehow Emily knew that this might be the only lifeline that would be thrown to her, that if she didn't grab for it now, all would be lost. She stood abruptly and picked up the phone.

1950

Emily's eyes were squeezed shut as she lay on Father Devlin's desk. There was no longer any "tutoring" with the priest, since she had been confirmed in sixth grade along with her fellow students. All pretense was gone now; Emily was forced to come to his office week after week so that Father Devlin could use her body for his perversions and sick desires. She had learned not to fight it—the more she resisted, the more frenzied he became. She had learned to just get it over with, to stare at the ceiling and recite poetry or times tables in her head, or relive special moments with her mother, recalling snowball fights or trips to the park or watching the stars from Mrs. McGill's back yard. Occasionally, the humiliation of what was happening to her would overwhelm her, and she would start to whimper. This always made the priest angry, and he would tell her quietly but fiercely to shut up. Then he would go back to his odd murmuring as he went about the violation of her body. But today, just as he was removing her panties, she heard him exclaim out loud.

"Well, look what we have here! Somebody is turning into a young lady."

Confused, Emily looked straight at him, something she ordinarily tried not to do. "What do you mean, Father?"

Devlin turned her panties inside out and showed her a blood stain in the crotch. "You've started your menstrual period. You're a woman now."

Emily was almost thirteen. She didn't feel like a woman, and she certainly didn't understand how that had anything to do with blood in her panties. In fact, the blood was a little scary. "What's a period? And how did there get to be blood in my underwear?"

"Well now, that's a conversation for you to have with Mrs. Hutton. All girls around your age should learn about this part of growing up from their mothers. Now get dressed and go back to class. Tell Sister Mary Francis what's happened and ask her to get you a sanitary napkin. She'll know what to do."

Startled and relieved that the abuse had ended almost before it got under way, Emily hopped off the desk and hurriedly put her clothes on before Father Devlin changed his mind. But as she walked down the hall toward her classroom, her steps grew slower and slower. She thought about how embarrassing it would be to tell her teacher what was happening, especially when she didn't know what was happening herself. What if some of the other kids overheard her? And she certainly couldn't tell Mother who was lost in her own world most of the time now. Nor could Emily tell Father. That would be even more embarrassing. Emily hoped that the blood would stop pretty soon so she could wait until she got home to figure out what to do. She sidetracked into the bathroom so she could wipe herself and maybe slow the flow, but she found that there was even more blood now. Alarmed, Emily folded up several layers of toilet paper and put it in her underwear. She wasn't sure what she was more afraid of, bleeding to death or getting blood on her desk chair. And she was starting to feel some cramps in her abdomen. She prayed for the day to end quickly and went back to her class.

Emily barely heard a word as Meg chattered beside her on their way home from school. Her mind was focused on what she was going to do about the bleeding. All she wanted was to go to bed and curl up in a ball, but then who would keep an eye on Joey? Then the answer occurred to her. She could ask Fannie! Fannie was eighteen now, which Emily thought might qualify her as a woman. Maybe she would know what all this was about.

The minute she walked in the door, she hustled Meg upstairs then went into the kitchen to find Fannie. When she was greeted by Fannie's big smile, Emily almost collapsed from relief. "Fannie! Thank God! I need to ask you something before you leave."

Concerned, Fannie asked, "What is it, Emily? You look like the world is ending."

Emily pulled Fannie to a chair, sat next to her and began whispering in her ear. As Fannie listened, her eyes widened in understanding, and then she smiled. "Oh, it's alright, lassie. No need to be afraid. It's perfectly normal, and I promise you won't bleed to death. Fannie will get you fixed up right quick." Leading Emily upstairs to the bathroom, she pulled out a thick, white pad from a box in the linen closet and showed her what to do with it. After she was finished educating Emily on the onset of puberty and womanhood, she found an aspirin bottle in the medicine cabinet. "Now, take two of these, and those cramps will feel better in a flash. I've got to run now, so put on your happy face for Mrs. H, and I'll see you tonight when I get home. You're going to be just fine."

1959

When Emily opened the front door to let in her friend, Lottie's jaw dropped. "Emily! What's happened? Are you sick? You look terrible!" She drew Emily into her embrace and held her tight. Emily felt a dam break inside her and began to sob in Lottie's arms. She had forgotten how it felt to be hugged by someone who truly cared about her. For the first time in ages, she felt safe. Eventually, she pulled away and led Lottie into the kitchen, embarrassed by the shambles the house was in and then realizing that Lottie wouldn't care. Her parents' home had been like this most of the time when the kids were little. She poured coffee for them both and sat down at the table, lighting another cigarette.

Lottie took a moment to absorb Emily's frail frame, her shaking hands, the dark circles that indicated many sleepless nights. "Okay, Emily. I'm here. Please tell me what's going on."

Emily stared at her for a long moment before responding, "I don't even know where to start."

"How about the beginning?"

"The problem is, which beginning? One beginning when we were kids at school, and one beginning now." She took a deep breath and let it out slowly. "I guess the way that makes the most sense is to tell you about George and I. We wanted children desperately and couldn't figure out why I wasn't getting pregnant. George was getting more and more irritable with me, and I was depressed and feeling like I must be doing something wrong. It was pretty awful. Then George made me go to the doctor to see why we weren't conceiving. I didn't want to go, in fact, started having dreadful nightmares and just felt more and more anxious. And then we went, and it was every bit as awful as I expected it to be. But the worst thing was that the doctor apparently found scar tissue inside me and told George I must have been a prostitute before I met him."

Lottie interrupted with a loud gasp. "What?! That's insane! Did George believe him?"

"Yes. Just took the doctor's word for it with no hesitation. And he was so furious, it scared me. He'd never been that furious before. I mean, he can really have a temper, and he never hesitated to express it, even slapped me a few times, but this . . . this was different. He . . . when we got home . . . he, well, he bent me down over the table and . . . Lottie, he raped me! In the behind."

Lottie gaped at Emily with horror writ large in her eyes. "Emily! That's horrendous! I can hardly believe it! What would cause him to do that?! Oh Emily, I'm so sorry! Why didn't you tell me sooner?"

Emily took another drag on her cigarette and shook her head. "I couldn't. I was too ashamed. I mean, things like that just don't happen in polite society. I felt dirty . . . and disgusting. But that's not all." She stared out into the yard for a moment, trying to dredge up the strength to tell her friend the next part. "It's about Father Devlin. You remember how he insisted on doing lice checks on me so Mrs. H. wouldn't have to? Well, when George was raping me, I suddenly had a rush of memories of Father Devlin doing the same thing . . . and other things . . . during tutoring, confession, the lice checks."

"Father D. *raped* you?!"

Emily nodded wordlessly.

"Oh, my God, Emily! I had no idea! Oh, honey, I don't even know what to say!"

"I was too scared to tell you, Lottie. He threatened that if I told anyone, he would make sure I was sent to an orphanage. And I felt so filthy, like nobody would want to be around me if they knew the things he was making me do." An errant sob escaped Emily's throat. She covered her hand with her mouth, trying to pull herself together before speaking again. Lottie reached over and laid her hand on Emily's arm, giving her a squeeze of encouragement. Emily continued, "You know how I always hated confession? And how I was always last? Because as soon as everyone was gone, he would make me come over to his side of the booth and do stuff to him."

Lottie's eyes widened. "My God, he was a monster! How could he have done those things to you?! I wish I had known. I mean, I remember how he seemed to pay special attention to you and that it made you uncomfortable, but . . . .. That bastard! It makes me sick to think about it. Did you tell any of this to George?"

Emily shook her head. "He wouldn't have believed me. He was so convinced, and he wanted to have someone to blame for not having children. He's gone completely round the bend, Lottie. He kicked me out of our bedroom, and now I have to sleep on a pallet of boxes in the spare room. He felt so betrayed after he had tried to live such a straight and narrow life, following all the rules, doing everything right, and then this happened. He had been a virgin when we married and thought I was too. When he found out I wasn't, I think he figured why should he try anymore when he had sinned without even knowing it. Now, he goes out drinking almost every night and brings prostitutes home for sex in the middle of the night. I hear them in the next room, and it brings back all the memories until I think I'll go mad."

"Emily, that's outrageous! You have to tell someone about this! Can you go to Father McCaffrey?"

"I couldn't possibly! It's too embarrassing and implausible. He'd never believe this of George. I actually ran into Father McCaffrey last night when I left the house to avoid hearing George and his latest hooker. I wasn't looking where I was going, just running blindly, and I literally bumped into him and fell down. When he bent down to help me up, all I could see was his collar, and it scared me so bad I started screaming like a banshee. He took me into his kitchen to make sure I was alright, and he wanted to know what was wrong, but all I could say was that George and I are having problems. I've been so defiled at this point, I don't feel like I could even enter the sanctuary of the church again, much less tell the priest about it. And I'm sure God has written me off completely."

"Oh, Emily, I'm sure that's not true. God loves you. You

were not to blame for what happened."

"How do you know? And where was God when all this happened in the first place? First, both my parents die, and then I end up with a perverted priest who destroys my childhood and any chance of having children. It must be punishment for something. You know how some people are just bad eggs from the beginning? That's me. I deserved it."

"No! That's not true. You didn't deserve what that deviant did to you, and you don't deserve what George is doing to you now. I can understand that it would be hard to feel safe with a priest after what you've experienced, but what if I came with you? Would you go talk to Father McCaffrey then? I've known him all my life. Even though he was never our parish priest, he was a good friend of my father from his volunteer work at the diocese, and I swear you can trust him, Emily."

Emily stared at Lottie, thinking about what she had said. What Lottie was asking of her felt like an enormous leap of faith, and she wasn't sure she had the strength. On the other hand, she felt she didn't have much to lose. Maybe it would help. She had so many questions, so many feelings, so much doubt that needed to be addressed before she could even start moving on with her life. Could she stay with George like this forever? The thought made her shiver with dread. She lit another cigarette, her new form of courage. "OK, Lottie. If you go with me, I'll tell Father M."

1950

Father Devlin was waiting for Emily at his office door when she walked down the hall. His eyes wore a hungry look as he grabbed her arm, pulled her into his office, and shut the door. There was a vibration of excitement emanating from him like electricity crackling in the air. This intensity was matched only by Emily's fear. She had no idea what was about to happen, but she knew it couldn't be good.

As he pulled her toward his desk, he said, "You know, Emily. Now that you're a woman, things have changed. Our love is going to have to be expressed in a different way." He moved to stand right behind her. "Now, bend over." He pushed her down until her face was pressed against the scattered papers on his ink blotter. A pen dug into her cheek as he pulled her panties down to her ankles. Fear overwhelmed her. She had no idea what was coming next. And then came excruciating pain as something penetrated her backside. A howl burst uncontrollably from her throat, and Father Devlin quickly covered her mouth with his hand, squeezing so hard she couldn't breathe.

"Don't. Make. Another. Sound." Each fierce word was accompanied by another agonizing thrust. The pain seemed to go on and on, pain without end. Desperately, Emily tried to focus on the objects on the desk, the smell of his cigars—anything but the pain and the sounds he was making. Then, one final excruciating stab, his uncontrolled cry of pleasure, and it was over. The priest stepped away from her and pulled up his pants. Emily felt unable to move.

Father Devlin helped her stand and straightened her clothing before guiding her over to the couch. Arm around her, he began to murmur in her ear. "That was so beautiful. I love you so much, Emily. Thank you for giving yourself to me in that way. It was exquisite. I know that it hurt a little, but next time won't be so bad." Emily cringed to think there would be a next time. He handed her his handkerchief to wipe the tears from her face. "Remember that this is our secret. Nobody would understand what we have together. If you tell, the Huttons will be very upset with you. I don't know what they might do, but if they find out, I won't be able to protect you." After several more minutes of the priest's protestations of love, he indicated it was time for Emily to return to class.

Still wiping at her cheeks, she closed Father Devlin's door behind her and walked down the long hallways that would take her to the door and allow her to escape. As she walked past Mrs. Northrup's desk, the woman gave her a long glance that took in Emily's red face, her damp cheeks, the still rumpled look of her jumper. What Emily saw in her eyes was not disgust or judgment, but sympathy. She paused for a moment then looked down at the floor and hurried back to class. The other students were working quietly on an assignment, so they didn't look up when she walked into the room and settled at her desk. Sister Mary Francis, now teaching English for the upper grades, couldn't help but notice Emily's red eyes and trembling hands. She had become accustomed to seeing her favorite student return from tutoring looking upset and withdrawn, but today something was markedly different and far worse. Not for the first time, she wondered what was really happening in Father Devlin's office. Emily had long ago caught up with her classmates in catechism, so her continued tutoring sessions made no sense. Shaking her head, the teacher turned her attention back to the class for another twenty minutes. "OK, times up. Please pass your papers forward. Your homework for tonight is on the board. See you tomorrow."

As the other students filed out, Sister Mary Francis asked Emily to stay back for a moment, ostensibly to fill her in on the work she had missed. Perching on the edge of her desk to strike a casual note, she took a deep breath and spoke. "Emily, you were later than usual getting back from your tutoring sessions. I can't help but to have noticed how often you seem upset after you've been at the rectory, today especially. Are you alright? Can you tell me what's wrong?"

Emily looked at her with troubled eyes, hesitating as she pondered how to answer. Deciding on a partial truth, she said, "Well, sometimes, after we're done with a lesson, we just talk about me losing my parents and how things are with my foster family and stuff. And I was feeling really sad today, so Father Devlin was comforting me." Emily watched her teacher closely to see if she believed the explanation.

Sister Mary Francis struggled to keep her face composed. "Well, I'm sure it must be nice for you to have Father Devlin giving you such personal attention. I'm sorry that you got so upset today. Is there anything I can do to help?"

Emily shook her head. "No, Sister, I'll be alright."

"Okay, then. You'd better go. I'm sure Meg is waiting for you to walk her home."

She watched her favorite student walk out the door, wondering what to do. Thoughts tumbled through her head remembering the many times Emily had returned from tutoring visibly upset and unable to focus on her lessons. But today was the worst. Emily's excuse was obviously false, and if Father Devlin truly were counseling her, the nun would eat her wimple. He had never been the epitome of compassion. Then she nodded as if a decision had been made and marched straight to the rectory.

She entered just as Father Devlin was conferring with his secretary. "Ah, Father! Just the man I want to see. Can I have a moment of your time? It's about Emily Snow."

Devlin nodded. "Certainly, let's go to my office. Mrs. Northrup, we'll finish this later." The priest led the way down the corridor and into his office but failed to shut the door all the way. "Now, Sister, what can I do for you?"

Curious, and still bothered by how Emily had looked as she left Devlin's office this afternoon, Mrs. Northrup had meanwhile crept quietly down the hall, hoping to eavesdrop on the conversation.

Sister Mary Francis spoke. "Well, Father, I have some concerns about Emily. She is fully caught up with catechism, in fact has been for a while now, and I'm wondering whether continued tutoring is really necessary. It's very disruptive to the whole class when she returns from her sessions with you, and it's not good for her to miss parts of lessons and have to try to make them up. I've tolerated it for a long while now, but as the material gets harder, it is more and more imperative for her to be in class. Can you help me understand what this is all about?"

Clearly annoyed, the priest stretched to his full height, looming over the diminutive teacher. "I find it quite impertinent that you would challenge me in this manner. But if you must know, I'm no longer tutoring her. Mrs. Northrup has more work than she can keep up with here, so Emily has been helping her out in the office. She's a very capable girl."

"I have no doubt of that. If she's needed here, I certainly don't want to stand in the way. I just wish I had been notified. And I hope you will consider my concerns about her classwork. Perhaps there is a better time for her to come, perhaps during P.E.?"

"Well, when you're principal of the school, Sister, I will take your thoughts into consideration. Until then, you need to stick to your teaching duties and not interfere in parish business. Now, if you don't mind, I have work to do."

"Yes, Father." Struggling to collect herself, Sister Mary Francis turned to leave. Mrs. Northrup had scurried back down the hall ahead of her and was seated at her desk when the sister walked by her. The secretary caught her eye and slowly shook her head. The woman had no idea what exactly was going on behind the priest's closed doors when Emily was there, but it wasn't tutoring, nor was the girl providing the secretary any kind of clerical help as he had claimed.

Sister Mary Frances held Mrs. Northrup's gaze and nodded her head, acknowledging the silent message. "I'll be back," she said quietly and left the rectory.

1959

Lottie pulled her car into a parking spot in front of the church and turned to look at Emily. "Are you ready?" It had taken almost half an hour to coax her into the car in the first place, so Lottie was by no means confident that she would be able to get her friend into the church now that they were here.

Emily shook her head. "I can't do this." It was at least the twentieth time she'd said it in the last hour.

"Yes, you can Emily. You can. I'll be right there beside you. You *need* to do this. What's happening is eating you up inside, and you have to get it out."

"Why can't I just talk to you?"

"You *can* talk to me, but it's not enough. I can't leave the baby with my mother so often, and you need someone who can give you some spiritual guidance, who can help you make sense of what's happened to you. You need someone older and wiser than me."

"But he's a priest, Lottie! What if he doesn't believe me, or defends Father Devlin, or tells me to just get over it?"

"That's not going to happen. Trust me. I know this man, and he is the kindest, gentlest person I know. He's going to know the right things to say. He's going to be on your side. I can't believe he would ever sanction what was done to you."

Emily was starting to falter. "Are you sure?"

"I'm absolutely sure. Please, Emily. I can't stand how much this is tearing you apart, how much it's hurting you. Please."

Lottie's eyes had filled with tears as she spoke. Touched by the depth of her friend's concern, Emily gave in. "Okay. I'll do it. Let's get in there before I change my mind." Lottie hustled her friend out of the car and up the sidewalk, praying all the while that their meeting with the priest would give Emily some comfort.

Father McCaffrey ushered them into his office and sat down behind his desk, again sensing that Emily needed a certain amount of distance to feel safe. After their encounter the other night, while he didn't know the whole story, he did suspect that there was a lot more to it than just a troubled marriage. Emily was clearly terrified, and he wanted to ease her fears as much as possible. "Before we start, ladies, I want to assure you that whatever we talk about today will be held in the strictest confidence. The only one who will ever hear about this conversation is God. And speaking of the man upstairs, let's pray, shall we?" The women bowed their heads as the priest prayed. "Heavenly Father, we ask for Thy presence here. We ask for Thy compassionate heart to receive the story that Emily has to tell and to give her comfort. And grant me the wisdom and the right words to ease her suffering. Help Emily to know that she is Thy beloved child. Amen."

The priest turned his eyes toward Emily expectantly, wordlessly inviting her to begin. Lottie reached over and gave her hand a reassuring squeeze. Emily took a deep breath and began. "Father, I didn't tell you the whole truth the other night. I mean, George and I are definitely having trouble, but that's not all there is. I . . . we . . . um, I wasn't getting pregnant, so George took me to a doctor, and . . ." Falteringly, Emily told the story of their fights, the doctor's diagnosis, and George's pinch-lipped silence in the car on the way home. She told him about George raping her, watching the priest's reaction closely for skepticism or judgment. Instead, there was compassion and outrage on her behalf.

"Dear God in heaven, Emily! He ravaged you? You poor thing! I'm so sorry! No wonder you are struggling so. And how do things stand between you now?"

Emily went on to talk about being banished to the second bedroom, the prostitutes and drunkenness, the cold and steely silences. "But Father, there's more. There's a reason that I screamed so loudly when I ran into you the other night. The only thing I could see in the dark was your collar, and . . . I thought you were someone else, someone who hurt me years ago. He's the reason for the scars Dr. Merritt found."

Father McCaffrey went utterly still. Emily watched as the import of her words sunk in, fearing she had said too much, wanting nothing more than to run from his office, but it was too late. The words had been spoken and couldn't be taken back.

Finally, he spoke. "Are you saying that a priest did unspeakable things to you when you were but a child?" Emily nodded. The Father took a deep breath and spoke softly. "I believe you, Emily. I want you to know that right now. I believe you. I've seen the fear in you, and I suspected that it had to come from something truly horrifying. The fact that it was caused by the actions of a man of the cloth literally turns my stomach. I assure you that I am not one to believe that every priest is without reproach, so don't imagine for one moment that I will try to defend one of my own. And now, I think I'm ready to hear the rest of the story."

And so Emily continued, stumbling over words, pausing many times to pull herself together, tears streaming down her face. She spoke until the whole story was out, a tangible thing, like an invisible tumor pulsing in the middle of the room. Lottie was crying silently, and even Father McCaffrey had tears in his eyes. After a long silence, he spoke. "My dear Emily, I am wounded to my core that anyone could have done such depraved things to you. As priests, we are taught that we are a brotherhood, but the man who did this to you is in no way my brother. You did not deserve that, nor do you deserve the treatment that George has visited upon you."

"I don't know if I can believe that, Father. I feel so ashamed. I must have done something terribly wrong, or maybe I was just born bad in order to bring all these horrible things upon myself. I feel dirty—contaminated—and I don't know how either of you can stand to be around me."

"That's where you're wrong, Emily. You didn't allow or cause these things to happen. You were forced by someone older and stronger, someone in a position of authority over you who threatened you with dire retribution if you ever dared to tell anyone. There's no way you could have possibly stopped this from happening. The man who did this made a choice, and he carried out his vile deeds completely against your will and against God's will. God knows it wasn't your fault, Emily. There is nothing you need to be forgiven for."

"I want to believe that. It's nice to hear you say it. But there's a part of me that still feels defiled and disgusting. The shame is so overwhelming at times, I can hardly bear it."

"I can understand that. We just need to find a way to counteract the shame, so that it doesn't have such a strong hold over you. Tell me, before you started having these memories, what did you do to feel better when you were feeling low?"

Emily thought for a moment. The memories were so overpowering now that it was hard to remember any of her life before they came roaring to the forefront of her consciousness. She shook her head, at a loss to imagine anything that might possibly help her. Then Lottie blurted out, "Emily, I know! You used to write poetry. All the time! Remember? You loved to write poetry. It helped you express your feelings about losing your parents and dealing with Mrs. H."

Father McCaffrey leaned forward. "Is that true, Emily? Did the poetry help you?"

Emily nodded, remembering. "It did. George made me stop for a while, but when I couldn't get pregnant, I would secretly write poetry about my depression and loneliness, and I would feel better for a while. It made things seem more manageable."

"Well then, let's give that a try. When you go home, sit down and write a poem about your shame. See if that cuts it down to size for a little while. And let's plan to talk again next week. I have no illusions that one conversation and a poem are going to be enough to ease the pain you've been carrying around for so long." He stood and walked around to the front of his desk. "I'd like to give you a hug, if you'll allow me."

Emily hesitated for a moment then stood and felt herself enfolded in the priest's gentle arms. She rested her head on his ample chest and felt comforted to her core. A memory from many, many years ago nudged its way into her mind, a memory of being held on her father's lap as he comforted her over a skinned knee. Tears came, the first in a long time that weren't accompanied by the dark images of her abuse.

Shame

Shame is a river that flows
through my veins,
spreading to the farthest reaches
of my being.
It is all I am now.
Shame is a putrid flood,
washing away every trace
of innocence.
Horrific memories feed its waters,
like tributaries,
each one a groundswell of black sludge
rising up to choke all light.
They condemn the girl
I used to be,
the one with happy memories,
savored like treasures,
to be brought out
when the world turned harsh.
Taken!
The hiding place is destroyed,
the treasure tossed into the torrent,
and I am set adrift
on the current of my pain,
forever lost,
forever exiled
from a girl named Emily.

Chapter 10

"Rage, rage against the dying of the light."
—Dylan Thomas

1959

Emily awakened to the now familiar sounds of George "entertaining" a woman of the night in the next room. For once, it didn't immediately send her into a flashback of Father Devlin's abuse. What she felt, maybe for the first time, was disgust. Instead of feeling guilty for forcing George to get his sexual needs met in this way, she saw the choice he was making to exert his power over women. And she felt pity for the woman who was reduced to prostitution in order to get by. She even wondered if the prostitutes had experienced abuses like her own that caused them to believe this was all they were good for. Suddenly, her musings were interrupted by a loud and agonized scream. At first, Emily wondered if it had come from her own throat, so familiar did it sound. Placing her hand at her neck, she knew that it hadn't. The guttural sound came again, and in that moment, she realized what was happening. She knew, because it had happened to her.

Rage began rising in Emily like a great flood of white-hot flame. Without premeditation, she jumped up from her makeshift bed and ran to the door, flinging it wide and bursting through the door opposite. The scene she witnessed was as she had expected, George in much the same position he had been in when he raped her on the kitchen table. The woman—girl, really—was screaming and crying out, "Stop, stop! You're hurting me, you son of a bitch!"

Emily rushed over to the bed and pushed George away from the young woman. "What do you think you're doing, George! Are you crazy? How dare you commit rape in my house! How dare you take advantage of this poor girl! You disgust me!"

"Who are you to talk about disgust? You're no better than

her! Just a no-account whore that deserves what she gets. What gives you the right to interfere in my sexual predilections? Just for that, I ought to make you finish the job." George reached out to grab Emily's arm as the prostitute clutched her clothes to her and ran from the room.

Emily pulled her arm away and slapped George on the cheek. "No! Don't you touch me! I tolerated it once, but you are never going to do that to me again." Outraged, George grabbed her by the shoulders and threw her onto the bed, but she rolled off before he could climb on top of her. "Don't imagine that I am the same placid woman who married you. I've had enough of your abuse."

George once again attempted to wrestle Emily onto the bed, but she thrust her knee into his groin and watched him topple to the floor. "You bitch!" he exclaimed as he rocked back and forth in pain. "I will get you for this! If you think your life has been bad so far, just wait. You're still my wife, and I have a right to marital privileges, which I promise are going to be more painful than anything you've experienced before."

"I doubt it," spat Emily. "I endured the pain you inflicted on me for years. And that wasn't even the worst of it. Did it ever occur to you to ask ME about the scars? I wasn't a prostitute; I was abused and raped by a priest! I was eleven when it started—eleven! Can you imagine what that feels like? No! You cannot. Any more than you can imagine what you just did to that poor girl or to me. You don't know how to feel pain, but you sure enjoy dishing it out. You love the feeling of power it gives you. But trust me, you are never going to exert that power over me again, even if I have to get a gun to defend myself. You are far worse than the prostitutes you hold in contempt. You are lower than the belly of a snake!" She stormed out of the room, entered her own and slammed the door, chest heaving from the ferocity of her anger. Quickly, she started pushing the boxes that had been her bed against the door, knowing George would not give up easily.

Soon enough, he began pounding on her door, bellowing obscenities at her. "Just wait! You're going to have to come out sooner or later, bitch, and when you do, I'll make you sorry you ever dared walk into my room tonight. You'll pay, you filthy whore! I promise you'll pay." Eventually his shouts turned into mutters, and

Emily heard him slide to the floor, his rage spent, at least for now. She listened until she heard him begin to snore loudly, then wrapped her blankets around her and fell fast asleep.

The next day, after George had left for work, Emily bathed and dressed. Despite the short night's sleep, her anger seemed to have had an energizing effect that cleared her mind while she planned out what to do to protect herself. She went into George's room and pulled out the drawer where she knew he kept his secret stash of money. Smiling at the large wad of cash wrapped in a sock, she removed what she thought she would need and left the house, walking with determination toward the hardware store. She took a deep breath of fresh air, taking in the trees dripping with melting snow and realized with surprise that it was March.

Bells jangled as she entered Pratt's Hardware. Mr. Pratt himself was behind the counter and smiled when he looked up to greet Emily. "Good morning, Mrs. Edwards. I haven't seen you in a while. How can I help you?"

"And a lovely morning it is, Mr. Pratt. I am in need of a lock and key set for our shed. The old one finally just broke into pieces, and George hoped that I could get one today, so he can install it tonight after work. You know how much he values his tools and wouldn't want them to be stolen."

Mr. Pratt helped Emily find the right lock, chatting cheerfully all the while, then asked if there was anything else.

"As a matter of fact, there is, but you'll have to promise to keep it a secret." Intrigued, the store owner nodded eagerly. "Well, it's George's birthday soon, and I want to surprise him with a shotgun. I know it sounds a little funny, as fastidious as he is, but he has fond memories of going rabbit hunting with his father when he was a boy, and I want him to be able to relive those happy times."

Soon, Emily was leaving the store with a long bundle in her arms that included gun, shells, and instructions on its use, "in case George has forgotten how to load it." There was a satisfied smirk on her face and a desire to shout her defiance from the rooftops. She was determined not to allow George to make good on his threats.

1950

Life in the Hutton home had settled into a different kind of routine now that Mrs. Hutton wasn't able to drink any more. She alternated between irritability and deep depression, often weeping quietly in her room. On irritable days Mrs. Hutton would create busy work for Emily—scrubbing bathroom floors, polishing silver and crystal that were never used, bringing her tea and cookies that were never touched. On her depressed days, Mother would beg Emily to come and sit with her as she talked about the pain of losing a child, her body racked by deep sobs. At those times, Emily would often resort to reading poetry to calm her and lull her into a fitful sleep. All the chores and time spent comforting her foster mother left little time for schoolwork, so Emily would often have to stay up until late at night finishing her assignments. Worst of all, the lack of sleep often caused her to nod off in class, inviting reprimand and embarrassment. The only improvement in her life was Father Devlin's apparent decision to stop tutoring her. Inexplicably, she was no longer called to the rectory to be violated by his idea of love. He wasn't even taking advantage of the privacy of the confession booth to grope her or force her to otherwise satisfy his hungers. Nonetheless, Emily lived in a constant state of dread, waiting for the next expression of his perversion.

One afternoon as spring break approached, Sister Mary Francis called the children to attention just before the final bell. "Students, I have an important announcement to make. I am saddened to inform you that Father Devlin will be leaving our parish. I am told he has a medical condition that will no longer permit him to fulfill his duties here, so the diocese has placed him on indefinite medical leave. They have found a priest to take his place, a Father Novak, I believe, but he is currently serving a parish in Oregon and will need some time to relocate. We may be able to expect him to join us after Easter vacation. Father Devlin's last day will be Friday, so let's all make sure to let him know how much we have appreciated his leadership and that we will miss him and wish him well. And now, let's bow our heads and pray for healing and comfort for him during this difficult time."

Emily bowed her head with the rest of the class, but her mind was whirling with so many thoughts that the words of her teacher's prayer could not be heard. Elation, fear, doubt, and relief all fought for supremacy in her head. Was this real? What if this mystery illness was cured quickly and he came back? Oh, my goodness, he'll be gone in two days! No more "lice checks" or "tutoring" ever! But what if the next priest is just as bad? Or worse?! Is it possible that the violations of her body could be over?

After school, Emily and Lottie waited until they were out of sight of the school before Lottie grabbed Emily by the arms. "He's leaving!"

"I know," cried Emily, and the two began jumping up and down in their glee. "No more Father Devil! Hurray!"

Meg looked puzzled at the girls' excitement. "What are you talking about?" she asked.

Emily crouched down to explain. "Did your teacher tell you that Father Devlin isn't going to be our parish priest anymore?" Meg nodded. "Well, we're not glad that he's sick, but Lottie and I didn't like him very much, so we're just excited that we'll be getting somebody new."

"Oh. I didn't really like him either. He was kind of creepy. Can I jump up and down, too?" The older girls laughed and took Meg's hands to help her jump as high as she could go.

The week passed slowly, but Friday arrived at last. There was a school assembly to say farewell to Father Devlin. A few students spoke, expressing their gratitude for his knowledge and guidance. Emily listened with an odd sense of detachment. It seemed strange for her to be so relieved at his impending departure while some of the other students seemed to be genuinely sad. Or maybe they were just good actors, since almost everyone had complained about his exacting expectations in catechism. Lottie and Emily weren't the only ones who had called him Father Devil under their breath. But no matter how hard she tried to dredge up some regret, all she felt was numb. She glanced towards Lottie who stifled a smile and winked at her. Emily smiled and looked away quickly lest anyone witness their exchange. *Thank God for Lottie,* she thought. *She makes everything bearable.*

Two weeks later, the new priest entered Emily's classroom to lead catechism. The man who walked toward the lectern couldn't have been more different than Father Devlin. He was short and round, and his white hair was a mere fringe around his balding head. His rosy red cheeks and twinkling smile reminded Emily of popular images of Santa Claus. Sister Mary Francis introduced him as Father Jacob Novak, going on to tell the students a little about him. He thanked the sister for her kind words and turned to the students. "I'm looking forward to getting to know each of you. I love the catechism, and I enjoy helping students learn not just the words but the meaning behind the words."

Emily felt some of her anxiety begin to ease. *Maybe he won't be like Father Devlin,* she thought. Nonetheless, she was determined not to let down her guard. Looks could be deceiving.

As the days went by, students were surprised to find Father Novak occasionally wandering the halls on days he was teaching catechism, stopping to chat with the students, poking his head into classrooms, just to observe for a few minutes and say hello. This was highly unusual, as Father Devlin had spent as little time in the school building as possible. On one of such days, he was walking down the hall as Emily was returning from lunch, and he called out her name. "Emily, is it?"

Emily froze. This was it. She had gotten complacent, but now he was going to ask her to come to the rectory, and the horrors would start all over again. "Uh, yes, Father?"

"Nice to meet you, young lady. I just wanted to tell you how impressed I am with your grasp of the gifts of the Holy Ghost. Most of the students have them memorized, but you seem to actually understand them. Well done."

"Uh, thank you, Father. They just speak to me, I guess. Does that sound silly?"

"Not at all, Emily! It sounds like a very mature observation from someone of your age. I look forward to hearing more from you in class."

Emily blushed with pleasure at his praise, forgetting her caution for a moment. "Well, I guess I'd better get to class before I'm late. See you tomorrow, Father." Then she remembered that tomorrow was confession, and she quailed at the thought. What kind of penance would Father Novak demand? Lottie always talked about having to say a bunch of Hail Mary's or perform an act of kindness, but Devlin had never asked her to do any of those things. What he extracted from her was far worse. Would the new priest do the same?

The next morning, Emily vacillated between faking illness and just getting it over with. The problem with skipping school was that Mrs. Wisener, the school secretary, would probably call Mother if Emily didn't show up for class. And where would she go for the day? Ultimately, she was too afraid of getting caught to try it. Mother and Father would be furious, an outcome she would rather avoid. And the reality was that Emily couldn't skip out on confession forever. She would have to go eventually, and it might as well be now. She tried to focus on Father Novak's kind eyes and cheerful nature. Maybe it wouldn't be so bad. Maybe it would only be the things Father Devlin did in the beginning, before the really awful stuff.

And so it was with determination that Emily entered the chapel with the rest of her class on Friday afternoon. Distracted by her anxious thoughts, she failed to notice when Ralph Riggs stepped out of the confession booth and slipped back into the pew beside her. She was startled out of her reverie when Sister Mary Francis called her name. "Emily, it's your turn. Snow comes after Riggs, remember?"

She trudged to the confession booth and stepped in, dropping to the kneeler. "Forgive me Father, for I have sinned. It's been two weeks since my last confession." She waited for him to tell her to come onto his side, although she wondered how she would fit in the tiny space with his bulk. Father Devlin had been much skinnier, but tall and frightening in his intensity. Yet, he didn't say a word. Stumbling through her list of "sins," Emily's anxiety mounted. Nothing was going as expected.

"Well, my child, I don't think any of those trespasses are exactly cardinal sins. Let's just do ten Hail Mary's and call it a day, shall we?"

"W-what? That's it? I mean, yes, Father. Thank you, Father. And I'll try to do better, I really will."

"I'm sure you will, dear. Now, go back to your seat and wait with the rest of your class. I'm sure that young Mr. Sullivan is going to have quite a long list."

Stunned, Emily exited the booth. *What just happened? He didn't touch me! He didn't make me touch him! Maybe he really isn't going to hurt me. Maybe this nightmare is truly over.*

1959

Emily was sitting in Father McCaffrey's office again, tears coursing down her face as she related the continuing nightmares and memories of what she had endured at the hands of Father Devlin. She had been visiting the priest almost weekly for about a month, and although difficult and painful, she found that she felt some relief afterward. Most of the time he just listened and nodded and reassured her that the abuse wasn't her fault, that Devlin was one hundred percent to blame for what he did to her. She liked that he didn't try to fix anything but just let her tell her story, the story that had been bottled up inside her for so many years. The words seemed to come in a torrent, rushing to get out.

"I just feel so lonely, Father. My parents are gone, my foster family abandoned me, and George ignores me completely, which is just as well. If it weren't for you and Lottie, I would have no one. And Lottie can't just drop her responsibilities and come running every time I'm having a bad day."

"I know it's hard, my child, but don't forget that God is with you."

A wild rage suddenly sprang up in her like a roaring fire, taking her over and erasing all self-control. "Is he!? Is he? Where? You tell me where! And where was he when my parents died? Where was he when one of his chosen priests took it upon himself to brutalize me? Where is he now, while George is making my life a living hell? Do you know what he did the other night? He raped a prostitute in the backside while I was right there in the next room. I heard her screams and immediately knew what was happening. And when I burst in there to stop it, he threatened to do the same to me since I had dared to interrupt him. I barely escaped! Where was God then? Apparently, God despises me, because he's dished out nothing but pain my entire life! Don't *tell* me God is with me."

Emily flopped back down in her chair, anger draining out of her as quickly as it had come. She clapped her hands over her mouth, utterly ashamed of yelling at her priest. "I'm so sorry, Father. My God! I can't believe I said that. Please forgive me. You've been nothing but kind to me, and you didn't deserve that outburst."

"I can take your anger, my dear, and so can God. We both understand the deep wounds that it comes from. There's nothing to forgive." He paused in thought for a moment. "Who were your angels, Emily?"

"What? What do you mean?"

"Well, God can't stop someone who chooses to sin egregiously against another human being, but he can put people in the lives of those who are suffering—people who are kind and loving and supportive, even if they don't know what's happening to you. I would call those people angels, and I believe that God must have sent some to you. I was just wondering if you could look back and recognize them."

Emily thought for a long time. "Well, my mother was my first angel. Even after she was gone, just thinking about her could make me feel better. And then, I would say that our landlady, Mrs. McGill, was an angel. She took me in rather than letting the state take me to an orphanage, and she was kind and motherly to me. Her hugs gave me so much comfort. And there's Fannie, the live-in help at the Huttons. Even though she's not much older than me, she was a great friend and someone I could talk to when Mrs. H was on one of her tirades. Oh! And I can't forget Sister Mary Francis! She was wonderful! She was my favorite teacher, and she encouraged my poetry and listened when I needed someone to talk to. I'll be grateful to her forever. And Lottie, of course. She brought me to you." Emily smiled. "I guess I had more angels than I thought."

"I would say so. And I'm glad. But I'm afraid none of those angels can protect you if George decides to get violent with you again. Nobody would blame you if you left him, Emily. He has irrevocably broken his marital vows, and God does not expect you to stay in this marriage that is so damaging to you in body and soul."

Emily looked surprised. "What? Do you mean that? I hadn't even considered leaving. I just assumed that marriage is forever, for better or for worse. And I guess I have felt that I deserved George's abuse, since he always blamed all our problems on me. I really don't know where I would go, Father. I have no money. I don't even know if I could find a job at this point. I mean, I can see what I look like in the mirror. Who would hire me? I could have a random memory of the abuse in the middle of work and collapse in a heap. I'd be fired on the spot."

"I know it seems like too high a hill to climb right now, Emily, but I think you're getting stronger every day. Perhaps you could just think about it for a while, consider what you might do, who might help you with money so you can get away from here, someplace where you can begin to heal without constant reminders of both George and Father Devlin, and get a new start."

"I'll think about it, Father, I will. But I'm afraid that it might take another angel to make that happen. Maybe you could pray for a miracle." Emily smiled feebly, surprised at the small glimmer of hope that was flickering inside her.

1955

Emily walked down the halls of her school at the end of January, marveling at the fact that in a few short months she would be leaving, graduating, and moving on to a new stage of life. The years had passed swiftly, and she would miss the life she had here, the friends she had made, the excitement of learning, her close relationship with Sister Mary Francis. She would even miss Father Novak, who had been just as cheerful and kind as he had appeared when she first saw him and thought he looked like Santa. Her home life had not been as kind, but she had learned how to cope with Mother's ups and downs. Fannie had moved on to another nanny position once Joey had started school and no longer needed someone to be with him during the day. As the children had grown, Emily's workload had decreased, leaving more time for her studies and for her writing. Emily smiled as she thought of the pile of diaries stashed in her closet, filled with pages and pages of poetry. Now that Fannie was no longer in the house, Emily had a bedroom to herself, and even though she missed her friend, she loved having a refuge to which she could retreat from the tensions in the household when Mother was particularly difficult.

Emily collected Meg and Joey from their respective

classrooms, and they walked home together, making scuff marks on the sidewalks that were covered with a light dusting of snow. Snow sloughed off the branches of fir trees as they passed. Pale sunlight caught the tiny particles and turned them into diamonds falling from heaven. As always, witnessing the grandeur of nature gave Emily a deep sense of peace and well-being.

"What are you smiling about, Emily?" asked Joey, now nine and naturally inquisitive.

"Oh, nothing much, Joey, just happy, I guess. Don't you love the snow in the trees?"

Joey shrugged, then turned his attention to a squirrel that was racing up a nearby tree trunk. "Look! Did you see that big pinecone he had in his mouth?"

Emily and Meg laughed and gave each other a look that said, "Typical Joey—always off on a tangent!" Soon they were at the front door, stomping the snow off their feet before entering. Emily shooed the children upstairs to get started on their homework and headed towards the kitchen to see what she could round up for dinner.

After the evening meal, Father followed Emily into the kitchen. "Why don't you leave the dishes to soak, Emily, and join Mother and me in the bedroom. There's something we need to discuss with you."

Emily nodded her assent and dried her hands on a towel, wondering what this might be about. As she entered the room, she saw that Father had brought in two chairs, one for himself next to the bed and one for her opposite her foster parents. Father looked awkward, and Mother just looked blank. Wary and anxious, she sat down and waited.

Father spoke. "Emily, you will be turning eighteen next month, at which point you will be considered an adult, and as such, will no longer technically be our foster child. The money which the state has been paying us for your keep will stop. As you know, much of our money goes for Mother's doctor bills and medications. This means that our financial situation is not solid enough for us to be able to afford to support you anymore. I'm sorry to tell you that we are going to have to ask you to find another place to live once you turn eighteen. Given your experience here with us, we are confident that you will be able to find a job as a nanny or housekeeper. We would give you excellent references. Of course, we want to wish you well in whatever you choose to do." Father looked down at his hands as though embarrassed. Mother stared into space, almost as though she wasn't part of the conversation.

Emily sat perfectly still, hardly believing what she had just heard. Her thoughts and her stomach churned. "But what about school? Can't I just stay until the end of the school year? How can I finish school if I'm working?"

Mother finally spoke in a tight voice. "In my day, getting a high school education wasn't all that important. You already know how to do all the things that matter for finding a husband and raising a family."

"Now, Vivian, I don't think that's the point. We care about you, Emily, and we wish we could afford to help you finish your education, but we just can't." He paused as if unsure what to say next, then added, "I know this is upsetting to you, Emily, but you're a smart and capable young woman. I'm sure you won't have any trouble finding a job and supporting yourself. And we hope you'll stay in touch. We'll give you until the end of February to find another place to live. That should be plenty of time. You can get back to your chores now."

Stunned, Emily stumbled into the kitchen and slumped down into a chair. What would she do? How could she just walk away from school after how hard she had worked to excel? How could she leave Meg and Joey? Tears welled up in her eyes, and Emily laid her head on her crossed arms and let them come. She heard footsteps and looked up. Father was standing behind her. He put his hand on her shoulder and said, "I'm sorry, Emily, truly sorry." And then he walked away.

The next day, Emily stayed after school, having told the children to walk home without her. She needed to talk to the only adult she truly trusted—Sister Mary Francis. The nun was now teaching high school English, which had allowed the two to see each other often. She was not surprised to see Emily, as they often talked after school, discussing books, poetry, and religion. However, her student's facial expression suggested that these topics were not what was on her mind today.

Emily plopped down onto a desk chair in the front row and

blurted out the events of the previous evening and the situation she faced. She ended with an agonized, "What will I do?"

The nun was fuming inside, but tried to appear calm and collected for Emily's sake. "Oh Emily, I'm so sorry this is happening to you. It's a scary proposition to be suddenly cast out into the world without a safety net. And quitting school is just not an option. You are far too smart to set aside your education. You mentioned that the Huttons thought you could get a job as a nanny, but is that even something you would like to do?"

"No! I mean, I love Meg and Joey, but I can't imagine doing that kind of work forever. I want to do something that challenges me. I've thought about being a teacher, but I don't know how I would ever be able to afford college."

"Well, let's just look at the immediate future, shall we? We need to find something you can do after school that would pay for another place to live—something like a business that operates twenty-four hour a day so that you could do shift work and still attend school."

Sister Mary Francis' practical approach helped Emily's overwhelming situation feel a bit more manageable, and the two women talked for some time about the possibilities for employment. Even though full-time work seemed daunting, Emily realized that she had been putting in nearly that much time doing all the cooking, cleaning, and childcare at the Hutton household. And living on her own would certainly relieve the anxiety generated by the constant tension caused by Mother's highs and lows. They also discussed possibilities for room and board, so that by the time Emily left for home, she had a list of potential employers and rooming houses to check into. Nonetheless, Emily quailed at the thought of facing the world on her own, without benefit of anyone to lean on, to counsel or guide her. How could the Huttons do this to her?

When she walked into the house, Emily marched straight into the kitchen where the family was eating. Thankfully, Meg had become fairly adept at pulling together a simple meal and had covered for Emily's absence. "Father, I need to talk to you. In the living room."

Mr. Hutton looked astonished at her tone. "I'm in the middle of dinner, Emily. Can't it wait?"

"No, it can't. We need to talk *now*." With that, Emily turned her back on him and left the room. Waiting in the living room, she took a deep breath to steady herself. She was just as surprised at how firm she had sounded as Father was, but there was an anger burning in her that would not be suppressed.

"Now, what's this about, Emily? This imperious tone is not like you, and I have to say that I'm rather annoyed by your interruption of my evening meal with the children."

"Well, perhaps you have forgotten that for a little while longer, I'm one of your children, too. And the situation you've put me in requires me to make plans for my future with very little notice. So, given that urgency, I am informing you that I will not be performing my usual chores on Saturday so that I can go look for work and housing. I hope that won't *inconvenience* you."

"Now, look here! There's no need for that kind of disrespect."

"Really? What are you going to do to me, Father? Throw me out?"

Outrage and shame fought for supremacy on the man's face, and finally he let out a deep breath and looked down at the floor. "I'm sorry, Emily. I guess I deserved that. I'm sure we can do without you on Saturday and on future Saturdays if it comes to that. I wish you the best with your search."

As he left the room, Emily's sense of triumph quickly faded into sadness at the loss that was facing her. While Mrs. H. had often been a trial, it had been lovely to feel part of a family, to watch Meg and Joey grow up and to have a father figure who was gentle and kind, even if often absent. She knew he couldn't love her as he loved the children, but he had never been uncaring or cruel. He had tried to give her a break from Mother's needs when he could, but his long work hours didn't give him much time for that. Emily would miss them all, even Mother. And now she faced an uncertain future on her own.

Armed with her list and a letter of recommendation from Sister Mary Francis, Emily spent the following Saturday beating the pavement, looking for a job. Tentative at first after several employers turned her away, she found herself growing bolder. One of the owners had read the letter of recommendation aloud, and the nun's glowing words gave Emily confidence to speak more boldly about her skills and knowledge. Hopping on yet another bus, she thought about her next stop, the telephone company. Operators were needed twenty-four hours a day, and if Emily could get a job on the night shift with fewer calls to handle, she might even be able to study while she worked.

The bus deposited her right in front of the imposing edifice of the phone company. Gazing up at the Art Deco architecture, she took a deep breath, realizing that this was the job she really wanted. The other jobs she'd applied for would have been adequate in terms of making a living, but they would have been dull and boring. The idea of interacting with people and helping them make important calls seemed interesting and might even yield a good plot for a short story or two. She walked in the door with fingers crossed. When she walked back out, she had a job. She would start Monday after next, which would allow her to save up for a deposit on a room in a boarding house. Suddenly, she was actually looking forward to being independent. A door to the wider world was opening.

1959

"Who did you tell? Who did you tell, you little slut?!" Father Devlin held her by the shoulders of her jumper, lifting her almost off her feet as he hissed a mere inch from her face. She felt drops of his spittle on her skin, but it was his eyes burning fanatically out of a beet red face that scared her the most. They looked wild, almost insane.

"Nobody, Father! I swear I didn't tell a soul."

"I don't believe you! You must have told. That's why they're sending me away. And it's your fault! I thought you loved me. Trust me, you'll be sorry."

Emily was filled with terror. He proceeded to wreak his revenge, raping her savagely, covering her mouth so hard that she thought she would die of suffocation. But that was better than when he thrust himself into her mouth so violently that she choked and almost vomited on him. She wished she could just fade into oblivion, but that was too much to ask. And so she bore it, took a trip in her mind to another world where children were safe and loved.

Emily awoke to her own screams. Her entire body seemed to

be in excruciating pain, and Father Devlin's presence was so real that she couldn't stay where she was. The only thing she knew was that she had to run. Panicked and overwhelmed by the vividness of her memories, Emily ran out of the house and rushed wildly through city streets, eyes searching for danger in every direction. She felt as though she was alone in a dark and threatening wood, being stalked by a madman. The threat was everywhere and nowhere, the devil himself hiding behind every tree and bush. Emily stumbled over a crack in the sidewalk and fell against a hedge. Its branches caught at her clothing, causing her to thrash about as if she were trying to escape the claws of a monster. When she had finally freed herself from its clutches, she ran blindly until she tripped again and fell onto the freshly cut lawn of a neighboring yard. Emily sprawled there, face-down, gasping for breath. Gradually, her breathing slowed and quieted. The smell of the grass penetrated her consciousness, and, slowly, she rolled onto her back. On this dark night, the stars were like diamonds scattered on a carpet of black velvet. Emily had the sensation of her mother's hand sliding into hers, and suddenly she was a child again, lying in the back yard on a summer's night, stargazing with her mother . . .

The young girl stretched her arm up as if to touch the stars. "Mama, how can the stars feel so close and far away at the same time?"

"Well," responded Maddy, "I guess they're a little like God that way. God is always in heaven where he can look down and watch over his children, and he is also just as close to us as I am right now, holding your hand. The stars remind us that God's light will always conquer the darkness. I love the part in Psalm 139 that says, 'Yea, the darkness hideth not from thee . . . the darkness and the light are both alike to thee.' Like the stars, God is always there, even when the clouds block your sight. Remember that, Ladybug. God will always be your light, even in your deepest darkness. No matter what happens in life, God will be there in the midst of it, guiding the way . . ."

Her mother's words echoing in the adult Emily's head, she took a deep breath and released it slowly, feeling her body truly relax for the first time in weeks. Her eyes searched the stars, seeking guidance and reassurance. Gradually, they focused on Orion, blazing in the southern sky, the hunter's bow and arrow pointing westward. Was this God, showing her the way? Words formed unbidden in her mind, "It's time to leave, Emily. Follow the stars."

* * *

Standing at the street, Emily looked at the house she hadn't entered in four years. It hadn't changed much except for a general air of neglect. She felt nervous, unsure of how she would be received, yet knowing this was really her only chance of escape. Taking a deep breath, she approached the front door and knocked. After a moment, the door was opened by a lovely young woman with soft, blond curls falling around her shoulders. In another second, Emily found herself nearly knocked over by an enthusiastic embrace.

"Emily! Oh, Emily! It's so good to see you! I've missed you so much! How are you? You look, um . . . "

Emily laughed. "Don't worry, Meg. I know how I look. And I've missed you, too. I've come to see your father."

Meg turned to shout into the kitchen, "Father, Father! It's Emily! She's here to see you. Joey, Emily's here!" Brimming with excitement, she grabbed Emily's hand and pulled her into the house. Mr. Hutton and Joey emerged from the kitchen, the older man smiling a welcome as Joey ran past him to throw his arms around her.

Joey was thirteen now and taller than both Meg and Emily. It was startling to see him almost grown up when the last time Emily had seen him, he was an awkward fourth-grader. She gave him a delighted smile and reached up to tousle his hair as she had when he was a toddler. "It's a little higher of a reach than it used to be, isn't it?" he said.

"Indeed. You're quite the young man now, Joey. I'm sure there are any number of girls clamoring for your attention."

Joey blushed. "Naw, I don't pay them any attention. I'm playing basketball now, and between practices and homework, I don't have any time for girls."

Mr. H. chimed in, "And let's just make sure it stays that way, shall we?"

Emily turned toward the older man. "Hello, Father. It's good to see you."

"Hello, Emily. To what do we owe the pleasure?"

"I'd like a word with you privately if I may."

A look of puzzlement crossed his face before he responded. "Certainly, let's talk in the living room. Kids, off to your chores! You can catch up with Emily after we've talked." He ushered her into the living room and took a seat, gesturing her to her usual place on the settee. "What's on your mind, Emily?"

She paused, trying to formulate the right words as if she hadn't rehearsed them endlessly the night before. She took a deep breath and plunged in. "I need your help, sir. My marriage is irretrievably broken, and I fear that if I stay, my life will be in danger. My husband is not the man I thought him to be, and a certain, uh, situation has sent him off the deep end. He has taken to drink, brings prostitutes into our home, and has assaulted me on more than one occasion and threatened my life."

"My God, Emily! Are you alright? Don't answer that—I can see that you're not. What is it that set this off?"

In halting words, Emily related her infertility, the visit to the doctor, and George's reaction to what the doctor found. Steeling herself, she locked eyes with her foster father and said, "He raped me."

Slack-jawed, Mr. Hutton looked at her with horror. "Good God! Tell me where he is, and I will hang him from the highest tree!"

Emily gave a hint of a smile. "I don't need your vengeance, Father. Let's leave that to God. What I need is money enough to get away from him. And there's something else I need to tell you." She went on to explain the memories unleashed by George's abuse, the horrifying tale of what Father Devlin had done to her, and the hell her life had become. The next time she looked up, Father's jaw was clenched in a mixture of anger and pain. He buried his face in his hands.

When he was finally able to speak, he said, "I hardly know what to say, Emily. I'm so sorry. I never knew. I *should* have known. But I was so caught up in my work and dealing with Mrs. Hutton that I just wasn't paying close enough attention. It's unforgivable really. We took you in and promised to care for you, but this happened under our very eyes, and we didn't see it. We failed you. *I* failed you."

The reference to Mrs. Hutton caused Emily to ask, "Where is Mother?"

"You don't know? Oh, of course you don't. Another failure on my part. Mother is gone. She died last fall. She had another stroke, much worse than the others, and she wasn't strong enough to withstand it."

"I'm sorry, Father. You must miss her very much."

"I do. She was my wife, and I loved her, but I am also aware of how difficult she was for you. She could be quite demanding at times."

"Yes. She blamed me for you finding out about her drinking, so there were times when she would get angry and take it out on me. I know what kind of misery she lived with day after day, so I tried to look past it, but there were days when it wasn't easy."

"I'm so sorry. I think we both expected way too much of you. Looking back, I am horrified by the way we used you and, in some ways, treated you more like a servant than a daughter. It was inexcusable. And then to throw you out on your ear the moment you turned eighteen! I didn't want to. I knew it was wrong, but she kept harping on how we couldn't afford to keep you. And I allowed her strength of will to overshadow my better instincts."

"It's alright, Father. I forgive you. No one knows better than I what a strong will she had. I'm sorry she's gone for the children's sakes, but I can't pretend that I will grieve her."

The two sat in silence for a moment, taking in all that had been said, and in some way experiencing healing in the things that had been shared, the repentance offered, and the hurts forgiven. Then Mr. Hutton cleared his throat and broke the silence.

"So tell me what you need. I will help you however I can."

And so Emily told him her plan. They talked a long time, and when she left, she turned her gaze up to the darkening sky, looking for the evening star. Quietly, she spoke, "I'm going to be okay, Mama. God is shining light on my path."

Chapter 11

*What is this voice
that whispers underneath
the roar of doubt and fear?
Urgently it speaks,
It's time to go, time to escape
the chipping away of your soul,
time to save the only life you can,
time to fly.*
—Emily

1959

Emily stood staring at the boxes that had served as her bed for all these long months. Many emotions swept through her as she contemplated the tasks that lay ahead, sorting through her belongings, packing up what she could and leaving the rest behind, finding a place to live, traveling across the state to start a new life. She felt apprehensive, excited, sad, scared, and overwhelmed. She gave herself a mental shake and thought, *nothing's going to happen if you just stand there.* She sighed and bent over to open the first box.

When she had been thrown out of her marriage bed, Emily had tossed her things in boxes so hurriedly that there was no order at all. The boxes were a mix of unmatched clothing, old embroidery projects, some books and journals she had kept hidden from George, and memorabilia from childhood all thrown in together. Slowly she began to sort the clothing into piles according to season. Reaching into the bottom of one box, her hand encountered the soft, nubby feel of an old sweater. With a frisson of recognition, she pulled it out and buried her face in it. It was her mother's sweater, the one Mrs. McGill had brought down from their apartment the night Mama had died. It had comforted her then, and it comforted her now. Emily pulled the sweater on and wrapped her arms around herself. It felt almost as though her mother was holding her, just as she had so many times in childhood. Memories ran through her mind unbidden—a seven-year-old Emily heartbroken over the loss of her father, a third-grader angry over the bullies who had called her a baby, stubbed toes, scraped knees—all those moments when her mother's hug had made all the difference and comforted her beyond measure.

Still wearing the sweater, Emily sank to the floor to look through the books and papers that had been haphazardly tossed aside as she sorted her clothes. She fanned out the papers with her hand, and her attention was caught by the corner of a black and white photo. Pulling it out from the pile, she was surprised to see that it was a class photo from fifth grade. There was Sister Mary Francis with that loving smile, there was Lottie—her jumper a little rumpled as usual—and next to Lottie stood the eleven-year-old version of herself. A mixture of emotions stirred in her—fondness for Sister and Lottie, distress at the stirring of painful memories, sadness over the lost little girl she had been. As she looked more closely at her own image, she saw a frightened child, one who looked as though she was trying to disappear. There was a haunted look in those wide eyes, and a wariness that came from constantly scanning her environment for danger. Tears began to fall, not tears of rage or fear or pain, but tears of grief for a lost childhood and for the suffering the girl in the photo had endured. She brushed her fingers over the photo in a caress, a gentle touch of comfort. "I'll take care of you now," she whispered, "You're safe."

Wiping the tears from her cheeks, Emily set aside the photo and picked up an old school folder. Inside were pages and pages of poetry, some her own, others copied meticulously from library books of Emily Dickinson, Carl Sandberg, Elizabeth Barrett Browning. Immediately she was lost in the words and images of another time, another world where beauty and pathos combined and spoke to a young girl's heart. Here were the words that had lifted her when life was at its lowest. Here were the images that had given her strength. Here were the words she herself had written, encouraged by the gentle coaxing of Sister Mary Francis. *Oh, how I loved her,* Emily thought. *I'm so grateful God put her in my life.* With absolute certainty, she knew that she could not have survived those years without the constant light and love of her teacher and mentor. Emily was filled with a sudden resolve to see her beloved Sister again. She began sorting in earnest, filled with energy and purpose at the thought of their reunion.

Two days later, Emily walked hesitantly through the front door of her old school. She had waited down the block first, listening for the closing school bell and watching as the children emerged, laughing, and running down the sidewalk as she and Lottie used to do. She sighed at their innocence and prayed that nothing dire would happen to destroy it. It was the first time she'd been back since graduation, and though four years had passed, it felt as though nothing had changed. Mrs. Wisener still sat behind her desk in the school office. She looked up from her typewriter when Emily walked in, looking puzzled at first as though trying to place her. Then recognition dawned, and a smile lit up her face. "Emily! It's so good to see you! What brings you here?"

Emily answered the kind woman's smile with one of her own. "I just thought I'd drop in and visit with Sister Mary Francis for a while. Is she still here?"

"Of course, she's still here! I think they'll have to take her out of this school feet first. It's hard to imagine her ever retiring. Go on down and see her. She's still in the same classroom."

"Thanks, Mrs. Wisener. It's been lovely to see you as well."

She walked slowly down the hall, looking at the pictures and schoolwork of the children taped on the cement block walls. It was odd to think that this place held some of her happiest memories and some of the worst at the same time. School had always been such a delight for her, feeding her hunger for knowledge and her love of words, while also being the place where such horrifying acts had been perpetrated against her. Yet such was the change in atmosphere Father Novak had wrought after Devlin's departure, she did not feel her tormentor's presence in this place. Despite her initial apprehension, she was not sinking into the flashbacks she had feared. Nonetheless, she had no intention of visiting the chapel that was home to the confessional booth where so many abuses occurred.

Reaching the door to Sister's classroom, she poked her head around the door frame to get a first glimpse of her beloved teacher. Sister Mary Francis sat at her desk, which occupied its usual place, her head bowed over a pile of papers, red pen in hand. There were a few more wrinkles at the corners of her eyes, but the kindness in them remained the same. Emily knocked gently on the door frame, and the older woman looked up. Delight transformed her face. "Emily! Oh, Emily, please come in. You look . . . well, you look too thin to my eyes, but I'm so happy to see you. How are you? What brings you here? Come and give me a hug. You've just made my day!"

The two women embraced, and Sister pulled out one of the student's chairs for Emily to sit, then pulled her own chair closer and leaned forward to close the distance between them. "Okay, my dear. Tell me everything."

"Well, Sister, I came to say good-bye. I'm leaving soon and moving to Seattle to start over. My marriage is irretrievably broken, and I need to get away from the painful memories."

"Oh Emily, I'm sorry to hear that. You looked so happy on your wedding day. What happened?"

Emily took a deep breath. Now that she was here, she wasn't sure she had the courage to tell the whole story. But remembering how much it helped to speak of it to Lottie and Father McCaffrey, she sat up straighter and began. "Well, the story actually goes back much further than my wedding day. It begins with the day I first stepped through the door of this school. It starts with the secret and awful things that Father Devlin did to me." As she continued to speak, the sister's trembling hand moved up to cover her mouth, and her eyes welled up with tears. With her other hand, she reached over and covered Emily's, imparting comfort and strength to her beloved former student.

When Emily finished, there was a long silence while both women struggled to compose themselves. Finally, Sister Mary Francis spoke. "I feared as much. I saw all the times you returned from tutoring and confession red-eyed and upset. One of the last times, you were shaking so badly, I thought you were going to disintegrate before my very eyes. That was the day I asked you why you were so upset after tutoring, and your answer was so ridiculous, I knew it couldn't be true. So I marched over to the rectory after school and confronted that vile man. He gave me a completely different response than yours, and that just confirmed what I feared. And then there was Mrs. Northrup, who must have overheard our conversation, sitting at her desk and shaking her head as if to say, 'Don't believe a word he says.' The next day, she and I both made reports to the diocese, and incredibly, they took us seriously. When they put him on medical leave, I was so relieved—you have no idea. I didn't know exactly what was happening, and I certainly didn't imagine anything as serious as what you are telling me, but I knew something was terribly wrong. And then, when Father Novak arrived, I could see you starting to come out of your shell. It was only when your fear started to leave you, and your smile came back that I realized how bad it must have been. Not that you were happy exactly, because who could really be happy with your situation at home. I know Mrs. Hutton was a real trial for you, God rest her soul."

Emily looked somberly at her teacher. "Sister, with all my heart, thank you. Truly! I don't know what would have happened if Father Devil hadn't left when he did. I shudder to think about the further atrocities he would have inflicted on me. And the trouble was, it was so confusing. He would tell me he loved me and shower me with praise and then do such terrible things to me. And I still struggle with wondering if I deserved it or wanted it. I was so desperate to be loved, which is probably why I married George too quickly. But I don't think I could have survived Devlin's abuse much longer. As it was, I got to have a few good years in which to put those memories out of my mind in order to survive. Mrs. H. was definitely a challenging woman, but her troublesome moods pale next to what Devlin did to me."

Emily and her teacher talked on for over an hour as Emily shared the wreckage of her marriage and her plans for a new life. She shared her gratitude for the gift of the nun's mentorship and for encouraging her love of poetry. When the light began to dim, the two women realized it was time to say good-bye. They embraced once more, promising to write each other often, then Emily took one more look around the classroom and walked out the door, resting her hand on the door frame as she left as though to capture the spirit of this place and the woman who had presided over it for so long.

1955

Emily and Meg were chopping vegetables for stew when Mother hollered for Emily from her bedroom. The girls exchanged glances, and Meg nodded to indicate her readiness for what both were sure was coming. Emily walked down the back hall and went into Mrs. H's inner sanctum. "What is it, Mother?"

"Come and fix my pillows. You never do it right! You'd think that after all these years you could learn a simple thing like the proper placement of my pillows. How am I expected to read a book or write my correspondence when I am slouching so?"

"I'm sorry, Mother, but I am no longer in your employ. I will be starting a new job tomorrow at the phone company, and I will be unable to wait on you in the manner to which you are accustomed. If you'd like, I will let Meg know that you need some assistance."

"You impertinent and ungrateful little witch! Get over here right now and do what I tell you. My daughter is not going to wait on me like a servant."

"Well, that is certainly a dilemma, isn't it? You might have thought of that before you decided to throw me out. Did you even consider the fact that you are losing your hand maiden? I did, and I have been advising Meg about your daily needs, so she is well prepared to help you should you so desire. Shall I send her in to attend to your pillows?"

"No! I'll do it myself! Now get out of my sight, you ingrate!" Much of the venom behind her words had evaporated as the woman began to ponder for the first time what impact Emily's absence would have on her daily life.

Back in the kitchen, she shrugged her shoulders at Meg and said, "Just wait."

It wasn't long before a voice came from down the hall, "Meg, darling, could you come in here for a minute?"

1959

A few nights after Emily had installed the padlock on her bedroom door, George came home from work and knocked on her door, demanding that she come to the kitchen to cook his dinner.

"There's a plate in the refrigerator that you can heat up in the oven, George. Set it for 250 degrees and let it warm for about fifteen minutes."

He had rattled the doorknob and cursed, "Godammit, Emily, I don't want leftovers! I want a real home-cooked meal. Now open this door and get out here!"

"I don't think so, George. The last time we were in a room together you tried to assault me. Do you really think I can trust you after that?"

"You're crazy! I did no such thing."

"Yes, you did. You just don't remember, because you were blind drunk at the time. Now go and heat up your dinner. You know how cranky you get when you're hungry."

George had pounded on the door for a few more minutes, but finally the swearing dwindled to mumbling, and then he finally gave up and left the house, presumably to eat at the local diner.

Since that time, he had given up trying to lure her out of her bedroom when he was home. He seemed to be drinking less, and the parade of hookers had slowed to an occasional episode of drunken sexual antics on weekends. The change was explained by a phone call Emily overheard between George and Caruthers one evening. "Yeah, old Matthews read me the riot act this morning. He claimed he could smell booze on my breath and suggested that my drinking was the real reason I'm late all the time. He refused to believe that it's because of Emily's illness. He said I needed to either show him a doctor's note explaining the situation or start showing up for work on time. He even told me I looked sloppy and disheveled! The nerve of that guy! Anyway, I guess I can't go out tonight. I can't afford to lose my job right now. Maybe Friday." Emily had almost laughed out loud. She had been wondering how George was getting away with his tardiness after all the nights of drinking until the wee hours.

The relative quiet had lulled Emily into a sense of complacency, and she had grown lax about locking her room. Her preparations for leaving were nearly complete one evening when she was awakened by George slamming the kitchen door as he came in from an evening of drinking and began shouting her name. "Emily! EMILY! It's time you started satisfying my husbandly urges! I'm not going to stand for your refusals any longer."

Eyes wide, she rushed to her door and fumbled with the lock. Fortunately, the key was already inserted, so all she had to do was turn it. She managed to lock it just in time, because George was suddenly there, turning the knob as hard as he could. "Open this damn door! If you won't open it, I'm going to break it down. I'm sick of having to pay for women! You're my WIFE, dammit! I want satisfaction, and I want it NOW!"

"No! I said you were never going to touch me again, and I meant it! Now get away from my door."

"You bitch! How dare you withhold your body from me! You promised to love, honor, and obey, and I'm telling you to come out here and satisfy me or you will regret it. I'm going to get a sledge hammer right now. Don't imagine that your little lock is going to stand up to that!"

Emily began to tremble violently. Sweat broke out on her brow, and she could barely breathe. The thought of George raping her again threatened to send her into another one of her flashbacks, but she couldn't afford to let that happen. She rushed to the closet where she kept the shot gun and checked to make sure that it was loaded and the safety off. She turned to face the door just as George returned from his shed.

"George, you get away from my door. I have a gun, and I'm not afraid to use it."

"You're lying, bitch! You don't have the guts to use a gun against me. You're just a cowering little mouse. I'm coming in." His first heave of the sledge hammer put a hole in the door.

"George! Stop! I'm not kidding!"

"You wouldn't dare shoot me, you witch!" Another blow landed.

Emily was terrified. She knew that the cheap, hollow door wouldn't hold up for long, but she still couldn't bring herself to shoot. Another blow landed. She could now see George's face on the other side of the door, twisted into a hideous caricature of himself.

"No! George, please stop. I don't want to shoot you." He ignored her and landed another direct hit to the door. Emily cocked the shotgun. George appeared to be laughing at the idea of his wife thinking she could possibly defend herself against him. The hole was now nearly large enough for him to push through. Emily pointed the gun at the ceiling and fired.

"Jesus Christ, Emily, are you nuts?! What the hell?!" His face registered shock and disbelief. Emily placed another shell in the chamber and cocked it again.

"Don't come through that door, George. You underestimate me. You always have. I may not want to, but I will shoot you if I have to. I mean it." Emily put as much venom in her voice as she could.

George's voice shook with impotent rage. "You're a lunatic, Emily! I'll have you committed. You're a flaming lunatic! When I tell the authorities what you've done, they will lock you up faster than you can count to ten. I'm done with you!" With that, he turned and left the house, kitchen door slamming behind him.

Emily collapsed to the floor, body heaving with a mixture of fear and relief. Then she gave herself a mental shake. *I don't have time for this,* she thought. She rushed into the kitchen and dialed Mr. Hutton. As soon as he picked up, she said, "Plans have changed. We have to go now! I don't have time to explain, just come as fast as you can." She raced back to the bedroom and threw her last-minute things in a duffel bag, grabbed the trunk she'd packed from the closet, and dragged both of them into the living room. She took a quick look around the house to make sure there was nothing she was forgetting, and her eyes fell on the framed marriage certificate that George liked to keep on the mantel. He had often pointed to it as a way of reminding her of all the ways he felt she wasn't living up to their wedding vows. In an impulse born of rage, she grabbed it, smashed it against the stone hearth, and let it fall from her hand. "And I'm done with *you*," she said with determined finality. The honk of a car horn told her that Father had arrived. Her new life was waiting.

The next morning, Emily embraced Meg and Joey as she wished them a tearful good-bye. She had no idea when or whether she would see them again. Mr. H. had loaded her luggage into the car and was waiting behind the wheel. She took one last glance at the house that had been her home for seven years, then ran down the walk and climbed into the car. Minutes later, they arrived at the bus station. Father walked up to the window and bought her ticket then joined her on the sidewalk. "Do you have the money safely hidden?"

"Yes, Father. It's rolled up in my socks. I only put enough money in my purse to pay for lunch in Ellensburg and for the first night in a hotel. I'll get the rest into a bank as soon as I can."

"Good. Are you nervous?"

"Terrified," Emily responded. "The thought of starting life over again on my own is absolutely overwhelming. There will be so much to do, and I won't know a soul. Part of me just wants to go back to your house and curl up in a corner. But then I think of all the reasons to leave, and what I've accomplished so far, and I realize this is the best thing for me. Nevertheless, my stomach is regretting the breakfast I ate!"

Mr. Hutton smiled and gave her shoulder a squeeze. "You're going to be just fine, Emily. When I think of all you've endured over the years and all that you've accomplished despite it, I know that you are capable of achieving anything you set out to do. And all you have to do is call, and I will help you however I can. You know that, don't you?"

"Yes, Father, I do. I don't know how I can thank you enough for everything you've already done. Truly, you saved me when I thought all was lost. You're one of my angels."

The bus rumbled into the station, brakes hissing as it stopped in front of the station. Mr. H. enfolded Emily in his arms, holding her there for a long moment before her held her at arm's length and said, "Time to go. Your future awaits." Emily nodded with tears in her eyes. Mr. H helped her stow her bags in the luggage compartment of the bus, then she handed the driver her ticket and boarded the bus. From her seat she could see the man who had been a substitute father to her still standing on the sidewalk, unwilling to leave until the bus pulled away from the station. She held his gaze as the other passengers climbed on board, and even as the bus began to move, she watched until he was out of sight. Turning then to face forward, she squared her shoulders and set her jaw with determination. No longer was she subordinate to anyone, no longer a prisoner of others' expectations. Today felt like the beginning of a journey to find herself.

As the miles rolled by, Emily felt her anxiety beginning to ease. She had feared that George might have actually gone to the police to accuse her of discharging a weapon inside their home. She had imagined a police car, siren blaring, driving up behind the bus and forcing it to stop. Now she realized that he had been so inebriated that either he would have passed out on the way to the station or been so belligerent and rambling that the police would have written him off as a crazy drunk and thrown him in a cell to sleep it off. Fears assuaged, she began to be more aware of her surroundings, taking in the wide plains of Central Washington and the gentle rolling hills as they approached Ellensburg. Vague memories of a trip with her mother in an ill-fated attempt to reconcile with her grandparents came to mind. It had been early spring then, too, the hills covered with the pale green velvet of grass bursting forth from the earth after a cold winter. Emily identified with those tender shoots, feeling the rise of new growth, hope, and a new beginning. After a short stop for lunch, the bus began to climb into the mountains. Emily's eyes grew heavy, and she fell into a deep sleep, unaccompanied by specters of the past.

PART II

SEATTLE

1959—1962

Chapter 12

Hope is the thing with feathers
That perches in the soul,
And sings the tune without the words,
And never stops at all . . .
     —Emily Dickinson

Spring 1959

Awakened by the stops and starts of the bus on city streets, Emily realized they were entering the outskirts of Seattle. She sat upright and gazed out the window which was streaked with rain, filled with a mixture of excitement and anxiety at the same time. *How will I ever find my way around in the big city? Will I be able to find a job? Will I have enough money to pay for lodging?* Mr. H. had given her what seemed like a lot of money, but she had no idea how much things would cost here. She just hoped it would last until she found a job that would pay the rent. But then the larger reality dawned on her. She was free! She was now three hundred miles away from George, from the place where so many painful things had happened, from the memories of Father Devlin's abuse. Emily straightened her shoulders as she felt her burdens fall away like the shedding of an impossibly heavy load. She realized that she was smiling. There would be time for the postmortem later, but for now she would celebrate her freedom and the adventure that awaited her.

The bus neared the city center, traversing streets across a steep hill. Between buildings, Emily caught glimpses of the waters of Puget Sound below. Just then the sun emerged from behind a cloud, and one narrow ray cast a trail of diamonds glittering across the bay. Emily caught her breath, transfixed. The Spokane River had been the backdrop for much of her life in Spokane, flowing through the heart of the city and dividing it into north and south, but it was merely a fixture in Emily's life, as invisible as wallpaper and just as taken for granted. However, this vast expanse of water took her breath away, surrounded as it was by misty green hills off in the distance and tall buildings crowded right up to its edge. Wherever she found to live, she hoped it would be near the water.

A large brick structure with a tiled roof soon came into view, and the bus turned in and pulled up underneath its portico. They had arrived at Central Terminal. Emily's nerves returned as she stood with the other passengers to disembark the bus. Suddenly freedom and independence didn't seem like such a good idea. Nonetheless, she put one foot in front of the other, carried along by the tide of travelers until she reached the stairs and descended to the sidewalk. She waited with the others as the driver opened the cavernous storage space beneath the bus and began tossing bags onto the pavement. She slung the strap of a heavy duffel over her shoulder, then picked up her suitcase, and a smaller bag. Standing there on the sidewalk, she looked around for someone who could help her with directions. Mr. H. had obtained a map of Seattle for her, and she pulled it out of her purse. Then, chin up, she walked to a ticket window where an older gentleman with a pleasant smile greeted her. "How do you do, miss? What can I do for you? "

"Well, I just arrived from Spokane, and I've never been in Seattle before. Can you help me find a nearby hotel that wouldn't be too expensive? I have a map here, if you could show me where I am and where I need to go."

"Sure thing, ma'am. I think the Firestone Arms might fit the bill, and it's only a few blocks away. It's old but clean, and the proprietors are careful about the kind of people they let in, so it's safe for a woman on her own, if you get my drift."

"Yes! Thank you. I hadn't thought about that. I guess this is the big city, isn't it?"

"Yes, indeed. You want to be careful around here, especially after dark. Give me your map, and I'll show you how to get there."

Directions fixed in her head, Emily set off. Waiting for a green light before crossing the street, she looked around and noticed the spire of a church just up the hill. She paused for a moment, a flicker of some vague longing rising in her. She turned to a man standing next to her and said, "Excuse me, do you happen to know what church that is up there?"

"Yes, miss. That's Gethsemane Lutheran. The spire is lovely, isn't it?"

"It certainly is. Thank you very much."

The light changed, and they crossed the street together, but the man continued straight as Emily turned to head down the hill towards the hotel. The weight of her bags soon pushed thoughts of the church out of her mind. The hill was steep enough that she had to lean back on her heels to keep from going tail over teakettle. She soon discovered that the ticket agent's idea of a few blocks was an understatement, but eventually she found her way to the doors of the Firestone Arms. The building's exterior was dingy, and the brass nameplate on the wall hadn't been polished in a while, but Emily had no desire to try to find something else. Her arms and shoulders were screaming, and the sky was threatening more rain. She wanted nothing more than to set down her bags and fall onto a soft bed behind a closed door.

When she entered the lobby, she was pleasantly surprised by the warm colors and lighting. Sure, the rugs were frayed and worn, but the overall impression was of gentility and welcome. A portly man with a handle bar mustache greeted her from behind an old-fashioned desk with elaborate scroll work. His round face and abundant waistline spoke of a cheerful demeanor, but his dark suit and pomaded hair lent him an air of dignity. "Good afternoon, ma'am. How can I help you?"

"I just arrived in Seattle on the bus, and I need a room for a few days. I'm not really sure how long, because I need to get my bearings and find a place to live first."

"Well, you are in the right place. If you rent by the week, it's less expensive than our nightly rate, and I do have a room available that you can get into right away. Will you want meals?"

"Oh, yes please. That would be lovely!"

"Fine. Let's get you checked in then. Supper is served promptly at six in the dining room to your right, but if you're too tired to join us, I can have my wife bring you up a bowl of soup and a slice of her freshly homemade bread, which is heavenly if I do say so myself."

The desk clerk, who Emily discovered was Mr. Firestone himself, escorted her to her room, thankfully carrying her bags up the stairs to the third floor. He unlocked the door with an ornate key, pressed it into her hand, and opened the door into the room that was to be her home for the near future. It was just as welcoming as the lobby had been. The furnishings had seen better days and the drapes and rug were slightly threadbare, but the room was clean, and the lamps gave off a warm and inviting light. Suddenly realizing she needed to tip Mr. Firestone, she fumbled in her purse, but before she could find some coins to press into his palm, the man put his hand on her arm and said, "No, no, my dear. That's not necessary. I can see that you're tired. You've had a long day, and you need to rest. I'll leave you to it, and the missus will be up with your supper in an hour or so."

The door closed, and Emily was alone. She walked to the bed and tested the mattress. It gave way under the pressure of her hands, and she immediately fell across it, feeling the heaven of softness. No more sleeping on boxes for her! Within moments she was asleep.

An immense roar startles her awake, just in time to witness the slashing of her door by a giant claw. Through the opening she sees a dragon with George's face, breathing fire. Another slash, and the door is demolished. The dragon, black as coal with an iridescent purple belly, pushes through the doorway, pulling the wall down as it comes. His glowing red eyes lock on her as she scrambles into the corner, huddling in terror. His voice, a howling basso, echoes through the room, "How dare you leave me? You belong to me. And now, I am going to swallow you whole." Maniacal laughter comes from the hall. It's the devil wearing a priest's collar and wielding a pitchfork. Through his laughter, he urges the dragon on, prodding its whipping tail with his pitchfork. The dragon's jaws open wide as he hovers over her, teeth already dripping with the blood of another victim. Emily screams.

Emily awoke to find herself curled up in the corner where her bed met the wall. She was gasping for air and sweating profusely. Her eyes darted around the room, half expecting to see it in shambles, expecting to see the monster of her dream. Instead, all she saw was the gentle light of a lamp on the bedside table and the tidy room with its worn appointments. The door was solidly intact. *I'm safe*, she thought. *I'm in Seattle, and only three people in the world know where I am. I'm three hundred miles from George. He can't hurt me anymore. He's probably drunk on a barstool somewhere, chatting up another prostitute to take my place.*

Her breathing began to slow, and then she heard Father

McCaffrey's voice in her head, telling her, "You're stronger than you think." Her mind went back to all the things she had done despite such long odds, the way she had stood up to Mrs. H., surviving Father Devlin's abuse, finishing high school while working nights, protecting herself from George, planning and making her escape. *I am strong!* She was surprised that she had said it out loud. Then she said it again. "I am strong!"

Just then there was a knock at the door. "Miss Edwards, it's me, Mrs. Firestone. I have your soup for you."

"Oh, yes. Please come in Mrs. Firestone." Emily stood up and straightened her rumpled skirt as the woman entered with a tray. She was as plump as her husband with hair drawn into a bun at the back of her neck. Splashes of tomato and broth on her apron gave testimony to the freshness of the soup she bore.

"Good evening, dear. I hope you got some rest. I'll just put your soup over here on the table. Did you hear screaming a moment ago? It was quite disturbing."

"I'm so sorry, Mrs. Firestone. That was me. I had a bad dream, that's all. I'm fine. No need to worry."

The older woman frowned. "Well, I'm glad you're alright, but I hope you are not in the habit of screaming in your sleep. It wouldn't do for our other guests to be awakened from their slumbers by your shrieking."

"No ma'am, it won't be a problem. I'm sure it was just the result of my long trip. I came all the way from Spokane today, and I'm not accustomed to being so far away from home. I assure you, it won't happen again."

"Well, see that it doesn't. Enjoy your soup, dear. Breakfast is at seven. You can bring the tray down when you come."

"Thank you so much. Oh! And do you perhaps have some stationery I could use? I have some letters I need to write, and I forgot to bring paper and pen."

"Well, yes. There should be a few sheets of paper and a pen in the desk drawer over there. Good night, Miss Edwards."

Emily let out a sigh of relief. She hoped her nightmares wouldn't continue. She really didn't want to have to change hotels every time George and Father Devlin visited her dreams. This also made the choice between living in a rooming house versus finding her own apartment clearer. She preferred to have privacy anyway, but wasn't sure she would be able to afford the extra cost. Realizing she was famished, Emily sat down at the small table to eat her meal. The soup was heavenly, and the bread was everything Mr. Firestone had said it would be.

When every drop of soup was gone and every crumb of bread consumed, Emily went to the small desk Mrs. Firestone had indicated and pulled out the simple white stationery she found there. She might have letters to write, but that could wait. There was a poem lurking in her mind that needed to be put on paper.

> No more!
> I lift my sword to fight
> the two-headed monster—
> One who stole my innocence,
> One who stole my dreams.
> You took too much.
> You will not take more.
> No more hiding in the underbrush,
> no more cowering in fear;
> instead I parry and thrust,
> taking back my life.
> Your fiery breath doesn't scare me
> anymore.
> I am strong,
> powerful beyond measure.
> I drive my blade into your heel,
> and you fall, helpless against my rage.
> Both of you,
> Helpless.
> I am stronger than you ever knew.

Having slept soundly and dreamlessly, Emily arose in the morning to her first full day in Seattle. She dressed quickly and went downstairs to join the other guests for breakfast. Mrs. Firestone continued to live up to her reputation by serving the most mouth-watering cinnamon rolls Emily had ever tasted. Alongside were bacon, fried potatoes, and a soft-boiled egg served in a little egg-shaped cup. Emily ate every bite. It was as if her release from the captivity of fear had restored her appetite, and now she was making up for the semi-starvation of the past several months.

After yesterday's showers, the sky had cleared, and a gentle sun shone over the rain-washed city. Emily was determined to explore her new home, so armed with her map and purse she exited the Firestone Arms and turned toward the water. Navigating the steep hill without luggage in hand was much easier than yesterday's arduous trek, and she walked briskly, breathing the fresh salt air as she went. Reaching the waterfront, her steps slowed as she took in the sights and sounds of the docks. She enjoyed the frenzied pace of the fish market, where buyers jostled for space at the counter, shouting their orders to the men behind it. Another shout was given to workers near huge crates full of ice and fish. Soon there were fish flying through the air to the men at the counter who wrapped them in butcher paper and made change with the customer before turning to the next impatient buyer. Nearby was a large public market where vendors hawked their food and wares—fresh fruits and vegetables, breads, cheeses, and meats, as well as pots, dishes, and dry goods of all kinds. Circling around to Pioneer Square, Emily discovered a pharmacy, a clothing store, and a stationer's.

Relishing her new-found freedom with no one to care where she was, what she bought, or for how much, Emily walked into the stationer's. She walked the aisles, her eyes alight with pleasure at the wide variety of colors, textures, and designs. She had never dreamed of such a selection, and after having spent years writing on used envelopes and paper napkins, this bounty filled her with delight. Ultimately, she decided to be sensible until she had a job and bought several pages of simple off-white paper, a few envelopes, a pen, and stamps. She really did need to write Mr. H. and Lottie to let them know she had arrived safely and where they could contact her until she found something more permanent.

A noon whistle blew, and Emily realized she was hungry again. She went into the pharmacy where she had noticed a lunch counter and slid onto a stool. The man behind the counter was wearing a white uniform with a jaunty cap resting on his wavy brown hair. "Good afternoon, miss. Aren't you a breath of fresh air!" Then he winked at her.

Flustered by his flirtatious behavior, Emily replied, "It's missus, actually."

"My apologies, ma'am. I didn't see a ring."

"Oh! Well, uh, I must have forgotten to put it on this morning. The rain makes my fingers swell."

"Right-o. What can I get you then?"

Emily ordered a hamburger and malted strawberry shake. As she waited, she pondered her marital status. The night Father had picked her up from George's house, she had removed her ring, wrapped it in a napkin and shoved it into her purse. She found she couldn't stomach wearing it. She had no desire to wear something that would constantly remind her of the man who had promised to take care of her forever and then done everything but. Now she was questioning her decision. A married woman would gather less unwanted attention from the likes of this soda jerk, but being married could be a disadvantage when seeking a job. She knew that employers hired married women less readily, assuming they didn't really need the job, enjoying the financial support of their husbands as they did. Management also might assume that married women would only stay in their employ until they became pregnant and left to raise their children. Reasoning that she needed a job more than she needed protection from flirts like this, she decided that nobody in Seattle needed to know that she was married and likely to stay that way unless George keeled over from a heart attack, wishful thinking but improbable.

The next day was devoted to searching for a job. Emily bought a newspaper from the corner newsstand and searched the want ads diligently for anything she might be qualified to do. Using her map to locate the addresses of ads she had circled, she created a grid and began walking to the closest businesses first and then fanning outward from there. She filled out application after application until her fingers were cramping and walked many miles without a single flicker of interest. A few employers took down the number of the Firestone Arms in case they decided they wanted to interview her later, but the look on their faces told Emily they were just being polite. It was the same thing the next day and the next and the next. After the fourth full day of job-hunting, Emily plopped wearily onto her bed, discouraged and frustrated. She had begun to question her own abilities, feeling that perhaps she should have taken more classes in typing and shorthand rather than focusing so much on literature and writing in high school. Apparently, her excellent grade point average didn't count for much with employers who just wanted someone who could take dictation.

The next day was Sunday, and even though businesses would be closed, at least she could scour the large section of classifieds in the Sunday paper in hopes of new job listings. After another satisfying breakfast, Emily bought the thick Sunday edition of the Seattle Post-Intelligencer. She loved the name of this newspaper; it sounded so dignified and authoritative. For a few minutes, she read some of the articles to familiarize herself with the goings-on of her new city and fantasized about what it would be like to have something she'd written appear in the pages of a paper like this. Sighing, she finally opened it up to the Help Wanted section. The second page jumped out at her. It was a full page of job openings for the Seattle Post-Intelligencer itself. How wonderful it would be to actually work for this newspaper! Emily pored carefully over the listings, hoping she might find something she had experience for. She didn't imagine that the paper had any need of someone who could take care of children or clean or cook, and probably not someone who wrote poetry either. Then her eyes fell upon a listing for a switchboard operator. Here was something she could do! After all, hadn't she worked for the phone company from the time Mother threw her out of the house until she married George? Finally, a job she was actually qualified for!

Emily was out of bed bright and early on Monday morning and caught a bus (thanks to some guidance from Mr. Firestone) that took her right to the building that housed the newspaper. It wasn't open yet, but Emily wanted to be the first one through the door when it did. While she waited, she studied this impressive building topped by a giant globe with an eagle perched on top, wings raised as if in flight. Rotating around the globe was a neon banner with the words "It's in the P-I." Emily suddenly knew that she wanted desperately to work in this place. Just then, the doors were opened, and she entered with a determined step.

At a large reception desk in the center of the modern lobby, a blond woman wearing a tailored blue skirt and jacket looked up at her through dark-framed glasses. "How can I help you, miss?"

Emily squared her shoulders and responded, "I'm here about the job opening for a switchboard operator."

"Oh! Right. You'll want to go up those stairs to your left and straight down that hall. The personnel department is about halfway down on your right. They'll be able to help you there." As Emily walked toward the staircase, the receptionist called after her, "Good luck!" Emily turned and smiled, feeling suddenly less intimidated and anxious. She took a deep breath to inhale the scent of ink that lingered in the air and felt at home. She easily found the personnel office and entered a large room with several desks arranged in rows where people were speaking on the phone, typing, or consulting their colleagues. Smoke rose from hands clutching cigarettes as they gestured in animated conversation. A woman at the nearest desk looked up and asked Emily her business then invited her to be seated in one of the three folding chairs lined up against the front wall. She then walked over to a gentleman in a worn tweed jacket and spoke with him briefly. He nodded, and the woman returned to her desk, telling Emily, "Mr. Kendall will see you momentarily."

Emily continued to survey her surroundings, noting both the sense of purpose and friendly banter that pervaded the room. She was reminded of her co-workers at the phone company and the relationships she missed so much. *Please God, let this be the place for me.* Soon Mr. Kendall was approaching her. "Miss, you're here about the switchboard job?" When Emily nodded, he motioned her toward his desk. "Come right this way."

When they were seated, he said, "Before we do anything else, tell me about your job experience. I really need someone experienced, and I don't want to waste your time filling out an application if you're not qualified." Emily proceeded to describe her job duties at the phone company, and before she knew it, the man had pulled out a form from his desk drawer and was quickly filling in information as Emily answered question after question. "And why did you move to Seattle?" he asked.

"Well, my mother died recently, and I couldn't bear to be in Spokane where I was surrounded by memories of her everywhere I went. I had been taking care of her, you see. That's why I had to quit my job at Ma Bell. So I decided I needed a fresh start in a new environment, and here I am." Emily was surprised by the ease with which she spoke these falsehoods, but knew it was necessary to explain the gaps in her job history without mentioning George.

"I'm so sorry. And what about your father?"

"Oh, he's gone, too. He died in the war when I was seven, which is why I was so close to my mother. It was just the two of us, and we took care of each other." This much was absolutely true.

Mr. Kendall stood up, saying, "Well, I think that's all I need. Let's go downstairs, and I'll show you the switchboard and introduce you to the supervisor, Mrs. Lake." As they walked toward the door, there was another young woman seated there waiting. "Are you here for the switchboard job?" he asked. The girl nodded, and he said, "Sorry, but the position is taken," and escorted Emily out into the hall. She had the job! Her momentary sympathy for the other applicant was quickly pushed aside by elation. For once, it felt like her prayers had been answered.

As she scurried after Mr. Kendall, he began rattling off the terms of her employment. "I can pay you fifty dollars a week, and we can consider a raise after you've been here six months. We have two shifts a day since we have the office workers and advertising reps who start early and the reporters and editors who are scrambling to meet deadlines late in the evening. You'll need to rotate shifts with the other girls, and Mrs. Lake will let you know which shift she needs you on for now. I guess you're going to need to find a place to live, too. The area between here and the waterfront is called Belltown, and you should be able to find something there. It's a working-class district, so there are lots of sailors and longshoremen who can be unruly at times, but also the shopkeepers and such that can't afford to live right downtown. There are plenty of boarding houses and apartments. If you ask some of the other girls, I'm sure they could help you find something suitable."

A short time later, Emily found herself back on the sidewalk outside the P-I building shaking her head at the rapidity in which events had unfolded. She was now in possession of a job, a list of her shifts, and some recommendations of possible living accommodations. She had met her new boss, Mrs. Lake, who was a tall and thin middle-aged woman with her hair pulled back tightly into a bun at the nape of her neck. She was pleasant but reserved and clearly had high expectations for the girls under her supervision. Emily had already sensed that she would brook no nonsense, in a way that reminded Emily of some of the nuns who had taught her in high school. Except, of course, for Sister Mary Francis.

Eager to tie up the remaining loose end in her new life, Emily decided to begin looking for a place to live right away. It was barely 9:30 with the entire day ahead of her and nothing else she needed to do. There was a bench at the corner bus stop, so she sat down to consult her map and locate some of the apartment buildings that had been suggested by her new co-workers. Marking the possibilities with X's, she plotted her route and set off. At first, she walked briskly, eager to accomplish the task of finding a place to call home. Then gradually the sights, sounds and smells of the neighborhood began to penetrate her consciousness. As it had on her first day in the city, the moist sea air tantalized her senses, and then the aroma of baking bread from a corner bakery caused her footsteps to slow. Music from a radio floated out of an open window, and brightly-colored crocuses waved from a balcony down the block. As she crossed the street, she caught a glimpse of the waters of Elliott Bay far below.

A sudden sense of freedom came over her, the awareness that she now had choices for the first time in her life, that she could live the way she wanted without having to answer to anyone. She also realized that she wasn't afraid in this moment. Fear might come as she encountered circumstances outside her control, but for now, this minute, she was without fear. Emily's pace slowed even more, until she stopped right in the middle of the sidewalk. She wanted to fully experience what it felt like not to have a sense of dread accompanying her everywhere she went. Looking back, she thought that fear had been her constant companion since the day her mother died. Tears of gratitude formed and coursed down her cheeks, and a sound that was half sob, half laughter escaped from her lips.

"Are you alright, miss?" A young man in dirty dungarees and a pea coat was standing in front of her looking concerned.

Again, Emily laughed. "Yes, I'm fine. It's just such a lovely day, isn't it? Good day to you." And she walked on, still smiling. She glanced up at the bright blue sky, the same sky she and her mother had gazed upon so many years ago. It was indeed a lovely day.

Chapter 13

Savior! I've no one else to tell —
And so I trouble thee.
I am the one forgot thee so —
Dost thou remember me?
    —Emily Dickinson

Spring 1959

A week later, Emily sat at her station at the switchboard, amazed by the whirlwind of events that had brought her to this place. After only two days of hunting, she had been able to find an affordable one-bedroom furnished apartment within walking distance of the paper. She had moved herself and her meager belongings the next day. Mrs. Lake had given her two days of training on Thursday and Friday, and now here she was on her first actual day of working at her own switchboard. The other girls welcomed her with an ease that made her feel at home right away. After suffering the isolation and repressive environment of the home she shared with George, their smiling faces were a welcome sight. Even so, the sheer number of phone jacks in front of her and the names underneath each one were a little intimidating. She hoped that she would be able to learn them quickly and keep up with the many calls she would be expected to handle in a day. Right on cue, a flashing light on her switchboard indicated an incoming call, and Emily plugged her cord into the appropriate jack. "Good morning, Seattle Post-Intelligencer. How many I direct your call?"

For her first few weeks, Emily was assigned to the early shift, from 6 AM to 2 PM. This allowed Mrs. Lake, who only worked the early shift, to supervise her work more closely and make sure Emily was catching on well enough to work independently. More accustomed to working the swing shift from four to midnight at the phone company, Emily was finding it difficult to get up so early in the morning, but it did allow her most of the afternoon to explore the city. She loved traversing the hills of Seattle, catching glimpses of the water, exploring the little shops in her new neighborhood, or wandering the waterfront and taking in the sights, smells and sounds of this bustling metropolis. Most of these sorties into her surroundings were short jaunts, but her days off allowed Emily the opportunity for longer expeditions.

One Sunday, Emily set out on the long trek to China Town. She carried her now well-worn map with her, but it was no longer absolutely necessary. She had gained a sense of direction that helped her navigate as she explored, and the map was mostly just a security blanket in case she took a wrong turn. Emily stayed on upper streets for a while to avoid the heavier traffic closer to the Sound and soon found herself not far from the bus station where she had arrived not so long ago. Caught up in the realization of how much her life had changed in such a short period of time, Emily's thoughts were interrupted by the sound of church bells. She looked around and saw the steeple of the church she had noticed on her first day in Seattle, a Lutheran church if she remembered right. The bells stirred memories of going to church with her mother as a young child—sitting in the wooden pews swinging her legs back and forth, feet clad in black patent leather, listening to the Reverend read the liturgy, and studying the stained glass depiction of Jesus in the garden of Gethsemane. Suddenly Emily was filled with longing for the peace and comfort she had always found in those moments when she still trusted that God was near.

As if of their own volition, Emily's feet turned uphill toward the church. As she approached, she saw people streaming toward the open double doors and, without hesitation or thought, found herself joining them, mounting the concrete steps and entering a beautiful sanctuary. From the outside, one could see hints of Gothic architecture, but inside the soaring pointed arches and elaborate stained glass windows exemplified the Gothic style in all its glory. And the best part was that there were no confessional booths. Slipping into a back pew, Emily craned her neck to try and see every detail at once and breathed in the smell of wood polish and candle wax. Organ music was playing, and the velvet tones of a familiar hymn wrapped around her like a lullaby. Suddenly, she noticed that everyone was standing to sing the opening hymn. As she stood, Emily looked down for a hymnal and realized that she was wearing the casual clothes meant for a weekend outing, not exactly appropriate attire for church. She was tempted to slip out of the pew and leave before she was noticed, but just then a young couple stepped into the pew beside her, blocking her escape. Embarrassed, she buried her face in the hymnal and tried to be invisible.

Soon the organist was playing the final "Amen," and the Reverend stepped to the pulpit. "Holy is the Lord, the Almighty."

Without thought, Emily joined the congregation in the response, "He was, he is, and he is to come."

"He is worthy of glory and honor and power. . . ." The long-forgotten words, hidden in the recesses of memory, washed over her like cool refreshing water. They were as soothing as her mother's hand holding hers as they sat together in the pew, two souls intertwined and held together in the hand of God. How could she have lost this feeling so utterly? How had these memories been erased so completely until this moment? Tears of both sorrow and joy welled up—sorrow for the absence of her mother, joy for the gift of remembrance and rediscovery of something so precious. For the first time in many years, Emily felt that God was a tangible presence, a safe and loving sanctuary in which to abide. She may have forgotten God, but she knew now that God had not forgotten her.

A sense of peace accompanied Emily all week, and the following Sunday she donned her best dress and returned to Gethsemane Lutheran. Still not wanting to be noticed, she sat in the back pew, and again, words of comfort and reassurance lifted her spirits:

> Blessed are you, O Lord our God, king of the universe,
> For in your wisdom you have formed us.
> You feed the hungry and clothe the naked.
> We bless you and praise your name forever.
> You set free those who are bound.
> We bless you and praise your name forever.
> You raise up those whose courage falters.
> We bless you and praise your name forever.

It felt as though the words were spoken just for her, to remind her of how fortunate she was to have been set free from the bondage of fear and pain, and the gift of courage she had been given in order to flee from her horrific circumstances and to find hope again. After worship, instead of rushing out of the church before the notes of the closing hymn faded away as she had the previous week, Emily filed out with the rest of the congregation and found herself shaking hands with the Reverend as he greeted his flock at the door. He was a middle-aged man with a graying crew cut and stocky build. Sparkling brown eyes looked out from beneath bushy eyebrows as he greeted her with a smile. "Welcome! I'm Reverend Patterson. Is this your first visit?"

"Well, not exactly. I was here last week, but I left early. I'm Emily Edwards, and I just moved here from Spokane a few weeks ago."

"Lovely! I look forward to getting to know you. Why don't you stop by the church office sometime for a chat?"

Emily hesitated for a moment, then nodded. "Yes, I think I'd like that."

"Wonderful! I'll hope to see you soon, then."

Emily walked down the steps wondering if this pastor might be someone she could talk to in the same way as she had with Father McCaffrey, helping her muddle through the confusing maze of questions about God that arose out of all that had happened to her. Maybe she would try to find time after work this week to come by and see whether she could feel safe enough with him to share her story.

Thursday morning dawned sunny and bright, a perfect Seattle summer day. It was Emily's day off, and she had planned to go visit with the Reverend at Gethsemane Lutheran. She awoke with both a sense of panic and a small thread of hope. It was scary to contemplate telling her story to a perfect stranger, and yet she had missed her regular conversations with Father McCaffrey and hoped that Reverend Patterson might fill that void. But, what if he didn't believe her or thought she was to blame for the abuse? What if he suggested that she was over-reacting? Emily took a deep breath. *Slow down, Emily,* she thought, *you don't have to tell him everything all at once.*

Take your time, and see if he feels trustworthy. Emily sat at the small table next to a window overlooking the street below to eat her breakfast. She gazed at the people walking by, the baker opening his shop as patrons waited to purchase the tempting donuts and sweet rolls on display in his window. The tantalizing aroma and peaceful morning activity helped to calm her, and soon she was ready to venture forth, drawing on the courage she was beginning to discover within herself.

Reverend Patterson's face brightened as Emily entered his office. "Welcome, Emily! I'm so glad you stopped by. You've rescued me from my research for Sunday's sermon." He pointed to the large tome that lay open on his desk. "I was hoping you would take my invitation seriously. Please sit down." He gestured toward two dark blue cushioned chairs in one corner of the office, then took her elbow and escorted her to her seat. The vigor and enthusiasm of this man was a little intimidating and likeable at the same time. Emily found that she truly didn't know what to expect, but she was ready to find out.

"So, Emily, tell me a little about yourself."

"I hardly know where to start, Father, I mean, Reverend. Sorry, I've spent a lot of my life in the Catholic church, even though I was raised Lutheran until my mother died when I was ten. My foster parents were Catholic and sent me to Catholic school, so I guess the Catholic terms come pretty automatically to me. But I have happy memories of going to the Lutheran church with my mother, so it has been like a homecoming to come here these past couple of weeks."

"I'm glad to hear that. I wish everybody understood church to be a place of homecoming. I like to think that's what God intended for it to be. Especially for someone who lost a parent too soon. What about your father, Emily?"

"He died in the war. I was only seven at the time, so I don't have many memories of him. I do remember that he was playful and fun. He used to take Mama and me to the park on Sunday afternoons and push me on the swings or pretend to race me to see who could get to the top of the slide fastest. And he always sang to me at bedtime. I always felt so safe when he tucked me into bed."

"He sounds like a wonderful father. And then you lost your mother three years later! What a sad thing for you to go through! I hope your foster parents were good to you?"

Emily faltered. "Well, they, uh, I guess they did the best they could. My foster mother had health problems, and they basically took me in to care for their two younger children. My foster father was okay, but he was at work long hours, and his wife was, well, she was difficult to please, I guess you could say. She had lost a baby in childbirth, and suffered from melancholy and nerves and often took that out on me."

"I'm so sorry, Emily! Did you have anyone who showed you affection or looked out for you? Grandparents? Aunts or Uncles?"

"Both my parents were only children, and my dad's parents died before I was born. My mother's parents were also Catholic and basically shut us out of their lives when my mom left the church to marry my dad. But there *was* someone who made a difference for me, one of the nuns at the Catholic school, Sister Mary Francis. She's the one who taught me to love poetry and encouraged my love of writing. I'm eternally grateful to her. In many ways, I feel like she saved me." Emily's voice trembled as she spoke, remembering the true extent of what she had been saved from. "I wouldn't be here if it weren't for her."

Reverend Patterson looked thoughtful. "It sounds like there is more to this story than you're saying. I know you've just met me, but I want you to know that whatever you share with me will be held in the strictest of confidence. However, I will certainly understand if you'd prefer to stick with less serious topics."

Emily held his gaze, struggling to decide whether she dared to tell him the whole story. He had opened the door without trying to push her through it. She believed that if she refused his invitation, he would respect that, but would the opportunity come again? She found that despite her wariness, she did feel safe with him. And so, she opened her mouth, and her story emerged, bit by horrifying bit. When she finished, Reverend Patterson was visibly shaken, and her own cheeks were damp with tears.

"Emily, I am so sorry that you suffered such appalling acts by a man who represents the church. It's no wonder that you felt compelled to leave Spokane and escape the memories of what he put you through. It's a wonder that you were able to walk through the door of this church, when your experience of church has failed you so completely. I don't know how you had the courage to tell me all this, given how you have been betrayed by a man of the cloth. I'm honored, truly. Anytime you feel the need to talk again, I would be glad to listen. I hope Gethsemane Lutheran can be a safe haven for you."

"Thank you, Reverend. I'd like that very much. There was a priest that I trusted in Spokane who served as my spiritual advisor during a, uh, more recent difficulty, and I do miss having him to talk to. Our conversation today has helped to fill that gap in my life. But I think that's enough for today. I'm emotionally spent, and you look like you might be too. Perhaps your research will be a welcome respite now."

The Reverend laughed out loud. "You might be right about that, Emily. That might be just the thing. And I imagine that a walk in the sunshine will lift your spirits better than staying here in this gloomy office. Here, let me escort you out."

As Emily walked back to her apartment, she was acutely aware of what she had left out, her marriage to George and all that had ensued. She wondered why that seemed to be the part that was more difficult to share. However, she determined to set aside those thoughts for now and enjoy the sunshine. As she walked past a nearby park, she watched as a father pushed his small son on the swings. Their laughter brought a smile to her face and a pang of regret as well.

Chapter 14

Far from love the Heavenly Father
Leads the chosen child;
Oftener through realm of briar
Than the meadow mild,
Oftener by the claw of dragon
Than the hand of friend,
Guides the little one predestined
To the native land.
>   —Emily Dickinson

Autumn 1959

Summer passed, the nights became cooler, and autumn winds rustled the trees, color beginning to dapple their leaves in shades of yellow, orange and red. Emily felt more and more at home in her adopted city and continued to love walking its streets whenever she could. She was also gaining confidence in her job and making friends with the girls who worked the switchboard with her. Even so, she missed Lottie terribly, so she was delighted to find a letter from her friend tucked in her mail slot one afternoon after work. So eager was she to read it that she ripped it open right there in the lobby.

> Dearest Emily,
> It was so wonderful to read your last letter and hear how well you are doing. I can't tell you how happy it makes me to know you are safe and content in your new surroundings. It appears that things are not going so well for George however. I was in the bank the other day and noticed that someone else was seated at George's usual desk, and the name plate was not George's. One of the tellers goes to our church, so I asked her where he was. She's a bit of a gossip, so I

knew I could get the real skinny. Believe it or not, he
got fired! Apparently, he had shown up to work still
drunk from the night before and wearing a rumpled
suit that smelled of vomit. No doubt Mr. Matthews
had had enough of George's tardiness and shoddy
work, and this was the last straw! Truthfully, I'm
surprised it took this long. He has been going
downhill for a while now, even before you left.
Anyway, just thought you would want to know.
Everything is fine here, and the children are growing
like mad. I wish you could see them. I miss you!
Please take care, and write soon.
Love, Lottie

When she finished reading the letter, Emily realized that her
hands were shaking. Even the mention of her husband's name
brought back unwanted memories. While a part of her felt
satisfaction that George's life was in freefall, she also felt fear
flooding back. It would be just like George to blame her for this
further disintegration of his life, and now that he didn't have a job to
go to, there was nothing to stop him from trying to find her and
exact revenge. Still, she wished she could have been a fly on the wall
when Mr. Matthews told George to clear out his desk. Despite her
anxiety, a slight smile quivered on her lips as she walked up the stairs
to her apartment.

That night, Emily slept restlessly, haunted by dreams of
George stalking and chasing her, his ravenous hands outstretched to
grab at her clothes. Her legs tried to run but felt like they were stuck
in a dark sludge that oozed everywhere. Again and again, she woke
up moaning unintelligible cries for help, and then the nightmares
would pull her back down into tortured sleep. Sunrise came as a
welcome relief from the difficult night, but she couldn't shake the
sense of dread that remained as a shadowy residue of her dreams. As
she washed her face to get ready for work, she noticed dark smudges
under her eyes and a pallor that dimmed the healthy glow she had
acquired since living in Seattle. She hoped nobody would notice or
comment on her appearance, as she had no idea how she would
respond. Maybe the switchboards would be busy enough to deter

conversation among her co-workers.

Somehow Emily got through the day without anyone commenting on her fatigue. The constant work of connecting incoming and outgoing calls had taken her mind off her renewed worry about George, but the anxiety returned as she walked home, and she found herself peering into alley ways and looking furtively behind her every block or so. She knew she was being irrational, but that knowledge did nothing to ease her mind. After a light dinner and a scribbled note to Lottie, Emily decided to call it a day. She climbed into bed and closed her drooping eyelids, but her head immediately began scrolling through an imaginary list of what-ifs. Determined not to have another night of troubled sleep, she got back up, rummaged around in the closet for her mother's old sweater, wrapped it around herself, and clambered out onto the fire escape. Perhaps a few minutes of gazing at the stars would ease her fears and bring peace.

It was a different world here on her lofty perch. The clamor of daytime gave way to the gentle sounds of an occasional murmur of conversation from neighboring apartments, a dog barking in the distance, and a breeze ruffling the leaves of the trees. Emily took a deep breath of the sweet, cool air and looked heavenward. Dimmed only slightly by nearby streetlights, she could pick out the Big Dipper and Orion easily. She felt as though she were in a cozy nest of her own, far above the cares and concerns of life. Her mother's gentle presence came to her with a sense of comfort and protection. In this moment, Emily felt safe. Soon her eyes began to close, so she went back inside, closed the window and slipped between the sheets of her bed where she slept deeply and dreamlessly until morning.

The next few days alternated between her renewed anxiety and the reassurance she had gained from her evening on the fire escape. She knew that the odds of George finding her were slim. He didn't know her well enough to have any idea where to begin looking for her. Their marriage had always been about him, and what Emily's interests, wants, and needs were had been utterly inconsequential to him. Even if he was looking for her, he would start looking in Spokane. He had always underestimated her and would never imagine that she might have the courage to move away from her familiar environment. Nevertheless, a mild sense of foreboding still accompanied her and was with her when she went to church the following Sunday.

For the first time, she became aware of the vast difference between herself and the other people that were worshipping in the pews. Families entered with husbands in suits and ties, wives with their nice dresses and hats, well-behaved children at their sides. Older couples held hands as they made their way to their pews, the husband supporting his wife's elbow to ease her into a seat. Everyone was smiling as Reverend Patterson greeted them, and when the prayer of confession and pardon was spoken, Emily knew that the sins they confessed were mere trifles in a comfortable and happy life compared to the life of abuse and disintegration she had experienced. No one could possibly know what she had gone through without viewing her with horror and revulsion. None of the unattached men here would ever consider her a good prospect for marriage, nor could they fail to be appalled by some of the things she had done to survive. A deep sadness overcame her as she faced for the first time the thought of living the rest of her life alone. And even though the words of worship were a comfort to her, she could not imagine ever feeling a sense of belonging in this place. Even salvation seemed out of reach.

After church, Emily waited in line as the congregation filed out to shake hands with Reverend Patterson. Remembering how good it had been to tell him about her abuse, she wondered if it might be helpful to speak to him about this sense of alienation and loneliness she had experienced during worship. When it was her turn, she asked if he might have time on her day off to talk.

"Certainly! I have been hoping you would come and chat with me again. My office is always open to you. Wednesday morning will work just fine." He smiled as he held her hand in both of hers.

Emily felt her spirits lift as she met his kind gaze. "Thank you, Reverend. I'll look forward to it."

As she walked to the church on Wednesday, anxiety slowed her steps. She realized that she needed to tell the cleric the rest of the story—her disastrous marriage to George and the repugnant way in which it had ended. Only the full story would explain what she had felt during worship on Sunday. And yet, she kept walking, longing to find a way back to the simple faith of her childhood—if that were even possible.

As before, Reverend Patterson greeted her with warmth and

ushered her into his office. "Now then," he said, "tell me what's on your mind today."

Emily paused on the brink of this precipice, gathering her courage for the story she was about to tell. Then, taking a deep breath, she began. "Well, I guess you need to know the part that came after the abuse by Father Devlin and after I finished school and left the Hutton's home. I lived in a boarding house for a couple of years and continued working at the phone company. Then I met a man at my bank who courted me and made me feel cared for and not so alone. I had never dated before, and I was so flattered to have him pursue me. And in my innocence, I didn't pay much attention to his need for control and his patronizing ways. So I married him, and at first it wasn't so bad. He expected me to cook and clean to his high standards, but as long as I did what he asked, everything was fine.

"Then after a while, he began wondering why I wasn't getting pregnant. He became more and more demanding and more and more obsessed. He blamed me and felt that I wasn't trying hard enough. Finally, he forced me to go to a doctor, which terrified me, but at the time I didn't know why. You see, over the years I had shoved away all my memories of what Father Devlin did to me and had no recollection of them at all. The doctor found scarring in my, um, private parts and assumed that I had received them from being a prostitute. This is what he told George outside of my hearing, so I had no idea why George seemed so angry as we drove home. As soon as we got home, he slapped me hard, yelled accusations at me, and—and he…" Emily stopped abruptly. She looked at the gentle man seated across from her with anguish in her eyes.

"It's alright, Emily. You don't have to say it. It's clear that whatever he did, it was terrible."

"No. I need to say it. He raped me right there on the kitchen table and left me battered and bleeding on the floor. His attack brought all my memories of abuse flooding back, and I was absolutely overcome with horror and shame and shock. I felt each memory in my body like it was happening all over again, and I couldn't get off the floor for hours. I woke up the next morning on the cold kitchen floor in a pool of my own vomit."

"My God, Emily! I'm so sorry! What a nightmare!" He fished into his pocket for a clean handkerchief and handed it to her. Then he waited patiently as she pulled herself together. After a few moments, Emily continued, relating the rest of the saga—George's long slide into drinking and consorting with prostitutes right under her nose and the final decisive confrontation.

"And so, here I am, a married woman in name only, a victim of the depraved acts of a priest and an obsessive husband, and trying to make a life for myself. It has made a big difference to be on my own and away from the reminders of my past, and I was doing so much better until I found out that George lost his job. Now I've been having nightmares again, imagining him looking for me and exacting his particular brand of revenge. So this was all on my mind on Sunday, and I suddenly felt so alienated from the church and from the people around me who are living normal, happy lives, while I struggle with darkness and despair. It felt so good to come back to church initially, and I was starting to feel closer to God, but now this. The only thing I could think of was to come and talk to you."

"And I'm glad you did. But I promise you that there are a lot of people in this church whose lives are far from normal or happy. Church can often be a place where people put on a good show in order to hide the pain and struggles in their lives. As their pastor, I often know more about people than they let on to others. But it certainly makes sense that you would feel alienated, Emily. You have gone through things that most people can't even imagine. And the fact that your abuse happened in the church where you should have been able to feel safe and loved makes it doubly difficult. It taints your entire sense of what church is or should be."

The cleric's words settled into Emily's soul and began to ease her mind and heart. There was a momentary silence as she assimilated all that he had said. Then he began to speak again.

"You know, Emily, I have a thought. If I'm remembering correctly, you told me last time that you love poetry, right?" Emily nodded. "Then how familiar are you with Emily Dickinson?"

"Oh, I love Dickinson! She's my favorite! I felt a kinship with her from early on, partially because we share the same name, but mostly because so much of her poetry felt like she was writing it directly to me. Why do you mention her?"

Patterson smiled. "Well, you have more in common than you realize. She also struggled with issues of faith. She loved God and

221

believed Jesus' teachings devoutly, but she never felt like she really belonged in her church. Overwrought altar calls were common in her time, and her natural reticence prevented her from joining her contemporaries in their fervor. She felt that her failure to have a conversion experience placed her outside the embrace of the church and maybe even excluded her from heaven."

In amazement, Emily responded, "Really?! I think I sensed that in some of her poetry, but I was too young at the time to truly understand it. So we share that, too."

"Yes. She never fit in with her more conventional friends, but she did feel a kinship with Christ, especially his suffering on the cross. She too suffered in many ways, and I like to think that she felt the way I do, which is that Christ's death on the cross was a declaration of God's solidarity with human suffering in all the ways in which we experience it. It was through the cross that Jesus removed the gulf between God and humanity for all time. Through Jesus, God knows exactly what you and every other person who has suffered is going through."

Emily looked thoughtful, then spoke slowly. "I never thought of it like that, but it makes sense. I'm going to have to ponder this for a while. It feels like it might be a guiding principle for me and a means for me to heal this spiritual part of my abuse."

"Indeed. And it's notable that Dickinson found joy and divine connection through Creation. She often writes of the birds she delighted in, the changing of the seasons, the sunshine and rain, all those ordinary things that captured her imagination and fed her soul. In a way, she's a kindred spirit to Saint Francis of Assisi. I think one of her lines of poetry goes like this—'Who has not found the Heaven below, will fail of it above.' She certainly lived life acutely aware of the spiritual truths found in nature."

"Yes! I feel that. I've always loved that she writes about Creation so much. It's like she understands that the natural world and the spiritual world are not that far apart. Since I've been here where I don't have to be so afraid anymore, I'm more able to notice my natural surroundings more, like the sun sparkling on the waves of the bay or a tiny songbird alighting on the fire escape. Those things give me joy and peace, but I'd never consciously thought of them as spiritual before. Thank you. This has been more helpful than you know. And now, I've taken up too much of your time today. I will be on my way and let you get back to work."

"This is part of my work, Emily, and you're welcome to come again anytime. If you need a sounding board for your ponderings, I'm happy to oblige."

"Thank you so much, Reverend. You've helped me so much today, and I feel a lot better. I'll see you on Sunday with bells on!"

Chapter 15

The path of healing
Never does run straight,
But winds through thickets,
Tripping over stones,
Stumbling in the dark.
But there are also clearings
And sun,
And the sweet song of a nightingale.
                    —Emily

Winter/Spring 1960

It had been weeks now since Lottie's letter about George losing his job, and Emily had gradually become less anxious about the possibility that he might come looking for her. It seemed silly really, to think that he would consider searching in Seattle, much less that he could find her in a city of half a million people. She didn't have a telephone, so he couldn't find her in the phone book either. Immersed in her work and her enjoyment of the freedom to explore, read, and write as often as she wanted, there were sometimes days when she didn't think about George or Father Devlin at all. Nightmares and flashbacks happened less and less frequently. She continued to visit with Reverend Patterson regularly and was beginning to find her footing in this new life she had created for herself.

One afternoon, as she worked the late shift on the switchboard, Emily was approached by Mrs. Lake. "Emily, a friend of yours just called. Lottie, I think? It sounded rather urgent. Anyway, I told her I would have you call her on your break, which is in ten minutes. You'll have to call collect, I'm afraid."

Emily's heart started racing. She couldn't imagine what was so urgent that Lottie would try calling her at work. She hoped nothing had happened to the children or Bradley, Lottie's husband. The ten minutes seemed like an hour, but finally her relief nudged her away from the switchboard, and she raced into Mrs. Lake's office to place the call. It took the operator another eon to make the connection, and then there was Lottie's voice on the other end of the line, saying, "Yes, operator, I'll accept the charges."

"Lottie! What's wrong? What happened?"

"Oh, Emily, you'll never believe it! George was just here. I was just starting to fix dinner when I heard someone pounding on the door, and when I opened it, there was George, drunk as a skunk."

"What?! Oh, my God! What did he want?"

"He accused me of harboring you in my house, insisting I let him in to search for you. I told him to leave or I'd call the police, but he was still trying to push past me. I kept telling him you weren't here, but he wouldn't believe me. I didn't know what to do. I'm not strong enough to hold him back, and I was so afraid of him scaring the kids, I didn't know what to do."

"Oh, Lottie, I'm so sorry. I never imagined he would do something like this. What *did* you do?"

"I did the only thing I could think of; I told him you had moved to Portland. I figured that would get him to leave and also send him in the wrong direction. And then I called the police after he stumbled away and reported the incident. They took down his name and address, so I'm pretty sure he will be getting a visit from them before long. I was so scared, Emily."

"Trust me, Lottie, I know how scary George can be. You did the right thing. It just makes me cringe to think he put you in that position. And I fear that this won't be the end of it. Can Bradley install a peep hole in your door so you can see who's standing on your doorstep? Maybe even an extra lock would help. I'm serious, Lottie. You don't know him like I do."

"I hadn't thought of that. I'll talk to Bradley when he gets home. I'm sorry I told George anything, even if it was a lie. I hope you'll forgive me."

"Please don't fret about that. You did what you had to do to get him away from you. And if he even considers going to Portland, he won't have a clue where to start looking, much less think about expanding his search to Seattle. It's okay, Lottie. You just keep you and your family safe, and don't worry about me. I'll be fine. I'll take extra precautions too, but I really doubt that it will be necessary."

"Thanks, Emily. I was afraid you'd be terribly upset. We'll be careful here. I'll let you know if I hear anything else from the police or if that maniac shows up here again. Take care of yourself. I've got to run. The natives are getting restless!"

The two friends said goodbye, and Emily put the receiver back in its cradle, then collapsed into Mrs. Lake's desk chair, heart pounding even harder than before. She wouldn't admit it to Lottie, but she was terrified upon hearing that George was actively searching for her.

Just then, Mrs. Lake walked into her office. "Goodness gracious, Emily! What happened? You're as white as a sheet!"

Emily took a deep breath and let it out, brain scrambling to decide how much to share. She looked her supervisor in the eye and knew that this woman was someone she could trust. "Mrs. Lake, there's something I need to tell you, and I need your word that you will keep this in utmost confidence."

"Of course! You're one of my best operators, and whatever this is, I want to help."

"Well, first of all, I'm not a single woman as I wrote on my application. I left Spokane to get away from an abusive husband, because I truly feared for my life. The woman who called is my best friend, and my husband showed up at her door today, drunk and demanding that she tell him where I was. She lied, so I'm not in imminent danger, but the fact that he is still intent on finding me months after I left does cause me alarm."

Mrs. Lake took this news in stride with barely a blink. "Alright then, we cannot let this bastard get anywhere near you again. What can I do?"

Emily almost laughed at her boss's language and her steely aplomb. "Actually, just knowing that you know helps a lot. I trust that if I don't show up for work one day without calling you, you will sound the alarm. And if you see a man harassing me in the lobby or something, you will know to call security. If someone were to phone reception asking if I work here, would they be given that information?"

"I don't think so, but I will find out. And if I get the wrong answer, I will make sure there is a change in policy immediately. I will go straight to the top if I have to—without letting them know who you are. Will that do?"

"Yes, Mrs. Lake, that would certainly make me feel safer. If I think of anything else, I will let you know. Sincerely, I feel better just knowing I have someone in my corner that will be keeping an eye out. I'm so very grateful. Thank you!"

"Don't think anything of it, Emily. I'm not unfamiliar with the ugly side of marriage, so I'm just glad I can help. Now, you'd better get back to work before the girls start wondering what's going on."

Emily smiled. "Yes, we don't want those girls to start gossiping, or who knows where it will lead!" She returned to her station and was soon immersed in her work, connecting call after call. Before she knew it, it was quitting time. She pulled on her winter coat and gloves, picked up her purse, and left the switchboard along with the other girls.

Outside, it was cold and damp, a typical Seattle winter evening. Without work to focus on, Emily's mind immediately went back to Lottie's phone call and George's attempt to locate her. Instantly her anxiety rose up like bile in her throat. Irrational though it might be, she scanned her surroundings for anyone lurking in dark doorways or alleys. She had never liked walking home in the dark, but this night was even more fraught than usual. She imagined that every shadow was George waiting to pounce, to force her to return home with him. And she knew that she couldn't go back to that nightmare. She was beginning to build a life here with a job she enjoyed, friends she could talk to, a church that fed her spirit, and most of all, a life without fear. But now, George's alarming visit to Lottie's home threatened to change all that. Emily suppressed a shudder and decided to splurge on a cab ride home. She knew she couldn't afford to do that every time she worked the late shift, but walking in the frame of mind she was in seemed overwhelming.

George's raging face populated her dreams that night— crashing through her door, taking her by force, violating her body, laughing maniacally at her pleas for him to let her go. She awoke in a pool of sweat, more exhausted than she had been when she went to bed. It was still early, but Emily knew she wouldn't be able to get back to sleep, so she rose and went to the window. The streets were quiet and peaceful, no one stirring, no lights in windows other than the baker across the street who would already be in his kitchen kneading the dough for his renowned sourdough bread. Emily rested her forehead against the cool windowpane, breathing in the silence. The horrors of her dreams began to dim, blurring around the edges as the familiarity of her neighborhood and the stillness of early morning seeped into her soul. The smooth touch of the glass beneath her hand brought her more fully into the present moment, a present in which George was three hundred miles away, sleeping off a hangover. If he was intent on finding her, he would be looking in the wrong place, if he even remembered the incident when he woke up. Peace overcame her bit by bit, but Emily knew that the fear could return in a heartbeat if she let it. Perhaps it was time for another visit with Reverend Patterson.

"You must think I'm crazy, Reverend! I know I'm being illogical, But I can't seem to reason my way out of it."

"Far from it, Emily. Think about this. You spent most of your life feeling unsafe; first, when your father died, then your mother, then being a token member of the Hutton family, abused by your priest, and finally by your husband. It wouldn't be logical for you to *not* be afraid when you found out your husband is trying to hunt you down."

Emily thought about that for a moment. "When you put it that way, I guess it does make some sense. But how do I keep this fear from paralyzing me? I don't want to spend the rest of my life looking over my shoulder. I mean, literally, it's like my head is on a swivel every time I am walking down the street, checking out every recessed doorway, every alleyway, every possible hiding place. When I get on a bus, I scan every face before I sit down. It's exhausting!"

"I can see that it would be. The pastor in me wants to tell you to just pray and trust God to protect you, but I also think that some practicality is in order here. I seem to remember that when you finally realized you needed to protect yourself from George, you marched straight to the store and bought yourself a shotgun. Where is that fierce part of you now?"

"Are you suggesting I buy a gun? I don't think people would

appreciate me walking down the street with a shotgun over my shoulder!"

Patterson laughed. "No, I don't think a shotgun would be very practical. I was thinking in terms of a more portable means of protection and also an attitude you project. George did ultimately learn that you were not to be taken lightly, and some of that came from your determination as well as your willingness to cause him harm if necessary. I notice that the handbag you carry isn't very big, but what if you found one large enough to carry a big wrench, for example, something that could do real damage when swung at George or anyone else who tried to harm you?"

"Oh! I hadn't thought of that. I could definitely do that! There's a hardware store just down the street from my apartment building."

"Good! And keep in mind that determination I've seen in you. Walk tall, head held high. Let people know you are a force to be reckoned with. And a prayer or two wouldn't hurt!"

Pastor and parishioner laughed together at that. As Emily prepared to leave, Reverend Patterson added, "And maybe a short passage from Psalm 18 would be helpful as well—'The Lord is my rock, and my fortress, and my deliverer; my God, my strength, in whom I will trust.'"

Emily smiled in gratitude. "Thank you so much. You have helped me beyond measure. I'll see you Sunday, and in the meantime, I have some shopping to do!"

With new protections in place and armed with a restored confidence in her ability to handle adversity, Emily's fears that George might find her began to ease. As time passed with no sign of him and no repeat of his drunken visit to Lottie's home, she felt a sense of safety growing. Thoughts of her past life became seldom as she focused on the life she had and the future she believed might be possible. Nightmares became few and far between.

Spring was beginning to encroach on winter's grip with warmer breezes and buds developing on the many cherry trees along city streets. The fresh air no longer nipped at her nose but brought a hint of warmth and spring fragrances. Nonetheless, one blustery day, Emily decided to take the bus part of the way home and strolled to the nearest bus stop. A gentleman in a gray felt fedora was seated on a bench nearby. When he saw Emily approaching, he stood and turned toward her to offer her a seat. It was then that she noticed the port wine birthmark splashed across his left cheek. Suddenly, her throat started to close up and dizziness overcame her. Her knees buckled, and the gentleman reached out to take her arm. Emily cried out and jerked her arm away as she collapsed onto the bench.

Devlin's hands were around her throat, thumbs pressing into her windpipe as he thrust himself into her mouth. Terror and disgust flooded her. She could barely breathe and was sure she was going to die. He was moaning with pleasure and murmuring words that she didn't want to hear. The sounds and sensations were so horrific, so brutalizing that she struggled to find something— anything—to focus on. And there on his belly was a purple splotch on his skin. She studied it intently, pondering its odd shape and color. Is this the mark of the devil, she wondered? It must be, she thought. It was the only thing that made sense. And then with one final thrust that bruised the back of her throat and an emission that caused her to choke, he was finished. "Don't withhold yourself from me again," he said as he zipped up his pants. He cracked the door to see if the hallway was clear and left the closet, closing the door behind him.

"Miss, miss! Are you alright?" A woman was crouched in front of Emily, shaking her shoulder gently. Emily startled and lifted her head, looking at her surroundings as though they were completely foreign to her. Only slowly did she become aware that she was not in a closet at Saint Ignatius, but on a Seattle street, seated on a bench just as a bus was pulling up to the stop. Her body was still shaking in the grip of her memory, but she forced herself to focus on the woman and others who were looking quite concerned.

"I'm fine. Really. Just give me a few moments to pull myself together. I, um, I get panic attacks sometimes, and it takes time to come out of them. Please go ahead and get on the bus. I'll just sit here and wait for the next one. Thank you for giving me a little shake. It helped me realize where I was. I'll be fine now. I promise."

The woman looked at her doubtfully, but clearly needed to catch this bus so climbed the stairs, still looking back. As the bus pulled away, Emily could see her craning her neck to watch until the bus took her out of sight. Emily put her face in her hands, utterly embarrassed and still feeling the effects of what she had remembered. She took a few deep breaths, sucking in the fresh air to counteract the imagined cutting off of oxygen she had experienced during the flashback. She hadn't had a memory that powerful for several months, and it was a new one. She was horrified by what it had revealed. Nausea threatened to embarrass her even further, and she swallowed hard to hold back the threat of spewing on the street as people walked by. Finally, she felt calm enough to stand. Deciding not to wait for the next bus, she started to walk home, posture erect, head held high. Under her breath, she whispered, "The Lord is my rock and my fortress, in whom I will trust."

One of the things Emily enjoyed about the switchboard was the relationships she was building with the reporters and editors she helped as they placed their calls to pursue a story or verify facts. She was even beginning to recognize some of their voices, some pleasant, some more abrupt. One of the more pleasant voices was that of Mr. Graves, head supervisor of the copy-editing department. One morning, Mr. Graves' light flashed, and Emily immediately plugged in. "Good morning, Mr. Graves. What can I do for you today?"

"Good morning. Can you connect me with Sunset 4-2679?"

"Certainly. One moment while I try that line." Then, "I'm sorry, sir. That line is busy. Shall I keep trying and notify you when I am able to get through?"

"That would be most helpful. Thank you. By the way, what's your name? I know you've been with us for several months, but I haven't had a chance to meet you yet. I like to put names to the voices I hear on the switchboard."

"Yes, sir. My name is Emily Edwards. Thanks for asking. Oh dear! I've got another light flashing. I'll connect you with that call as soon as I can."

A few days later, as Emily walked toward the lunchroom, two men in white shirts and ties were talking in the hallway. Emily recognized one of the voices immediately, and slowed to get a look at his face. The man was short and slender, with light brown hair and brown eyes with a hint of fun in them. They gave the impression that he didn't take himself too seriously. He had apparently noticed the slowing of her steps and looked directly at her. "Can I help you with something?"

Emily blushed, embarrassed to have been noticed. "No, Mr.

Graves, it's just that I recognized your voice. I'm Emily from the switchboard. I didn't mean to interrupt your conversation."

He extended his hand to shake hers. "No, no, I'm glad you stopped. Good to meet you, Emily. It's about time, I'd say. And this gentleman is Bob Burnett, one of our popular columnists. Bob, this is Emily, and she is an excellent switchboard operator."

"Mr. Burnett, nice to meet you. I admire your work. And now I will let you gentlemen get back to your conversation. Good day to you."

Emily scurried down the hall, feeling as though she had made of a fool of herself, yet pleased by Mr. Graves' compliment. This kind of attention was not something she was accustomed to, and it was both uncomfortable and heady at the same time. Mr. Graves seemed like a genuinely nice person. He reminded her of someone, someone from long ago, but she couldn't quite think who it could be.

A few days later, Emily was coming back from her lunch break with a few minutes to spare when she saw Bob Burnett rushing down the hall with a file folder in his hand. In his hurry, he bumped into her, and the file was knocked loose, spilling papers onto the floor. Flustered, he apologized profusely. "Oof! I'm so sorry! Are you all right?"

"I'm fine, Mr. Burnett. Please don't concern yourself. You must be on an important errand." They both bent down to pick up the scattered pages.

"You're right about that. It's Emily, right? The girl Paul introduced me to the other day? I've got to get my column up to Paul for editing, but I just received a call from an important source on a story I'm working, and he wants to talk to me urgently. Say, do you think you could run this up to Paul for me? It would be a big favor. Can you spare the time?"

"Of course, I'd be glad to Mr. Burnett. I think I have just enough time before I'm due back from lunch."

The columnist grinned. "Super! But if you catch hell from Mrs. Lake, just let her know you were doing me a favor, and she'll ease up. She holds us journalists in high esteem." He handed Emily the file folder and raced off.

Emily smiled, then looked down at the file in her hands. She was holding the work of a writer she admired in her hands. Curiosity got the best of her, and she decided to take the elevator rather than the stairs so she could read Mr. Burnett's latest column on the way. She started reading while waiting for the notoriously slow elevator, then stepped on without looking up from the pages she held. So engrossed was she that she almost failed to get off at the correct floor and had to put her arm between the doors before they closed on her. Now, which way to Mr. Graves' office? In the months since her hire, Emily had explored the halls of the massive building to get a feel for all the different functions of the paper, but she hadn't quite memorized the locations of all the offices yet. Taking a guess, she turned right. Soon enough, she found the copy-editing office and opened the door into a rabbit's warren of desks. She scanned the room until she spotted Mr. Graves at his desk in a glassed-in corner office. Before she could reach his door, he looked up from his work, saw her approaching and stood to greet her.

"Emily! So nice to see you. To what do I owe the pleasure?" The smile and twinkling eyes were very much on display.

Emily felt herself blushing. "Good afternoon, Mr. Graves. I just ran into Mr. Burnett downstairs as he was rushing off to meet with a source, and he asked me to deliver this to you." She held out the file folder, then pulled it back. "Um, I hope you won't mind, but I took the liberty of reading this in the elevator."

"Well, that's certainly no crime. What did you think?"

"Oh, it's wonderful as usual, but, well, I'm sure this is terribly presumptuous of me, but I did notice some grammatical and spelling errors. Of course, I have no doubt that you will catch them yourself. That's your job." Abruptly, she thrust the folder into his outstretched hand and turned to go.

"Wait, Emily! Show me what you mean. I'm not above having someone help me do my work. Heaven knows, I have a big enough pile on my desk to go through today."

Hesitant, she turned and asked, "Are you sure?"

"Absolutely! Please." He pulled out one of the chairs opposite his desk, and when she was seated, sat down in the one next to it. "Let's see what you've got."

The two sat and bent over the typed pages, Emily gaining confidence as she pointed out the minor errors she had noticed. "And truthfully, I think this paragraph would be stronger if he left off this last sentence entirely. It takes away from the punch of the previous sentence, which seems to me to be the crux of the entire piece."

Paul Graves turned to look directly at Emily. "That is a very keen observation, Emily. How much schooling have you had?"

"Oh, just high school, but I really loved my English courses, especially the writing part."

"And I'm guessing that you got straight A's, too. Thank you so much for sharing your thoughts with me. You've definitely saved me some time on this." He grinned. "Not to mention brightening my day."

Emily suddenly looked at the clock on the wall and jumped up. "Oh, dear! I have to go. I'll be late getting back from lunch, and Mrs. Lake will not be pleased."

"Not to worry, Emily. I'll call down to her right now and tell her I detained you. She might not be happy with me, but she won't take it out on you. Now, get on your way, and I'll take it from here."

"Thank you, sir. Have a good day." As she turned to leave the office, Graves watched her thoughtfully for a few moments before picking up the phone to call Mrs. Lake.

Two weeks passed, in which Emily completely forgot about the incident other than feeling a bit of pride when Burnett's column appeared in the paper. Then one afternoon, Mrs. Lake stopped by her station and placed a hand on her shoulder.

"Emily, would you mind coming in a bit early in the morning? There's something I'd like to talk to you about."

"Certainly, Mrs. Lake. Have I done something wrong?"

"Oh, no. Far from it. Don't fret, and I'll see you at 7:30 in the morning."

Nonetheless, Emily did fret, so it was with a bit of anxiety that she entered Mrs. Lake's office the next day. Surprisingly, Paul Graves was sitting in a chair to the side of her supervisor's desk. He stood to greet her and pulled out the chair that was usually where girls sat when they were being called on the carpet. "Good morning, Emily. How are you this lovely morning?"

"I'm fine, thank you." Emily looked from Mr. Graves's smiling face to Mrs. Lake's sour countenance and wondered what exactly was about to take place. Fortunately, she didn't have to wait long.

Mrs. Lake began speaking. "I'm sure you're wondering why I've asked you to come in so early, Emily, and why Mr. Graves is joining us. I'm not particularly happy about what is about to transpire, but what I want is not the issue here. Mr. Graves, perhaps you will enlighten us."

"Well, Emily, do you recall the day you delivered some of Bob Burnett's copy to me? And the audacity you showed in telling me how I should edit it?" Emily nodded and looked down at her lap in embarrassment, certain that she was about to be fired. "Well, I was very impressed with your grammatical knowledge and your initiative in sharing your observations with me, so two days ago, when one of my copy editors put in his notice, I immediately thought of you." Emily's head came up in astonishment as Mr. Graves continued. "I've been speaking to Mrs. Lake, and though she hates to lose an excellent employee such as yourself, she agreed that your skills might better serve the newspaper in the copy-editing department. So what's happening here is that I'm offering you a job. If you want it."

Speechless, Emily stared wide-eyed at him, then turned to look at Mrs. Lake, who was now smiling, then back to Mr. Graves. "I—I hardly know what to say! I never dreamed I would get an opportunity like this! I—are you sure? I mean, I've been here less than a year!"

Mrs. Lake, in her typical sardonic way, chimed in, "So do you want the job or not? Because, if not, I will gladly send you straight back to your switchboard. But if you do, then I have to get busy finding a replacement for one of the best switchboard operators I've ever had. So spit it out, girl!"

"Yes! Oh my goodness, yes! Thank you! Thank you both so much!"

Her new boss was chuckling now. "Curb your enthusiasm, Emily. It will be hard work, and much will be expected of you, but given your love of the English language, I'm sure you will enjoy even the most tedious of assignments. We'll start you off with the less important stories for now and see how you do. You'll get a bit of a raise, and your hours will be more regular—eight to five, Monday through Friday, but there will be some overtime on heavy news days. So, are you up for it?"

Emily felt like she was floating as Graves' words drifted over her. Her face was beaming as she answered with another enthusiastic "Yes!"

Mrs. Lake's voice barely penetrated when she added, "You can finish out the week here on the switchboard and say good-bye to the girls, then you'll start up in the rarefied air of the copy room on Monday morning. Now, get to your station before the phones start lighting up!"

The rest of the week went quickly, and soon it was Friday and time to say good-bye to the other girls in the switchboard room. Many of them hugged her and wished her well, and Emily promised to come down and visit them on her breaks when she could. Even Mrs. Lake gave her a hug, her usual stern look replaced by a mixture of affection and pride. "Mind your P's and Q's up there, young lady! Show them you deserve the confidence that's been placed in you. I'm going to miss you down here. I don't know where they're going to find me a replacement half as efficient as you! Now get out of here and enjoy your weekend. You've got a lot of hard work ahead of you." She cleared her throat to hide her unexpected emotion and shooed Emily away with a wave of her hand.

Emily walked to work with a bounce in her step despite the early morning fog that swirled around her. This was the first day of her promotion to the copy department, and she was both excited and nervous, hoping she wouldn't disappoint Mr. Graves. The idea of being engaged with the written word again filled her with anticipation. Perhaps she would be inspired to return to her poetry. When she entered the P-I's big front door, she had to fight her feet to turn them away from their habitual path to the switchboard room. Soon she was in the hall outside the copy room where she took a deep breath before entering. Mr. Graves was already there, and he looked up as she walked back toward his office.

"Good morning, Emily! Welcome. Let me show you to your desk." He walked her over to an empty desk in the middle of the room, then clapped his hands. The other employees raised their heads from where they stood—some at the water cooler, some settling in at their desks, others chatting with a co-worker. "Good morning, people! I want to introduce you to our newest assistant,

Emily Edwards. She's coming to us from the switchboard department, which isn't the likeliest place to find a good copy writer, but take my word for it—her skills are top-notch. Please take time during the day to introduce yourselves and welcome her to the office." Emily saw a few people smile at her, while others returned to their conversations without a second glance. She guessed that some might not be pleased about her apparent lack of qualifications, so she planned to tread carefully until she got the lay of the land.

Mr. Graves handed her a pile of papers on top of which he placed a list of editorial terms followed by symbols. "Today is a training day, so I'm giving you some old copy to edit, so you can practice the symbols we use to indicate how the manuscript should be changed. For example, this squiggly line indicates a transposition, and the letters "sp" indicate a misspelling. Study the list and then see what you can do with these. And don't be nervous. You'll do fine."

Emily gave a half-hearted smile and took the pages from him. "Thank you for the confidence, Mr. Graves. I'll do my best." She settled herself at her desk where she saw that several pencils had been sharpened and placed there for her. She bent over her work and was immediately absorbed.

So intent was she that she was startled when one of her co-workers cleared her throat and touched Emily on the shoulder. "It's lunch-time, Emily. Twelve o'clock. I'll show you to the break room if you'd like. My name is Sandra."

"Oh! Is it noon already? Thank you, Sandra. I'd appreciate you steering me in the right direction. I haven't been on this floor very often, so I don't really know my way around. Just let me grab my lunch." She pulled her sack lunch from a drawer then followed Sandra down the hall where others were already pulling out sandwiches or thermoses of soup. Whereas the level of conversation in the copy room had been a low murmur, here the talk was louder as co-workers chatted about their weekend or their families. In this atmosphere where everyone seemed to know everyone else, Emily felt like a stranger in a strange land. She sat down a little apart from the others and unwrapped the sandwich she had made this morning. Just as she was mid-bite, Mr. Graves sat down next to her.

"How's it going so far, Emily? You have certainly been absorbed in your work. I didn't see you lift your head from your desk all morning. It's okay to get up and get a drink of water at the cooler every once in a while. You'll go blind if you never look up!" He grinned to let her know he was joking.

"I think I'm getting the hang of it, Mr. Graves. It's fascinating work, really. I feel like I'm back at school in a way. A good way."

"Glad to hear it. I'll look at what you've done later this afternoon, and we can go over any issues to make sure you're clear on the symbols and editing terminology. But that's for working hours. We don't talk shop during lunch. Tell me a little about yourself."

Emily froze. There was so much she didn't dare share that she could hardly think of what to say. "Um . . . well, I moved here from Spokane last spring. My mother had died about a year before, and I needed a change of scenery. I used to work for the phone company there, which was why the switchboard was a natural fit for me. But my favorite subject in school was English, so reading, spelling, and grammar come pretty naturally to me."

"What about other family? Did you move here all by yourself?"

"Well, yes. My dad died in the war, and both of them were only children, so I have no aunts, uncles, or cousins."

"And no siblings either?" Emily shook her head. "I'm so sorry, Emily. It must feel overwhelming to be all alone in the world. You're very intrepid moving to a new city all by yourself."

Emily was relieved when her boss moved on to less personal topics, and they chatted throughout lunch. Gradually Emily found herself feeling more comfortable, even when co-workers joined in. Nonetheless, she was glad to get back to work where she felt on more solid ground. Mr. Graves's scrutiny of her work at the end of the day resulted in high praise, and he told her he was going to give her real assignments the next day. She left the building at the end of her shift on cloud nine.

Chapter 15

If I can stop one Heart from breaking,
I shall not live in vain;
If I can ease one Life the Aching,
Or cool one Pain
Or help one fainting Robin
Unto his Nest again,
I shall not live in Vain.
—Emily Dickinson

Autumn 1960

As the weeks passed with no hint of George still looking for her, Emily had become less anxious about walking home after work even as the days shortened. Even so, a woman alone should always be alert to potential danger, and she was still carrying the wrench Reverend Patterson had suggested the last time they spoke. One evening, Emily was walking home through a drizzling rain as dusk settled when she heard a muffled sound coming from an alleyway as she passed. She stopped cold, listening. It sounded like someone or some*thing* had moaned. She wavered between the urge to run and the compulsion to see what or who was there. Then in the stillness, the sound came again, a cross between a moan and a whimper. Emily looked up and down the street to see if anyone else was around, but the streets were empty. Another moan, this time perceptibly human. Holding her purse tightly under her arm, she took a step toward the alley, and then another. Inside, she paused for a moment, allowing her eyes to adjust to the deeper gloom. When the sound came again, she looked in the direction from which it emanated and was able to see a dim figure huddled on the ground.

Emily rushed over and knelt down to get a closer look. "Are you hurt? Can I help you?"

A feeble female voice answered, "Please . . . he beat me . . . it hurts!" The woman gave another guttural cry and curled up in pain.

Alarmed, Emily asked, "Oh, my! Do you think he'll come back? We need to get you away from here." She put an arm around the woman's back and under her armpit and hoisted her to a seated position. "Okay. Can you get to your knees? Put your arm around me, and if we both lift at the same time, maybe we can get you on your feet." After a few moments of struggle, the woman was upright and supported heavily by Emily. "Good. Now let's get you someplace safe and see how badly you're injured." Step by step, they left the alleyway and walked toward a nearby streetlamp so Emily could assess the woman's wounds. Now in better light, Emily was stunned to see a young girl, probably no more than thirteen. Her face was battered and bruised, and one eye was swollen shut.

"What on earth happened to you? Who could do such a thing?"

The girl responded with a single word, "Dad."

Emily stared, astonished. The girl whimpered, and Emily saw that now was not the time for a longer explanation. "Okay let's get you to my apartment building. It's only a couple of blocks from here. Do you think you can make it?"

A slight nod was all the teen could manage, so Emily took a firmer grip and guided her gently down the street. Her umbrella had been left forgotten in the alley, so by the time they reached the apartment building, both women were drenched. Emily settled the girl onto a small bench in the foyer where there was a phone for emergencies. "You rest there while I call for an ambulance."

"No! No ambulance!" Her eyes were wide with terror.

"But why not? You need medical attention right away."

"No! If I go to the hospital, they will ask me a million questions. I'll have to tell them who I am, and they'll call my parents. Then my dad will come, and he'll just beat me again and dump me somewhere else. Please. Can't you take me to your apartment? I won't be a bother. I just need a good night's rest, and then I'll get out of your hair in the morning."

Emily looked at this young girl, pondering what to do. Realizing she didn't have the heart to refuse, she said, "Alright then. I'm two floors up. If we take it slow, you can make it. I'll clean you up and bandage you as best as I can, and then we'll figure out what to do from there. Ready? Up we go."

It took fifteen minutes of tedious climbing to get up the two flights of stairs. They had to stop frequently to let the girl rest. It was obvious that each step caused her pain, and Emily worried about the possibility of internal injuries. Eventually they reached her apartment and collapsed on the couch, both panting from the exertion of the climb.

After they had caught their breath a bit, Emily turned on more lights to get a better look at the girl's wounds. As she helped her off with her threadbare coat, she was stunned to see a slightly swollen belly on a girl who was otherwise stick thin. "Are you pregnant?" she asked.

The girl nodded. "My dad . . ." Her voice broke. "It's his."

Aghast, Emily responded, "Your father got you pregnant, and then he beat you and tossed you in an alley?"

The girl nodded. "He wanted to get rid of me before I started showing more than I am already. He didn't want my mom to find out."

"That's appalling! I'm so sorry! Will you let me look you over and see the extent of your injuries? Then I will clean you up as much as possible. My mother was a nurse, and she used to talk to me a lot about her work."

Receiving a brief nod, Emily gently removed one piece of clothing at a time, trying desperately to retain her composure as a mosaic of bruises was revealed. In addition to the bruises on the girl's face, there were cuts that had bled and crusted over. Finally she said, "Other than the surface pain from the bruises, is there any internal pain? Does it feel like anything is bleeding inside? Cramping? Are you bleeding 'down there'?"

The girl shook her head to each of these questions. "Alright. So far, so good. I'm Emily, by the way. What's your name? How old are you?"

"Anna. I'm fourteen. And thank you . . . for rescuing me. I thought I was going to die in that alley."

"I'm just glad I heard you. Actually, I almost ran away, thinking you might be a robber lying in wait. It's a good thing I didn't."

241

Anna gave a slight smile that turned into a grimace.

Emily continued, "I think the easiest way to clean your wounds is to get you in the tub. Do you think you can manage that?" Another nod.

Emily started filling the bathtub, helped Anna walk to the bathroom, then supported her weight as she gingerly stepped into the warm water. Perhaps to take her mind off the fact that a complete stranger was bathing her naked body, Anna began to talk, and by the time she was done, her entire sad story had been revealed, and both she and Emily were crying. It was a story that Emily was all too familiar with. Anna's father had begun molesting her when she was seven—just touching through her clothing at first, but progressing gradually until he was forcing intercourse with her on a regular basis by the time she was eleven. The only breaks from the abuse came when her father left home for work in another state, often for weeks at a time. He was away from home when Anna had her first period, so he hadn't known that his incestuous behavior could impregnate her until it was too late. He'd left again before Anna started showing and hadn't returned until a few days ago. Even then, he didn't notice her swollen belly until he came to her bed that night.

Anna's mother had been at her job waiting tables. When the implications of her pregnancy sank in, he became enraged. He shouted accusations and called her a tramp, blaming her for the pregnancy and denying his part in it. Then he decided to take matters into his own hands in an effort to eliminate the problem before his wife and neighbors began to suspect. He had beaten her and dumped her in the alley, yelling, "And don't come crying home to me. I never want to see your face again. You're dead to me!" The evidence of his handiwork was there for Emily to see, and she understood now that Anna's father could never know that she, and hopefully the baby, were still alive.

Father Devlin's face loomed before her, his foul breath turning her stomach, his glowing red eyes piercing her, his thin lips opening wide as he tried to kiss her. "Stop struggling, Emily! You know you want this. Kiss me!" Devilish claws pawed at her, ripping at her clothes and mauling her breasts. "You can never escape me! If you run, I will find you. I am not finished with you yet. You belong to ME!" Try as she might, Emily could not pull herself away from his painful grasp. His hands were holding her down, his body crushing her until she feared that she would suffocate. Terrified, she struggled against him and cried out, hoping that someone . . . anyone would hear.

"Emily, Emily! Wake up!" With a start, Emily awoke to a strange face leaning over in the dim light. Instinctively, unaccustomed as she was to having someone in her apartment, she scrambled to get away only to be stopped by the arm of the sofa. "Emily, it's me, Anna. You were screaming in your sleep."

Only then did the events of the previous evening come flooding back and the frightening images of her dream recede. "Oh! Anna. I'm so sorry. Did I wake you? What time is it?"

"It's early yet, maybe six or so? But you didn't wake me. I had to get up and use the bathroom. That's when I heard you screaming. Are you okay?"

Emily sat up and looked around her living room in an attempt to erase the vestiges of her dream. She remembered that she had offered her bed to Anna, knowing that would be more comfortable for her in her condition. "I'm fine. It's just . . . well, I do have nightmares sometimes, but this was the first in a long time. I guess hearing your story last night brought back bad memories of my own."

"I'm sorry. I didn't mean to cause you so much trouble. I'm feeling much better this morning, so I'll just go and get out of your hair." Anna started to straighten up, but winced as she did so.

"No! You're still in a lot of pain. There's no way I'm going to turn you loose on the streets with a baby coming. What do you think you're going to do when the time comes, have the baby in an alley somewhere?"

"But I don't want to be a burden to you. This isn't your problem. You've already done way more than anyone else would have, and I'm grateful, but I think I need to go."

Emily was silent for a moment, trying to figure out what to do. Finally, she spoke. "Look, you're hurting, and you need some rest. Neither of us is in any shape to make decisions right now. Why don't you stay here at least for today? I've got to go to work, and when I get back, we'll talk about it and figure out a plan. How does that sound?"

Anna sighed. "I guess I don't feel all that great. I felt a little flutter during the night, but I don't know what that means. Do you? So maybe I should just rest here for the day if you're sure you want me to."

"I'm sure. And it's possible that what you felt was the baby kicking, which is a positive sign that your father didn't inflict as much damage as I feared. Now, I bet you are hungry. Let's rustle up some breakfast."

The everyday tasks of putting on coffee and frying eggs helped both women regain a sense of normalcy in the unusual situation in which they found themselves. As they ate, Anna asked, "So did your dad abuse you, too?"

"No, my real dad died in the war. Then my mother was killed in a bus accident, so I went to a foster family. They sent me to Catholic school, and it was the priest there who molested me for years."

"Oh, my gosh, Emily! A priest? That's awful!"

"Yes, it was. My life has been a mess for a long time, but I finally feel like I am breaking free of all that and can create the life I want to have." As Emily spoke the words, she suddenly realized that they were true. She really was in the process of creating a new life for herself. She smiled at Anna. "I hope that someday you'll be able to do that, too."

"I don't know. It's hard to imagine right now."

"Just give it time. You'll figure it out." Emily looked at the clock. "Oh! I have to get going. Can you take care of the dishes?"

"Sure, Emily. I do almost all of the cleaning for my mom, because she has to work so much. You go get ready, and I'll handle it."

The copy-editing department was inundated with a rush of urgent articles to edit, and Emily spent the day working at top speed. It wasn't until she was walking home that night that she remembered Anna. She began pondering what to do about the unfortunate girl. She couldn't imagine just turning her out onto the streets with no money, no home, and a baby on the way. Was there a home for unwed mothers in Seattle? If so, Emily had no idea how to find it. And if she allowed the girl to live with her, how would she explain it to her landlady? Could she even afford to feed an extra person, especially one who was eating for two? Then Emily reminded herself of the raise she had received when she got promoted to copy-editor. There had been money left over at the end of each month since then, not a lot, but maybe enough to feed another person if she was frugal. She remained in deep thought the rest of the way home, and by the time she climbed the stairs to her apartment, she had made up her mind.

When Emily opened the door, her nostrils were met by the tantalizing smells of something simmering on the stove. Anna turned from the pot she was stirring to greet her. "Hi Emily, how was your day? I hope you don't mind. I just thought it might be nice for you to come home to a meal already prepared instead of having to fix something after a long day. I rummaged around in your refrigerator and cupboards and found enough to make a pot of soup. Truth to tell, I was getting a little restless, so it was good for me to have something to do."

"This is lovely, Anna! The soup smells wonderful, and you're exactly right. It's nice to come home to a meal on the stove. In fact, I don't remember the last time someone cooked for me. I did most of the cooking for my foster parents, and then I got married, and was the chief cook and bottle washer for someone who wouldn't know how to boil water if he had to."

"You're married? Where's your husband then?"

Emily made a grimace and said, "I guess there are lots of things we don't know about each other. But my marriage is a story for another day. Let me go wash up, and then we'll eat. I'm famished!"

Over dinner, Emily probed Anna for more information about her family situation, about the fights her parents had, the physical abuse, the lack of any kind of affection. Money problems had led her father to pull Anna out of school when she was ten to supplement the family income by cleaning houses. "I really miss school," she said. "It was my safe place. It was warm, and I got free lunch, and nobody beat me if I didn't give the right answer. I miss learning new things. I got good grades, and that was at least one thing that I could feel good about. At home, I was always made to feel worthless and shameful, which makes sense, considering what my dad was doing to me."

"He pulled you out of school? That's horrible! I guess that's

245

one thing I can be grateful to my foster parents for. Education was not optional in their mind until my senior year when they kicked me out of the house."

"Well, I guess foster care is better than living on the streets." Anna sighed as she gazed past Emily to the windows where the rain had started again and was lashing against the glass.

"Yes. Which leads me to the conversation we need to have about your future. Have you had any thoughts about that today?"

Anna sighed. "I can't think about anything *but* that. I'm a good worker, but nobody's going to hire me in the shape I'm in. And even then, I couldn't afford a place to live, assuming a landlord would rent a room to a 14-year-old. Which they wouldn't. I don't know. I guess I'm up a creek without a paddle."

Emily reached across the table and put her hand over Anna's. "Well, Anna, I've been thinking too, and I want you to stay with me." Anna opened her mouth as if in protest, but Emily stopped her short. "Before you start listing all the reasons not to, give me a chance to explain. First of all, the simple truth is that there's nowhere else, and I can't in all good conscience turn you out with a baby coming and winter approaching. If not for my foster father helping me escape from my husband, I could have been living on the streets myself, just to get away from him. And to tell you the truth, it was really nice to have you here when I got home and a delicious meal waiting for me. As glad as I was to get away from George and be on my own, I miss having someone to talk to."

"But can you afford to feed another mouth? Even with two incomes, my parents could barely afford to put food on the table for us."

"Well, I did just get a raise a few months ago, and that should be enough to help pay for a little extra food. And having you here isn't going to impact my rent. We don't need anything bigger than this apartment, because the sofa is perfectly comfortable. Except for the nightmare, I slept well last night. I don't think my landlady will have an objection, since several people in this building are already sharing an apartment to cut costs. If you did the cooking and cleaning, that would be more than enough compensation. As your pregnancy advances, you won't be able to do the heavy work, but that's not an issue. I've been cleaning since I was ten as well, so I'm used to it. What do you think?"

"Are you sure? I mean, I'm truly grateful to you for saving me from that alley and taking me in, but staying here long term just seems like too much to ask."

"Anna, I need you to hear this. When I look at you, I see myself. Sure, I never got pregnant, but only by the grace of God. You have suffered enough in your short life, and if I can give you a chance at a happy ending, I want to do it."

Deeply moved, Anna replied, "Thank you so much. I can't tell you what a relief it is to know that I won't have to go back and beg my parents to take me in. I couldn't face any more of my dad's abuse. I have actually felt safe today for the first time in years."

"Well then, it's decided," Emily said briskly. "Let's clear the dishes, and then we can talk more about how this is going to work."

The next morning, Emily knocked on her landlady's door. Mrs. Benson opened the door a crack to see who was there, then pulled it wider to invite Emily in. "Good morning, Emily. What can I do for you? Is there a problem with the apartment?"

"Oh, no, Mrs. Benson. I just wanted to let you know I'm taking in a roommate. Actually, it's my niece. She's had a rough time of it and needs a soft place to land. My sister, her mother, died about a year ago, and her father is quite the ne'er-do-well. Anna, my niece, had to quit school and work in order to help make ends meet. Anyway, she was working in a diner, and the bus boy took a shine to her and eventually forced himself on her in the back alley one night after closing. The boss had already locked up and left, so nobody was there to protect her, and her dad had taken off to get some work logging and was gone for months. When he got home and found her pregnant, he beat her and threw her out of the house, refusing to believe her story of rape. I know this is probably more than you wanted to hear, and this is asking a lot, but I just can't turn her out in this condition. Anna is a good girl who's in a horrible situation and needs some kindness right now. I owe this much to my sister; God rest her soul." Emily paused, taking in the gleam in her landlady's eye. As she had expected, Mrs. Benson couldn't resist juicy gossip, and really, Emily hadn't lied too terribly much. She just hoped she would be able to keep all her lies straight in the future.

"That poor girl! Of course she can stay with you, Emily. Just make sure she understands the rules. The other tenants wouldn't thank me if she made an undue amount of noise. I hope you won't get behind on your rent, what with another mouth to feed. How far along is she? We'll have to revisit the issue once the baby's born, but for now I have no objection to her presence."

"Oh, thank you, Mrs. Benson! You are such a good-hearted soul. I knew you would understand. I just wish I had known about this situation sooner. My sister and I weren't always close, because she was so much older than me, and I hated being around that detestable husband of hers, so I avoided visiting, and of course, I feel horrible about that now. I'm just glad I can help Anna when she needs me most. Bless you for allowing me to provide a home for her."

"You're most welcome, Emily. Now I'm sure you must be getting along to work. Have a good day."

Emily rushed back upstairs to tell Anna the good news, then walked briskly to work so she wouldn't be late. Even in her rush, she noticed the damp smell of decaying leaves and the smoke coming from chimneys along the route. She breathed deeply and smiled. The sky was gray, but that did not dampen her mood. She wondered why she felt so right about this decision when many might think she was a fool to take in a total stranger. Nonetheless, she knew she didn't have it in her to turn away someone whose suffering was so similar to her own. And even though Emily couldn't have a baby herself, it might be nice to have a baby around, at least for a little while. But that was a plan and a decision for another day.

Saturday broke with a promise of sunshine. After checking Anna's bruises, cuts, and scrapes, which looked awful but showed signs of healing, Emily asked the girl if she felt up for a walk. "I always like to be out and about on my days off, and I'm sure you're tired of being stuck in this apartment for four days. There's someplace I'd like to take you."

When Anna asked where, Emily just smiled and said, "Wait and see." At first, the two seemed to walk aimlessly, turning this way and that to look at a tree ablaze with fall color or catch a view of Elliott Bay below them. However, the wandering wasn't entirely random, as eventually they found themselves on the doorstep of the main city library.

"What are we doing at the library?" Anna asked.

"Well, I've been thinking," Emily said. "You told me how much you miss school, so I thought maybe we could find some textbooks to check out, and I could tutor you in the evenings after dinner. How does that sound?"

Anna beamed. "That would be wonderful! And it would give me something to do during the day, since it doesn't take much time at all to clean your apartment. I don't know why you are being so good to me, but thank you. I'm so grateful for all you've done already." Before long, they had found a fifth-grade math book, a spelling book, and a collection of short stories for young readers. These disappeared into a tote bag Emily had brought as she led Anna determinedly toward their next destination.

As Emily pulled open the doors of the Goodwill store, she ignored Anna's protests. "You need some clothes. You've been wearing the same torn clothing all week and washing your underwear every night. I'm sure you'd like to never see them again, given what happened to you while wearing them. I still have a little money set aside from my foster father, so let's see what we can find you to wear."

Anna began to cry. "I haven't had new clothes in so long. I mean, I know these clothes aren't 'new', but they'll be new to me, and I get to pick them out myself. I don't know if they'll have maternity clothes though, so we'll have to buy stuff that's extra large for when I get bigger."

After much searching, trying on, and debating, they left with a few outfits, some underthings, a coat, and a warm nightgown. Tired and hungry, they entered a small diner nearby and ate lunch, discussing potential lesson plans and chattering about their purchases. As they returned home from their expedition, Emily realized that the last time she had had so much fun shopping was with her mother. Grateful tears welled up as she remembered a mother who had made her early childhood a delight despite the demands of financial hardship and single parenthood.

On Sunday, Emily took her laundry to the local laundromat after a brief tussle with Anna, who wanted to do it for her. "Over my dead body, Anna! I am not going to have you carrying a heavy basket of clothes down these stairs in your condition. They are dangerous enough for you as it is! You were lucky that your father's assault didn't cause you to lose the baby, and I'll be damned if I let something happen to it now."

Anna looked taken aback at Emily's use of profanity, but Emily just laughed. "My mother wasn't so proper that she didn't use a few choice words when the situation warranted it. My husband would have had a fit if I used a swear word in front of him, so this is my own belated rebellion. And it got your attention, didn't it? I'm fine with you doing some minor cleaning and cooking, but you are not to do my laundry until that baby arrives safely." Anna gave a mock salute and a smile as Emily went out the door with a load of wash in her arms.

The afternoon was spent looking through the library books they had checked out. Emily made a list of reading and math assignments for the week as well as a vocabulary list for Anna to study. It was strange being the teacher rather than the student, but it felt good. She thought fondly of Sister Mary Francis and wondered what she would think about Emily's current situation. Life has a way of surprising you, she mused.

Chapter 17

I can wade Grief —
Whole Pools of it —
I'm used to that —
But the least push of Joy
Breaks up my feet —
And I tip — drunken —
Let no Pebble — smile —
'Twas the New Liquor —
That was all!

> —Emily Dickenson

Autumn 1960

"So, I seem to be over my fear of George tracking me down, but now I'm having more nightmares about Father Devlin. I think Anna's abuse by her father is stirring up old memories. I feel like I'm reliving those days all over again."

Reverend Patterson rubbed his chin thoughtfully. "And how do you feel when you wake up from these dreams?"

"Well, obviously, there's the terror and disgust, but mostly it's the shame. I feel so dirty, like I should have been able to stop it, but didn't."

"And how old were you when this started?"

"Just eleven, but old enough to know right from wrong."

"Don't you think priests know right from wrong too? And wasn't he bigger and stronger than you? Wasn't he a frightening figure even before he started molesting you?"

"I suppose so, but he kept telling me that I wanted it, and there were times when my body responded in ways that made me feel so ashamed. And before he started touching me that way, I kind of liked the attention he was giving me, even though it made me uncomfortable. It was just so confusing! I must be bad for letting him

251

do those things."

"I'm sure it *was* confusing. He probably did that on purpose to make you more compliant. Do you have any idea why he chose you as his victim?"

Emily paused for thought. "I don't know. I never thought about that. You know, he made such a big deal about me being an orphan and how precarious my position was with the Huttons. He always wanted me to see him as a listening ear and someone who could offer comfort, but in hindsight, it seemed to reinforce my sense of being alone in the world."

Reverend Patterson pondered that for a moment. "So it sounds like your loneliness and sense of being different than the other kids might have made you more vulnerable to his predations. He believed that you would be less likely to tell anyone what was happening."

"You mean he didn't molest me because he thought I would be willing? He didn't see me as bad or in want of his sexual attentions?"

"I highly doubt it! There is nothing about you that communicates that. I think it was because he thought you would be more malleable due to your situation. Your being an orphan and an outsider at the school made you more easily singled out for 'special attention'. Ask yourself this—was there ever a time when you actually wanted him to engage in sexual acts with you?"

"No!! Never! Even when my body responded to it, I always felt sick to my stomach and wanted it to stop."

"And if you had told him to stop, do you think he would have?"

"Not a chance! For one, I was too scared to, and even when I tried a couple times to refuse his phony lice checks, he always had a reason why he needed to do them. He convinced me they were for my benefit."

"Then, if you never wanted it and tried to say no, there is nothing for you to be ashamed of. He's the one who should be ashamed, but I'm pretty sure he never would. You couldn't have stopped him, and you didn't want it, no matter what he told you!"

Emily felt a weight start to lift off her chest. "Thank you, Reverend Patterson. That's such a relief to hear you say that, especially as a man of God. I'd never looked at it from that perspective before. I'm truly grateful to you for taking so much time out of your busy schedule to listen to me. You're a godsend."

"You're welcome, Emily. This is why I became a pastor in the first place, to bring hope and healing to people who are hurting. It's my privilege to listen to your story and help if I can."

Emily rose from her chair with a light heart and gave him a spontaneous hug before leaving the church.

Arriving home one clear and cold autumn night, Emily was welcomed by a warm apartment and the aroma of pot roast. Immediately she was transported back to the apartment she shared with her mother, coming home from school and being greeted by the sounds and smells of home. Then Anna turned around from the stove, disrupting her daydream, and Emily felt a sudden surge of longing for her mother. She gave the young girl a half-hearted smile and hurried into the bathroom, ostensibly to wash up for dinner. But instead of washing, she sat on the edge of the tub and buried her face in her hands, swamped by a tidal wave of grief. It had been a long time since she had felt this ache, this sense of loss. For a moment, she gave in to it and allowed the tears to flow. Then she splashed warm water on her face, washed her hands and took a deep breath before joining Anna in the kitchen for dinner.

As Anna chattered about her day, her studies, and the book she was reading, Emily gradually felt her inner pain ease. It was nice to have someone to talk with over dinner again. Towards the end of her marriage to George, he hadn't come home for dinner at all, and even before that, the strain over her inability to get pregnant had made for many awkward silences at the dinner table. Emily reached over and laid her hand on Anna's arm. "I'm so glad you're here," she said.

Anna looked surprised. "What brought that on?"

"Oh, just being grateful for my blessings tonight, that's all. It's nice to have someone to talk to at the end of the day."

"But you're not talking very much. I'm doing all the talking."

Emily smiled. "That's perfectly alright. I'm in more of a listening mood tonight." The two cleared the table and washed the dishes together before Anna pulled out her books to show Emily what she was working on. "You're doing so well, Anna. You are learning quickly, and taking the initiative to move to the next lesson even if I'm not here. Excellent work!"

"You think so? I'm really glad to be studying again and making up for lost time. Is there anything else you want me to do tonight, or can I read my book for a while? I'm at a really good part."

"Of course! I may read a bit too." Anna fetched her book and settled at the table, while Emily curled up on the sofa. Book in hand, her eyes were drawn not to the written words but to the night sky outside her window. Maybe it was the remnants of her grief that made the stars seem to sparkle more brightly than usual, but she could almost feel the touch of her mother's hand in hers. And then she noticed that if she put her face right against the window and looked straight up, she could see the slender curve of a new moon. This had always been Emily's favorite phase of the moon, evoking as it did a glimpse of new beginnings, a shimmer of light promising the fullness yet to come. Magically, she felt a sense of peace steal over her and something that felt like hope. The words of a poem began writing themselves in her head until she felt compelled to write them down. She borrowed some paper from Anna and allowed the words to unfold on the page. Then she read what she had written and sighed with contentment. It felt like she was returning to the person she used to be.

Cathedral
New moon shimmers in the sky,
a slender tear in the soft dark fabric
of night.
Stars strewn across the eternal expanse
beckon me with their light.
I long to reach and touch
this Holy ceiling, the face of God,
revealed in breadth and height.
I could once,
while holding my mother's hand.
I had forgotten—
the firmament and the familiar
are both God's handiwork.

Emily awoke the next morning, still bewitched by the night sky of the previous evening, the memories it drew from her distant past, and the poem that resulted. It was the first poem she'd written in a long time that wasn't about her pain. She wanted to honor it somehow, to reclaim her love of poetry and her right to use her time however she pleased. This was something George had taken away from her, and she wanted to make a statement that he couldn't demean her passion anymore. In the past, she had written poetry on scratch paper, napkins, even the margins of discarded newspapers. It occurred to her that she could take it to work and use one of the typewriters there to create a clean copy for herself. Excited, she got up quickly and hurried through her morning routine so she could arrive before the rest of her co-workers.

Once there, Emily quickly typed up the poem, pleased with the imagery and her word choices. She finished just as her colleagues began arriving and took the poem to her desk. Her friend Sandra waved and scurried over to share details of her date with Gary in the typesetting department. Mr. Graves walked in and stopped at Emily's desk to wish her good morning. He looked down, paused, then picked up a piece of paper. "What's this, Emily?"

Emily froze for what seemed like an eternity, color draining from her face. Certain she was about to be reprimanded, she hurried to explain. "I'm so sorry, Mr. Graves. I just used the office typewriter for a few minutes. I won't let it happen again"

"Did you write this?"

She blushed in shame. "I-I did, sir. It's just a silly little poem. I'm sorry I misused office resources on such a paltry thing."

"You're not in trouble, Emily. I just wondered who wrote this poem. It's really quite lovely."

Emily realized she was shaking. "You're just saying that to be polite. It's only some scribblings I wrote last night while looking at the moon. I wanted to have a clean copy for myself, but I fear that it was inappropriate. I won't do it again."

"Emily, there's nothing wrong with using a typewriter here before the workday starts. Sometimes people need to type up a personal document or something, and I don't have a problem with that. But what I really want to know is, can I have your permission to show this to the Features editor? Sometimes we print poetry in the paper, and I think this is publishable material. Would that be okay with you?"

Stunned and breathless, Emily replied, "Do you really mean that?? I mean, I'm not a real poet. I've never even shown my poetry to anyone before, except for school assignments. I just play around with images and how they impact me sometimes."

"Well, these images and your thoughts are very touching, and I think our readers would very much appreciate your work. I understand if you feel it's too private, but I'd love to see this in print if you'll let me."

A smile spread across her tremulous lips. "Yes! If you truly think it's worth sharing. I've never had anything published before. I would be honored." Emily spent the rest of the day floating on a cloud. She couldn't believe that something she wrote might actually get published in the paper. Her thoughts fluttered between how excited Sister Mary Francis would be and how much she wished she could wave the newspaper in George's face and say, "Just how frivolous do you think my poetry is now?"

When Emily arrived home that night, Anna was sitting on the couch urgently beckoning her benefactress to come over. "Come sit! Put your hand right here." Anna took Emily's hand and placed it on her belly. "Feel this!" Emily did as asked, intently waiting for something to happen. And then she felt a very slight twitch against her hand.

"Oh! I felt it! Is that the baby?" Anna nodded with a smile.

"I think so. It's been happening on and off for the last couple of days."

"Oh, my goodness! That's wonderful!" Overwhelmed by the events of the day, culminating in this experience of the miracle of life, Emily radiated joy. Then she took in the glow on Anna's face and laughed. "Aren't we a pair, getting all goo-goo eyed over a little flutter," she exclaimed, then pulled her ward into an embrace.

A week later, Mr. Graves waved Emily into his office when she arrived at work. Her thoughts immediately began reviewing her recent assignments to pinpoint anything she might have done wrong. She stood before her boss's desk with a touch of anxiety. "Yes, sir?"

His pleasant glance eased her fears but not her curiosity.

"Good morning, Emily. Please sit down." As she did so, he continued, "So, I've spoken with Harold Stone, and he was very impressed with your poem. He definitely wants to print it in the Sunday paper this week. And if it is well-received, he would like to see more of your work for future publication. We can pay you ten dollars for it. I know that's not much, but it's the standard rate for items on the features page."

Emily sat with her mouth agape, her eyes sparkling. "I-I can't believe it! The paper is going to *pay* me to print my poem? How can I ever thank you?!"

Her boss smiled broadly. "I thought you'd be pleased. Thanks are not necessary. It's not much, but I thought a few extra dollars here and there might be welcome. So anytime you feel the urge to wax poetic, be sure to bring me the result, and I'll pass it along to Mr. Stone."

Breathlessly, Emily assured him that she would. "Thank you so much! I never would have dreamed that my little poems might be worthy of publication. You have no idea how much this means to me. I have loved poetry since I was a little girl and my mother was reciting *Jabberwocky* to me."

"Well, clearly that had a deep impact on you. I'm sure she would have been proud." He stood and escorted Emily to the door. "I see a pile of work on your desk, so you'd better get to it." And he winked.

Chapter 18

I shall know why—when Time is over—
And I have ceased to wonder why—
Christ will explain each separate anguish
In the fair schoolroom of the sky—
—Emily Dickinson

Late Autumn 1960

Saturday was a day for chores and grocery shopping. The local market sat opposite a plain white church Emily had never paid any attention to. On this particular day however, as she and Anna walked by, Anna stopped short. "I used to go to this church."

Surprised, Emily turned to Anna. "What? What do you mean?"

Anna responded bitterly, "Me and my parents. We went to church here sometimes. All those people talked just like my Dad—all about sin and eternal damnation. I guess it's okay to hit your wife and molest your daughter if it's meant to punish them for their sins."

"Oh, my goodness, Anna! I'm so sorry! It's hard to believe in a loving God when all you hear is how God is going to pounce on your smallest infractions of the law."

"You can say that again! Truthfully, I don't care if I ever walk through the doors of a church again. It's all hogwash as far as I'm concerned."

Emily paused. "I can certainly understand that. Tell you what. Let's get our groceries, and when we get home, we can talk about this some more."

Anna shrugged. "I don't know what there is to talk about, but I guess."

Back home with groceries put away, Emily sat down and patted the couch cushions next to her. "Come sit down, Anna. Let's talk."

The girl shook her head. "If this is a lecture coming on, I'm not interested."

"Not a lecture. I'm not your mother, just someone who has been where you are. Please, Anna."

With great reluctance, Anna came and sat next to Emily. "Okay, let's get this over with."

"I guess I don't have to tell you how I felt about God when I was getting molested by a priest. After all, priests are representatives of God in the Catholic church, so if this is what Father Devlin was like, I figured God was like that too—sadistic and cruel. Here I am, getting raped and sodomized, while at the same time, the nuns were trying to impress upon me that God loves us all unconditionally. Talk about confusing!" Anna gave a small nod that Emily hoped was a sign that she was listening.

"Then later, when I got married, my husband was a strict Catholic who would lecture me every time I did something that was the slightest violation of his rigid interpretation of God's commandments. He would punish me if I didn't go to confession every week, and confession was the hardest thing for me to do, because of . . . well, let's just say it was really hard. So I had some pretty negative ideas about God. Then one night when things had gotten so bad in my marriage, I ran out of the house in a panic and ended up bumping into the local parish priest—not the one who abused me, but the one at the church George and I were attending at the time. He saw that I was terribly upset, so he took me into the rectory and tried to get me to tell him what was wrong. I couldn't tell him then, not yet, because I was so afraid of how he would feel about me after I told him my story. He was kind, you see, and gentle, and I knew that if I told him what a messed-up person I was, that would change. But he kept inviting me to come and talk to him, and eventually I did. At first I only told him bits and pieces, but ultimately the whole story came out, and he was so sympathetic and understanding, and he didn't judge me at all. He helped me to see that Father Devlin and my husband were not what God is like. They didn't hurt me because I deserved to be punished, but because they were sick and twisted inside, and what they did to me was not something that God would ever condone."

"But God let it happen, didn't he? Why didn't God stop it? If you are a good person and obey the Bible, isn't God supposed to reward you and protect you?" Anna asked.

"Well, that's certainly the idea that some people have, that God is like Santa Claus and the candy man rolled into one, but the world is more complicated than that. Jesus said, 'God makes the rain to fall on the just and unjust alike.' Bad things happen to everyone, because people choose to hurt you, or accidents take your mother away from you, or war kills the fathers of countless thousands of children. God does not cause all the horrible things that happen in the world, but God is there to help you get through them. I hadn't been to church for a long time when I moved here, but then I started going to the Lutheran church by the bus station, and being there reminded me of the comfort and sense of God's presence I felt when I went to church as a child."

"But what about all the commandments and laws and stuff? Doesn't God get mad when we sin? My dad was always telling me I was going straight to hell for disobeying him or telling lies or sassing back."

"Apparently your dad skipped all the Bible passages about grace and forgiveness. God knows we're not perfect, but if we keep trying and resolve to do better, God keeps loving us and helping us to do the right thing. That's all. So, would you consider going to church with me sometime? It doesn't have to be tomorrow. I want to give you some time to think about it, and I'm not going to force you, but I think you will find that the Lutheran church is very different than the one you grew up in."

Anna looked doubtful, but she nodded and said, "I guess so. But if I don't like it, I won't have to go back?"

"Of course not, it will be up to you. I promise."

"Okay, I guess it wouldn't hurt for just one time."

A few days later, Emily arrived home to find the kitchen and living room empty and no dinner simmering on the stove. Puzzled, she stood still, listening for some sign of Anna's presence. A muffled sound emanated from behind the closed bedroom door. Walking over to the door, she put her ear against it and heard the unmistakable sounds of sobbing. Emily knocked lightly. "Anna, are you okay? Can I come in?" She heard something that sounded like an assent and opened the door. Anna was curled up on the bed, face in her pillow, shoulders heaving in her distress. Emily moved quickly to the bed, sat down beside the distraught girl and placed a steadying hand on her back. "I'm here, Anna. Please tell me what's wrong. Is it the baby?"

Anna shook her head. "No. It's not that."

"Then what is it? Are you ill? Did something happen to upset you so?"

Anna nodded, face still buried in the pillow.

"What then? You're worrying me! Please sit up and tell me what's disturbing you."

Slowly, the girl pushed herself upright, eyes downcast. Her face was red and wet with tears. She took a deep, shivery breath and let it out in a whoosh. "I went to see my mother."

Emily's face blanched. "You did what? Why would you do that? Did you tell her where you've been? You're not thinking about going back, are you?"

Anna shook her head. "No. Don't worry. I didn't tell her about you. I just miss her. I mean, she wasn't the best mother, but she did the best she could. I wanted her to know I was okay. I have no idea what's going to happen to me, how I can manage a baby on my own, where I will go, how to pay for the birth. I don't know anything about babies, and you aren't going to want me around forever. I just . . . I thought that if I told my mom everything, I could persuade her to leave my dad, so she and I could start over somewhere. I was hoping she might know where my big brother is, so we could be together as a family, and between us, we could make a living and share in taking care of the baby."

"You have a brother? Why don't you know where he is?"

"I guess it's just never come up until now. He's four years older than me, and he ran away a couple years ago, got tired of getting beat up by my dad. His name's Jack. I miss him a lot and wonder where he is all the time. I know that if he were here, he would want to help me."

"Okay, so tell me what happened with your mom. Obviously not anything good."

"It was awful! First of all, she was shocked to see that I was pregnant. She hadn't noticed before or at least didn't want to see. When I told her about what Dad had been doing for years and that he had beaten me up and left me in an alley, she wouldn't believe me. She said it was not possible for him to have done that, as if he doesn't beat on her all the time. And I know he has forced her to have sex when she didn't want to. I've heard them through the walls. She called me a slut, no better than a prostitute! Then she said that even if I was telling the truth, it was my fault, that I must have done something to encourage him. As if I wanted this to happen! And she completely shot me down about leaving him and helping me with the baby. She said she couldn't leave him, because the Bible says a wife has to submit to her husband no matter what. And then she told me to get out of her sight; she didn't want to have anything to do with me or my bastard child." Anna started sobbing again.

Emily put her arms around the distraught girl and rocked with her. "Oh, Anna! I'm so sorry. Those are such ugly words. You didn't in any way deserve to be treated like that. What your father did to you was *not* your fault! His behavior was his choice alone. He was the one with all the power. Please don't worry, honey. We'll figure this out, I promise we will. I am not going to abandon you or put you back out on the street. Everything will be alright. You'll see."

The sobs gradually reduced to sniffles and then a deep sigh. "But I'm getting farther and farther along, and we haven't talked about what's going to happen when the baby's born at all! I know you are just barely able to support me as it is, much less pay for the hospital and all the stuff baby's need. Oh Emily, what are we going to do?" The last words came out in a wail.

"I apologize, Anna. This is my fault. I have been so wrapped up in my job and the pleasure of having you here that I failed to think about how anxious you might be about your future. But you're right; we don't have time for me to keep sticking my head in the sand. We need to start planning and exploring possibilities. I'm not exactly sure where to start, but I'll figure it out. My mother told me once that God has a special concern for widows and orphans, and in this case, I think our situation counts. Your parents aren't the only ones who can quote Scripture! I think it's in Psalms somewhere, 'Father of the fatherless and protector of widows is God in his holy habitation.' My mom quoted that verse to me when we had to move from the home we'd lived in since I was born, because we couldn't afford the rent anymore. I hated the idea of moving, but we found a little apartment above someone's garage that cost half the rent we were paying before, and the landlady became a good friend. In fact, she was the one who took me in after my mother was killed. I don't know what I would have done without her."

"But God wasn't there when your mom died, or when that priest was doing terrible things to you. How can you say he protected you?"

"Oh, sweetie! Bad things happen to everyone. Even my friend, Lottie, who had a wonderful family, lost a baby sister to polio, and my favorite teacher, Sister Mary Francis, had a brother who was blinded in a logging accident. Suffering is everywhere, but God is there to help you through it."

Anna looked doubtful. "I don't know about that. I don't see how God is going to get me out of this mess my life is in."

"Wait and see, Anna. We just need to put our heads together and figure this out. Maybe, if you give me some clues about where Jack might have gone or what kind of work he might be doing, we can find him. And I can definitely talk to the landlady again to see if she is willing to let us stay here on a conditional basis to see how the neighbors feel about a baby crying in the night. But one thing I know we need to do on Sunday is go to church. Your parents have shown you a poor example of what it means to be a person of faith, and I want you to experience a God who is more loving and merciful than the one they worship. Can we do that?"

Anna nodded as she wiped her eyes with the corner of a tangled sheet. "I guess if God is anything like you, he can't be all bad. I don't know where I'd be if you hadn't rescued me, Emily. I owe you so much." She threw her arms around her benefactress and hugged her tight.

That Sunday dawned cold and gray. Though it wasn't raining, steely clouds threatened. It was tempting to stay in bed, huddled near the radiator for warmth. Nonetheless, Emily was determined to take Anna to church. She pulled a blanket around her shoulders and padded into the kitchen to start a pot of coffee. Soon the aroma wafted under the bedroom door and awakened its teenage occupant, who wandered out, eyes bleary and hair mussed. "Brrr. I'm cold! Are you sure we have to go to church today? What if it rains?"

"That's what umbrellas are for! I know it's not the best day for it, but I promise you won't be sorry. Now let's get some breakfast and make ourselves presentable."

Before long, swaddled in heavy coats and scarves and armed with umbrellas, the two women were walking briskly up the street leaning into the wind. It was a relief when they could turn right on Fifth Avenue where the buildings blocked the chilly gusts. Soon they approached the church, and Anna paused, craning her neck to take in its lofty spire. "It's beautiful! I've never been in a church like this. It's a little intimidating. What if people stare at me? Aren't they going to disapprove of someone my age being pregnant?"

"Anna, I promise you they won't. First of all, with your heavy coat on, you can hardly tell. They'll just think you're on the heavy side. And second, if someone does judge you, that reflects more on them than it does you. They don't know your story, so they don't have the right to judge. Jesus taught people *not* to judge. Besides, most people have enough of their own problems without fretting about someone else's."

Reassured, Anna straightened her shoulders, lifted her chin, and started up the stairs toward the arched doors. Emily allowed a small smile to play on her lips as she followed. They walked in together and slipped into a pew toward the back. Anna gazed in awe at the high arched ceiling and ornate stained glass windows. Organ music swelled in the vast sanctuary and seemed to calm her. Emily reached out and squeezed her hand, praying silently that today's worship would touch Anna's heart and help her know that God was on her side. The worship began with the comforting words of invocation that had always given Emily a sense of peace and hope. The service progressed through prayers and hymns until it was time for the scripture reading and sermon. When Reverend Patterson stood to read from the large Bible on the altar, Emily held her breath. "Hear this reading from the book of Isaiah, chapter 49:

Sing for joy, O heavens, and exult, O earth:
break forth, O mountains, into singing!
For the Lord has comforted his people,
and will have compassion on his afflicted.
But Zion said, "The Lord has forsaken me,
my Lord has forgotten me.
Can a woman forget her sucking child,

that she should have no compassion on the son of her womb?

Even these may forget, yet I will not forget you.

Emily turned to look at her young charge and saw tears glimmering in her eyes. She glanced heavenward and breathed a silent thank you for the providence that led Reverend Patterson to choose the perfect passage for Anna to hear. The cleric went on to speak of suffering, of the hardships that lead people to believe God is indifferent or absent in times of trouble. "Our Lord is never far away from us. It is just harder for us to sense His presence when we are hurting. We are turned inward in our misery, and it takes all our energy to get from one moment to the next. We feel lost and can't see anything but what is right in front of us. We can't imagine the light will ever dawn in what feels like unending darkness. Yet our God is a creative God, One who transforms and redeems even the most desperate situations. Even the disciples thought that Jesus' death on the cross was the end of the story, but God had another ending, another *beginning* in mind. God did not forsake Jesus or the disciples. Neither will God forsake or forget you. You are written on His palms, engraved on His heart. The author of Lamentations tells us, 'The steadfast love of the Lord never ceases; His mercies never come to an end; they are new every morning.' Trust in this promise. Trust in God's faithfulness and mercy. Believe that a new day will come. Amen."

As the two women filed out of the church, they were greeted by Reverend Patterson. "Hello, Emily. It's so good to see you. And who is your young friend?"

"This is Anna, my niece. She's living with me for a while. Thank you for your uplifting message this morning, Reverend. It was just what we needed."

"I'm glad it spoke to you, Emily. I've learned over the years that God's timing is always impeccable. Nice to meet you, Anna. I hope you'll come back. Have a lovely day."

Anna was silent for several minutes on the way home. Finally, she spoke. "That was different than any service I've ever been to. I didn't know church could be like that. I'm used to pastors who shout and pound the pulpit and talk about going to hell. All the hymns we sang were about the blood of Jesus, not how much he loves us. I've never heard 'What a Friend We Have in Jesus' before. It was so beautiful I almost cried. And the preacher was so good! I didn't want it to end. He made me feel like there was hope for me. I see now that God sent you to me so I would know He hadn't forgotten me. Just because my parents failed me in so many ways, doesn't mean that God will fail me too. Maybe I can stop worrying so much and trust that things really will be okay. Thank you for making me come, Emily. I really didn't want to, but now I can hardly wait to go back."

The next morning, Emily awoke to the sounds of Anna puttering in the kitchen. The smell of frying eggs began to permeate the room. Emily smiled as she snuggled deeper into her blankets on the couch for a few more minutes of laziness before starting the day. A strange feeling settled over her, vaguely familiar and foreign at the same time. Pondering, it took her a while to realize, surprisingly, that what she was experiencing was contentment.

> I am washed up, gasping,
> on the shore of Hope,
> spit out at last
> from the maw of the tempest,
> from the inky and merciless waters
> of despair.
> I floundered so long
> in the crashing waves of memory,
> wave after wave,
> I feared I would drown
> in their relentless violence,
> swallowed whole
> by their dark appetites.
> And yet, here I am,
> fingers clutching
> the sand beneath me,
> no longer tossed by anguish and pain,
> daring to hope for calm,
> daring to hope for peace—
> against all odds, catching a glimpse
> of Happiness on a shimmering horizon.
> I'm alive.

Chapter 19

The first Day's Night had come –
And grateful that a thing
So terrible—had been endured—
I told my Soul to sing—
        —Emily Dickinson

Late Autumn 1960

Two days later, Emily was sitting in the lunchroom when Patsy, one of the girls from the switchboard, came in and looked around, then rushed over to Sandra. "Sandra! My sister had her baby Saturday! I've been dying to tell you, but we were so swamped yesterday I couldn't get away. It's a girl, and Janet named her Grace, after Grace Kelly, you know, because she's so beautiful!"

Sandra got up to embrace her friend, squealing with delight at the news. "Did you get to see her right away? Is she just adorable?"

"I can't even tell you how cute she is! And I got to be with Janet through the entire labor and birth. The midwife kicked Roger out of the house for the duration, and I got to help her! It was so special. Janet was a real trooper, and the baby was in just the right position to make it easier for her. It only took six hours from the time the midwife got there."

The women continued talking for a few minutes, but Emily was deep in thought, wondering how much money might be saved by using a midwife rather than going to the hospital when it came time for Anna's baby to be born. Out of the corner of her eye, she saw Patsy leaving the room and jumped up to follow her. Before the woman could get to the stairs, Emily called out, "Patsy! Do you have a minute?" Patsy turned and walked back.

"Sure. I don't have to be back at my switchboard just yet. What's on your mind?"

"Well, I couldn't help but overhear your conversation with

267

Sandra about your sister's baby. Congratulations, by the way. It sounds like it was a wonderful experience. What I was wondering was if you could give me the name of the midwife your sister had. My niece is expecting in a few months, and we've been trying to figure out how she is going to afford all the doctor and hospital bills. I hadn't thought about a midwife, but that just might be the solution to our problem."

"Of course! Her name is Dorothy Hough, and she was wonderful. I don't have her phone number, but I can ask Janet and get back to you. She's probably in the phone book though."

"Thank you so much, Patsy. I'll check the phone book, and if I can't find her listing, I'll let you know. It would be such a weight off my mind if we had a plan in place for my niece's delivery."

Lunch only half eaten, Emily rushed into the office to find a phone book and locate a number for the midwife. She turned to the H's, ran her finger down the page that began with Horton, and there it was—Leon and Dorothy Hough! She scribbled the number down on a piece of scratch paper and tucked it into her skirt pocket.

Emily walked home briskly that evening in her excitement to share her news with Anna. When she opened the door to the apartment, Anna looked up from the stove and noted Emily's flushed cheeks. "You're early. You must have run all the way home. What's going on?"

"Oh, Anna! I think I might have found the solution to our problem! One of the girls at the paper just attended her niece's birth, which was delivered at home by a midwife. I'm certain that a midwife would cost less than a medical doctor, and we could cut out the expense of a hospital altogether! I have the woman's name, and I'm going to try to call her after dinner to find out more information. We can't get too excited yet, but I'm very hopeful."

"That would be super if it worked out. To tell you the truth, I'm not all that excited about a doctor mucking about down there, if you know what I mean. I'm not sure I'd be able to handle that after what my dad did to me."

"I understand. I'm sure I would feel the same way. Let's just pray this works out."

An hour later, Emily was standing in the foyer of her apartment house, dialing the midwife's phone number with fingers crossed. A woman answered the phone after the second ring. "Melrose 4-2-5-9. Dorothy Hough speaking."

"Hello, Mrs. Hough. My name is Emily Edwards, and I am looking for a midwife for my niece, Anna. You were recommended to me by Patsy Cook. You just delivered her sister's baby on Saturday."

"Yes. Beautiful little girl! How old is your niece? Do you know when she's due?"

"She's fourteen, and truthfully, we're not exactly sure about a due date. We were hoping you might help us with that. The pregnancy was the result of an . . . um, assault, you might say, and her parents are no longer in the picture. That's why her care has fallen on me, but I have no experience in this kind of thing, so we could really use someone to help us through the process. We should probably talk about fees, too, as money is a little tight."

The two women conversed for several minutes before deciding that Miss Hough would make a house call the next evening to examine Anna and coach them both on how best to care for mother and baby until the birth. Emily ran upstairs to fill her young ward in on what she had learned. Anna looked up from the book she had been studying. "What did you find out, Emily? I've been trying to read, but not a word is sinking in. I'm so anxious to know what she said!"

Emily smiled and sat down next to Anna on the couch. "Well, I really liked her, and I think she is going to be the answer to our prayers. Her fees are very reasonable, and she's quite knowledgeable. So, she's coming to meet with us tomorrow night and examine you. And she can give us some idea of when we might expect this baby to arrive."

"Tomorrow? That's so soon! I don't know if I'm ready yet. That makes it feel so real."

"Yes, I know, Anna, but it *is* real, and we have to start making some decisions. Having a plan in place and some knowledge about what to expect is going to go a long way towards relieving your fears. I know it's a little intimidating to think about a strange woman examining you, but it's a necessity that you are going to have to accept. You can't deliver this baby on your own, and I certainly don't have the wherewithal to do it either. This is the right thing to do.

Trust me."

The young woman sighed, "I know. It's just so scary. I guess I'm going to have to buck up and soldier on. And you'll be there to encourage me. I know I can count on that."

Emily smiled and squeezed Anna's hand. "Yes, you can. I'll be there every second, I promise."

Anna was silent for a few moments, deep in thought. Emily waited quietly, hand still cradling Anna's, giving her space to assimilate all that was ahead of her. The stillness lengthened, both women lost in their own thoughts, yet feeling the deep connection between them. Finally, Anna spoke, "Emily, I've been thinking about this a lot, and I know it's too much to ask, after everything you've already done, but . . . I want you to raise my baby." She put up her palm to forestall Emily's response. "You don't have to answer me right now. Just hear me out. I'm not ready to be a mother yet, and I think you'd be a great mother. I want to go back to school so I can make something of my life, maybe be a teacher or a nurse. I don't know how that would work or what we would do about money or even what the laws are about that, but I don't want to give the baby up for adoption to a perfect stranger. How could I trust that they wouldn't abuse him or her like my dad did to me? You're the only person in this world that I trust. So, would you just think about it?"

Emily nodded slowly. "I am honored by your trust. I'm completely caught off guard by your request, but I suppose I shouldn't be. I have been so focused on the birth, I never considered what would happen after. I guess that's how I've been approaching my own life for the past several months, just dealing with what was right in front of me without looking ahead to the next thing. Obviously, that's going to have to change. I *will* think about it and about how to get answers to the legal questions. There's so much we will need to figure out. And we *will* figure it out. But right now, I think we both need some rest. Tomorrow is going to be a big day."

Promptly at seven the next evening, a brisk knock was heard at the door. Emily opened the door, and her gaze was met by a dark-haired woman wearing the crisp white uniform of a nurse. Emily gasped and cried out, "Oh!" raising her hand to her heart, overcome by a vision of her mother. On second glance, the similarities were superficial. Mrs. Hough had green eyes and not the deep brown eyes

270

of Maddy Snow, and her features were round and soft, where Maddy's had been more angular.

Mrs. Hough looked puzzled. "Do I have the right apartment? I'm looking for Emily Edwards."

Emily let out the breath she hadn't known she was holding. "Yes. I'm she. I'm so sorry. Please come in. I guess I wasn't expecting you to be wearing a uniform, and for a moment you reminded me of my mother. She was a nurse as well."

"Was?"

"Yes, she died when I was still a child."

"I'm so sorry to hear that. And now, where is my patient?"

"Of course! Please forgive my manners. Anna is right over here." Emily stepped away from the door so the midwife could see Anna who was struggling to get upright from the couch.

Mrs. Hough reached out her hand as she approached Anna. "No need to get up this minute, Anna. Please sit. It's not so easy to get up at this stage of the game, is it?"

Anna sank gratefully back to her seat and smiled tentatively. "Nice to meet you, Mrs. Hough. Thank you for coming."

"I'm glad I can help. Now let's see what we can see." The woman glanced around the room, still holding the large brown carry-all she had in her hand. "Is there a bed in the other room? I think we'll both be more comfortable with you lying down." With an affirmative nod from Emily, Mrs. Hough bent over, put her arm around Anna's back and, with surprising strength, hoisted her out of the couch and supported her as they walked into the bedroom.

An embarrassed Anna blushed. "Forgive the mess. I guess I wasn't expecting that we'd need to come in here."

"Oh, posh! I've got children at home that can make a mess twice as bad in a matter of minutes! As long as there's room on the bed for you to lie down, we're perfectly fine. Now, let's see if we can narrow down when you can expect your little bundle to arrive. Do you remember when your last period was?"

"Well, it was my first and my last. I didn't write it on the calendar or anything, but it was just before school got out for the summer. I didn't know what was happening, so I went to my mom, and she just said, 'Well, now you're a woman, God help you,' and handed me some pads. I didn't have the first idea how to use them, but eventually figured it out. My dad was away working, so he didn't know. He showed up about two weeks after, climbed into my bed in the middle of the night as usual, and left three days later. He'd found out about a job with a big logging operation in Montana, and off he went. By the time he got back in September, I was starting to show, and he went crazy. That's how I ended up here with Emily."

Mrs. Hough's face had turned as white as her uniform. "Are you saying that your own father is the father of this child?"

"Yes, ma'am. I've never been with anybody else, never even had a boyfriend. I was too afraid of what my parents would do. They're holy rollers, and they preached at me all the time about preserving my chastity, which is a big joke considering what Dad was doing when Mom wasn't looking."

The midwife slowly shook her head, and Emily thought she detected a slight shudder going through her body. "Well, I think we should be able to narrow our dates down a bit between what you've told me and what I learn from the examination. Let's have you lie back and pull your blouse up to your breasts." Mrs. Hough pulled out a measuring tape which she stretched from just under Anna's breasts to the top of her pubic bone. She nodded her head as if satisfied with the results. "Good! The measurement matches your timeline, so I think we can expect this little bundle to show up in early March, God willing. Has there been anything unusual about your pregnancy so far? Anything that could affect the health of the baby?"

A look passed between Emily and Anna. Emily began to speak. "You should probably know that when I found Anna, she was lying in an alleyway after having been beaten and left there by her father. She had a number of abrasions and bruises, a few of them on her abdomen, and a cut just below her eye. I cleaned her up as best I could and iced the places that hurt the most, but she was in a lot of pain for the first few days. Even so, she felt the baby moving, so we knew he or she was still alive."

The midwife swallowed as if trying to keep from being sick, clenched her fists for a moment, then took a deep breath and relaxed her shoulders. "And is the baby still kicking and active?"

Anna nodded. "Oh, he's an active one alright. I think he's probably going to be a football player or something. And at night, he pushes at my ribs something fierce!"

"Excellent! That's a good sign. It sounds like you are a very lucky girl. And Emily, it appears you learned a few things from your mother. Now Anna, I'm going to listen to the heartbeat, and then I'm going to have to do a pelvic examination. It might be hard for you, bring back memories of what your father did, but I will be as gentle as I can. Alright?"

Anna glanced at Emily with trepidation, but Emily took her hand and squeezed it. "I'm right here, Anna. Just keep telling yourself that you're safe now, and that nobody here is going to hurt you." Anna nodded.

Mrs. Hough got out her stethoscope and placed it on Anna's belly. She moved the chest piece from place to place, listening intently until she stopped in one spot and listened for several seconds. Then she smiled. "Your baby has a strong and steady heartbeat, dear, just what we were hoping for! Do you want to listen?"

Eyes widening, a speechless Anna nodded emphatically. The midwife placed the earpieces in her ears and watched as a beaming smile spread across the young woman's face. "I hear it! Oh, my goodness! I can hear my baby's heart beating!"

"Yes, indeed. The slower swooshing you hear is actually your own heart, but the faster beats are the baby's."

"Is it supposed to beat that fast?"

"Yes, all babies have a much faster heart rate than adults. It's completely normal. Okay, now it's time for me to check you on the inside. Are you ready? Squeeze Emily's hand if it feels uncomfortable. I'll try to do this as quickly as I can." She pulled a latex glove on over her right hand and squirted a clear jelly from a tube on her index and middle fingers. "Pull your feet up next to your bum now, Anna, and let your knees fall to the sides. That's a girl. Good. Now you're going to feel me touching you."

For a moment, Emily felt herself going down the rabbit hole of memory, reliving her own examination by Dr. Merritt in another lifetime, but shook the images from her head. Anna was trying to hold back tears and needed her full attention at this moment to avoid remembering events that were much more recent Emily's. "You're doing great, Anna. Just think about the baby. You're doing this for the baby. Your dad is never going to hurt you again. Take a deep breath and feel my hand holding yours. That's my girl!"

Before they knew it, the midwife was withdrawing her hand, and it was over. "That's it. All done. Now that wasn't so bad, was it."

Doubtful, Anna nevertheless shook her head. "Is everything okay?"

"Everything is perfect. Your pelvis is wide enough to make room for the baby's head, so delivery should be relatively smooth. Go ahead and sit up, and we'll go back into the living room to chat."

For the next half hour, Mrs. Hough talked to them about what to expect in the next four months, what kinds of food Anna should be eating to provide healthy nutrients to the baby, and when she would be returning for follow-up visits. When she finished, she handed Anna a bottle of special vitamins and admonished her not to forget. "You're getting a late start on these, so you need to be faithful in taking them daily. Do you understand?"

The young woman nodded. "I do. Every morning like you said. Thank you so much. I feel a lot less scared now I know the baby's alright. I'm so grateful, Mrs. Hough. Truly."

"Alright, now that we've gotten all that over with, please just call me Dorothy. I know a lot of other midwives prefer to be more formal, but I always find it puts my patients more at ease to call me by my first name. I'll be off then. I'll see you again in a month."

Emily escorted the woman to the door with a smile. "I can't tell you what a huge help you've been, Dorothy. You have really eased our fears and prepared us for what's to come. Many thanks. See you soon."

The two women shook hands. "It was my pleasure, Emily. Goodbye, Anna." The door closed, and she was gone. Emily joined Anna on the couch and the two sat in silence for a very long time, absorbing the reality of this baby coming into the world and what it would mean for both of them.

For the next few days, Anna alternated between happiness and anxiety. The visit from the midwife had made her pregnancy very real and exciting, and she began to be more alert to the baby's movement and to wonder if it would be a boy or girl. But the reality also caused anxiety as she worried about the birth, the prospect of breast feeding, and how they were going to afford all the things a baby needs. In order to distract her, Emily plopped down at the kitchen table one evening while Anna was studying, and said, "Okay, tell me more about Jack. If we're going to find him, I need to know about his personality, his interests, anything that would help me know where to look."

Anna shrugged. "I don't know. He was my big brother. He looked after me as best he could, but he didn't know what Dad was doing in the middle of the night. He was feisty though. He didn't back down from an argument with Dad, and they both ended up with black eyes and bruises when it got bad. He loved being outdoors, and he hated school, so he didn't mind too much when Dad made him quit when he was twelve and get a job to help out with money."

"So, what kind of work did he do?"

"I'm not sure exactly. I was only eight at the time, so I wasn't paying all that much attention. Sometimes he and Dad would talk about it at the dinner table, and I think they said something about 'the mill,' but that's all I really know."

"Well, that's a good start. What kind of clothes did he wear when he went to work?"

"Um, I think long-sleeved flannel shirts, and he always came home a mess. Mom was forever yelling at him to brush off the sawdust before he came in the house. Then she'd grab a broom and start sweeping, muttering under her breath the whole time."

"See, you remember more than you thought! This is a big help. I'll start asking around the local sawmills and see if anyone there has heard of Jack. What does he look like? That will help too."

"Um, he was pretty tall and lanky. But he was strong, and he could defend himself in a fight. Dark, curly hair and brown eyes like me. And he had a dimple in one cheek. Girls thought he was dishy, which bothered my mom no end. She was constantly on him about being careful not to fall into temptation. He'd just tell her she was his only girl, and she'd laugh and wave him away." Anna's eyes glittered with tears. "I miss him so bad."

Emily got up and hugged her. "I'm sure you do, honey, and I'm going to do my best to find him for you. But that's enough for now. Let's go over your spelling words, shall we?"

When Saturday dawned, Emily resisted the desire to stay in bed for just a while longer and instead rose to dress for a day of visiting local sawmills. She donned corduroy slacks, sturdy walking shoes, and a pullover sweater. Considering the low clouds, she added her oilskin jacket, which Mr. Graves had recommended she buy the first time she'd shown up in the office soaking wet from a sudden downpour. She reached for a canister on the top shelf of a kitchen cabinet and withdrew a few dollars from her dwindling emergency cache. The bus wouldn't take her all the way to Lake Washington, where most of the lumber industry was centered, so she was going to have to take a taxi for part of the trip. Then, armed with a list of mills she had procured from the paper's business editor, she left a note for the still sleeping Anna and pulled the door closed behind her.

At the first mill, Emily was overwhelmed by the noise and frantic activity. She looked for an office, but when she finally found a small room with a desk and chair, it was empty. She returned to the main yard and tried to flag down one of the many men driving forklifts, running from one building to the next, or sweeping tailings from the floor of a vast warehouse. She was chagrined to find that, far from standing out as a woman in a man's world, it was as if they didn't see her at all. Finally, a gruff voice behind her shouted, "What are you doing here?" She turned to see a large and angry man bearing down on her.

She felt a flash of panic before logic told her it was doubtful this man would assault her in the middle of the yard. She squared her shoulders and spoke. "I need to speak with a supervisor. I'm looking for someone, and I was told he might be working here." The last part wasn't exactly the truth, but she doubted she would be given the time of day if she admitted that this was a shot in the dark.

"Well, I'm the crew boss, so I'd be the one to know who's on the payroll and who's not. Who is it? I ain't got all day."

"I'm looking for Jack Beecher. He'd be about eighteen, tall and dark-haired. Do you know him?"

"Nah, never heard of 'im. Sorry, lady. Now you best get out of the way before you get run over around here."

Emily thanked the man and turned away in disappointment. Realistically, she knew the odds were long that she would find Jack the first place she stopped. She would be lucky if she found him at all. Steeling herself for a long day, she checked her list for the next mill and strode down the rutted and muddy road. By mid-afternoon, she had been to three more mills with the same result and more or less the same level of resentment for her interruption of the men's work. Discouraged and weary, she decided to try one more yard before calling it quits for the day. This last establishment seemed larger than the others and had an air of prosperity they had lacked. The movements of the workers seemed more purposeful than chaotic, and the moment she entered the yard, a man in a yellow hard hat lifted his eyes from a clipboard and asked, "Ma'am, are you lost? What can I do for you?"

"No, not lost, just looking for somebody. Is there a Jack Beecher that works here?"

"Nope. Not anymore at least. Why are you looking for him? Did he run out on you?"

"Oh no, not at all. I'm, uh, his older sister, and he's been estranged from the family for a while, but there is a family situation that he needs to know about. Do you know where he is?"

"No, ma'am. I'm sure sorry. He worked for me for a year or so—a real hard worker, but boy, did he have a temper! Anyway, he got into it with one of the other guys six months back. They went at it pretty good. Jack busted the guy's nose and then up and quit. Haven't seen him since."

"Oh, dear! I had so hoped to find him. I don't know what we're going to do now!" Emily brushed away an imaginary tear, shocked at her ability to be so disingenuous.

"Now, now. Don't give up hope. I'm sure he'll show up eventually. Tell you what. You give me a phone number or an address, and I'll let you know if he comes back here or if I hear anything about him through the grapevine. You never know."

"Oh, sir! That would be so kind of you." Emily pulled a wrinkled piece of paper out of her purse, along with the pencil she kept with her in case inspiration for a poem struck at an inopportune moment. She scribbled her contact information down and added the name Anna Beecher. She handed it to the man and thanked him profusely. As she strode down the yard and out the front gate, she marveled at the renewed energy she felt from just this little spark of hope.

The following Saturday, Emily got up for round two of her search for Jack. She had decided that the next best place for a young man without specialized skills to find work might be on one of the fishing boats that supplied seafood to the local markets and restaurants. She hadn't had time to visit the waterfront since she had taken Anna in, and as she dressed, her anticipation let her know how much she had missed it. In her pocket were several pieces of paper with Anna's name, the address of the apartment building, and the number of the pay phone in the lobby that tenants used when needed. After having to scramble to find a piece of paper and pencil the week before, this time she planned to hand out contact information to everyone she talked to, whether they knew Jack or not.

As Emily stepped off the bus, she took a deep breath of the salty air. The sun was shining for a change and light glittered on the choppy water of the bay. She felt something shift in her, a lightening of breath, a calming of the whirling thoughts she'd been experiencing since Anna had asked her to raise her baby. She realized that she couldn't avoid the decision too much longer, and this lovely day was as good a time to ponder as any. After making the rounds of commercial fishing vessels with no results, she began to stroll along the wharf, enjoying the strange mixture of beauty and grittiness that characterized the harbor. A pair of harbor seals cavorted on a weathered dock, their loud barks adding to the cacophony of shouting dock workers and ferry blasts. A nearby bench beckoned, and she sat down to rest. Setting aside mundane thoughts, Emily slowed her breathing and stilled her mind in hopes of hearing the voice of wisdom that had sometimes guided her in the past. So many questions arose. Will Anna change her mind once the baby is born? Is this what's best for the baby and for Anna? Am I prepared to be connected to Anna through this child for the long term? Would I be a good mother? Is this what I want?

It was at this last question that Emily realized the answer was an emphatic "Yes!" Through all the months of trying to get pregnant with George, it was the prospect of having a baby of her own that kept her going. Despite the trials of living with the Huttons, she had adored caring for Meg and Joey. She knew that the same traits her own mother had possessed were in her as well, and that she would be a good and loving mother. It occurred to her that the practical question—how can I afford this— had not been a part of her thought process. They could cross that bridge when they came to it. She remembered her talk with Anna about God providing for orphans and widows and decided to have faith in that promise. She began to imagine what it would feel like to say yes. Warmth started to spread through her body despite the chill wind. She felt impossibly happy and realized that she was smiling widely. She glanced around, but nobody was paying her any attention. She laughed out loud. She couldn't wait to get home and tell Anna.

Chapter 20

'Tis the absence of fear
that opens my eyes
to Beauty,
however ephemeral,
however small.
Each vision imprints itself
on my soul,
reawakened to grace,
to light glittering on water,
to the countless moments
when the holy
meets and transforms
the profane.
Daily miracles sing,
sparkling windows on shabby walls
revealing heaven—
so much closer
than we think.
　　　　—Emily

December 1960

With several months of working in the copy-editing department, Emily was feeling comfortable in the hectic environment and confident in her work. Her co-workers were accepting and friendly, and Mr. Graves was proving to be an exceptional boss. The office flourished under his benevolent management style of praise and encouragement rather than criticism. He was kind and considerate, and he shied away from authoritarianism. The staff respected him and worked hard to gain his respect in return. While completely professional when on the clock, his demeanor during breaks and lunch hour was more casual, which allowed the workers to relax and truly enjoy their break time. He showed an interest in the lives of his employees and joined in their friendly banter. In this atmosphere, Emily found herself more and more at ease and able to come out of the shell that had developed over years of social isolation and anxiety.

Thanksgiving had come and gone, and the talk had begun to turn to Christmas. One day at lunch, someone called out, "Hey! Who's going to the Christmas Ship Parade this year? It's coming up next weekend." Others chimed in with enthusiastic assents and memories of past years' events. After a few minutes, Mr. Graves noticed that Emily hadn't joined in the conversation.

"Emily, I keep forgetting that you're new to the Seattle area. You probably have no idea what we're talking about! The Christmas Ship Parade is a parade of boats—sailboats, motorboats, tugboats, even canoes and rubber dinghies—that cruise around Lake Washington every Christmastime. All the boats are decked out in Christmas lights and ornaments. Some even have a Santa or nativity scene. It's quite a spectacle and something every Seattleite should see. It's our tradition for everyone in the office to go together, and it's great fun. You should come with us! I'd be glad to pick you up—I doubt you could find our secret vantage point on your own." The rest of the office chimed in, urging Emily to join them.

At first hesitant and unsure how it would be to go on an outing with her boss, the general atmosphere of excitement and camaraderie infected her, and she nodded her head. "It sounds wonderful. I'd love to go!"

As Emily got ready for the event the following Saturday, she realized that she was quite nervous. She looked over her scanty wardrobe with a jaundiced eye, fearing that nothing there would be appropriate for the evening. Attempting to strike a balance between warmth and attractiveness, she thought she would probably fail at both. Finally, she settled for the same outfit she had worn while searching lumber yards and the waterfront looking for Jack, grateful that she had laundered them in the meantime. Clean and warm would have to do. Anna was oddly quiet and failed to answer Emily's goodbye as she left the apartment and ran downstairs to meet Mr. Graves.

He pulled up promptly in a blue and white Ford Fairlane that had seen better days. Her boss hopped out and went around to open the door for Emily, greeting her with a smile as he took her elbow to help her into the car. "Good evening, Emily. I'm glad to see that you're dressed for the cold. I brought a couple of blankets for us, as it can get breezy near the water. I've got a thermos of hot chocolate too, so we should be plenty warm."

He got back in the driver's seat and pulled away from the curb. Emily was surprised that there was no one else in the car. She had assumed that there would be others riding with them. An awkward silence ensued as Emily glanced around the car, trying to think of something to say. Her eyes fell on Mr. Graves's hands as they gripped the steering wheel, and for the first time, she noticed he wasn't wearing a wedding ring. For some reason, she had always assumed that he was married, even though she realized now that she had never heard him mention a wife or children. Finally, she spoke. "Will we be meeting the others there?"

"Yes, most of them live farther away from the paper, so it's easier for them to go straight to our usual meeting place. I'm glad you are coming with us tonight. I'm anxious to see what you think of our unique celebration of the holidays. Did Spokane have any special traditions that you enjoyed?"

"Nothing like this," Emily responded, "All our focus was on the Lilac Festival in spring. There were two parades—the Torchlight Parade on Friday night, and the main event the next day. The streets were lined with people for blocks and blocks."

"Sounds like a great tradition! What was your favorite part?"

"Oh, definitely the floats! They were so beautiful, decorated with all kinds of flowers, not just lilacs." They continued to chat about their respective hometowns until they arrived at a dead-end street where a few cars were parked.

Mr. Graves pulled up behind one of the cars and said, "Good! The others are here. Let me get the door for you."

He again took Emily's arm to help her out, grabbed a thermos and blanket out of the back seat, then pointed with a flashlight in the direction of a rough path that lead up a hill to the right. A few large homes loomed above them, Christmas lights glowing in the dark. Soon they heard familiar voices as they rounded

a corner and saw their co-workers seated on a pile of boulders.
Everyone greeted the latecomers enthusiastically and made room for
them to sit. Emily had kept her eyes on the trail until then, but now
was able to gaze at their surroundings. Lake Washington spread out
before her, a mere stone's throw away and slightly below their perch.
The surface of the water was ruffled by a slight wind, causing
reflected lights to scatter into shimmering pieces of glass. She gasped
with delight.

"It's beautiful, isn't it," Mr. Graves remarked.

"I didn't expect to be this close to the water. This is a lovely
spot! How on earth did you discover it?"

"John Berger's aunt and uncle live just above us and don't
mind us sitting here for the parade. It's a perfect vantage point. Now,
keep your eye out. If you look over to the left, you'll see the lead ship
appearing through the Montlake Cut, and then the other waiting
boats will follow."

Across the lake, Emily saw what appeared to be a flotilla of
boats gathered, ready to begin their circumnavigation of the
shoreline. Lights from the houses above began going out so as not to
compete with the lights that were beginning to be turned on in the
boats. The banter of her co-workers diminished in expectation of the
spectacle about to begin. And then a single large sailing vessel
appeared, arrayed in hundreds of lights, and turned to follow the
shoreline. Soon, one by one, the line of boats that had been waiting
peeled off to follow the lead ship around the lake. Still too far away
to see details, Emily was nonetheless mesmerized by the chain of
colored lights. She shivered, and someone put a mug of hot cocoa in
her hand.

The impact of this moving string of boats scattering light
across the water was breathtaking. By the time the first vessel neared
their vantage point, Emily was barely breathing in her anticipation.
And then it was there, gliding past them in all its glory. White lights
were strung along every mast, and blue lights lined the gunnels. A
large Christmas tree served as the mast head, and wreaths adorned
the sides of the boat. Emily exhaled with a reverent "Ohhh . . . ."
Boat after boat followed, each a unique expression of the season.
Santas and elves were followed by angels and manger scenes,
followed by snowmen, stars, and giant Christmas packages made

completely of lights. Some boats had passengers who sang familiar Christmas carols, and the watchers on shore joined in. There was a sense of connection and peace like nothing Emily had ever experienced. Time lost all meaning in the face of such beauty. Even after the last boat had passed, no one moved, each reluctant for the evening to end. They continued to watch as the parade began to break up, each boat returning to its own moorage, the uniform circle turning into a series of lines across the water, reflections scattering into a thousand points of light.

Finally someone stretched, stood, stomped their feet, rubbed buttocks numb from sitting on the rocks. Conversation started up again: "This was even better than last year;" "The tugboat was my favorite;" "Wasn't that manger scene beautiful?!"

Mr. Graves turned to Emily, who was still silent. "How did you like it?"

"I'm speechless! It was the most beautiful thing I've ever seen! Thank you so much for bringing me."

"It was my pleasure, Emily. It really was delightful, wasn't it?"

She nodded with a beaming smile. Everyone began gathering their belongings and making their way back down the trail to their cars. The ride back went quickly as Emily and Mr. Graves compared notes on their favorite displays. Before she knew it, he was parking the car at the curb in front of her building. Again, he came around to open the door for her. He placed his hand at her elbow to help her out, and Emily stood and stepped away from the curb. She became aware that his hand was still there as he walked her to the entrance. She turned to face him.

"Thank you again for a lovely time, Mr. Graves. I enjoyed it very much."

"Please, when we're outside the office, you can call me Paul. I'm so glad you came tonight. It was wonderful to see the parade through a newcomer's eyes." He paused. "Would you consider having dinner with me next weekend?"

Emily's heart fluttered in her chest, and suddenly she couldn't catch her breath. She opened her mouth to speak, and nothing came out. Finally, she caught hold of one possible response from out of the maelstrom. "I . . . um . . . are you sure that's appropriate?"

Paul smiled. "If you're worried about appearances, there's no policy against dating co-workers. In fact, I can name at least four inter-staff marriages I've attended in the ten years I've been with the paper."

Emily looked down and took a deep breath, brain spinning. What could she possibly say? Part of her wanted to say yes, and part of her was terrified. The only thing she could think of to explain her reluctance was the truth. "It's not just that. I . . . one of the other reasons I left Spokane was because of a relationship that ended badly. I guess it's made me a little gun shy. Would you let me think about it before I give you my answer?" It was the truth, just not the whole truth.

Paul gave her a look of concern. "I'm sorry. That must have been very painful. Of course, you can think about it. Take all the time you need."

"Thank you, Paul. I appreciate your understanding. Well, I guess I'd better get inside before my toes fall off. Good night."

"Good night, Emily. Sleep well."

She smiled and turned to unlock the door. With one more backward glance, she went in and ran up the stairs. Her arm still tingled where Paul's hand had been. He watched her go, lingering for a moment in the light of the streetlamp, then walked to the car and drove away.

For the next few days, Paul's dinner invitation was all Emily could think about. She felt flattered that he would think of her in this way and had to admit to herself that she was attracted to him as well. And yet, hadn't she felt the same way about George, and look how that had turned out. Still, this felt different somehow, and she felt she knew Paul better from working with him for the past several months than she had ever known George. But how could she begin a relationship with Paul when she was still legally married to someone else? It felt dishonest to keep a secret about something that had the potential to ruin everything when the truth ultimately came out. What if the relationship became serious, and Paul asked her to marry him? Then what would she do? And then a voice in her head chided her for making too much out of the situation. Just one date couldn't hurt, could it?

When she walked into work on Tuesday, she saw Mr. Graves

waving her back to his office. Anticipating that he was going to press her for an answer, her heart began to pound. When she entered, he greeted her with a broad grin and said, "Just the person I wanted to see! Please sit down."

"What is it you need, Mr. Graves?"

"Well, I've been thinking about your reaction to the Christmas Ship Parade and about that poem of yours we published recently. So, I called Mr. Stone down in Features and asked him if he would be interested in an article about the parade through the poetic eyes of a newcomer to the city. He was very excited about the idea and would love to see what you could come up with. No guarantee of making it into the paper of course, but I have confidence that you will write something he will want to print. What do you think?"

"Oh, my goodness, I'd be honored! I would love to write something about the parade! I'll do my best not to disappoint you or the paper."

"I don't think I could ever be disappointed in any of your work, Emily. And by the way, have you thought about my dinner invitation yet?"

There it was. And without even thinking, she said, "I, uh, yes, I have. I accept your kind invitation. Unless, of course, you've had second thoughts."

"No second thoughts or third thoughts! In fact, I'm delighted! How's Saturday? Seven o'clock?"

Emily nodded. "That would be lovely. I look forward to it." As she walked back to her desk, she realized she was smiling. Nonetheless, there was a whisper of doubt inside her head, saying "What have you done?" This whisper was quickly pushed aside by her excitement about having an actual writing assignment.

That night over dinner, Emily told Anna about both her work news and her date, excited to share her happy news. But instead of the pleased response she expected, she was surprised by an outburst of anger totally uncharacteristic of her young friend.

"I knew it! You've been distant ever since your outing on Saturday, and now you have a date? I can just see it now. You're going to fall in love with this guy, whoever he is, and then it's all over for me. I'll be on the street again, and this time with a baby to feed and clothe. You promised to take care of us, and now you're prepared to throw it all away."

"Anna! I have no intention of backing out on my commitment to you and the baby! I have no idea whether this will lead to a relationship or not, but for now it's just one date. Let's not get ahead of ourselves. I care about you, and I am committed to raising this baby. Please believe me."

The younger woman seemed to calm down a little. "I'm sorry. It's just that you've been so different the past few days, staring off into space and not responding when I ask you a question. I've had to say things two and three times before you even realize I'm in the room. I can see the look on your face, and it's clear that you really like this man, even though you've never mentioned him to me before. I worry about my future all the time, and my mom's example of putting my abusive dad ahead of her own daughter doesn't exactly give me confidence that you won't do the same."

"Oh, honey, I'm sorry that I've been distracted. Now that you say it, I realize that you've been a little irritable these past few days. I should have been more observant and asked you what was wrong. I completely understand your fears, but I have made a promise to you, and I'm going to keep it. And 'this man' as you call him, is my boss, and he is a very good man. I doubt it would ever come to a point of having to choose between him and you, assuming this even goes beyond the first date. Let's not put the cart before the horse."

Emily got up and walked around the table to give Anna a hug. Anna's response was lukewarm, as if she was still distrustful of the situation but willing to wait and see. "Now," Emily said as she returned to her seat, "how did your studies go today?"

As Saturday approached, Emily became more and more anxious. She remembered George's inquisition on their first date and tried to figure out how she would respond if Mr. Graves asked personal questions about her past. Then there was the question of what she would wear. Nothing in her meager closet seemed appropriate for a date, and her budget didn't stretch far enough for a new dress. On the off chance she might find something both appropriate and affordable, she stopped in at the Goodwill store immediately after work on Friday when they had extended hours. She looked through several racks until she found a woolen emerald green sheath with a jewel neckline. It was slightly worn, but not so badly that a man would notice, especially in a dimly lit restaurant. Thus it was that she walked down the stairs on Saturday evening, feeling confident in her appearance if not in her ability to navigate the first date she'd had in years.

Paul was already waiting at the curb as Emily emerged from her building. He greeted her warmly and held the door open for her. As they drove off, he said, "I hope you like Chinese."

"I do! I hadn't ever eaten it before I moved here, but I've come to love it. Not that I eat out very often, because that's not in the budget, but the couple times I tried it were very good."

"Well then, you're going to love this place! It's not the poshest restaurant in town, but the food is out of this world. I eat there so often everyone knows my name."

Soon he was parking in front of a dimly lit area of Chinatown and helping her out of the car. The storefront was less than inviting, but the interior was warm and cheerful despite the aging wallpaper and worn fabrics of the decor. As predicted, Mr. Graves was greeted by name and immediately led to a table in the corner. Menus were presented, and after one look, Emily was overwhelmed at the huge selection. Noticing her dismay, Paul said, "That's how I felt the first time I ate here. It's a lot to take in. Since you're relatively new to Chinese food, do you mind if I order for you? Is there anything you particularly don't like?"

"I don't mind at all, in fact, I'd be glad if you did. The only thing I'd prefer to avoid are dishes that are too spicy."

Just then the waiter appeared, and Paul began reeling off their order. He and the waiter bantered like old friends as Emily looked around the restaurant. She couldn't help but compare it to her first date with George at the Davenport Hotel. She much preferred this casual but homey atmosphere to the stuffiness of the Davenport's elegance.

As they waited for their meal, the two chatted easily about work and co-workers. Soon, several platters arrived, and Paul began dishing portions from each one onto Emily's plate. She looked at the pile of food with dismay. "How am I ever going to be able to eat all of this?"

Paul laughed. "Wait and see. And if you don't finish, you can take the leftovers home with you. Now dig in!"

Upon tasting her first bite, Emily closed her eyes and moaned with pleasure "Oh, my! This is wonderful!"

"I knew you'd like it."

Just then, their waiter appeared with a pot of tea. As he pushed aside some of the platters to make room for it, he accidentally slopped a bit of the tea onto the table. Emily froze in anticipation of an angry scene. The waiter apologized, and Paul just laughed. "Don't worry, Chen. Accidents happen. I doubt that a few drops of tea on the table are going to ruin our dinner. Now, if you had spilled it on my shrimp chow mein, that would have been a different story!"

Chen smiled. "I thought that's how you liked it!" Then he walked back into the kitchen flipping the damp towel over his shoulder. Emily let out her breath with relief. Both of them dug back into their food and were silent for several minutes as they enjoyed the meal.

Then, taking the bull by the horns, Emily asked Paul, "So you said you've been at the paper for ten years. Tell me about your life before that."

"Well, I was born and raised right here in Seattle. My dad worked at the P-I doing maintenance on the presses, so I spent a lot of time there as a kid, and it got into my blood. I went to college right here at UW, got a scholarship for crewing, and didn't do too bad. Of course, not as good as the famous crew team that went to the Olympics in '36. Those guys were heroes around here when I was a kid."

"Um, I hate to sound ignorant, but what's crewing?"

"Oh, sorry. I forget that not everybody knows the sport like we do here in Seattle. It's basically competitive rowing. The boat is called a scull or shell, and it's quite long and narrow. It can be done as an individual sport, pairs, or a team. I'll take you down to Lake Washington in the summer so you can see the rowers practicing. It's beautiful to watch, very graceful, and the teamwork is poetry in motion. I think you'll love it."

"It sounds wonderful. I'd love to see it."

Paul met her eyes, and said, "Now, what about you? You're something of a mystery woman around the office, because you never talk about yourself. You do what you just did with me—ask everyone else about their lives while avoiding any questions about you. Other than that you came from Spokane, and you write beautifully, I know almost nothing about you."

Emily met his gaze but didn't immediately respond. She wondered if there would ever be a time when she wouldn't have to think so hard about how to answer personal questions, how much information to share, what to keep in the dark closet of her mind, and what she would have to fudge the truth about. She found that she didn't want to do that with Paul but wasn't ready to tell her story either. She took a deep breath as she began to speak.

"It's a long and sordid story, Paul, one that I'm not quite ready to share. I fear that it would just be depressing and ruin our lovely evening. Is that alright with you?"

Paul looked at her intently for a long moment. "Of course, it's alright, Emily. It's your story. I've sensed that life wasn't always hunky-dory for you. There's a haunted look you get sometimes when someone else is talking about their own difficulties or when there's a tragic news story in the paper. Tell you what—let's try this. I'll ask you a question that I think wouldn't require you to delve too deeply into your troubles, and you can decide whether you want to answer or not."

"Thank you for understanding. Sometimes I feel on the outside of so much that goes on in the office, but I don't know how to belong when I carry around all this darkness. So yes, ask your question, and I'll answer as best I can."

Paul placed his hand over hers where it lay on the table. His smile was somewhat melancholy, and then his normal cheerful expression took over. "Okay! Let's see . . . how about this. What is your happiest memory?"

Emily's eyes brightened. "That's easy! Stargazing with my mother! We used to go outside at night in the summer when the house was too hot and lay on the grass looking up at the stars. She would hold my hand and say, 'What do you see up there, Ladybug?' And we would make up different names for the constellations. Like, when she first showed me Orion, she didn't tell me it was supposed to be a hunter, and I said it looked like a lopsided butterfly. From then on, that's how we always referred to it. It wasn't until I was studying the stars in sixth grade that I learned its real name!"

Paul laughed. "That's a great story, Emily. I love how your mother called you Ladybug. Is there a story behind that?"

"I'm not sure really. She had called me that ever since I can remember. It's hard to say what came first, the nickname or the fact that I always liked ladybugs and would let them crawl around on my hands until they flew away. Thanks for reminding me of that."

"You're welcome! And here comes Chen with our fortune cookies. Let's see what our future holds."

Paul looked seriously at his fortune and intoned, "Your companion will achieve greatness someday."

Emily grabbed the slip of paper out of his hands. "It does not say that! It says your family will prosper."

"You never know. Both could be true." They were both still chuckling as they went out to the car. There was a comfortable silence as Paul drove Emily back to her apartment. He escorted her to the door and gazed down at her. "I had a lovely time. Thank you for agreeing to come out with me. I hope we can do it again soon."

Emily smiled. "I'd like that." He leaned toward her and kissed her gently on the cheek, then bade her farewell. Emily watched until he was out of sight, then rearranged her expression so that Anna wouldn't see just how much she had enjoyed her date. "I just need to give her time to adjust," she thought, unaware that this meant she had already decided to see Paul again. She floated up the stairs.

A couple days later, Paul caught up with Emily in the hall at work. "Hey, what do you think about going down to Pike Place Market on Saturday? It's a great place to go if you still have Christmas shopping to do, and there will be holiday lights and Christmas carolers all over the place. We can eat lunch at Ivar's Acres of Clams. They have the best clam chowder in the city and a great view of the bay. What do you say?"

Without even thinking, Emily said, "I'd love to! It sounds wonderful."

"Great! I'll pick you up at ten. And now I'd better scurry to my meeting with the big boss. Talk to you later." Emily watched him walk down the hall, a bemused look on her face, ignoring the internal whisper that she was walking a dangerous path.

At breakfast Saturday morning, Anna barely spoke, a stormy look on her face. In fact, she had been in a bad mood since Emily had informed her of another outing with her boss. She was trying to hang on to Emily's promise that she wouldn't abandon her, but a second date so soon after the first did not bode well for the pregnant teen. She tried to be polite, not wanting to do or say anything that would make Emily mad, but it was hard to maintain a cheerful demeanor. Wisely, Emily chose not to comment on Anna's silence. She tried to tamp down her excitement, knowing that would only make the tension worse.

By the time Paul and Emily arrived at Pike Street, crowds were already milling around in the square outside the popular market. After driving in circles for several minutes, Paul finally found a place to park several blocks away. Emily shivered in the chill air as they walked and turned up the collar of her winter coat. Paul took her hand, and it seemed like the most natural thing in the world. She turned to look at him and smiled brightly. Christmas lights blinked from the many shops they passed, and Emily could hear carolers ahead of them, strains of "falalalala" reverberating from the canyon of tall buildings as they walked. They spent the morning browsing the many stalls filled with gifts, foodstuffs, and Christmas decorations. Emily bought Anna a book and a pair of gloves plus a small manger scene to decorate the apartment. While she was looking at a particularly delightful selection of Santa figurines, Paul disappeared for a few moments, then returned looking like the cat that ate the cream.

"Are you getting hungry for lunch? I know I could stand to be inside where it's warmer. Let's head over to Ivar's." Emily nodded her agreement. The walk took several minutes, but soon they were being seated in a booth overlooking the water.

"This is beautiful! I love the nautical decor." Emily looked around at the fishing nets draped on the walls, the glass floats arranged artfully among the nets, old anchors and diving helmets placed here and there.

Paul smiled. "I love seeing things through your eyes. I think I take the beauty of Seattle for granted most of the time, but you make me appreciate it in a whole new way. Speaking of which, I have some news for you. I spoke to Harold Stone yesterday, and he was very pleased with your piece on the Christmas Ship Parade. It seems that he has already received a number of letters from readers saying how much they enjoyed the article and wanting to see more of your take on Seattle's places and events. So, Harold wants you to write a monthly feature on your explorations of the city. You would be paid per line just like our other contract writers. What do you think?"

"What? Are you teasing me? That would be marvelous! I'm so grateful for your championing me with Mr. Stone. I never dreamed I would be able to make money doing what I love to do."

"I thought you might be pretty tickled by this news. And you sure deserve it. The way you describe things makes readers feel like they are right there with you. It's like you're painting a picture with words."

Their conversation eventually moved on to other topics—favorite foods, music, and Christmas plans. When Paul mentioned his family traditions, Emily asked, "You didn't mention any siblings last time we went out. Do you have brothers and sisters?"

Paul grinned. "You might say so. I have two older brothers and a sister. She's the youngest, and believe me, she is completely spoiled. All of us boys were so glad not to have another brother to compete with, we treated her like a little princess. In fact, sometimes we still call her that. What about you?"

"No siblings. I'm an only child, and both my parents were too. I always thought it would be great to have a brother or sister, but it wasn't to be, I guess."

"Okay, am I allowed another question?" Emily nodded. "What is your favorite Christmas tradition?"

Smiling, Emily responded without having to pause to think about how to answer. "Oh, definitely the department store Christmas displays! My parents used to take me into downtown Spokane at night to see them, especially the windows at the Crescent. I could have looked at them for hours if they'd have let me. Elves making toys and Santa loading the sleigh, children skating on ponds made of giant mirrors or sledding on hillsides of fake snow. It was magical!"

"I loved those too. Frederick and Nelson still create Christmas displays here. In fact, the store isn't that far out of our way. Maybe we could go see them on our way back to the car?"

Emily clapped her hands in delight. "I would love to!"

Lunch over, the pair decided they'd had enough shopping for one day and walked hand in hand toward the big department store.

Christmas music was playing from loudspeakers along the sidewalks, and occasionally Paul would sing along in a rich baritone voice, prompting Emily to join in. Sometimes they would stumble over the words and laugh. However, when they reached Frederick and Nelson, they grew silent except for Emily's whispered, "Oh!" In an instant, both of them were transported to childhood, entranced by the scenes in the windows—a gingerbread village, a winter wonderland, giant toys under a massive Christmas tree, ballerinas and snowmen and a sleeping Santa next to a sign that said "December 26th."

Finally, Emily turned to look at Paul, face glowing. "Thank you so much for bringing me here. I can't tell you what this means to me."

He smiled. "It really is wonderful, isn't it? And I bet I know what your next column is going to be about."

Before long, the winter light began to fade, and it was time to go. When they arrived back at Emily's building, Paul turned to her and said, "Will you let me escort you up to your apartment? I feel like a real heel just dropping you off outside."

Emily paused, caught off guard by his request. "I, um, that's probably not a good idea. I have a roommate, and, uh, she's very shy."

He looked puzzled but didn't push the issue. "Okay, maybe some other time. Let me just get the car door for you." As Emily stepped out of the car, he took her elbow. "As usual, I had a swell time. We'll do it again soon."

She smiled. "I'd like that. It was a great day. Thank you again."

He walked her over to the vestibule and again kissed her gently on the cheek before saying goodbye and returning to his car. As Emily watched him go, she thought, "I could get used to this."

On Tuesday afternoon, Paul stopped by Emily's desk and spoke quietly. "Since we only work a half-day on Christmas Eve, do you want to have lunch with me before we race off to our Christmas engagements?"

"That sounds lovely! Count me in."

And so it was that the two were seated across the table from one another at The Dog House restaurant, a popular Seattle hangout. Paul reached across the table to take Emily's hand. "I'm glad you agreed to this. I wanted to spend at least a little time with you to celebrate Christmas. I would have invited you to my parents' annual Christmas Eve bash, but I fear it would have overwhelmed you. They ask everyone they know, and it can get a little wild. My parents don't drink much normally, but this party is the exception. To say the booze flows freely would be an understatement, and that just doesn't seem like it would be your scene. And then the whole family gathers for Christmas Day dinner, and I didn't think you'd enjoy having my siblings and their spouses staring at you and speculating about our relationship. They have been trying to get me married off for years!"

"I'd say your instincts are on the money." Emily replied. "The last party I attended was for my ninth birthday, and the punch was made with cherry Kool-Aid and ginger ale!"

Paul laughed. "Then I definitely don't want to expose you to some of my parents' friends and neighbors." Then he reached into the inside pocket of his overcoat and pulled out a brightly wrapped gift. "But I did want an opportunity to give you this."

"Paul! You didn't have to do that. I didn't get you anything. Oh, dear!" Emily's face turned red with embarrassment.

"No need to fret, Emily. I wasn't expecting you to. It's just something I saw when we were at the Pike Street Market, and I knew it would be perfect for you. Please open it."

Emily carefully peeled back the wrapping paper to reveal a flat white box. She lifted the lid and pulled away the tissue paper that covered its contents. Inside was a beautiful leather-bound book with the words "Emily's Journal" in gilt letters embossed on the front. Inside were lined parchment pages just waiting to be written on. "Oh, Paul," she gasped, "it's beautiful!"

"Seeing your face right now is the only gift I need. I'm glad you like it. I've seen the scraps of paper you write your poetry and articles on, and I think your writing is worthy of something much more elegant. You really are a wonderful writer, Emily, and I want you to believe it, too. Maybe this will help you do that."

Face alight with pleasure, Emily thanked Paul profusely. "This is perfect! Sincerely, it's the best Christmas gift I've received since my parents bought me my first baby doll. I will treasure this."

He reached across the table to take her hand. "I hope you know how fond I am of you. I'm glad this makes you happy." Just then their food arrived, saving Emily from the need for a response. The two dug into their food, and the moment passed, but Emily was intensely aware that this was no longer a casual dating relationship. It felt like the point of no return had passed, and that a time was coming when she would have to tell Paul the truth of her life. Underneath her happiness was a quiver of fear that she was headed for heartbreak.

Later that night, Emily and Anna walked to church under a clear starlit sky, turning their collars up against the cold. Anna had never been to a Christmas Eve service, since her childhood church had ignored the Christmas story in favor of an emphasis on sin and salvation. When they entered the church, Anna gasped at the sight of candles twinkling everywhere in the darkened sanctuary. Huge swags of evergreen boughs were draped along the front railings, and a giant Christmas tree decorated with golden stars dominated the chancel. Anna turned to look at Emily with wonder in her eyes, and Emily smiled and squeezed her hand. The two women sidled into a pew and sat, entranced by the beautiful sound of the choir singing "O Come All Ye Faithful" to begin the service. Familiar words washed over Emily as the service progressed, the scripture passage of the nativity and Christmas hymns speaking of peace and joy and sparking memories of Christmases long past, before the world had become a harsher place.

Even though it was late by the time Anna and Emily returned home, they made hot cocoa and sat near their simply decorated Christmas tree, enjoying the colored lights shining in the darkness. There was little conversation, but a sense of quiet companionship that had been missing in recent weeks settled over them. Emily thought back on what her life had been like two years ago and marveled at the changes since she had first arrived in Seattle. Peace crept in like a silent but welcome guest, filling her with an assurance that, despite the challenges ahead—the looming birth of Anna's baby and the deepening relationship with Paul—all would somehow be well.

Chapter 21

If lies were truth
And truth were lies,
I'd never have to tell.
But lies keep building
On themselves
Until the wall's so high,
I find myself lost
On the other side,
And losing
What I sought to gain.
———Emily

Winter 1961

Shortly after Christmas, winter began in earnest. Gray clouds camped over the city, dropping rain almost daily, making Seattle's inhabitants feel claustrophobic and moody. The only ones seemingly unaffected were Paul and Emily. They continued to see each other almost every weekend, much to Anna's chagrin. Emily hummed as she puttered around the apartment, getting things ready for the baby. She made regular trips with Anna to the local thrift store to buy diapers and sleepers, putting off other clothing until they knew the baby's gender. Stacks of supplies occupied empty corners until there was no room left. In the meantime, Anna continued her studies to keep her mind off her concerns about the future. She tried to stay focused on the experience of pregnancy, the wonder of another human growing inside her, and the anticipation of the day when she would be holding this baby in her arms.

Paul continued to ask Emily innocuous questions about her childhood, which she sometimes answered and sometimes dodged. One evening, they stopped at a local malt shop for ice cream sundaes after catching a movie. Paul cleared his throat, a signal that he was about to ask another of his questions. "Okay, Emily, how about this one? What was your biggest disappointment as a child?"

Seconds ticked by as she tried to come up with a truthful answer that didn't reveal too much. Finally, she answered, "Well, I always wanted a puppy . . ."

Paul sat back in his chair and gazed at her thoughtfully. He let out a sigh, and said, "Emily, I am a patient man. I'm pretty sure that the lack of a puppy is not your deepest disappointment in life, but it's all you feel you can give me for now. I know that your lack of trust has nothing to do with me, so I am willing to keep asking these questions until the time comes that you feel safe enough to reveal more. I can wait however long it takes. Obviously, I'd prefer it to be sooner rather than later, but it is entirely in your hands."

Waylaid by his thoughtfulness and understanding, Emily found herself on the verge of tears, not knowing how to handle the gentleness with which he spoke. The moment lengthened, until at last she spoke, "Paul, I'm so grateful for your patience. I know I've been asking a lot of you, and it's natural for you to want to know more about me. I'm not yet ready to tell you the whole story, but maybe I can make a start." She took in a deep breath and released it slowly, looking down at the table to ground herself. "My dad worked for the railroad, and he met my mother when he injured his arm in an accident and wound up in her hospital ward. They fell in love and married, and I was born a year later. They were great parents—fun, affectionate, nurturing. I truly never felt that I was lacking for anything. Then Pearl Harbor happened, and my dad felt a duty to help defend his country, so he enlisted in the Army. Two years later, he was killed on Normandy beach in the D-Day invasion.

"My mom had to go back to work to support us, and we moved to a small apartment above our landlady's garage. I learned to clean and cook so I could help Mom out, since she often had to work late at the hospital. Even so, we had a good life together. Then the winter I was ten, she just . . . didn't come home. There was a major snowstorm that day, and the bus she was on slid through an intersection and drove right into the corner grocery store. My mother was standing at the front of the bus, and the impact threw her through the windshield, killing her instantly."

Paul reached out and took her hand. "Oh, Emily! I'm so

sorry. I can't imagine what it was like for you to suddenly be alone in the world. What happened then? Where did you go?"

"Well, I lived with the landlady for a while. She was so motherly and kind, but I was not easy to handle at that point. She didn't want me to have to go to an orphanage, so she kept me as long as child welfare would let her until they found a suitable foster situation for me. Then I went to live with the Huttons. It wasn't an ideal situation, but it was a roof and a family. I'll tell you more about that part of my life some other time. It's . . . complicated. And I'm a little tired. Will that suffice for now?"

"You don't have to tell me anything you don't feel ready for. I feel privileged that you would share this much. I had no idea! Thank you, Emily. Sincerely. Now I know where your bravery comes from. You are an amazing woman, and I feel lucky to be with you."

Paul drove Emily home and walked her to the door, but instead of his usual kiss on her cheek, he took her face in both hands, leaned down and kissed her tenderly on the lips. "I hope you know how beautiful you are," he said. "Sleep well, my love." When he left, she could still feel his lips on hers.

Winter continued without let-up—a gray ceiling, heavy with mist that permeated every nook and cranny and immediately dampened the clothing of anyone who dared to step outside. The gloom darkened moods and shortened tempers as it continued day after day. On one such Saturday morning, Emily awoke and lay lethargically, waiting for the energy to rise and fold up the couch. The bedroom door creaked open, and Anna emerged, belly first. Seeing her in this way awakened Emily's awareness that the baby's birth was almost upon them and that much needed to be done before his or her arrival. With a wrench of her stomach, she realized that she could not put off any longer telling Paul about the way in which her life was about to change.

Anna rubbed the sleep out of her eyes and made a face at the unremitting gray outside the window. "Great! Another day of being stuck inside. And I'm sure you'll be out with Paul again tonight, and I'll be here alone again. I am so sick of this apartment I could scream! It feels smaller and smaller each day I'm trapped in here with nowhere to go and no one to talk to. I feel like I'm going crazy!"

"Oh, Anna, I'm so sorry. I should have realized how closed in you must be feeling. Tell you what, I have to go down to the fish market today to buy some things for dinner tonight. I'm cooking for Paul at his house. Anyway, why don't you come with me down to the pier. We'll splurge and take a taxi with the money I earned from my most recent column. What do you say?"

"Well, it looks pretty miserable outside, but anything's better than staying here all day. So sure, I'll go with you. But why are you cooking for Paul anyway?"

Emily laughed. "Oh, he was moaning about how tired he is of eating out and longed for some good home cooking. He eats with his family every Sunday, but apparently his mother isn't the best cook. His paternal grandmother used to preside over family dinners, and she was an excellent cook, but when she died last year, his mother took over. So, I told him I'd cook to give him a break from all the restaurant food he eats."

The two prepared breakfast together, and Anna's mood seemed to brighten as they chatted. Emily realized how long it had been since they had felt so comfortable together. She felt a twinge of guilt for leaving Anna alone so much as her relationship with Paul deepened. Before long, breakfast finished, they bundled up and descended the stairs to catch a cab. Despite the threatening clouds, there was no rain falling, and they soon arrived at the fish market.

Anna took deep breaths, reveling in the fresh air after long days in the stale fug of the apartment. Even the chill and damp did not discourage her from enjoying this rare outing. The two women queued up at the end of a long line at the open-air counter where fish were tossed from a back area into the nimble hands of the clerks. Anna enjoyed the shouts and the sense of vigor in the men who worked with such skill. Her glance skipped from one man to the next until it suddenly rested on one who looked vaguely familiar. Then her eyes widened, and she cried out, "Jack! Jack!"

Emily's eyes swiveled toward Anna and then toward a young man who gave an answering cry, "Annie? Oh, my God! Annie!" In a flash, he jumped over the counter and pulled Anna into a crushing embrace. Encountering the obstacle of her swollen belly, he stepped back in surprise. "What the . . .?"

Tears streaming down her face, Anna answered, "Oh, Jack, it's so good to see you! We've been looking for you." Jack's eyes swiveled to Emily then back to his sister. "I, uh..." She put her hand on her abdomen. "It's a long story. I don't suppose you could take a break for a few minutes?" He glanced at the long line waiting at the counter, then toward a man who was glowering at him from inside. "Um, not now, but tell me where you live, and I'll come see you later. I get off as soon as we sell all the fish. At this rate, I'd say I could be through here by mid-afternoon." His eyes went back to Emily.

Emily introduced herself and gave him the address of the apartment. "Jack, my name is Emily Edwards, and Anna has been living with me for the past several months. I promise she is in good hands. We had just about given up hope of finding you, though. You have no idea how good it is to meet you!" Jack nodded, gave Anna another quick hug, then returned to his place behind the counter.

Sure enough, shortly after three o'clock there was a knock at the door. Despite her bulk, Anna raced to the door to greet her brother. Jack looked around the apartment with a critical eye as if assessing the situation in which his sister had found herself. Apparently judging it satisfactory, he sat on the couch at Emily's invitation.

"Welcome, Jack! You must be cold from working out in this miserable weather. Can I get you some coffee?"

"Sure. Coffee would be a treat. I'm chilled to my bones." Once a mug was placed in his hands and Emily and Anna were also seated, Jack said, "Now tell me what on earth is going on. Anna, why are you here, and how in the hell did you get pregnant?"

Anna took a deep breath and let it out slowly. "Well, you know as well as I do how horrible Dad was to us—the yelling and the beatings—but what you didn't know is that he had been coming into my bedroom at night and, uh, doing stuff to me. Touching my privates and . . .."

Jack jumped to his feet, fists clenched. "I'll kill him! I swear I'll kill him."

Emily stood and touched his arm gently. "I know this is upsetting, Jack. I'm sure you had no idea. But there's a lot more to this story, and you don't want to make this any harder on Anna than you need to. Please sit down and let her finish."

Jack reluctantly sat back down, but his face remained stormy. Anna continued. "It got worse as I got older until finally he was, um, *doing it.* And then I started my monthly . . . you know . . . while he was gone chasing after a big job. After a couple weeks, he came home to see Mom and give her some money, and then forced himself on me while Mom was at work. Then he left again. It took a while to realize I was pregnant, because I didn't know anything about becoming a woman or where babies even came from, so I just thought I was getting fat. Then Dad came home again a couple months later, saw that I was pregnant, and got furious. He beat me up pretty bad, tossed me into an alley, told me not to come home ever again, and left me for dead. That's when Emily found me and took me in."

Jack leaned over and put his face in his hands, overwhelmed by what he had just heard. After several ragged breaths, he looked up at his sister and said, "Annie, I'm so sorry this happened to you. I should have been there. I should have seen it. I should have stopped him. And instead I just ran away. I want to kill him, but then where would you be? You need me now more than ever. I can't apologize enough for abandoning you, and I promise I'll never do it again." He turned to look at Emily. "And I can't thank you enough for saving my sister. You have done way more than most people would ever think of doing. How will we ever be able to repay you?"

Emily smiled. "Well, let's tell you what we've been planning and see how you might fit into that, shall we?" The threesome talked until it was nearly time for Emily to go, filling Jack in on their plans for Emily to raise the baby, Anna's desire to go back to school, and their need to figure out a new housing arrangement. Emily encouraged Jack to stay with Anna, so they could have some time to themselves and discover what Jack had been doing for the past three years. Emily packed up the things she needed for dinner at Paul's and rushed out the door, giving Anna a last-minute reminder of what was in the refrigerator for her and Jack to eat.

As Paul helped her into the car, he gave her a quick peck on the cheek, then pulled away from the curb, peering through the fog that had settled over the city. With him focusing on the road, Emily had a quiet moment to process all that had happened that day. She became even more aware that she couldn't keep this situation from

Paul any longer. She would have to tell him tonight and brace herself for the very real possibility that he might end their relationship. No man would want to be involved with a woman who was about to take on the task of raising someone else's child. The thought of losing Paul made her realize just how much she cared for him. So much about their relationship was completely opposite of her courtship with George, and it had been wonderful to feel cherished as well as respected. Paul never made her feel helpless or inferior in any way. The excitement of finding Jack gave way to a deep sadness for what she was about to lose.

Stopped at a light, Paul turned to her. "You're awfully quiet. Everything alright?"

"Oh, yes. I'm just tired. I think this weather is simply wearing on me."

Paul reached over to squeeze her hand. "Just say the word, and we can go out somewhere so that you don't have to cook."

"No, Paul. I'm fine. I'm looking forward to cooking for you. It's going to be a lovely evening."

Paul smiled and squeezed her hand again. "I'm looking forward to it, too."

Soon they were pulling into the driveway of a modest Craftsman home with a wide porch and gabled roof. The front yard was barren at this time of year but bore evidence of roses and rhododendrons along the porch area that would be a profusion of blooms in the spring. Bereft of leaves, a cherry tree stood in one corner and a dogwood in another. Emily couldn't help but think how much she would like to have a yard like this. Paul opened the door and ushered her in. As he took her coat and hung it in the coat closet, Emily looked around the living room. It was cozy and warm, neither too neat nor too cluttered, inviting guests to feel comfortable immediately. Books were piled on the coffee table, and family pictures adorned the walls. A large painting of a long, slender boat and several oarsmen took primacy of place above the fireplace mantel. Paul came and stood by her side. "What do you think?"

"It's lovely. Paul. It's just like you! Comfortable and welcoming."

"Well, it would have been even more welcoming if I had thought to build a fire before I came to get you! Let me show you where things are in the kitchen, and then I'll see to the fire."

The kitchen lay opposite the living room through an open arch. It was fitted with all the modern conveniences, which Emily found amusing, considering that Paul didn't cook. Nonetheless, she quickly found what she needed and began to prepare dinner. As Paul laid out kindling and small logs in the fireplace, Emily decided that she would try to keep the dinner conversation light, waiting to tell him about Anna until their meal was over, knowing it could be their last dinner together. As they ate, they chatted about work, the latest article Emily was working on, and the funny story that was circulating around the office. Occasionally, Paul's face took on a puzzled look, but continued with the conversation as though nothing was wrong.

After dinner, they cleared the table together, then Paul went in to put more wood on the fire. Emily was standing at the sink, filling it with warm, sudsy water for washing dishes, when Paul came up behind her and put his arms around her waist. Startled, she jumped and spun as if preparing to ward off an attacker. "Emily!" he said, "What's wrong?"

Trying to fight off the memories of George's assault in a kitchen very like this one, Emily responded, "I'm fine. I thought you were in the living room, and the running water covered the sound of your footsteps. You caught me by surprise is all."

Paul gave her a concerned look and pulled her into his arms. "Emily, you're shaking! You're safe with me. You know I would never hurt you."

Wondering if he knew just how close he was to understanding the source of her fear, she melted into his embrace, knowing it could be the last.

"Tell you what, let's leave the dishes to soak and go enjoy the fire." Paul took her hand and pulled her into the living room, taking a place beside her on the sofa. He put his arm around her, and without thinking, Emily put her head on his shoulder. They sat in silence for several minutes before Paul spoke. "Tell me what's going on, Emily. You've been acting strangely all evening. Are you alright?"

Emily took a deep breath and let it out slowly. "I guess the time has come to tell you the rest of the story, Paul. You deserve to know the truth about my life—all of it."

"Are you sure you're ready? I mean, obviously, I want to

know. I want to be able to support you better, but if you need more time, I can wait a little longer."

"Unfortunately, Paul, time is conspiring against me. I can't wait any longer."

"Okay. I'm here, Emily. Whatever it is."

Emily looked at him, knowing that he would change his mind about her once he heard the whole story. "Well, first, I need to tell you about my roommate."

Paul smiled. "Ah, the mysterious roommate. I've been waiting for this."

"Well, her name is Anna. She's fourteen years old, and she's almost eight months pregnant."

Paul's look of anticipation turned into a frown. "What? I don't understand. Who is she to you? And why is she living with you?"

And so, Emily related the story of finding Anna in the alley and taking her in. She laid out the details of Anna's abuse at the hands of her father and Anna's fear that if she went back home, he would kill her. She watched as Paul's expression went from dismay to horror to something she couldn't quite read.

And then he spoke, and his tone of voice was nothing she'd heard before—anger. "Emily, what were you thinking?! Do you know how dangerous it is for you to be harboring a girl whose father is clearly a homicidal maniac? Why would you do that?"

"Because it could have been me!" Unshed tears shimmered in her eyes.

"What? What are you talking about? Are you saying your father abused you? That all your happy memories of him were just a smoke screen?"

"No! I wouldn't lie about that. It wasn't my father. It was my parish priest. He taught catechism at my Catholic school, the one my foster parents sent me to, and he tutored me because I was so far behind the other students." Emily let out an uncontrollable sob. "He molested me for almost two years—in the confessional, on the desk in his office, one time in a closet—anywhere he thought no one would catch him. And he threatened that my foster parents would send me to an orphanage if I ever told them what was happening. I had to be absolutely silent while he did disgusting and horrible things to me."

As she spoke, Paul's face turned ashen, and when she finally stopped, he pulled her into his arms. "Oh, my God, Emily! My God! I had no idea. How could anyone be so cruel? I'm so sorry you went through this, so sorry." And then he fell silent and just held her as she wept.

When the tears turned to hiccups, Emily pulled herself together. She couldn't stop now. She lifted her head to look at Paul and sat back, putting a little space between them. "There's more. I've agreed to be legal guardian for Anna's baby and raise it as my own."

Paul stared at her, aghast. After a long silence, he said, "I don't even know where to start. I . . . obviously, I'm stunned. What could possibly possess you to do that?"

"I know this is hard for you to understand. I've become close to Anna over these last few months. I've been teaching her some at night, since her father had forced her to quit school after sixth grade. She's smart, and she wants to go back to school, have a normal life. It's not her fault she got pregnant. But how will she support herself and the baby and still get an education? She has an older brother, Jack, who had run away from home a few years ago, and we've been looking for him, but . . . amazingly, we actually found him today, down at the fish market. Hopefully, he can help out, but he's barely making enough to support himself, much less his sister *and* a baby. I just felt like this was the least I could do. And I love children. I've always wanted them, but I never believed anyone would want to marry me given everything that's happened to me."

Paul ran his fingers through his hair in frustration. "Emily . . . I don't know what to say. I'm just having a hard time wrapping my head around this. Around what this means for *us*. I thought you and I had a future, and now . . . .."

"It's alright, Paul. I never believed we could have a future anyway. I'm too damaged, too broken. You deserve someone better than me. I will never be normal, and if I'm honest, I could never give you children of your own."

Paul frowned, trying to make sense of what she had just said. "Wait a minute. You can't have children? How would you know that unless you'd tried? Emily, what are you saying?"

Emily felt herself falling into a pit of despair. Without

intending to, she had just boxed herself into a corner from which she couldn't escape. She hadn't planned to tell Paul about George tonight, and that would most certainly be the final straw for this man that she had come to love. Nonetheless, she could not hold back anymore. Paul deserved the truth. She stared down at her hands for a long moment, then looked into his troubled eyes.

"I'm married. I won't go into all the rationalizations for why I didn't tell you; there's no excuse. I just thought it would be a mild flirtation at first. I told myself one date couldn't hurt, and then I found myself falling in love with you. And I couldn't bring myself to tell you or to stop seeing you. And now I'm losing everything."

Paul just stared at her for long moments, his face a mask. "So, is this the relationship that 'ended badly' that you mentioned when I first asked you out?"

Emily merely nodded her head, eyes downcast.

"I need to understand this, so you're going to have to explain to me how the person I thought I knew could lead me on this way."

She wiped her tears away and squared her shoulders. She couldn't bring herself to look at Paul, so she stared unseeingly at the fire. "After the Huttons kicked me out when I was eighteen, I was on my own. In order to finish high school, I had to find a job on swing shift somewhere and live in a cheap boarding house. Enough time had passed that I had shoved my memories of the abuse in some corner of my mind where I truly didn't recall them. But I was young and scared to be on my own in the world, and one day I met this man at the bank. He saw how vulnerable I was and took advantage of that. He flattered me and promised to take care of me. It felt so good to be wanted and to have someone who was older and more experienced that I fell under his spell almost immediately. We married after only a few months, and it was only then that I discovered how controlling he was. My life became a rigid routine that revolved around him. There were rules about everything. I was not allowed to keep my job at the phone company, because it wouldn't look good for him to have a wife working outside the home. He wanted to be seen as someone who could be the sole provider, a real man.

"Worse, I couldn't read books or write poetry, because those were considered to be frivolous pursuits. I had to take up needlework like the other women in the parish, because he saw that as the only acceptable pastime for a woman. And he was so rigid about his religion! I was forced to follow every single bit of Catholic doctrine—weekly confession, no meat on Fridays, every genuflection, every recitation of the rosary, all of it! And in the meantime, I was starting to have panic attacks every time I entered the confessional booth.

"And the sex! He was rough and boorish and painful and insatiable! And then, when I failed to get pregnant, he decided we weren't doing it often enough. I was exhausted and depressed, and he was blaming me for all of it. He would rail at me about every perceived misstep, every mood, every failure, especially the failure to pray hard enough or have faith that God would give us a baby. Finally, he took me to a doctor. I didn't want to go. I was terrified, though I didn't know why.

"On the day of the appointment, George almost had to drag me to the car, and well, the examination was awful. I felt like I was falling down a deep, dark hole where something evil was waiting for me. And then the doctor took George to his office to share his findings and left me alone on the examination room. He didn't speak to me at all, and when George came to get me, he was clearly furious. He wouldn't say a word all the way home, even though I begged him to. Then, as soon as we walked in the door, he pushed me down over the kitchen table and . . . pushed up my skirt . . . and he, he raped me, from behind, like an animal." Emily gave out one deep sob, then drew in one long breath as Paul stared, speechless.

"And in that moment, all my memories of the abuse by my priest came rushing back. The pain was unbearable, and I screamed, and when George finished, I fell to the floor. He called me a whore and left, slamming the door behind him. I passed out and didn't wake up until the next morning."

Paul looked stunned, horrified. He worked his jaw as if trying to speak. Finally, he exclaimed, "Jesus! I . . . I don't have words. That is the most horrifying thing I've ever heard. What on earth did the doctor find that set George off?"

"George finally told me later that my insides were apparently so scarred up that the only thing the doctor could think of to explain it was that I must have been a prostitute before I met George. Which George assumed meant I had tricked him into marriage. He told me he'd never touch me again, but he started drinking a lot and bringing actual prostitutes into the house at night, and I would have to listen to them having sex in the next room. And that would stir up more memories of my abuse by Father Devlin. They felt so real I would end up screaming in terror. Then George would come to my room, slap me, and tell me to shut up. When I complained about the prostitutes, he would tell me that since he'd been sleeping with a whore all along, he might as well do it with one who enjoyed it.

"Anyway, the scarring made pregnancy impossible. There was a long period of George deteriorating into alcohol and depravity and me fighting the demons of memory and depression. Ultimately, I found the strength to escape with the help of my friend Lottie and my foster father. And that's how I ended up here. That's it. Now you know everything."

"Surely what George did gives you grounds for divorce!"

"You don't know George. He'd never allow that to happen. He's Catholic to the core, and his image is everything to him. He would say that I was lying and convince the judge that I'm crazy."

Paul was shaking his head in disbelief. "I knew there was something dark inside you, some deep pain that kept you from truly letting me in, but this . . . I just don't know what to do with this, Emily. I'm sorry this happened to you, really I am, but this might be more than I can handle—Anna, the baby, your marriage, the abuse, all of it is just . . . too much. I need some time to think."

Resigned, Emily just nodded her head. "I understand, Paul. I always knew it was too much to hope for. Please, just take me home. I'm tired, tired of it all. And if you want to transfer me back down to the switchboard, I'll understand. I'm sorry. I'm so sorry."

Paul stood slowly and went to retrieve their coats. No words were spoken as he drove her home through the gloomy night. He didn't come around to open her door, just said a terse good night and waited for her to get out. There was no backward glance as he drove away. Emily trudged slowly up the stairs, each footstep taking every ounce of energy she had.

Chapter 22

Except the Heaven had come so near—
So seemed to choose My Door—
The Distance would not haunt me so—
I had not hoped—before—

But just to hear the Grace depart—
I never thought to see—
Afflicts me with a Double loss—
'Tis lost—And lost to me—
　　　　　　—Emily Dickinson

Winter 1961

When Emily entered her apartment, Anna was waiting up, anxious to tell her more about her visit with Jack. When she saw Emily's face, however, her expression immediately changed to one of concern. "What's wrong, Emily? You look so upset!"

Emily sighed. "Well, you don't need to worry about Paul anymore. It's over."

"What?! What happened?"

"I told him the truth—about you, about the baby, about my abuse and my husband—all of it. And it was just too much. After all, what man wants a girlfriend who is about to become legal guardian of someone else's baby and who also happens to still be married to the man who raped her? It's amazing that Paul didn't just kick me out of his house and make me find my own way back home! I wouldn't have blamed him if he did."

"Oh, Emily, was it just awful?"

"Worse than awful. I should never have let myself get involved with him. I knew it would end this way, but I just couldn't stop myself from falling for him." She shrugged as if to dismiss the pain of her loss. "Anyway, enough about me! How was your evening with Jack?"

Anna beamed. "It was wonderful! I just can't believe we found him! I've missed him so much, and being together was just like old times. It was like we'd never been apart. And it's no wonder you couldn't find him all that time. He'd been up in Alaska, working on a big trawler for the past year and only just came back to Seattle a month or so ago. He's living in a boarding house down by the piers. It sounds like it's a dive, but it's cheap. We talked about the three of us, I guess four counting the baby, finding a place together. If we pool our money, we should be able to find something we can afford, don't you think?"

Emily gave a hint of a smile. "We'll see, Anna. More income would certainly help. I think we'll need to leave things as they are until the baby arrives. All we'd need is for you to go into early labor while packing and trying to move heavy boxes!"

"I suppose you're right. But we could at least start looking for someplace else, couldn't we?"

"Let's talk about this later. I'm so tired, and I just need some time to think. Okay?"

"Sure. I'm sorry. I know you must be feeling terrible about Paul. I'll see you in the morning. Are we going to church?"

"No. I don't think I could face it tomorrow. Good night, Anna. I'm so happy that you've got your brother back."

Emily waited while Anna used the bathroom to get ready for bed, then mechanically washed her face and brushed her teeth. Instead of hanging up her clothes, she just dropped them on the floor and put on her flannel pajamas. It took all her remaining energy to open up the couch and climb under the covers. When there was nothing left to do, she finally allowed the grief to come. It flooded her like a dark wave of sorrow, filling every corner of her soul. Her tears overtook her, and she abandoned herself to them, sobbing until nothing was left but a shell, hollowed out by the pain.

In the days that followed, Emily descended into a deep depression. Her feelings of loss over Paul were a physical ache in her chest that made it hard to breathe at times. She still got up and went to work every morning, but she kept to herself, eating at her desk when everyone else went to the lunchroom. She didn't make eye contact with anyone, especially Paul. She kept waiting for the ax to fall, to be transferred to another department, but it didn't happen. And so, she kept her head down, did her work and trudged home at the end of days that now seemed longer and colder than ever before. She and Anna looked through the classified ads every Sunday afternoon, searching for living quarters that would accommodate three adults and a baby at an affordable rate. Jack came over for Sunday dinner, and seeing him and Anna revel in their renewed relationship was the only thing that gave Emily a lift.

One day, when Emily checked the mailbox, there was a letter from Lottie. Eager to read what her friend had to say, she opened it immediately. It read:

> Dear Emily,
>
> I'm sorry it's been so long since you've heard from me. What can I say—the twins are walking now, and I can barely keep up with them. I seriously am going to have to keep my legs clamped shut when Bradley is "in the mood." I may be a devout Catholic, but these four kids are testing my commitment to not use birth control! I can't imagine trying to fit any more into this house!
>
> Anyway, I digress. I have news of George. He has been in and out of jail for the past several months on charges of drunk and disorderly, but now he's gotten himself in really deep trouble. He was arrested for aggravated assault a week ago. Apparently, he confused some lady standing on a street corner for a prostitute, and when she tried to fight off his advances, he beat her to within an inch of her life! The judge refused to allow him out on bail, so he is cooling his heels in a jail cell until trial. Of course, he can't afford a good lawyer, so he'll have to have a public defender, and who knows how that will go. I don't think there's any chance he'll be able to get himself out of this without a lengthy prison sentence. Hard to decide whether this is good news or bad news for you, but I thought you should know.
>
> I'll write again soon, but the twins are waking

from their nap, and soon all hell will break loose. Oh, damn, now I'm going to have to go to confession for swearing!
Love, Lottie

Emily stood motionless for quite some time until one of the other tenants came in from the street and glared at her for blocking the mailboxes. She apologized and walked upstairs in a daze. Anna was at the stove with her back turned; she announced that supper would be ready in a few minutes and returned her attention to whatever was bubbling on the burner. Emily dropped to the couch, letter still in her hand. She was stunned by Lottie's news and uncertain about what exactly she *was* feeling. A maelstrom of emotions swirled inside her—vindication, satisfaction, anger, regret, sadness—so that it was hard to identify which was uppermost. Certainly, there was a sense that he was getting what he deserved and that now people would see him for the monster he truly was. On the other hand, she wondered if she had played some small part in his downfall by failing to love him enough or be obedient enough. For a moment, she remembered the man he had been when they first met and felt sorrow that he had fallen so far from his own ideals. Lost in her thoughts, she finally realized that Anna had been calling her name. She looked up and said, "Sorry, Anna, I just received some troubling news. Did you say supper was ready? Let me wash my hands before we eat."

When she settled into her chair at the table, Anna looked at her with concern. "What's going on, Emily?"

"Well, it seems that my husband has gotten himself into some serious trouble."

When she finished telling the story, Anna spoke up. "Serves that bastard right! The things he did to you were criminal, and now somebody's caught him dead to rights. I hope the judge throws the book at him!"

Emily smiled at the young woman's vehement outrage on her behalf. "Well, he's not being let out on bail, so clearly, the courts are taking this very seriously. Apparently, the woman was badly injured, so I would imagine that the punishment will be severe. It's not like he's the upstanding citizen he used to be."

Content to let the topic die, Anna filled the remainder of their meal with chatter about her schoolwork, the baby's energetic gymnastics in her womb, and her anxiety about the upcoming birth. "It's going to hurt a lot, isn't it? I just know it is. And sometimes things go wrong. A woman at my parent's church died giving birth, and it was just awful! Of course, my parents said it was God's will, but I bet that didn't make her husband feel any better, did it? What a horrible thing to say! And if it's true, then God is just mean! A loving God wouldn't want that to happen to anybody. That lady was really nice, and she went to church every Sunday like a good Christian. And God knows I'm not that good. What if God decides to take away my baby?"

Emily reached across the table and placed her hand on Anna's cheek. "Take a deep breath, Anna. You're getting yourself all worked up. I know that you are anxious about the baby, but the vast majority of mothers and babies do just fine during the birth. It's true that sometimes bad things happen, but you are young and healthy, and Dorothy says the baby is doing great, so the odds of something catastrophic happening are very, very small. And God is not in the punishing business. God loves you and wants good things for you. Try to relax. Everything's going to be alright, and I am going to be with you every step of the way. Do you hear me?"

Anna placed her hand over Emily's as it rested on her cheek and nodded her head. She took another deep breath and let it out. "Thanks, Emily. I needed to hear that. Sometimes when I'm here by myself, my thoughts just get to spinning, and I don't know how to stop them. I get frantic thinking about all the things that could go wrong."

"I understand. It's not good for a girl your age to have to be alone so much. I'm sorry I can't be around more, but I need to work to pay the rent. Maybe things will be better once the baby comes and we are sharing a place with Jack. Plus, you'll be a lot busier taking care of the baby and won't have so much time to worry. Just hold on a little longer, okay?"

"Okay, Emily. I know I'm lucky to have you taking care of me. I don't think I'll ever be able to thank you enough."

When Emily went to bed that night, she lay awake, tossing and turning, her mind in a jumble. She was still feeling pushed and pulled by competing emotions about George, and now she was worried about Anna's emotional well-being too. On top of it all was her anguish over the loss of her relationship with Paul. Though it was better for Anna to have Emily's full attention, she missed Paul's smile, his gentle words, his tender treatment of her. His loss was an ever-present ache, a constant companion through her days and nights. Tears dampened her cheeks as she remembered the happy moments they had shared. She had so few people in her life that she could feel safe with, and now one of them was lost to her. Still unable to sleep, she finally got up and went to the window in hopes of gaining some kind of perspective and a modicum of peace.

After days of fog and drizzle, the skies had cleared, and the stars overhead shone brightly in the night sky. Low on the horizon, a crescent moon lay on its side, a curved filament of light cupping the sky. Its slender beauty touched something in her with its assurance of things yet to come. It was emptiness awaiting fullness. She suddenly found that she could breathe again. A shimmer of hope wrapped itself around her and reminded her that God was present in the midst of her turmoil. And she remembered then that she was not without people with whom she could share her burdens. It occurred to her that this might be a good time to talk with Reverend Patterson again. She hadn't been to see him in a while, and his wisdom had always helped her see things more clearly. As soon as she thought of him, Emily was filled with the urge to pour out her heart and receive the encouragement she knew she would find there. Resolved to call him the next day, Emily lay down and slid into a deep sleep.

At work the next day, Emily took advantage of the empty office during lunch to call Reverend Patterson and arrange for a visit. The following Saturday found her ensconced in his study with a cup of tea in her cold hands. "Ah, Emily. It's been a long time. How are you doing, my dear?"

"Well, life has certainly had some ups and downs since we spoke last, and right now mostly downs." Emily proceeded to tell him the truth about Anna, her relationship with Paul, how it had ended, and George's fall from grace. "I just don't know what I was thinking, allowing myself to care for Paul when a future wasn't in the cards. There is no way that George would ever agree to a divorce, even now with his legal troubles. In fact, he would probably see that as the last straw, yet another example of his failure to live up to the perfect life he envisioned for himself. And who would want to be with a woman who would be forever unattainable with no chance for marriage and a normal life? Especially when I am taking on the task of raising Anna's baby? It's all just so hopeless!"

The sympathetic cleric shook his head. "Emily, it's easy to understand how you could fall for someone who was kind and gentle and gave you the time and space to feel safe. It's so very difficult to resist love when you've had so little of it in your life. God understands that. And I've learned over the years that just when I think there's no chance that a bad situation will ever get better, something utterly surprising happens that turns my suppositions upside down. God still performs miracles, whether you believe in them or not. Either way, God will be with you through the bad times, even the difficulties that you think are of your own making. God knows your pain, Emily. He sorrows with you and will seek to give you hope. In fact, one of my favorite verses is this one from Jeremiah: 'For I know the plans I have for you, says the Lord, plans for welfare and not for evil, to give you a future and a hope.' Does that sound like a God who would leave you to deal with the muddle of your life by yourself?"

Emily slowly shook her head. "I've never heard that verse before. It makes me feel like I'm not so alone, that God really might stand by me through whatever comes. To think that God has a plan for me that is for my benefit is something that never seemed possible. Can you show me where that is in the Bible?"

For the next half hour, she and the Reverend pored through the Bible, writing down passages that would give comfort and reassurance as Emily came to terms with the difficult events of the past and her concerns for the future. As she walked home, she noticed a new feeling of calm. The turmoil in the core of her being was easing, at least for the moment. The responsibility for George's situation was his alone, and he would have to deal with the consequences himself. The feelings of loss over Paul were still there, but she didn't feel like she had to handle everything that lay ahead on her own.

When Emily walked into the copy room on Monday morning and saw Paul at his desk, she experienced the familiar pang of heartbreak and longing. Like so many other days, she felt the urge to walk into his office and fall into his arms, but she knew that was a hopeless dream. She sat at her desk and began her day, working through a pile of articles waiting to be proofed. When lunchtime came and her colleagues got up from their work to head to the break room, she opened her desk drawer and pulled out the brown paper bag that held her lunch. She started to open the bag, then stopped. She suddenly realized how much she missed the friendly banter of her work mates over lunch. How long was she going to keep up this self-imposed banishment in order to avoid Paul? Perhaps it was time to move on, to re-enter the land of the living. She stood up, grabbed her lunch and walked down the hall.

Her entrance was met by raised voices exclaiming, "Emily! Good to have you back! Where've you been? We've missed you!" There were smiles on their faces, and Emily couldn't help but smile, too, as she received this warm welcome. Even Paul was smiling. Her heart turned over as she looked at him, then quickly turned her head. The familiar conversations eddied around her, and she occasionally joined in with comments of her own. "Can you believe this weather? I can't wait for spring. How are the kids, Dean?"

Over the next few weeks, conversation between Paul and Emily became less awkward, and they settled into an amicable professional relationship. Emily was relieved at the lessening of tension in their interactions, but her heart never stopped hurting. She wondered how long it would take for this pain to go away and prayed for healing or at least a distraction that would divert her constant thoughts about what she had lost. That distraction finally came in the form of Anna's baby's impending arrival.

The midwife was visiting them on a weekly basis now that the baby was close to term. Dorothy continued to tell Emily and Anna that the baby was doing fine. The heartbeat was steady, and the baby had dropped into the right position for an easy birth. On this particular visit, she stood up from her examination and folded her stethoscope to stow it in her leather bag. "The cervix is softening and thinning. It's beginning to dilate as well, so my guess is that it won't be much longer. This weather isn't the best for walking, but walking is a good way to stimulate labor, Anna. Just don't wander too far from home. And make sure you have my phone number handy so that you can call me as soon as labor begins. I'll come right away so I can monitor the contractions and the baby's heartbeat throughout labor. I hope you two are ready! Do you have all the things I told you would be needed?"

Anna nodded. "We've been ready for a while. There's a stack over there in the corner with everything you asked us to get. I'm getting pretty nervous, though. Even though we've got everything prepared, I don't feel ready for this at all!"

"No mother ever does, Anna. Childbirth is a life-changing event, but you've got the best support you could possibly want in Emily here, and if anything remotely irregular happens, we will get you to the hospital right away." Dorothy patted Anna on the arm. "Try not to worry. You and the baby are both very healthy."

After Dorothy left, Anna was uncharacteristically silent for several minutes. Emily was washing the dinner dishes when Anna finally spoke up. "Emily? I've been trying to think of names for the baby, but I just can't come up with anything that feels right. And just now I realized that it's because I won't be the one raising him or her. I think you should be the one to name it. After all, it's going to be your baby."

Surprised, Emily turned from the sink, her hands dripping soapy foam on the floor. "I haven't even thought about that Anna. I just assumed you would. I'm not sure how I feel about this. On the one hand, I would love to be able to choose the baby's name, and on the other, I feel like I would be taking something away from you. Let me think about it for a bit, okay?"

Anna nodded. "Sure. Just remember, if Dorothy is right, you might not have very long to think!"

Smiling, Emily commented, "We can only hope! You look more and more uncomfortable by the day." She returned to the pile of dishes, thoughts swirling. Eventually, after pots and plates had been washed and dried, she sat down opposite Anna, who had been reclining on the couch with her feet up to reduce the swelling in her ankles. "Okay, here's what I think. I would like to name the baby after my parents—Madeline if it's a girl, or Daniel if it's a boy. But maybe you could choose the middle name. That way we'll both have had a part in naming this little person who is about to enter the world. How does that sound?"

Anna's eyes lit up. "That sounds perfect! Then we'll both be part of the process, just like we have been since you rescued me. Now, let me think . . .." She pondered for a few moments before blurting out, "Rose! I've always loved that name, and it sounds so pretty—Madeline Rose. Do you like it?"

"I do! It's a beautiful name! Now what about the name for a boy?"

"Hmmm. Daniel, Daniel, Daniel. That's harder. Daniel Robert, Daniel Matthew, Daniel Patrick, Daniel Joseph . . .."

Emily interrupted, "Daniel Patrick! I like that! It's a good Irish name, too. I think my dad would be pleased with that. Is it alright with you?"

"Yes! I like it too. That didn't take so long, did it? We're a great team, aren't we? Maybe we should go into the baby-naming business!"

Emily laughed at her young friend's silliness, and Anna joined in. Later, Emily wondered how long it had been since she had laughed so freely. For the first time in over a month, she fell asleep with a smile on her lips.

Hunched over her desk intently working on an edit of Bob Burnett's latest column, Emily barely noticed the sound of the phone ringing. A moment later, Sandra was calling her name. "Emily! There's a call for you on line two. It sounds urgent." Mind still focused elsewhere, she picked up the phone.

"Emily Edwards here. How can I help you?"

"Emily, it's me, Anna! I think I'm in labor!" Anna's voice sounded frantic.

All other thoughts flew out of her head at those words. "Okay, Anna. Don't panic. How far apart are the contractions?"

"I'm not sure. Maybe ten minutes? But they hurt already, and I feel like I might throw up."

"All perfectly normal, Anna. Don't forget to breathe. I'll come home right now." Just then, Emily heard a loud, male voice in the background. "What's that shouting?" Anna's muffled voice seemed to be engaged in an argument. "Anna! What's going on there? Is there something wrong?"

"Some guy wants me to get off the phone and doesn't seem

to understand the concept of an emergency." More yelling, then Anna's voice raised in alarm. "Oh, my God!"

The male voice, louder now, "Jesus Christ! What the hell is that? Did you just pee all over the floor?"

"Anna! Listen to me! Your water just broke. That's all. Calm down, and hand the phone to that creep." Muffled sounds of the phone being passed. "Sir. SIR! Listen to me!"

"Who the hell are you? This girl just gushed fluid all over the floor, and I need to use the phone. I'm going to hang up now . . ."

"Do NOT hang up! Now shut up and listen!" All eyes in the office swiveled toward Emily. "That girl is in labor, and she needs help. If you don't stop causing a scene, I am going to report you to the landlady, and you know how much she hates disturbances in her building. So, what you are going to do now is hand the phone back to Anna, and if you have any humanity at all, perhaps you can find some towels and clean up the mess." The man spluttered in protest, but Emily continued. "It won't be the worst thing you ever have to do; believe me! Now give up the phone and make yourself useful. Do you hear me?" A grudging assent was heard, and then Anna was back on the line. "Anna, have you called Dorothy yet?"

"No, I was too freaked out to think about it. I just wanted you here."

"Okay. I am going to call Dorothy, and then I will catch a cab and be home before you know it. Go back upstairs and lay on the couch. Don't worry about the mess. Remember to breathe slowly and keep track of the time in between contractions. Everything is going to be fine." Emily slammed down the phone, grabbed her purse out of her desk and raced into Paul's office. "I'm sorry to interrupt you, but can I use your phone? Anna's in labor, and I don't think the entire office needs to hear any more than they already have."

"Of course, Emily. Go right ahead."

With shaking fingers, Emily pulled the needed phone number out of her purse and buzzed down to the switchboard. One of the girls connected her immediately. The phone rang several times before a male voice answered. The wait had heightened Emily's anxiety to the point that her voice broke when she replied to his greeting. "He-hello sir, is this the number for Dorothy Hough? It's urgent that I speak with her."

"I'm sorry, she's out on a call. Can I take a message?"

"Oh, no! My niece is one of her patients, and she is in labor. Do you know how I can get in touch with Dorothy?"

"Are you Emily Edwards by any chance?"

"Why, yes!"

"Dorothy thought your niece's delivery was imminent, so she gave me the phone number of the house she's visiting now. Do you have pen and paper?"

Closely following the call, Paul pushed a note pad and pen towards Emily, who mouthed her thanks, then spoke to Mr. Hough. "Yes, I'm ready. Go ahead." She scribbled the number down and hung up. Another connection to the switchboard and another wait for someone to answer. As Emily waited, she saw Paul stand and remove his coat from the coat rack in the corner. Then somebody answered the phone on the other end. "Hello? This is Emily Edwards, and I need to speak with Mrs. Hough urgently." In moments, Dorothy was speaking into the receiver, and a quick conversation followed. When Emily hung up, Paul was standing by his office door, coat already on.

"I'm driving you. You'll have to wait too long for a cab in this weather. Let's go."

Emily looked at him gratefully and ran to get her coat. Without a word of explanation, the two raced out of the office, leaving a bewildered room full of co-workers behind. None of them had the slightest clue what was happening, and when the door slammed, the room erupted into questions, conjecture, and shock at the authoritarian way Emily had spoken to the person on the other end of the phone.

Paul drove recklessly in response to Emily's sense of urgency. There was little conversation other than an expression of gratitude from her, and Paul's reassurance that all would be well. In short order, he was pulling up to the curb, and she jumped out. "I don't know how long this is going to take. I'll call you when I can."

Paul nodded and waved her off, as if to say, "Don't worry about a thing." Then Emily turned and flung open the door to her building, racing up the stairs, two by two. She burst through the door of her apartment and rushed to Anna's side.

"I'm here, Anna, I'm here. It's going to be alright. Dorothy will be here shortly. How long between contractions now?"

"Five minutes, and they're getting stronger. I don't know if I can do this. They hurt!"

Emily actually laughed. "I hate to tell you, honey, but you can't back out now! This is happening, and we are going to get through it together." She took Anna's hands in hers and said, "Now let's breathe. In, two, three, four. Out, two, three, four. Again. That's it. You can do it. See, you're calming down already." Emily continued to count until Anna had quieted down enough to maintain the rhythm of breath on her own. Then she went to the window to watch for the midwife. A car pulled up on the street below just as Anna's belly began another contraction. "She's here, Anna! She's here. Keep breathing; you can do this. Good girl!"

When the contraction let go of its grip, Emily ran to the front door to let Dorothy in. Her professionalism put both of them at ease. She asked Anna several question, felt her belly, checked the cervix, and began barking orders at Emily. To Anna she said, "Now, at the end of the next contraction, we're going to move you to your bed, where you'll feel more comfortable. You're dilated to about four right now, so we still have a way to go, but don't you worry. The baby is in good position, and before you know it, you are going to get your first look at this child you've been carrying around for the last nine months." Her hand was resting on Anna's belly as she spoke, so she was the first to notice that another contraction was beginning. "Here we go, Anna. Just like we practiced. That's right. Keep it up. You're doing fine. Okay now, it's easing up. And there you go. Ready to walk to your room?"

Anna nodded. Emily and the midwife supported her on either side and walked slowly into the bedroom where Emily had placed several layers of towels near the bed in preparation for the birth. A pot of water was already simmering on the stove, and a tray for Dorothy's instruments was laid out on the bedside table. Over the next three hours, Anna labored on, weary and sweating, but bearing it with stoicism. It seemed that the immediacy of the baby's arrival made her able to tolerate the pain even when it ramped up and the contractions increased in frequency. Emily wiped Anna's forehead with a cool towel and murmured encouragement. She was also feeling the anticipation of meeting this child who she was going to raise as her own. Anna's labor made it real in a way that her swelling belly hadn't. There was very little conversation as the women waited for the baby's arrival, so when Dorothy performed another check of the cervix and declared, "Okay, ladies. It's time to push," Anna and Emily were startled out of their reverie.

Dorothy instructed Emily to help raise Anna's upper body and prop her up to lend support as she pushed. When they were in the proper position and another contraction began, Dorothy shouted, "Push! Harder! Push, push, push! Good girl! Okay, you can lay back now. But be ready to do it again as soon as I say." Moments later, "Here we go again! Push, push, push! That's a girl! Harder if you can. Okay, relax." For another hour, Anna pushed, and Dorothy and Emily cheered her on. Despite her evident exhaustion, there was a determined look on her face that said she would keep this up all night if necessary. Then suddenly, Dorothy exclaimed, "The baby is crowning! It's almost here! Let's go, Anna. PUSH! Yes! There's the head. Rest just for a moment while I maneuver the shoulders into position. Ready? GO! Keep going, keep going. Almost there . . ." And suddenly, the baby slipped out of the birth canal with a whoosh.

"It's a boy!" Dorothy tapped the bottoms of the baby's feet, which triggered an inrush of breath and the first squall of a new life. Anna and Emily were laughing and crying at the same time. With swift and sure movements, the midwife quickly swaddled him and placed him in Anna's arms. He quieted immediately, calmed by the tight wrapping and the sound of the heartbeat that had been his constant companion for months as he grew in the protection of her womb. Anna cooed at him, and Emily touched his tiny hands. The sensation caused him to close his fist around her pinky finger, as if cementing a relationship of love and care.

"Hello, Danny boy, "she murmured, "your namesake would surely be smitten with you. And your grandmother, too. You are such a beautiful boy. Yes, you are. Absolutely perfect." The baby's dark eyes stared intently at her as if memorizing her features, as she was memorizing his. The hair on his head was a very faint fuzz that hinted at blond locks to come.

Anna whispered, "Take him, Emily. He needs to know that you're his mama now." She transferred the little bundle into Emily's waiting arms. Tears glittered in her eyes, but her movements were sure.

    As Emily took him into her own arms, she felt something she hadn't felt since her mother died—that she belonged to someone. This tiny soul was hers to love, care for and protect as long as she had breath. And she knew without question that it would be the hardest thing she would ever do, and also the thing that would give her the greatest joy.

Chapter 23

And so tis joy that heals my heart,
And soothes my troubled soul.
This tiny child, his limpid eyes,
His petaled lips,
Have filled the gaping hole,
Which formerly did want for love
That proved so hard to find.
But now I'm pledged my love to give
Forever and a day,
Promising that I am his
And ever he is mine.
     —Emily

Winter/Spring 1961

As soon as Dorothy had delivered the afterbirth and cut the umbilical cord, she helped Anna put little Daniel to her breast. With her gentle guidance, soon his little mouth had latched on and was sucking vigorously. Emily watched with awe at this tiny miracle, a new life entering the world. Dorothy was bustling about, gathering soiled towels and rags and immersing them in the bathtub filled with hot water to soak. She then did a cursory cleaning of her instruments; she would sterilize them in her autoclave when she went home. Throughout the bustle, Emily and Anna were utterly unaware, focused only on the magic of this moment and the infant that had engendered it.

Anna looked up at Emily. "I thought I wouldn't have anything but resentment toward this baby because of what my dad did to me, but none of that matters now. I think I never really knew what love is until this minute, with Daniel in my arms." The two women beamed at each other, bonded by the moment, then both pairs of eyes returned their gaze to the object of their adoration. "Do you think Mary felt this way when Jesus was born? I feel like I'm in church."

Emily responded, "I think we are. There are stars overhead, and I can almost hear the sound of angels singing. Birth is a wondrous thing, Anna, and every new baby is a gift from God. Thank you so much for letting me be a part of this. I'll never forget it."

"Okay, ladies, is the little guy done eating? I need you to take him, Emily, so that I can get Anna cleaned up. The baby will probably sleep for a few hours at least. It's been a long day for him, too! And then I need to fill out the birth certificate so I can file it with the state."

Emily took Daniel and wandered the apartment with him, showing him his new home. She walked to the living room window and looked out at the stars. "Look, Daniel. See the stars? Aren't they beautiful? Stars are a very special part of this world we live in, shining light in the darkness and reminding us of God's presence. They remind me so much of my parents. I wish they could have met you. My mom and I used to gaze up at the stars together and imagine and dream. She said that sometimes, if we dream hard enough, we can bring the dream into being. You are a dream I had almost given up on, but now, maybe I can have faith in my dreams again and trust that they'll come true. What a blessing you are, little one."

Dorothy drew her out of her reverie to ask for her and Anna's input on the birth certificate. Emily gently laid the sleeping babe in his bassinet and returned to the kitchen table where Dorothy was seated. Anna remained on the bed in her room, but could see and hear the other women from there. Anna's name and birthdate were entered onto the form as well as the baby's name, date and time of birth, weight, and length. "Now, I know this is a troubling subject, but what should I put for the baby's father?"

Anna and Emily spoke simultaneously, "Unknown!"

"I understand your reluctance to put your father's name, Anna, but are you sure that's what you want?" Dorothy asked.

Anna was adamant. "I'm sure. I don't want him to ever know about this child. Let him think that I and the baby are both dead! I don't want him to ever come looking for me. Nor do I want anyone other than you, Jack, and Emily to know what really happened. I'd ask you to give me a fake last name, but I don't want to get you in trouble. I mean, I'm sure you could get into trouble for putting 'father unknown,' but how are they ever going to find out that it's not true?"

Dorothy nodded her assent and completed the form. "Now, as far as I know, once you receive the official birth certificate, you will need to go down to the courthouse and file a petition for legal guardianship, Emily. Since Anna's underage and she is the one requesting it, there should be no difficulty. They'll probably want to do a home visit to make sure the baby will be raised in a safe and clean environment, which is not going to be a problem in your case." She stowed the paperwork in a side pocket of her instrument bag. "Okay, ladies. It's been a long day for all of us. I'm going to go home and get some sleep, and I recommend the same for you. Who knows how long that little bundle will sleep, so you should catch some winks while you have the chance! I'll be back tomorrow to check on momma and baby and answer all the questions you will already have by then. But by all means, if you need me before then, don't hesitate to call. You both did splendidly tonight. Now, get some rest."

The midwife picked up her bag and left, pulling the front door behind her. Emily helped Anna get comfortable in her bed and then collapsed on the couch. She was fast asleep the minute her head hit the pillow.

The next few days passed in a blur of diapers and burp cloths, disrupted sleep, and moments of pure joy. Emily had found a used rocking chair at the Goodwill and brightened it up with a coat of paint, so Anna would have a comfortable place to nurse the baby. Once Anna was done, she would pass Danny off to Emily, who would sit and rock with him on her chest while he dozed. She never tired of staring at his sweet face, stroking his velvety head or patting his back. Sometimes, she would nod off too, yet at some level was always aware of the warm weight of him, trusting that he was safe in her arms.

Paul had given Emily the week off, knowing that Anna would need her there until she felt comfortable in caring for the baby on her own. On the day Emily returned to work, she reluctantly tore herself away from Daniel and reminded Anna several times to call if she needed anything. Never mind that she would have to navigate the stairs and then juggle the phone on her shoulder, feed the dime into the coin slot, and dial the number all while cradling the baby in one arm! When Emily entered the office, she was greeted with warm congratulations and questions about the birth. She had given Paul permission to tell her co-workers the circumstances of their mad rush out of the office when Anna had gone into labor. They had agreed that it was best to continue the story that Anna was Emily's niece for now.

Paul greeted her with a smile that was reminiscent of former days, when their relationship was first in bloom. Emily smiled back, mouthing a thank you for his help and support. Then she sat down at her desk and went to work. It did feel good to engage her mind again, playing with words and finding the best way to express what a reporter was trying to convey. Being away for just those few days and then returning had confirmed to her that this was work she loved to do.

Two weeks passed quickly as Emily dragged herself away from the baby every morning and rushed home at quitting time to take him into her arms again. Anna was recovering quickly from childbirth and feeling more and more comfortable with breast-feeding. She and Emily both were still tired from being awakened two or three times a night by the pitiful cries of a hungry baby, but they seemed to be adjusting to the routine and learning what Daniel needed and when. In short order, they had become a well-tuned team. Emily's feelings of loss over her relationship with Paul had been pushed into the background, though there were still times when he would smile at her that she would feel a pang of longing. And then the whirlwind of work and motherhood would catch her up in its pull, and the moment would pass.

On one day, when spring announced itself with a torrential rainfall, Paul stopped by Emily's desk just before quitting time. "Will you let me drive you home tonight? This rain is miserable, and I'm sure you'd like to get home without being drenched to the skin. You'd have to change clothes before you could hold Daniel, and I imagine you don't like to wait one minute more than necessary to have him in your arms."

Surprised, Emily faltered for a moment, then smiled. "Yes. That would be lovely, Paul. Thank you for being so thoughtful." He smiled and tapped her desk with his fingertips before returning to his office.

That night, the two raced across the street to Paul's car under umbrellas that did nothing to stop the wind from blowing raindrops sideways and dampening their coats, but at least their heads were dry. Once they pulled the doors closed, shutting out the rain, Paul sat still, staring out the windshield at nothing in particular, not making a move to start his car. Emily looked at him questioningly. He looked troubled and uncertain, as if something were weighing on his mind.

Finally, he spoke. "Emily, I know I hurt you badly when I dismissed you from my life that night. When I think back on the things I said, I can't believe how cruel I was. Here you were, baring your soul to me, something I had been wanting you to do for a long time, and then I confirmed your every fear that men would reject you because of what you'd been through. I wouldn't blame you if you decided never to forgive me." And then his voice broke. Emily started to speak, but he stopped her. "No, let me finish. I need to get this out." He seemed to struggle for a moment to regain his composure, then continued. "The thing is, these past weeks have been the most miserable of my life. I miss you. I miss being with you, talking with you. Maybe you can't help who you fall in love with, and it just so happened that I fell in love with someone who has been through the worst that life can offer and is still the warmest, kindest, smartest, and gentlest human being I've ever met. And you're married. And you have a baby who is not yours, but who you promised to raise as your own, because of that kindness, because that's who you are. You have so much love to give, and so many people who took it and reciprocated with cruelty. Why shouldn't you have a child to love and who will love you back?

"I guess what I'm trying to say is that I have come to understand that I can't live without you. I love you, and I want you back, whether you're married or not, whether you can bear my children or not. I don't have any idea what a future together will look like or how anyone else will feel about it, but I don't care. Being with you is all that matters to me. I'm yours if you'll have me." Finally, he turned to face her, and she saw that he had tears in his eyes.

"Oh, Paul! Of course, I forgive you. I think I've been in love with you since the moment we met. And I've missed you so much!"

The words felt like falling off a cliff, surrendering to gravity and trusting there would be a soft place to land.

Paul half laughed, half sobbed as he leaned toward her and took her into his arms. After an embrace that seemed to go on forever, he pulled away slightly and cradled Emily's face in his hands before bending his head to put his lips on hers in a kiss that was both tender and full of longing. Emily gave herself to it completely, feeling herself let go of all her fears, all her loneliness, all her self-doubt.

Finally, Paul pulled away so he could look into her eyes. "I guess I should take you home now, so I can meet your son."

Emily beamed. "I think that's a great idea!"

When they arrived at her building, Paul climbed the stairs with her for the first time. She made him wait outside so she could give Anna fair warning that they had company. Entering the apartment, Anna was bouncing Danny on her knees and patting his back, trying to get him to burp. "Oh, Anna! You're never going to believe this. Paul is here! He wants me back! And he wants to meet the baby."

"Here? As in outside the door right now? Oh, my gosh! Okay, here! You take Danny, and let Paul in. I'm going to go change my clothes, and then I'll be out. What wonderful news!"

Emily took the baby in her arms and smiled down at him. "Hello, sweet boy. Do you want to meet someone special? Let's go let him in." She went to the door and opened it wide. "Come in, Paul. Welcome to my home."

Paul entered and looked down at the infant in her arms. "Hello, little Daniel. You're a handsome fellow, aren't you? Yes, you are." He touched the infant's tiny fist which automatically opened and grasped the proffered finger. Paul met Emily's shining eyes. "He's beautiful, Emily! How on earth can you stand to be away from him all day?"

"Oh, trust me, Paul, it isn't easy. But I sure love the coming home part." She looked up as Anna came out of the bedroom. "And here's his mama. Paul, this is Anna."

Paul strode across the room to take the younger woman's hand. "It's so nice to meet you, Anna. From all I've heard, you are a very courageous girl. Emily said you were a trooper through the labor and delivery. How are you feeling?"

Having a male be solicitous of her was a new experience, and Anna paused for a moment before she could stammer out an answer. "I-I'm fine, thank you. Still a little tired, but that's to be expected with getting up three times a night to feed him. Luckily, Emily takes over with the burping, so I can go back to sleep. I don't know what I'd do without her."

"Well, I think the reverse is true as well, as far as I can tell. I'm not sure how she keeps from falling asleep at her desk though."

Anna excused herself then, rightly deducing that the couple might want to be alone. "Emily, do you want me to take him, or is he okay with you?"

"He's fine with me, Anna. Why don't you go lie down for a bit and see if you can get a short nap? Hand me out a clean diaper before you go, though, so I can change him if necessary, without waking you."

Once Anna had retired to her room, Emily and Paul sat down on the couch side by side. "Do you want to hold him?" Emily asked.

Paul readily agreed, and she placed the baby carefully in his arms. He settled Danny in the crook of his arm and began to chatter softly to him. "Welcome to the world, little man. What do you think of it so far? How do you feel about having a man around to play catch with and take you fishing? With these long fingers, you could be a great catcher! Maybe you could play for the Seattle Rainiers one day." Emily watched, enchanted by Paul's obvious delight in her son. Gradually, the soft tone of his voice caused Danny's eyes to glaze over and then begin to close. He was soon fast asleep in Paul's arms.

"Do you want me to take him, Paul?"

"No, he's fine right here. No need to disturb him."

Emily's smile deepened. "I think you're a natural at this."

"Yes, and I have another arm available for you." He put his arm around Emily, and she settled in beside him, resting her head on his shoulder. They sat together in silence for a long time, breath matching breath, each content in the presence of the other.

In the weeks that followed, Emily and Paul learned how to balance their desire to be together with the needs of Anna and the baby. Paul came to Emily's apartment a couple nights a week to spend time with her and Daniel; they went out to dinner on Friday or

Saturday night, then watched the baby on Sunday afternoons so Anna could get out of the house and do something fun with Jack. Nonetheless, the apartment seemed to get smaller and smaller as the days went by, and their living situation was on everyone's minds. So far, Emily's landlady had not expressed any complaints about the baby's crying disturbing the other tenants, but Emily didn't know how much longer she could count on Mrs. Benson's good graces.

One evening, as Paul and Emily were snuggled together on the sofa, Paul took the bull by the horns. "Emily, how do you feel about moving in with me? I know we can't get married, but why can't we live as though we are? I want to be with you, make a home with you, wake up next to you. I know it's not socially acceptable, but you're the woman I want to spend my life with."

Emily was silent for long moments, overwhelmed by Paul's love for her as well as the complicating factors that would go into such a monumental decision. Paul put his finger under her chin and turned her face to meet his gaze. Finally, she spoke. "Paul, I want that too. I just don't know how to make it work with Anna and Jack and the baby. I don't want to just take Daniel away from Anna completely. She's a part of my life now. And I want her to be a part of his. Jack had talked about wanting to get out of his boarding house and find a place that's big enough for all of us to be together, but that was when you and I weren't . . . together."

"Well, I've been thinking about that a lot, and then I saw a sign that made everything fall into place."

"A sign? What kind of sign? Like, a sign from God?"

"Well, I suppose it could be a sign from God, but I was being more literal. A 'For Rent' sign just went up on a house down the street from me yesterday. It's a little smaller than my place but would be big enough for Jack and Anna. We'd be close enough to them to share time with Daniel. I could pay the rent if Jack can't swing it, and then they'd only have food and utilities to pay for. Then Anna could go back to school as soon as Danny is weaned, and you could quit work to stay home with him."

"Oh, my goodness! That sounds perfect! But are you sure you can afford that? For people you barely know?"

"You don't need to worry about that. My grandmother left each of us kids a tidy sum when she passed away, and I used mine to buy that house. There's no mortgage on it, and my salary at the paper is more than adequate, even if I do pay Anna and Jack's rent."

"Paul, this is overwhelming! Jack and Anna are going to be over the moon! And I hadn't even thought about being able to stay home with Danny. Before you came into my life, I just assumed I would have to keep working and find someone who could watch the baby during the day. I would miss my work, though, and everyone at the office."

"Well, maybe I can speak with the boss and see if I can bring some work home for you to do while Danny is napping. And I'm sure that Harold will still want you to write a column for him from time to time. I know how much you love to write. And you don't have to be at the office to do that."

"The best of both worlds! You've thought of everything, haven't you? But what about your parents? What will they think? Are they going to accept the fact that we would be living together without benefit of marriage?"

"Sweetheart, let me worry about my parents. They probably won't like the idea at first, but once they meet you, it will be a different story. And they will understand the impossible situation you're in. The fact that you come with a baby for them to spoil will just be icing on the cake. You'll see."

"It *would* be wonderful for Danny to have grandparents, wouldn't it? I never did, and I feel like I missed out on so much. And it would be lovely to have a mother-in-law to get parenting advice from. Do you really think she'll like me?"

"I *know* she will. Now stop your fretting. Everything is going to work out; just wait and see. Right now, let's just savor the good things that are ahead of us."

He bent his head to kiss her, a long kiss that left them both breathless. Emily felt something stirring in her that she hadn't felt in a long time, something both exciting and frightening. "You know," Paul murmured softly, "I'm not just asking you to share my home, but to share my bed, too. I can imagine that might stir up some troubling memories for you, so I want you to know that I will give you as much time as you need to get used to the idea—hopefully not forever. We can go slow, and if I ever do anything that makes you uncomfortable or that hurts you in any way, you can tell me to stop, and I will."

Emily's eyes were wide and solemn as she nodded her head. "Given how I feel right now, I know that I want a physical relationship with you, too, but my brain is in a panic at the idea. I do feel safe with you. I just . . . have a hard time imagining love-making that is actually gentle and loving and not painful. Thank you for giving me time. I promise not to make you wait forever." In response, Paul kissed her again. And again, until the cry of a hungry baby interrupted them.

When Jack and Anna returned from their outing, Emily told them about Paul's idea. Jack was stunned. Looking at Paul, he said, "You'd really do that for us? I don't even know what to say. Nobody has ever been willing to put themselves out like that for me. I've had a pretty hard-scrabble life, and I never dreamed of a break like this. This gives Anna and I both the chance to make something of ourselves and to create the kind of life we never had growing up. And to have you two living nearby to rely on for advice and support— well, that makes it even better. Thank you, sir!" He reached out his hand, and Paul shook it in confirmation of a pledge made to serve as a father figure to this young man and his sister.

Anna was equally astonished and excited. She hugged Paul and then Emily in a tight embrace. To Emily she said, "Thank you so much! And to think I was afraid Paul would take you away from me! This is more than I ever dreamed of! Now, how soon can we see this house?"

Amid light-hearted laughter, the four of them started making plans for the new future that had opened up. They couldn't wait to begin this new phase of their lives.

The following days were a whirlwind of signing a lease on the house, giving notice to Emily's and Jack's landlords, and packing up belongings. In the midst of this, Paul invited Emily to his family's regular Sunday dinner. He had already told them that he had asked her to move in with him, and as expected, they were not very happy about it. "Just meet her," he had begged. "I know you will love her." Despite their reservations, they had agreed, and deep down they knew that once Paul had decided something, there was nothing they could do about it.

Emily took extra care with her appearance, choosing a pink

drop-waist shift with a white stand-up collar and low white heels. Her shoulder-length hair was brushed to a sheen and flipped up at the ends. When she opened the door to Paul's knock, he looked her up and down before emitting a whistle of admiration. "You look beautiful! My parents are going to think you're too good for me."

Emily laughed and swatted him on the arm. "You're just saying that because you know how nervous I am. The least I can do to impress is to dress appropriately."

"Well, you're impressing me, that's for sure!"

During the drive over, Paul tried to ease Emily's nerves. "Emily, I know my parents, and once they get past the idea of us living together, they're going to love you. I promise."

Sighing, Emily responded, "I sure hope you're right." Paul patted her leg reassuringly, and she took a deep breath then let it out. Too soon, Paul pulled into the driveway of a large Dutch Colonial home on Queen Anne Hill. As he helped her out of the car, Emily thought she saw a curtain flutter at the window nearest the front door. Feeling her tense up, Paul took her by both arms and looked her in the eyes. "Breathe, Emily. Just be yourself. My parents are open-minded, caring human beings. They are just disappointed that they're not going to get the big church wedding they had dreamed of for me. They'll get over it."

Emily's shoulders relaxed. "Okay, let's get in there before I decide to make a run for it!" She grinned at her attempt at a joke, and they turned and walked to the front door. Before they could even knock, the door opened, and a middle-aged blond woman appeared, wearing a hesitant smile.

She thrust out her hand and said, "You must be Emily. I'm Paul's mother. He's told us a lot about you."

Emily shook her hand. "Nice to meet you Mrs. Graves. Thank you for inviting me to dinner. I understand your Sunday dinners are quite the family tradition."

"Yes, they are. Please come in and let me take your coat."

When Paul and Emily crossed the threshold, they were met by the sound of numerous voices, some in quiet conversation, some louder as they commented on the baseball game playing on the television set in the next room. It seemed like Paul's entire family had arrived to get a look at his new girlfriend. Emily gave Paul a panicked look, then squared her shoulders and allowed herself to be escorted into what felt like the lion's den. Introductions were made amidst light-hearted banter and curious looks. Both of Paul's brothers were there with their spouses. There was a toddler running around adding to the chaos, and one of the wives was visibly pregnant. Apparently, the lone female sibling was absent, having gone to attend a baby shower instead. Paul's father pushed himself up from his deeply cushioned chair and extended his hand. When she took it, he leaned in so she could hear him over the din, as he said, "Welcome to the nut house, Emily. Don't mind the teasing. It means they are already prepared to like you."

Feeling a release of breath she hadn't known she was holding, Emily smiled brightly. "And I am fully prepared to like all of you as well. You raised a wonderful son."

Hearing the clattering of pots and pans in the kitchen, Emily went in and asked if she could help. "That would be lovely, dear. You can start carrying the food to the table." As she walked back and forth between kitchen and dining room, Emily noticed a beautifully embroidered prayer hanging on the wall in the dining room. She stopped for a moment to read it and was struck by its words:

"O God, seeing as there is in Christ Jesus
an infinite fullness
of all that we can want or desire,
May we all receive from him,
grace upon grace . . ."

Mrs. Graves commented as she passed with another steaming dish. "Isn't that a wonderful prayer? It's one of my favorites of John Wesley."

"Yes, it's beautiful, but I've never heard of John Wesley."

"He's the founder of the Methodist church, which we are members of. His teachings on grace are part of what makes me love the church so much. Did you attend church with your parents as a child?"

"Oh yes. We went to the Lutheran church, and I have many lovely memories of sitting in the pews with my mom and dad. My mom grew up Catholic, but she found its emphasis on being the only true church too exclusionary, so she left. That's what caused her parents to cut her out of their life. And then I ended up in a Catholic foster home after my mom died. Those were years I'd like to forget."

"Well, anytime you want to worship with us, we'd love to have you. The Methodist church welcomes everyone, no matter their background." Emily thanked her and went to get the bowl of mashed potatoes.

Soon, the large family was gathered around the dining room table, still chattering away. Paul reached for Emily's hand under the table and squeezed. Mr. Graves raised his voice to be heard above the clamor. "Alright, you hooligans, it's time for grace. Let's bow our heads." Hands reached out to join around the table, as he began to pray, "Heavenly Father, thank you for this meal and for all the blessings of life. Bless this food to our use, and us to Thy service. In Christ's Holy name, Amen." A chorus of amens were murmured around the table, and everyone began passing dishes.

Despite Paul's warning about his mother's cooking, Emily thought it was good, traditional comfort food. Sure, the roast was on the dry side, and the gravy a bit lumpy, but the warm family atmosphere made it special. In the midst of the meal, Mrs. Graves turned toward her. "This big family must be overwhelming for you, what with being an only child and all."

"Well, it is a bit, um, loud, but it's delightful! It actually reminds me of dinners at my best friend's house growing up. They were Catholic, so they had quite a brood. Always room for one more, though."

That opened the floodgates of the family's curiosity, and everyone took turns peppering her with questions, becoming somber when she spoke of her deceased parents, then moving on to questions about her work and her move to Seattle, asking her what sights she had seen and promising to introduce her to the sights she hadn't yet experienced. It was exhausting and wonderful at the same time. Finally, dinner over and bellies replete, Paul suggested it was time to go. His mother walked them out to the car to say her farewells. "Thank you for coming, Emily. I hope you didn't mind the inquisition. This family isn't afraid to pry, and Paul has never brought a woman to our family dinners, so you were bound to be bombarded with questions."

"It's fine, Mrs. Graves. I don't blame them. They love their brother, and they want to make sure he's making the right decision."

The older woman turned serious. "Paul has told us a bit about the difficult life you've had, and I want you to know how sorry I am that you suffered so much. It's a real shame. And yet, you've accomplished more than many women in your situation, and clearly it hasn't soured you on life. You are a strong and courageous woman. You'll be welcome in our home anytime."

Driving home, Paul was jubilant, and Emily was overwhelmed with the acceptance she had received from the entire Graves family. Tears glittered in her eyes at his mother's words. "Paul, did she mean it? Is she really accepting our relationship so quickly? I can't believe it! I wouldn't have expected this in a million years."

"I told you they would love you as soon as they had a chance to know you. Don't get me wrong. I think they will still be sad that marriage isn't in the cards for us, but I think my happiness is more important to them than respectability. And by the way, what did my Dad say to you when you were shaking hands?" When Emily relayed his words, Paul smiled. "Yeah, that's my dad. He's an expert at making people feel at ease. I knew he'd pull through for me."

"It seems he's passed that trait along to at least one of his sons as well."

Paul reached his arm out to pull her closer on the bench seat. "Scoot over here, my love. No need to be so discreet anymore." Emily gave a sigh of contentment as she rested her head on his shoulder.

Suddenly it was moving day. Paul had borrowed a pickup truck from one of his brothers to haul all their possessions from two different locations. Fortunately, the rental house for Anna and Jack was furnished, so they hadn't had to buy any secondhand furniture to fill up the rooms. Nonetheless, there were plenty of boxes to cart down the stairs between Anna's clothing and books, Danny's baby paraphernalia and the bassinet the women had found at a rummage sale. Somehow, Emily had accumulated more clothing than she had brought with her from Spokane, so that took up three boxes alone. Teasing, Paul shook his head, "I don't know if all this is going to fit in my house, woman! You might have to sleep on the porch!"

Emily laughed. "This was your idea, buster! If you want me,

you're going to have to accept all the baggage as well." They both smiled, their gaze acknowledging the deeper truth to her statement.

"I will take everything you've got and more, my love. I can't wait to wake up to that beautiful face every morning."

"Alright, you two lovebirds," Jack piped in, "We've still got work to do here."

Finally, they brought down the last load of belongings. Emily checked her mailbox one last time before turning in her keys to Mrs. Benson. Inside was a single envelope, a letter from Lottie. Emily knocked on the landlady's door and handed her the keys. "Thank you so much, Mrs. Benson. You've been extremely kind. I don't know what I would have done if I'd had to find another place to live on top of helping my niece through her pregnancy and birth. You are a gem. I hope you find another renter soon. Good-bye now."

She hurried out to the curb where Paul was waiting with motor running and climbed into the pickup. "Okay, let's go. I'm glad I remembered to check the mail. There's a letter from Lottie. I haven't even had a moment to let her know I'm moving, so this will remind me to write her with my new address and phone number. What a luxury it's going to be to have a phone in the house and not have to rustle up a dime every time I need to make a call!" Emily tore open the letter and began to read. She put her hand to her chest and breathed out a prolonged, "Ohhh."

"What is it, darling? Is something wrong with Lottie?"

"No, Lottie's fine. It's George. Here, let me read it to you."

"Dear Emily,

Well, George's trial kept getting delayed, but it's finally over, and thankfully, he was convicted. That poor woman will have some closure now. She is still walking around with a cane, because of the beating he gave her. Apparently, he kicked her in the spine and caused severe damage to her nerves there. They say she might have pain and numbness that affects her ability to walk for the rest of her life. I think the jury felt awfully sorry for her, and that's what swayed them and helped them realize what a dangerous man George was and would continue to be

339

toward anyone who crossed him. He really has gone 'round the bend, Emily. I hardly even recognized him! You would hate to see him now. Anyway, the judge sentenced him to twenty years in prison, I think because of the severity of his victim's injuries. He's being sent to Walla Walla state penitentiary, which I hear is a pretty rough place with lots of hardened criminals there. Not that he doesn't deserve it, but it's hard to reconcile this with who he was when you first met him.

       Better get this in the mail. I just thought you would want to know.

Love, Lottie."

Paul reached out to take Emily's hand. "Are you alright? I'd almost forgotten about George's upcoming trial with all that's been going on here. Twenty years is a long time. What are you feeling about that?"

"I'm not sure how I feel. In some ways, it's vindication that I wasn't just imagining how violent he could be, and now he's being punished, even if it's for something he did to someone else. I feel so sorry for his victim, and I guess sorry for him, too. He had such a horrible childhood with his alcoholic father who did nothing but criticize him and beat him for every perceived imperfection. It's no wonder he was so exacting and priggish, and then when it all fell apart, this ugliness came out. And I also feel relief that I won't have to worry about him trying to find me and seek revenge for ruining his life anymore."

"I can see why you would feel all those things, Emily, but don't forget—you had a horrible childhood, too, and it didn't turn you into a hateful monster. At some point, he made a choice to let his experiences shape how he treated others. And I personally can never forgive him for what he did to you."

Emily squeezed his hand. "I do love you, you know. It makes me feel safe and protected to know you feel that way. And that it's okay for me to have mixed feelings about this."

Paul was quiet for a long moment before speaking again. "You know, Emily, it seems like this conviction gives you grounds for divorce without needing George's agreement. No judge in the land would deny your right to divorce a violent felon. Then you would truly be free of him."

Emily stared at him, stunned by the truth of his words. "I never considered that! I had just resigned myself to living out my life forever tied to George by our marriage vows, almost like I deserved it. But it was he who violated our vows, not me! Oh, my gosh, Paul! This changes everything!" Her smile lit up her face even as tears of joy blurred her vision. "Drive faster, dear. I can't wait to start our life together."

At the end of a long day of loading and unloading the truck, making sure that the right boxes were carried into the right houses, everybody plopped down in Paul's living room, utterly exhausted. Danny, who had been a trooper through the entire ordeal finally declared his protest at the complete disruption of his usual quiet days. Anna began to nurse him, and after he had had his fill, he promptly fell asleep. Emily took him into her arms and quietly carried him into their bedroom, avoiding the boxes on the floor, to lower him into his bassinet. He grunted at the change of position, wiggled momentarily, then slid gently into a deeper sleep.

Emily returned to the living room where the others were debating dinner. No one felt like cooking, nor did they have any desire to go out. Finally, Paul sat forward in his chair. "Hey, I have an idea. Why don't I call Liu Chang at the Golden Dragon and have him deliver us something? Does everybody like Chinese?"

Though Anna had never tried it, she was agreeable as long as it meant she wasn't cooking or moving from the couch. Emily and Jack were definitely in favor, and so an order was placed, and soon a feast of steaming chow mein, sweet and sour pork, and egg foo young was delivered to their door. Before long, the cartons were empty, and the four tired movers were replete. Anna and Jack stood and made ready to walk down the block to their new home. "Do you want me to take Daniel with me, so you don't have to heat up formula in the middle of the night?" Anna asked.

"That's alright, Anna. I don't want to disturb him. He's a tired little peanut. I don't mind getting up with him, and you could use the rest. I'll bring him over in the morning, so you can nurse him. Now, off you go!"

The door closed behind them, and Paul drew Emily into his arms. "Welcome to my home, darling. Now it's your home, too. Any regrets?"

"None," Emily replied, resting her head against his chest. "It already feels more like home than anyplace I've lived since my mom died. Anyplace you are is home to me." She turned her face up to be kissed, and Paul pressed his lips against hers.

"Let's go to bed. It's been a long day." He took her hand and led her into the bedroom. Emily felt a flutter of nervousness stir in her belly. They had been too busy for her to think about what it would be like to sleep in his bed. She felt suddenly shy and awkward. Would she be expected to undress in front of him? He had told her she had all the time in the world to be ready for the intimacy of lovers, but would he get tired of waiting?

Almost as though she had spoken her worries aloud, Paul spoke. "If you want to change into your nightgown in the bathroom, it's perfectly alright. I figure it will take you a while to feel comfortable undressing in front of me."

Relief flooded her body. "Thank you, Paul. I was just worrying about that." She dug through a box to find her nightgown and disappeared into the bathroom.

When she returned, Paul was already in bed, sporting a pair of plaid flannel pajamas. He smiled and patted the bed next to him. "Climb in, my love. All I want is to fall asleep with you in my arms."

Emily got into bed and curled up next to him, her head nestled in the curve of his neck. His arms pulled her closer as he dropped a gentle kiss on her forehead. Emily sighed, feeling the comfort and safety of his embrace. She murmured an "I love you," and a minute later, they were both asleep, their breath mingling, their bodies entwined.

Chapter 24

Wild nights – Wild nights!
Were I with thee
Wild nights should be
Our luxury!

Futile – the winds –
To a heart in port –
Done with the Compass –
Done with the Chart!

Rowing in Eden –
Ah – the Sea!
Might I but moor – tonight –
In thee!

—Emily Dickenson

Spring/Summer 1961

Emily stirred in a strange bed, waking slowly then opening her eyes to find Paul lying beside her, leaning on his elbow, and gazing at her with a bemused smile. Returning his grin, she stretched. "Good morning. How long have you been watching me like that?"

"A few minutes. I'm just soaking in how beautiful you are and how amazing it is to wake up next to you." He leaned down to kiss her lightly. Emily rolled toward him for an embrace. Head on his shoulder, she suddenly caught sight of the bassinet and remembered the baby.

"Oh, my goodness! Danny's still asleep? Did he sleep through the night? He must be so hungry!" She tossed the covers aside to rush over to him.

"No, no, he's fine. He woke up around two in the morning, and you were fast asleep, so I got up and fixed a bottle for him. We

343

had quite the chat, and then he went right back to sleep."

"You fed him by yourself? And I didn't wake up?"

"Yes. I'm not completely helpless around babies. I am an uncle, you know. And I was half awake anyway. He had been grunting and rustling around for a while before he started to cry. I didn't realize that babies could be so noisy when they sleep!"

Emily chuckled at his naivete, despite his declaration of baby savvy. "I guess I've just gotten used to it, but I bet he'll be hungry again before too long. Thank you for handling night duty. It did feel good to sleep all night for the first time in a while. Do you want me to draw you a bath before I start breakfast?"

"Emily, I'm perfectly capable of turning on a faucet. You're not here to wait on me hand and foot, you know. I love you for who you are, not because I need a live-in housekeeper."

Giving a contented sigh, Emily stretched lazily and donned her bathrobe. "Okay then, I'll go rummage around in the frig and see what there is to eat. And I'll get another bottle ready in case he wakes up before Anna does. Hopefully, Anna is getting some good sleep, too. But I bet she'll want to nurse him as soon as she is up and dressed. Then we can start unpacking and rearranging."

"Good plan! And my vote is we start putting the crib together and getting Danny's room habitable. He can barely fit into that bassinet as it is."

"I know. It's unbelievable how fast he's growing." She yawned and shuffled barefoot into the kitchen to familiarize herself with the contents of the refrigerator. She pulled out some eggs and popped bread in the toaster. She didn't see a coffee pot but found some glasses for orange juice. Paul wandered in and walked up behind her, putting his arms around her. Emily turned and leaned into his chest, breathing in the smell of him and wondering at this new life she had fallen into. Then the smell of burning toast interrupted her reverie. She rushed over and pushed up the handle. "Oh, damn! I burnt the toast! I'm so sorry, darling. I'll be more careful next time."

Paul saw the touch of panic she tried to hide and took her face in his hands. "Relax, my love, no need to fret. I've eaten burnt toast more times than I can count. That toaster is finicky at the best of times. I'll just scrape off the worst of it and pile on the jam. It will taste lovely, because I'll be eating it across the table from you."

Taking a shaky breath, Emily dropped her shoulders and smiled. "I'm not used to such graciousness. Thank you. Between Mrs. Hutton and George, I'm more accustomed to catching hell for anything less than perfection. I think it will take some time to let go of those expectations, but I'm sure looking forward to it. Now, do you prefer charcoal or mildly scorched?"

The couple managed to get through breakfast before Danny woke up wailing for his bottle. Emily went in to change him, while Paul warmed up the formula she had already prepared. When she put it to his lips, he gulped eagerly and grasped her pinky finger in his chubby fist. Emily chuckled. "Oh my, you are a hungry little monkey, aren't you? Did you have a good sleep? Who got up with you in the middle of the night? Was that your daddy? He did such a good job! Yes, he did. We're going to fix up your nursery today, so you can have your very own room. And Auntie Anna is going to be here in a while, and we'll all help you get used to your new home. Won't that be fun? Now, let's think about giving me a good burp!"

Paul looked on in amusement and pondered this feeling of delight at being called Daniel's daddy. For so long, he had wondered if he would ever find someone to share his life with and if he was really fit for marriage and family. Yet here he was, in a most unconventional situation and finding it to be exactly what he wanted. Just then, Emily looked up at him and beamed.

At mid-morning, Anna walked over to take the baby off their hands for a few hours so Paul and Emily could start putting together the nursery. They worked together comfortably, with little need to discuss where to put things or who should do what. It felt perfectly natural to work in such harmony. In no time, the crib was up, and Danny's clothes and diapers placed in the used dresser Paul's mother had found. Mr. Graves had painted it for them—white with blue drawer fronts—and added a raised edge around the top to keep the changing pad from sliding around. In the midst of all this activity, the phone rang—Paul's parents offering to bring dinner over later. Paul and Emily were happy to accept, but neither of them was deceived that dinner was the primary reason for their visit. The older couple just couldn't wait any longer to meet little Daniel.

Anna and Jack brought Danny back over around five, as they

were planning to walk a few blocks to the local diner for a well-deserved break and to celebrate having a place of their own. The anxious looks that both of them had worn for so long had fallen away, replaced with their joy at being together and away from the abusive atmosphere of their family home. Hope had replaced worry and sadness, and they were looking forward to whatever the future might hold. As Anna handed the baby to Emily, she said, "He just ate about an hour ago, and took a short nap, so he should be okay for another couple hours. I just let him sleep on my bed, but now that you've got his crib set up, maybe we could take the bassinet to our house. I know he won't fit it in too much longer, but it will give us time to find a crib we can afford."

"Of course! Paul's parents are bringing dinner over later, but we can just bring it to the house after they leave. Now go have fun!" Emily grabbed Anna in an embrace. "I'm so glad you have a chance at a new life now. This is just the beginning for you!"

For the next hour, Paul and Emily moved as many boxes out of the living room and kitchen and into the upstairs bedroom as they could to make room for their guests. Soon, there was a knock at the door, and in walked Paul's parents. They quickly divested themselves of the food they carried, as well as a wrapped package and a large paper bag. Hugs were given all round, and then they rushed to the baby seat where Danny was lounging with a rattle in his hand.

"Oh, my goodness, he's adorable! Will he be okay if I pick him up? I just can't wait to get my hands on him!" Mrs. Graves exclaimed.

Emily chuckled at her eagerness. "Certainly, Mrs. Graves. So far, he hasn't been terribly clingy unless he's tired or not feeling well, so go right ahead."

The older woman gently lifted Danny out of his reclining seat and settled him into the curve of her arm. "Oh, look at you, little man! Aren't you just perfect?" She turned back to Emily. "And how's my son dealing with sudden fatherhood? Is he helping you with feedings and changing diapers and such?"

Paul piped up. "Mother, I'm right here! You act like I've never done this before. Remember I've babysat for Jeff and Louise a few times. If they trusted me to be alone with Bobby for a few hours, I think I can handle the basics with Emily looking over my shoulder."

Everyone laughed, and Emily went into the kitchen to set the table and make coffee. Mrs. Graves followed her. "That wrapped package is for you, a little housewarming gift, and the bags of clothes are hand-me-downs from Jeff and Louise. I think they're six-month size, so it might take Danny a couple months to grow into them, but I thought you would be glad to have them."

"Yes, indeed! It will be a gift not to have to go shopping every time I turn around as fast as he's growing." Emily carefully opened the wrapped gift, touched by her "mother-in-law's" thoughtfulness. Then her jaw dropped. She was holding the framed embroidery she had seen in the Graves' kitchen on her first visit, the John Wesley prayer on grace. "I can't take this! It belongs in your kitchen! It's so meaningful to your family."

"Nonsense. This isn't the original. I embroidered this for you as a 'welcome to the family' gift."

"But it's only been three weeks since I was there! How did you do this so quickly?"

"Oh, honey! I've been embroidering for years, and it's a fairly simple pattern, so I whipped it out in no time. I just thought, when I saw how much it affected you, that you might like to have one in your own kitchen."

"Thank you so much! It's beautiful! You and Paul and the rest of the family are direct evidence of God's grace. You've been so welcoming, and I'm grateful." Emily felt tears welling up, and she hugged Mrs. Graves tightly. When she pulled away, she saw tears in the older woman's eyes as well.

Paul walked in, clamoring for dinner, until he saw Emily and his mother's moist eyes. "Alright, what's brought on these waterworks, ladies? Are you crying because you know there won't be enough food for you when I'm done?"

Emily gave a half-laugh, half-sob and showed him the framed prayer. "Look what your mother made for us, Paul. Isn't it beautiful?"

"Wow, Mom! That's great! I've always loved that prayer, and it means a lot that we'll have one just like it here in our own kitchen. No wonder you were having a weep-fest in here!" He walked over and gave Emily's shoulder a squeeze. "Looks like you're not going to be able to back out now. You are officially one of the Graves clan."

347

On Monday, Paul and Emily went back to work while Anna watched Danny. Their co-workers had not been informed about the change in their relationship, but they would have been blind not to notice the stolen glances or the glimmer in the couple's eyes when they thought no one was looking. And anyone paying attention would have taken note of the fact that the two always arrived and left together. As the days passed, their lives settled into a routine, picking up Danny from Anna and Jack's place down the street, spending the evening playing with him until bedtime, then settling down in front of the fire to snuggle and chat about their day and their dreams for the future. They kept Danny with them on weekends so that Anna could have a break from babysitting duties to study the lessons Emily continued to give her, go for a walk, and on occasion go out for dinner and a movie with Jack.

The nights were similarly routine, with Emily changing into her nightgown in the bathroom before joining Paul in bed. Their kisses were becoming more and more passionate as time went on, but Paul seemed to know the exact moment when Emily began to pull back. He had promised to go slow, and he held to this promise. His hand would sometimes brush against the swell of her breast as he slid it down her side to rest on her hip or pulled her closer, and he noticed that her breath would quicken, but he didn't want to push further until she was ready. He longed for more but knew that patience was essential to her sense of safety.

On her part, Emily was feeling more and more comfortable with the intimacy of sharing a bed and of being seen in her nightgown. As spring turned into summer, she could no longer wear a flannel nightgown without sweltering at night, and she was aware that her cooler nylon gown clung to her body more closely, revealing more of her shape than flannel. And through all the waiting for her to be ready, Paul hadn't uttered a word of impatience or a given her even a glance of frustration.

One night, as Emily readied herself for bed, she gazed at her reflection in the mirror. She saw a woman with glowing skin, a glimmer in her eyes, and a perpetual smile on her face. Paul had done this. This man that was waiting for her to join him in bed on the other side of the door, waiting with arms open wide, loving her and cherishing her, willing to wait for her to give herself to him. He had been so patient, so gentle—nothing like George who, even when he still loved her, had been rough and unconcerned with her lack of pleasure at their union. How could she imagine that Paul would ever hurt her or be less than tender in their lovemaking? Why was she still holding back? Was she *testing* him? And she knew suddenly that it wasn't fair for her to make him wait any longer.

When she opened the door, Paul was reaching for his pajama top, upper body still bare. A curl of his dark hair had fallen onto his forehead, and he looked up at her with a roguish grin. Emily felt her heart turn over in her chest, and she caught her breath. "Paul," she whispered.

"What is it, darling?" He looked at her with concern.

Emily slipped the straps of her nightgown down over her shoulders, and let it slide gently to the floor. "I'm ready."

Paul dropped his pajama top and walked slowly to her, stopping a few inches short. "Are you sure?" he whispered. Emily nodded slowly, without hesitation. Paul took the final step toward her and cupped her face in his hands, kissing her deeply. Then his hands dropped to her breasts, stroking gently as he gazed into her eyes, watching for any hesitation, any hint of fear. There was none, only love and the gathering of breath. He scooped her up in his arms and carried her to the bed, shed his pajama bottoms and climbed in beside her. Hands explored, caressed, probed, breath quickening, desire building. Emily moaned in pleasure, and Paul could wait no longer. He entered her then and felt her legs wrap around him, drawing him deeper. "I love you," he whispered. "You have no idea know how much."

"Yes, I do," she said as she arched her back to meet his body stroke for stroke. After that, words were impossible and unnecessary, their bodies communicating everything they needed to know. When they at last fell gasping side by side on the mattress, hearts pounding, Paul took her hand in his. They lay in silence for long moments until Paul turned his head to look at Emily and saw tears coursing down her cheeks.

"What's wrong, darling? Did I hurt you? Dear God, I didn't mean to!"

Emily shook her head. "No, Paul. Don't fret. It was just . . . so beautiful. I never knew it could be this way. And it makes me sad.

That burst of pleasure at the end, I felt that a few times, with Father Devlin, but it was all mixed up with pain and shame, and I didn't know that it could be so full of love and beauty. George was so rough, and then he would fall asleep right away, leaving me alone and hurting in the dark."

She rolled onto her side to face Paul. "I'm sorry I made you wait so long. I'm sorry I thought for even a moment that you would be anything other than gentle and loving. I could sense you tonight, reading my every glance and movement to see if I was alright, to see if I wanted you to stop. And I didn't. Oh Lord, I did *not* want you to stop. It was exquisite, and if I weren't so worn out from it, I would want to do it again!"

Paul laughed. "Oh, don't worry, darling. Trust me, we have a lifetime together to do that as often as we want. We have some catching up to do!" He pulled her more tightly into his arms and wrapped his legs around her. They fell asleep that way, still naked, bodies intertwined.

Over the next days and weeks, Emily took Paul's words to heart and entered into their lovemaking with abandon. On the few occasions when Paul did anything she was uncomfortable with, she quickly learned that all it took was a tiny shake of her head for him to stop. One Saturday afternoon, while the baby was napping, Paul took Emily's hand as she puttered in the kitchen and pulled her into the bedroom. It was a beautiful day with the sun shining through the window above their bed, light playing across their bodies as they took pleasure in each other. Afterwards, Paul was still lying over Emily, elbows propping him up as they caught their breath. Sunlight shone on Emily's arms and face. Suddenly, Paul frowned and ran his fingers over what appeared to be scars on the underside of her forearms.

"What are these scars, Emily? I've never noticed them before."

Emily sighed. "I'd almost forgotten about them. It's going to sound strange, I know, but I made them myself."

"What? What on earth for? When did this happen?"

"It was shortly after George had raped me, and I was being bombarded with memories of what Father Devlin did to me. I felt so out of control, so ashamed and in pain. My body was actually feeling the sensations of what had been done to me as if it was happening right then. One morning, I was curled up on the bathroom floor, writhing in pain, screaming and crying, when I saw my comb lying there. Without even thinking, I grabbed it and began to rake it up and down my arms, over and over. Red welts raised up, and my arms started bleeding where the comb had broken the skin. It hurt something fierce, but surprisingly, it made me feel calmer. It was as if this was a pain I had control over. I could choose when it started and when it stopped, unlike the horrible abuses that had happened to me in both the past and present. And it was a way of punishing myself for being the person who deserved these things to happen. I just couldn't help but think that I must be innately bad and that my abuse was a punishment from God for just being me.

"After that first time, I started doing it whenever I felt out of control or overwhelmed by uncontrollable memories or by George's ongoing flaunting of his infidelity with prostitutes in our own home. Sometimes I used the comb, but there were also times when I grabbed a kitchen knife or George's razor. I can't tell you how strange it was to feel sweet relief at the same time as I was inflicting pain on myself. It's like another person entirely was taking charge of my body. I didn't think about the fact that I could have died of blood loss or that the cuts would leave indelible scars. I don't think I was even capable of rational thought in those moments."

Silent tears were running down Paul's face as he rolled to his side and pulled her close to him. "Oh, Emily, I can't bear to think of you doing this to yourself and believing that you deserved it. I can't imagine how desperate you must have been or how much pain you had to bear. If George wasn't in prison, I would be so tempted to track him down and beat him to a bloody pulp! But then, I'd be in prison, too, and I'd miss out on spending the rest of my days with you at my side." He took her free arm in his hand and began to kiss her scars gently and slowly from wrist to elbow, as if to draw the long pent-up pain from her marred skin before moving his lips to her face where her tears mingled with his own.

It was a warm weekend afternoon, and Emily was sitting on the floor with Danny, encouraging his efforts to roll over. He was on his tummy, grunting and wiggling and looking a bit like a backwards turtle who couldn't figure out how to stop rocking on his well-fed belly. Emily put her finger in his little fist and began to pull his arm upward, transferring his weight onto his side. Somehow sensing that he was headed in the right direction, he kicked backward with his leg, and suddenly, he was on his back and looking at his mother. He laughed with delight at the change in his position and view. Emily smiled broadly and called out for Paul, "Paul, come here! He did it! Danny rolled over!"

Paul rushed to her side, exclaiming to his son, "Good job, little man! What a big boy you are!" Both parents looked at each other, beaming at this latest accomplishment. In the midst of their delight over the baby's milestone, the phone rang. Emily stood and picked up the receiver.

"Hello, Graves residence."

"Oh, Emily, I'm so glad you're home!"

"Lottie? What's wrong? You sound upset."

"I—well—I don't know how to tell you this, but George is dead. He hanged himself in his prison cell. It was just in the Spokesman Review this morning, and I wanted to tell you before it hit the Seattle papers."

"What?!" Emily sank down on the couch as if her legs had suddenly given way. "I can't believe it! Are you sure? I—"

"Yes, Emily. It's true. I could hardly believe it myself, but then George wasn't exactly the type to adjust to prison life, was he?"

"No. You're right about that, but . . . oh, Lottie! I can barely take this in. It's such a shock."

"Yes, I'm sure it is. And it changes a lot of things for you. Do you know if George had a will? I'm sure you're still listed as his next-of-kin, and as far as I know, the house is still his."

"I hadn't thought of that. I guess I have a lot of thinking to do. Listen, I need to let you go. I have to tell Paul what's going on. I'll call you back soon. And—thanks, Lottie. You're a true friend."

"I feel the same way about you. I'll talk with you later. Take care of yourself, okay?"

"I will. I love you. Bye now."

Paul had walked over to sit next to Emily and took her into his arms as soon as she hung up the phone. "What is it, my love? What's happened?"

"You're not going to believe this. I—I'm a widow. George killed himself. He's dead." Emily said it as though to convince herself that it was true.

Paul stared at her in disbelief, a mixture of emotions coursing through him—shock, concern for Emily, and shame for the elation that was creeping into his head. They had not yet had time to consult an attorney about Emily filing for divorce, and now it would no longer be necessary. He held her tightly, her whole body shaking. "Are you alright? This must be a lot to take in. Tell me what you're feeling."

"Honestly, Paul, I don't know what to feel. Sadness, I guess, that his life had descended to this; relief that I no longer have to be afraid that he'll come looking for me some day and hurt you or the baby; guilt that I somehow contributed to his downfall. What I don't feel is grief. I suppose I should, but I'm not sorry he's gone. I can't be, not after everything he did to me. And I guess there's a part of me that feels nothing at all."

"That makes perfect sense, darling. He was a beast, and there's nothing you need to feel guilty about. He brought this on himself. I know he was a wounded child himself once, but he was the one who chose to react to the events of his childhood with power, control and violence, whereas you chose the path of kindness, generosity and love. And that's why I love you."

Emily lifted her head from his shoulder and save him a hint of a smile. "Thank you, darling. I don't know what I would do without you."

Just then, Danny let out a squall, outraged that he was no longer the center of attention. Emily rushed to pick him up and turned to Paul. "I guess we'll have to talk more later. I think this little guy is in need of some sustenance."

A few days later, just two years since she had made her escape from Spokane, Emily found herself on a bus that was taking her back into her past. After she had spoken by phone with George's attorney, she decided that she needed to go settle his affairs in person and put that part of her life to rest, once and for all. Paul had wanted to come with her for support, but she was adamant that this was something she needed to do herself. She wanted to make a clean break from all that had gone before, returning to Seattle purged of all the ugliness of her past. Paul and Danny were her future, and she wanted nothing to overshadow the brightness of it.

As she gazed out the window, she remembered the fear of her previous trip across the state, the sense of impending doom as she imagined the bus being pulled over by state troopers to take her into custody at George's behest. Looking back now, she realized how ridiculous that sounded, but at the time, George's control over her, his power and fury had seemed impossible to escape. So much had changed in such a short amount of time! When the bus finally pulled into the depot, Emily stepped off and was nearly bowled over by Lottie's embrace.

"Oh, my God, Emily! You're here; you're really here! I've missed you so much! Let me look at you." Both women were laughing and crying at the same time.

"Oh, Lottie," Emily said, "you haven't changed a bit! It's so wonderful to see you."

"C'mon. Let's grab your bags and get you home. The kids are nearly beside themselves with excitement. The boys have even given up their bed for you without a fuss. They think it will be fun to camp out on the floor in the girls' room. We'll see how long that lasts! How long do you think you'll be here?"

"Hopefully, just a couple of days. It depends on how long it takes to settle George's estate. And then I want to go visit my mom's grave and drive by Mrs. McGill's place. And I might stop and visit with Mr. Hutton if there's time. But for now, I want to hear all about you and your wonderful family."

"Oh, no. We can talk about that over dinner! I want to hear about Paul and that precious baby you're raising while the kids aren't around to interrupt!"

The two women gabbed non-stop until they pulled into Lottie's driveway. Within seconds, her children were tumbling out the front door, swarming Emily, and clamoring for hugs and kisses. Emily laughed at their eagerness, for a moment forgetting why she was here. Dinner was a feast of reminiscence, memories bubbling over like fine champagne. Just before bed, Emily called Paul. Though she had just left him and Danny this morning, she already missed them both desperately. The sound of Paul's voice when he picked up the phone made her heart beat faster. "Hello, darling. How are you? How's the baby?"

"We miss you! How was the trip? Are you enjoying your visit with Lottie?"

"I miss you, too. The bus ride was fine, and it's wonderful to see Lottie and the kids. I meet with George's attorney in the morning to sign some papers, and then he'll drive me over to the house to see what condition it's in. I'll call you again tomorrow night to report in. Oh, I'd better go now. Lottie's kids want me to tuck them in. Good night, darling. I love you. Give Danny kisses for me."

"I will, my love. Sleep tight and come home soon."

George's attorney looked much as Emily remembered him, though the intervening years had added more gray to his slicked back hair. His suit was clean but wrinkled, and Emily restrained an amused grin at how much this must have bothered George. Regardless, Mr. Neely was pleasant and professional, explaining in clear terminology everything that he put in front of Emily to sign. As expected, George had left no monetary assets, having spent all of his money on alcohol and prostitutes. His only remaining asset was the house. His car had been sold at some point to pay off part of his debt. When the paperwork was dealt with, Mr. Neely pushed back his chair and gestured toward the door. "Shall we go take a look? I have no idea what to expect, so I dare say, we'll both be surprised."

Emily nodded. She began to feel a rising anxiety at the thought of returning to her former home, site of so many painful memories. Yet, she was eager to get this over with and move on. If it weren't for the handful of people she cared about here, she wouldn't be sorry if she never returned to Spokane again. The attorney's office was located downtown, only minutes away from her former neighborhood, so there wasn't much time to dwell on her thoughts before they pulled up to the curb in front of house. Emily sat still for a moment, taking in the sight. The house hadn't changed much. The paint hadn't yet had time to fade, and blinds covered the windows, hiding whatever was inside. The only evidence of disuse was the overgrown yard and debris from windstorms that had tossed a few branches onto the lawn. Still, the house might be desirable to a potential buyer wanting a nice starter home in which to bring a new bride. She herself had been that bride once.

Mr. Neely waited patiently as Emily steeled herself for what she might find inside, what memories might lay in wait for her. Finally, she opened her car door and stepped out. The two walked side by side down the front walk, and the attorney pulled out a set of familiar keys, turned the lock and opened the door. A rank odor struck them before they could step over the threshold. Emily put her hand over nose and mouth, coughing slightly and exclaiming, "Good God! What is that smell?!"

Mr. Neely pulled out a handkerchief and handed it to Emily, which she quickly used to cover her mouth and nose. Then he gestured with his head to enter. She stepped across the threshold and into the front room. Even in the gloom, she could make out a scene of utter chaos and filth. Piles of dirty dishes were everywhere, clothing and newspapers strewn on almost every surface save the one chair that was George's favorite. Its cushion was sunken, fabric stained and covered with dust, which was everywhere, motes suspended in the rancid air. Emily reached over and pulled the drapes open to lend more light. "Holy Mother of God! He must have been insane!" The light had revealed more of the room—dining room chairs splintered into pieces, jagged arms and legs making it dangerous to navigate the room; the mirror over the fireplace shattered, shards sparkling in the light. Glancing down, Emily saw the pieces of their framed marriage certificate still lying on the hearth where she had flung it as she left.

Stunned, she walked toward the hallway and the room to which she had been banished after George had raped her. The door was hanging off its hinges, the top of it still bearing evidence of the shot gun blast that had prevented him from beating it down. Beyond, the room was empty. Other than the dust, it was just as she had left it. Between the two bedrooms, the bathroom was filthy, every enameled surface thick with the residue of bathing, shaving and who knew what. The stench here was overpowering, and Emily felt nausea begin to rise in her throat. She quickly stepped back and closed the door, eager to be done with this ghastly tour. She turned finally to the bedroom they had shared when their love was new, before the disillusionment began. Dingy gray sheets draped to the floor, even more clothes lay in piles and spilled out of dresser drawers. Empty liquor bottles crowded the top of the dresser and nightstand, and a stain on the door and broken glass underfoot spoke of a bottle thrown in anger. Small rubber circles lay on the floor near the bed, and it took a long moment before Emily realized they were used condoms. The nausea rose again, threatening to add to the horrid smell, but she was able to fight it down.

She turned to Mr. Neely, whose skin had turned to a sickly shade of yellow. "Let's get out of here," she said, and he nodded his vigorous agreement. They made their way through the obstacle course as quickly as possible, Emily casting a brief glance at the kitchen on the way out, eyes avoiding the table over which she had been so viciously violated. Mr. Neely closed the door and locked it in one swift motion, and they walked all the way back to the sidewalk before turning to look at the house one more time. Again, it looked merely benign and neglected, not reflecting the ugliness inside. "Just like George," Emily thought. "Just exactly like George."

She pivoted to the attorney and spoke in a steely voice. "Burn it down." She turned away then, opened the car and got in. As they drove away, she kept her eyes forward, not looking back.

On the bus ride back to Seattle, Emily reflected on the events of her trip and the emotional roller coaster it had been. When she and Mr. Neely had returned to his office after viewing George's house, he had tried in vain to convince her not to have it burned down. "It will reduce the value of the property, which you can ill afford considering the amount of debt he left behind. We can just hire professional cleaners to come in and get rid of all the junk. Maybe they'll even find something of value amongst the rubble. You never know. I urge you not to make such an important decision based on emotion."

Emily had responded, "I don't care if there's a million dollars hidden under the floorboards. I want it burned to the ground. I don't want anyone to have to live in a house where such abominable things happened. The very air in there reverberated with violence. You felt it too; I know you did. You said yourself that area has become a desirable neighborhood. I'm sure someone would love to buy a vacant lot on which to build their dream home."

"Well, I think you'll live to regret it, but it's your property, so I have no choice but to do as you wish. I'll keep you posted as to my progress in wrapping up the estate. And I'll let you know if anything unexpected crops up."

Emily had then said her goodbyes and returned to Lottie's home where she and her rambunctious children had done their part to chase Emily's emotional goblins away. The following day, she borrowed Lottie's car and paid a visit to the cemetery where her mother was buried. The sun shone brightly on beds of roses, snap dragons, and hydrangeas—their red, pink, yellow, and lavender hues lending a colorful counterpoint to the emerald green lawns. Giant oak trees dotted the landscape offering shade to those who had come to pay their respects to lost loved ones. Standing in front of Maddie's gravestone and thinking of her father's grave in a field in Normandy, Emily felt a sense of peace stealing into her heart. Gratitude overwhelmed her for the love they had given her. Though they had left her far too soon, she knew that their nurturance had given her the strength to survive all that had come after. It was that foundation of knowing herself to be loved that had sustained her through even the most difficult of times.

"Hi Daddy. Hi Mama. I just want you to know that I'm okay. There's a very special man in my life now, and he treats me like an equal, like Daddy treated you, Mama. He cherishes me, which I think is probably quite rare in this world. I wish you could meet him. And I—we—are raising a baby boy who feels like he is our own. I named him after you, Daddy. There probably won't be any more children, because I seem to be infertile, but Danny is more than I ever could have hoped for. I think of you both all the time, and I miss you so much. I hope you know how much I love you. Thank you for loving me and giving me so many happy memories in the time we had together." Then Emily had laid two yellow roses on the grave before walking away.

Afterwards, she had driven by Mrs. McGill's, and as luck would have it, her former landlady was outside watering her flower beds. Emily stopped and got out of the car to say hello. Mrs. McGill stared at her for long moments before it dawned on her who was walking up the sidewalk. Then she dropped the hose from her hand and rushed to pull Emily into an embrace. "Oh, my stars! Emily! Just look at you! You look wonderful. I haven't seen you in ages. How are you, love? My, you are a sight for sore eyes. Come in, come in! I want to hear all about you."

And so they had chatted in the woman's unchanged living room over iced tea. Emily glossed over the worst parts of her story but shared her love of Seattle and the work she was doing at the newspaper. Mrs. McGill had already heard about George's conviction and subsequent suicide. "I didn't lose any sleep over him. He deserved his fate. I'm just glad you were gone before he beat that poor woman almost to death. It sounds like he wasn't much of a husband to you at any rate, but I had suspected as much. I didn't like the look of him from the start. Too much of a prig for my taste. I suspected he would be hard to live with, too much of an unyielding taskmaster for your tender heart. I'm glad you're rid of him. And is there anyone special in your life now?"

Emily acknowledged there was and told her haltingly about Paul and Anna and the baby.

"Oh, bless your heart! You've got a baby to love! Well, I'm sure he is just precious. I'm so happy for you, Emily. You deserve every happiness this world can offer. You've done this old woman's heart a world of good today. I hope you'll keep in touch, and if you're ever this way again with your gentleman, please stop by to say hello. I'd love to meet the man that has put such a sparkle in your eye."

"I will, Mrs. McGill. And I just want you to know how grateful I am for what you did for me after Mama died. I don't know where I'd be if you hadn't gone to bat for me with the social services people. I will never forget it."

"Oh, darlin', it was nothing. Anybody else would have done the same. And you were a joy to have around the house. Now, I'm sure you have better things to do than sit around jawing with an old woman. I'm just tickled that you stopped by."

Afterward, Emily had dropped by Mr. Hutton's office, hoping he would have a few moments to visit. Luckily, he was in and happy to see her. She brought him up to date on George's estate, and he offered to be a liaison with Mr. Neely if needed. "And Emily, if there is any outstanding debt after the sale of the house, I want to cover it for you. I'm partner here now and not hurting for money. And I still feel so badly for how you were treated all those years ago. I know Vivian was hard to deal with, but I didn't know what to do about it. I feel like I failed you. I'm just so glad to hear that you are happy now and free of any fear that George could still come after you. I wish you the best, my dear. Be well."

Emily came out of her reverie and realized that the bus was entering the Seattle city limits, only a few short miles from the station. She smiled and sat up, checking her reflection in the window to make sure she looked her best for Paul, who would be waiting for her. Her beating heart told her how much she had missed him in just two short days. Soon the bus was pulling into the drop-off area and coming to a stop, brakes hissing. Emily could see Paul's eager face waiting for her on the sidewalk. Hemmed in by the other passengers who stood in the aisle pulling their bags down from the overhead rack, she waited impatiently to get off. Finally, they began deboarding the bus, and Emily rushed into Paul's arms. He kissed her eagerly. "I missed you so much! It feels like you were gone for a month instead of two days. You look wonderful!"

Emily laughed. "You're just glad I'm here to help with Danny. I hope he was good for you. Where is he anyway?"

"He's at Anna's. I thought he might get a little overwhelmed by the crowds and bustle. We can pick him up on our way home. Did I mention that I missed you?" He kissed her again, picked up her bag, and escorted her to the car. Once on the road, he asked, "So how was it? You look different somehow. It can't have been easy to go back to that house."

"No, it wasn't. It certainly brought up a lot of bad memories, but I also realized how much I've changed since then, how much stronger I am. I feel like I can close the door on that part of my life now and not look back. I feel . . . lighter somehow." She smiled. "I went to see my mom's grave. It was good to be there and feel her presence and Dad's too, even though he's not buried there. I got the feeling that they are happy for me, for where I am now, and that I have you and Danny in my life. I know that might sound odd, but I felt it very strongly. It was good."

Paul took her hand in his. "Lighter, I think that's what I sensed. If it's possible, you look even more beautiful than before. I'm glad you went, and even though it was hard to stay behind, I can see that it was a good thing for you to do this on your own."

The next morning was a Sunday. Though they had been attending church fairly regularly, alternating between Gethsemane

Lutheran and the Methodist church Paul's parents attended, Emily was exhausted from her trip and wanted to spend a lazy morning sleeping in and playing with Danny. When he woke up at six A.M., they brought him into their bed to give him his bottle and then dozed for a couple more hours. When he started to fuss, Paul took him into the kitchen to allow Emily another hour of sleep. When she finally emerged from the bedroom, yawning and stretching, Paul greeted her with a long kiss. "Hey, I have an idea. It's a beautiful day out. Why don't we pack up a picnic and the stroller and take Danny to the Washington Park Arboretum? I bet you haven't been there yet, and Harold has been asking when you were going to write another features piece on Seattle's landmarks. What do you say?"

"Mmmm. That sounds lovely. What do you think, Danny?" Emily said as she leaned over the baby's infant seat to plant kisses on his face and neck. He smiled and cooed at her. "I'm going to take that as a 'yes.' I'm all for it, darling. If you want to feed Danny his morning cereal, I'll fix us some breakfast and start making sandwiches."

Preparations complete, the small family loaded up the car and drove off. Soon Paul was turning into the parking lot of the arboretum with a flourish. Emily gazed around at old growth trees covered with moss, lush rhododendrons, brilliant Scotch broom, and velvet lawns. "Paul, this is beautiful! I never dreamt something like this could exist right in the middle of the city. It's magical!"

Soon they were strolling along winding paths through another world, Paul and Emily pushing Danny in his stroller. Each turn of the path led them to another scene of beauty and wonder. Finally, they reached a small pool with a trickling fountain in the middle. It was surrounded by mossy rocks and ferns, the varying shades of green creating an aura of serenity and stillness. Emily stood still for many moments taking in the beauty of the place when she heard Paul rustling around in Danny's diaper bag. She turned to look just as he slipped something in his pocket and walked over to face her with a serious look on his face.

"What is it, Paul? What are you up to?"

He put a finger under her chin and gently lifted her face to meet his gaze. "Emily darling, you know that I love you with all of my heart. I know our love story hasn't exactly unfolded in the usual

361

way, but I wouldn't want to change it for the world. I know without a doubt that I never want to be apart from you." He put his hand in his pocket, and when he took it out, he was holding a ring. "Emily Irene, will you marry me?"

Chapter 25

What strange emotion is this?
Contentment—
I'd thought it not for me.
So long I wandered the paths
Of grief,
Of anguish and of shame,
Never daring dream a life
As others do.
Yet boldly here it sits
On my doorstep,
Smiling at my surprise,
Inviting me in,
Welcoming me home.
> —Emily

Summer/Fall 1961

Reverend Patterson opened his office door and greeted the young couple warmly before ushering them to the chairs placed opposite his desk. "Emily, it's so good to see you! It's been a while. And Paul, I'm glad to have this opportunity to get to know you better. So tell me, what brings you to see me today?"

"Well, Reverend, a lot has changed since the last time I was in this office. Paul had broken off our relationship, and I was struggling with that loss. But the separation helped us both see how much we cared for each other, and so, even knowing the truth about my past, Paul asked me to take him back, and we have committed our lives to one another. Then, a few weeks ago, I learned that George had taken his own life while in prison."

The cleric's jaw dropped. "Oh, my goodness! How shocking that must have been for you!"

"Yes, it was. I would never have thought him capable of that, being the devout Catholic he was, but then in recent years he had been doing a lot of things that weren't in keeping with his beliefs. So yes, I was shocked, but also released. I went to Spokane to help in the settling of his estate, and as soon as I returned, Paul asked for my hand in marriage." She held up her left hand to show her pastor the ring sparkling on her finger.

"Well, this is quite the turn of events, isn't it? Congratulations, Emily! And you, too, Paul. I wish you both the best."

"Thank you, Reverend. We're not planning a big wedding. We didn't feel it would be appropriate under the circumstances. It will just be Paul's family and a few of our closest friends, and we're having it at Paul's parents' home in August. Hopefully, the summer weather will hold, and we can do it outdoors in their back yard, but if it doesn't, they have plenty of room for us to move indoors. But the main reason we're here is that we want you to perform the ceremony. It would mean a lot to me, after all the spiritual support you've given me, if you were the one to bind us together in holy matrimony."

"Emily, I would be honored. After all you've been through, to be a part of your new beginning would be a joy. You deserve every happiness, and I'm so glad I could play some small part in your healing process." The beaming pastor got up to walk around his desk and give Emily an enthusiastic embrace, then shook Paul's hand vigorously. "Congratulations, young man. You couldn't have found yourself a better woman to share your life with."

Paul smiled. "I couldn't agree more, sir. She's everything I could ever ask for—smart, beautiful, and compassionate. I'm pretty sure I'm getting the better part of this deal."

Emily swatted at his arm playfully. "Don't be silly, Paul. I'm the lucky one. Not many men would be willing to take on raising a baby that's not his own or a woman with a past like mine. You are able to look beyond that and take me for who I am here and now."

The Reverend then urged them to sit back down so they

could discuss the details of the wedding that would be taking place in a few short weeks. Once the formalities were dealt with, the men began to talk sports—both of them avid fans of crewing and baseball—and Emily's mind wandered to the delighted responses she and Paul had received to their announcement. After that day in the park, they had gone straight to Anna and Jack's house to share their news. The siblings had been ecstatic about the upcoming wedding, Anna especially. Not only was she happy for Emily, but it made her feel more secure in their situation, knowing that she and Jack were truly a part of this family. Paul's parents had also been overjoyed by Paul and Emily's engagement. Emily knew that they had dreamed of something more for their son, a more traditional wedding with all the pomp and circumstance, but his happiness took priority. She could hardly believe they had taken her into their family as much as they had, never giving her any hint of disappointment or regret. Being truly accepted as part of a family helped her feel a sense of belonging that she hadn't dared to hope for after all these years of being an outsider with the Huttons and even in her marriage to George.

And of course, the announcement in the office had been pandemonium! Everyone had jumped up to congratulate them—the women hugging Emily excitedly while the men vigorously shook Paul's hand. They were all talking at once, asking questions about when and where and how, just like good journalists would.

Just then Paul and Reverend Patterson broke into Emily's reverie. "Earth to Emily. Come in, Emily. I guess we got a little carried away with our analysis of the Rainier's pitching roster. Shall we get out of the Reverend's hair and let him get back to more godly matters, my love?"

"Yes, indeed. Thank you, Reverend—for everything. We'll be back in touch soon with more details about the wedding."

The following weeks flew by in preparation for the big day. Emily had asked Anna to help her pick out a wedding dress, and the two of them were in heaven at the opportunity to shop at Fredrick and Nelson instead of the local Goodwill. In a quandary about what would be considered appropriate for a widow who was already living with her husband-to-be, Emily decided to eschew white for something modest and pastel. She tried on several dresses, but time and again, one or the other of them would find something wrong—too short, too long, too traditional, too poufy, too plain. Finally, Emily walked out of the dressing room in a pale pink tea length A-line with a jewel neckline and sheer three-quarter length sleeves appliqued with pink daisies. Anna's jaw dropped. "Well," Emily said, "Don't just stand there with your mouth hanging open. What do you think?"

"Oh, Emily," she breathed, "it's absolutely gorgeous! You look beautiful. It's perfect. This is definitely the one."

Emily twirled in the mirror and beamed at her reflection. "I love it, too. It makes me feel pretty, and it meets all of our requirements. And it's not terribly expensive either. Some of those other dresses were a crime, they were so expensive. So, we're agreed, this is it?"

Anna nodded vigorously, still virtually speechless.

"Good! Now it's your turn."

"What do you mean, my turn?"

"Well, you're going to need a dress too, Anna. After all, you're my maid of honor."

"Really? I get to have a fancy dress, too?"

"Of course, silly! Now, what color do you think? Something that goes well with pink. Yellow, lavender, or—oh! How about light blue? To go with your eyes."

After a marathon shopping day, the two women returned victorious, having found Anna a lavender dress with similar styling, shoes for both, and a simple floral headband for Emily. They had even bought a cute little outfit for Danny. The boxes and bags got put in an extra closet at Anna and Jack's to prevent a curious groom from peaking before the wedding day.

In the meantime, Paul was planning a honeymoon to a secret destination and refused to give Emily hints, even though she pestered him relentlessly. The couple met with Reverend Patterson for pre-marital counseling and to finalize the details of the ceremony itself. Paul's mother helped Emily make decisions about flowers and the menu for the wedding luncheon, and in the midst of all of this, the demands of work and parenthood went on unabated.

And finally, the day arrived. Paul woke first and gazed for a moment at the face of the person he loved most in the world, wondering at the miracle that she would soon be his wife. Unable to wait a moment longer, he kissed her gently on the cheek. "Wake up, sleepyhead. I've got news for you."

Emily blinked her eyes and yawned. "Good morning, darling. What news is that?"

"We're getting married today. Can you believe it?"

A smile lit up her face. "No, I can't. But it really is happening, isn't it? I'm about to be one of the luckiest ladies in the world."

"Hmmm. And me the luckiest man. So how about we get up and get this show on the road? There's a lot to do before the 'I do's.'"

"Such a wordsmith! And you're right. We'd better get moving."

As if bestowing its blessing on Emily and Paul's wedding, Seattle had gifted them with one of its beautiful summer days, the kind that reminded residents of why they chose to live there. The sky was a brilliant blue, sun sparkling on rippling water, deep green trees dancing in a gentle breeze, a veritable rainbow of flowers gracing the Graves' back yard—pink begonias, lavender cone flowers, deep red geraniums, and purple sprigs of lobelia draping over the edge of hanging baskets.

Waiting in the family room with Anna and Lottie, who hadn't been sure she could come until the last minute and was wearing a borrowed dress, Emily watched as the guests gathered, butterflies fluttering in her stomach. Her throat tightened as she held back tears, in awe of this moment, of the people who had come to wish her and Paul well. Her eyes rested on Reverend Patterson, who had helped her beyond measure, Paul standing next to him, miraculously loving her despite everything, his brothers beside him, supporting his choice. She could see Mr. and Mrs. Graves in the front row, their generous acceptance of Emily a tremendous blessing to her. And then the music started.

Emily watched Anna and then Lottie walk across the lawn

to the arbor where the men stood, fidgeting in their suits. She took a deep breath and stepped across the threshold of the French doors. She felt as though she was floating up the grassy aisle, aware of little except the man who awaited her, gazing at her with love in his eyes. She suddenly felt her parents' presence powerfully, granting their approval, beaming at her from heaven, blessing this match, wishing her happiness. And then, the opening words, "Dearly beloved . . .."

More words—"I do"—"With this ring"—"I now pronounce you husband and wife." A kiss that communicated more than words could possibly tell, a walk back down the aisle, hands clasped, a new reality, a promise of forever. One quiet moment before they were inundated with congratulations to embrace, to kiss again, longer this time, to call each other by the names only dreamed of—Mr. and Mrs. Graves—to laugh with joy at this moment that life had led them to. And then they were surrounded by well-wishers, and the celebration began in earnest.

When all the toasts had been made, all the food devoured, all the gifts opened, and all of the guests had bid their farewells, the wedding party and Paul's family were finally able to collapse in the comfortable chairs and couches of the Graves family room. Emily cuddled Danny for several minutes, knowing she would be away from him for a week. "Mommy and Daddy are going bye-bye for a little while, Peanut, but Anna and Jack will take good care of you. Be a good boy, won't you, and sleep well. Anna gets cranky when she doesn't get enough sleep."

In response, Danny patted her face with a slobbery hand and said, "Mmmm," which everyone took to mean, "Don't count on it!" Emily handed him off to Mrs. Graves while she went to change into her traveling outfit. Emerging in her matching capri pants and crop top of emerald green linen, she and Paul said their good-byes with parting hugs to the Graves family, Anna, Jack, and Lottie. Emily gave Danny one last kiss on his pudgy cheek and felt herself choking up at the thought of leaving him.

Finally, Paul took her elbow, saying" C'mon, darling, we have a ferry to catch!" Reluctantly, Emily allowed herself to be pulled away, blowing kisses to everyone as they followed the newlyweds to the car and watched them drive off.

Settling in next to her husband, Emily laid her head on his shoulder. "Is this real? Are we really married?"

Paul smiled broadly. "Yes, indeed, Mrs. Graves. We really are. Ain't it grand?"

"Absolutely marvelous, Mr. Graves. So, where exactly are we going, sir? Is there a ferry that goes to Shangri-la?"

"Well, perhaps not quite that exotic, but I hope you'll find Victoria, B.C. to be an acceptable substitute."

"That sounds wonderful! I've heard Victoria is beautiful. And believe it or not, I've never been on a ferry before."

Before long, they arrived at the pier and got in a long line of other cars waiting to board. Despite her excitement, the frenzy of the past few days caught up with her, and she dozed off. The blast of a horn penetrated her consciousness minutes later, and Paul nudged her. "We're about to board, darling. I thought you'd like to be awake for this."

Emily sat up, craning her neck. "I would! Gosh, the ferry looks huge this close up, but there are so many cars. Are we sure it can hold all this weight without sinking?"

"It does so every day, all day long. We're quite safe. Now, do you want to go topside to see the view?"

"Yes, let's!"

Standing on deck and looking across the waters of Puget Sound, feeling the wind on her skin, and smelling the salt air was both peaceful and invigorating at the same time. All thoughts of sleep had vanished. The couple leaned on the railing and watched as trawlers, sail boats, and cargo ships plied the waters around them. They talked lazily about the plans Paul had made for their trip until they fell into a comfortable silence, not needing words to express what they were feeling.

When they sailed into Victoria Harbor almost three hours later, Paul pointed to a majestic hotel that dominated the waterfront. "See that building? That's where we'll be staying—the Empress Hotel, best hotel in the city."

"Oh, my goodness, Paul! It's beautiful! Are you sure we can afford this?"

"I'm sure. But that reminds me. Don't let me forget to take you to the bank when we get home and get you added as a signer on my account. I want you to be a part of the financial decision-making just as much as I am. We're partners now—in everything."

Emily reflected briefly on how George had refused to tell her anything about their finances, giving her a stingy allowance for food and necessities, but requiring her to ask permission for any other spending. Then she banished him from her mind. He didn't get to come along on this honeymoon.

The Empress Hotel was even more luxurious than it had appeared from the outside, with a grand lobby featuring dark polished wood paneling, burnished brass lighting fixtures, and richly appointed chairs in plush burgundy. Their room was equally exquisite and had a view of the waterfront where Emily could see people strolling casually along the boardwalk and small pleasure craft bobbing in their slips on the pier. "Oh, Paul! This is stunning! I couldn't have imagined anything half this wonderful."

Paul pulled her into his arms. "A stunning room for a stunning bride. How hungry are you? Because I know a good way to work up an appetite!"

Emily giggled and allowed herself to be carried to the bed where they celebrated their wedding in the age-old way.

The following days were filled with lazy breakfasts in bed, casual strolls along the waterfront, wandering through Chinatown, and driving to such sights as Craigdarroch Castle and Butchart Gardens. They even attended an evening concert at the gardens where classical music danced among the flowers that were lit with fairy lights. Emily had never in her life felt this spoiled or this relaxed. All her cares floated away for the first time since her father died so many years ago.

And then there was the food! Each meal was a feast attended by waiters that satisfied their every wish. And each time that Paul treated the wait staff with respect and gratitude, Emily smiled inside. At night, they fell into bed in a tangle of arms and legs, taking pleasure in each other's bodies again and again, only to wake in the morning and become aroused once more by a glance, a kiss, a touch.

Too soon, it was time to return to the real world. As wonderful as this idyll had been, Emily found that she was anxious to get home to Danny, to kiss his pudgy cheeks and hold him in her arms. The ferry ride seemed to drag, and even Paul seemed to share her urgency. When they encountered a traffic tie-up after leaving the ferry, he displayed uncharacteristic impatience, honking his horn at a car that was blocking an intersection at a green light. When they finally pulled up in front of Anna and Jack's, the couple raced to the front door. Danny was sitting in his infant seat, and when he saw them, he squealed and waved his arms excitedly. It didn't take Emily long to lift him out and hug him close. And Paul was right behind her, hand stroking the baby's hair as he spoke, "Hey there, little buddy! Mama and Daddy are here. Did you miss us? We sure missed you." Danny smiled widely and kicked his legs in delight.

Anna stood in the kitchen archway watching their reunion. "Hi, you two. Did you have a good time? It was sure different having you gone. I'm exhausted! Paul, I don't know what I would have done if your mom hadn't dropped by a couple of times to give me a break. This parenthood thing isn't for sissies!"

Emily laughed. "You're right about that. But we're here now, so you can relax until Monday when we have to go back to work. And just think, only another six weeks before you start school and get on with the life you've dreamed of. I guess Jack is at work, but why don't you two stop by tomorrow for dinner, so we can tell you about our trip. But for now, we're going to get out of your hair and let you take a breath."

"That sounds lovely," Anna responded. "We'll see you tomorrow then."

Soon, life settled into a normal routine, Danny spending his days with Anna and his nights and weekends with Emily and Paul. Marriage seemed to deepen Emily's contentment and her sense of safely and belonging. There were evenings when no conversation was necessary, when merely a glance or smile reassured her of Paul's love for her. Once Danny was in bed at night, they would often sit on opposite ends of the sofa, legs intertwining as they read the paper or listened to music unless there was a ballgame on.

As the summer hastened to a close, Emily helped Anna get ready to return to school. She was desperately in need of new clothes now that she was no longer pregnant. Anna also leaned on Emily to ease her fears about how she would do in high school after missing seventh and eighth grade completely. "You're going to do fine, Anna. You've been doing well in your studies, and your reading is already at tenth grade level. Your writing skills are good, and your math is passable. Remember, there's no shame in asking your teachers for help. They are usually pretty understanding as long as you show them you're willing to work hard."

"But I won't know anybody there. And what will I have in common with them? It's not like I've had a normal upbringing. What will we talk about? I can hardly discuss parenting tips with other girls my age!"

"Anna, the best way to make friends is to be interested in people and ask them questions about their likes and dislikes, their interests and goals. And yes, some of them might be silly and frivolous, but not all of them. All you need is one really good friend that you can count on for companionship and support, just like Lottie was for me. And she's still my best friend—besides Paul of course. Making friends takes time, but just keep being the caring and thoughtful girl you are, and it will happen. I promise. And just know that I'll always be here for you. Okay?"

Anna nodded, still anxious but somewhat comforted by Emily's words. Both she and Emily were facing big changes. Emily would be quitting work to stay home with Danny once school started. Anna knew how much Emily loved her job and wondered how she would handle the transition. Would she get bored at being a mom all day? In a way, knowing that Emily was also going through a significant shift took away some of Anna's fear. At least, she knew she would have someone to talk to who would understand.

As Emily's last day of work approached, she felt sadness creeping in. She had grown to care for the people she worked with, and she knew she would miss the camaraderie of the lunchroom, as well as the sense of purpose that came from their shared commitment to providing quality journalism to the Seattle P-I's readers. And yet she looked forward to embracing motherhood more fully, spending more time with her delightful son. She already loved him with a fierceness that surprised her in its intensity at times. It made her feel closer to her mother, knowing that this must have been how Mama felt about her. There was a certain kind of sadness that accompanied this, feeling deeply the absence of her mother for advice and understanding. Fortunately, Paul's mother had offered her help whenever needed and lived close enough that she could be there in minutes if an emergency arose.

Paul had offered to teach Emily to drive, and although she was hesitant at first, she finally conceded. Sometimes Seattle traffic could be challenging, and even Paul lost his cool at times. Even deeper was her irrational fear of buses. Buses were everywhere in Seattle. She'd ridden in them most of her life without a qualm, but the thought of driving a car alongside buses on the streets brought with it visions of being plowed into, just as the bus that killed her mother had crashed into the local grocery store. However, Emily could see Paul's point. Should an emergency with Danny arise, driving him to the hospital herself would be faster than waiting for Paul to come and get them.

Although she found shifting to be a challenge, Emily soon discovered that she enjoyed the sense of freedom and independence that driving gave her. No longer did she have to wait for a bus or rely on Paul to take her where she needed to go. It made her feel powerful, releasing one last remnant of the control George had exerted over her.

Finally, it was her last day at work. Although Paul still planned to bring editing work home for her when the office was overloaded, and Harold Stone had exacted a promise that she would continue to write feature columns, it would be the last time she would be part of the office family, and Emily knew she would miss her co-workers dearly. She spent the morning clearing her desk of any unfinished work and passing along longer-term projects to other editors. When she looked up, most of her workmates had already headed to the lunchroom. Emily grabbed her lunch pail from her desk and walked briskly down the hall. When she opened the lunchroom door, she was met by a chorus of voices shouting, "Surprise!" A large bouquet of flowers and a chocolate layer cake occupied the center of the table.

Emily's hands went to her face, and emotion squeezed her throat. "Oh, my goodness! You didn't have to do this!" She looked at Paul, whose eyes were sparkling. "Oh, this is so touching. Thank you! I'm going to miss all of you so much. You've become like family to me, and I will never forget your kindness, the way you've made me feel like I belonged." Her voice cracked. "Really, you have no idea what you've meant to me. And this is just icing on the cake."

Everyone laughed at her pun, then someone shouted, "You'd better eat your lunch, or the cake will be gone before you can get to it."

At the end of the day, one by one, her co-workers came to her desk to say good-bye. "Make sure you stop by with the baby from time to time." "Don't be a stranger." "I don't know what we're going to do without you around here." "Who's going to keep Paul on the straight and narrow now?" Emily's handkerchief was soggy by the time it was over.

On the way home, Paul reached over and took her hand. "What are you thinking?"

"I'm overwhelmed. Everyone has been so good to me. That send-off was beyond my imagining. Were you the impetus behind that?"

"Not at all. It was their idea. They really did come up trumps, didn't they? I think this is the best crew I've ever worked with, you included. I love that you're going to be able to stay home with Danny now, but I'll sure miss seeing you at work every day."

"Mm. Me, too. But we're married now. We might not have all of the days, but we'll definitely have all of the nights!"

Paul squeezed her hand and chuckled. "Don't go giving me any ideas. We still have dinner and playtime with Danny before we can think about that!"

Three days later, it was time for Anna's first day of school.

Emily had agreed to drive her to school after dropping Paul off at the office. When she pulled up in front of the house, Jack was just giving Anna a hug before taking off for work himself. Anna got in the car looking pale and nauseous. "I'm going to throw up. I just know it. And everybody is going to make fun of me, and I'll end up having no one to hang out with but other nerds like me. And of course, I'm getting a pimple on my nose. Just perfect!"

"Are you done? Because you sound ridiculous. I promise you that every other freshman in that school is feeling the same way right now. That's just the way it is. And you'll get over it about an hour after you get there. Remember that this is what you want. A chance to have a normal teenage experience, a chance to learn and to be something more than your parents thought you could be. Go prove to yourself that you are worthy of an education and a future that doesn't reflect your past. You've got a chance to BE somebody—whoever you want to be. And this is the first step. So take a deep breath and buck up, because I'm not taking you back home before your future has even started. Got it?"

Anna stared at Emily for a moment, letting her words sink in. Then she took a breath and exhaled. "Yes, ma'am. I've got it!"

Emily smiled widely, and Anna responded with a grin of her own. "Okay. We're here. Go learn something. And have a great day."

Anna reached for Emily's hand and squeezed it tight. "Thanks, Emily. For everything." Then she was out of the car and walking toward the big double doors. She looked back once and waved, then opened the door to her future.

At home, Emily put Danny down for his morning nap, started a load of laundry and went into the kitchen to wash up the breakfast dishes. She spent the day puttering around the house, dusting, picking up Danny's toys, straightening yesterday's paper. And at some point, she realized that she was smiling.

Chapter 26

The prophets cry, "Justice!"
The people cry, "Justice!"
The children cry, "Justice!"
Not with words or clenched fists,
But with pleading eyes,
Trembling hands clasped in prayer,
Huddled in a corner.
Theirs is a communal voice that whispers,
"How long, O Lord,"
And hovers like vapor in the air,
Like smoke from a candle.
　　　　　　　—Emily

Fall 1961/Winter 1962

As summer turned to fall, the clear skies abandoned the city, rain following in their wake bringing cooler than normal temperatures. One cold Sunday morning, Paul and Emily decided to skip church and have a lazy morning in. Paul started a fire in hopes of easing the chill in the house. Danny was napping, and his parents took advantage of the respite to curl up on the sofa with the newspaper, Paul laying claim to the sports page and Emily glancing through the local news. Suddenly, she sat bolt upright. "Oh, my God! Oh, my God! He's here! He's been here all along!"

Paul looked up and saw sheer panic on his wife's face. "What is it, Emily? What's wrong? Who's here?"

She thrust the paper at him with shaking hands and pointed to a headline, 'Missing Altar Boy Found Dead in Church Sacristy.' "It's him! It's Father Devlin—my priest at St. Ignatius! Oh, my God, it's him."

Paul dropped the paper and pulled Emily to him. "It's

alright. I've got you, and he can't hurt you now. You're safe with me."

"But what if we run into each other somewhere, and you're not with me? He's dangerous, Paul! You have no idea!"

"I have no doubt that he's dangerous and that he hurt you horribly. I also know that you're an adult now, and he probably wouldn't even recognize you. And while you may know *he's* here, he doesn't know *you're* here. You have a different last name now, and there's just no way for him to find you."

Emily allowed that reality to sink in and calmed herself enough to talk coherently. "I know you're right. It just caught me so off guard to see his name and realize that he's just up the road in Lynnwood. And I'll bet you anything he killed this boy."

"Okay, let me read through this and get the whole story, and then we can talk about what it means."

Missing Altar Boy Found Dead in Church Sacristy

LYNNWOOD—The body of Billy Clark, 11, who went missing yesterday afternoon, was found just hours later in the closet of the church sacristy at Church of the Holy Innocents on Walnut Avenue. The boy had been training with Father Anthony Devlin to become an altar boy and, according to the priest, left the church to walk home around 3 p.m. When he hadn't arrived home by four, his parents, John and Martha Clark, went to the church to pick him up. Finding him not there, police were called, and a search party organized immediately due to the boy's chronic health concerns which required regular medication. When a house-to-house search of the neighborhood revealed nothing, police turned their attention to the church itself, eventually discovering Billy's body in a closet in the church sacristy. No other details were available prior to press time.

Paul finished reading. "This is horrible! I can see why this is upsetting you so, Emily. The circumstances are highly suspicious, but there's little real information here. The good thing is, I'm in the perfect position to receive updates before they even hit the paper. I'll keep an eye out and share anything I can with you as more details are released. This is likely going to be all over the front page for a while. The suspicious death of a child is always big news."

Sure enough, by Tuesday the front-page headline read, 'Priest Questioned in Altar Boy's Death.' The article related the fact that Devlin had been taken to police headquarters to "assist the police with their inquiries" on Monday morning. The reporter had done some research on Devlin's history, and reported that he had been at this particular parish for five years, following assignments in three different parishes in Spokane over a twenty-year period. Not surprisingly, church officials declined to make a statement. Police reported that no arrests had been made but that the investigation was ongoing. Autopsy results weren't expected until the end of the week.

Over dinner, Paul and Emily discussed the case. Paul said, "The police didn't come right out and say he's a suspect, but that's certainly what it looks like. What do you think?"

"Oh, I know he's guilty. They don't really say how that boy died, but I guarantee you Father Devlin was abusing him. Looking back, I think his abusive behavior was absolutely compulsive, and he wouldn't have stopped just because he got put on medical leave. I'm not sure I ever told you this, but the last time I saw Sister Mary Francis, she told me that she and the parish secretary reported their suspicions that he was molesting me to the diocese. I think that's why they removed him from the school, using the cover story that he was being treated for a medical condition. He never looked sick to me, at least physically. Mentally, well, that's a different story!

"But if this reporter's timeline is correct, they sure didn't keep him away from a parish for long. How could they just put him back into a church where he would have more opportunities for molesting children? No wonder they're not commenting! He's like a wolf among the sheep. And they are the ones who set him loose.

Catholic parishioners admire their priests so much, they couldn't imagine them to be capable of such horrors. That kind of hero worship doesn't exactly allow room for suspicion or caution. I remember how stunned Mr. Hutton was when I told him what had happened to me. He had no idea. It just gives me the creeps that for the past five years, this monster has been living less than twenty miles away from me. What if I run into him when I'm out in public somewhere?" She shuddered.

Wednesday morning's headline read, 'Distraught Parents Convinced of Priest's Guilt.' The P-I's head reporter had obtained an exclusive interview with Mr. and Mrs. Clark detailing their suspicions. They stated that they had begun having doubts about Father Devlin, because Billy had recently been visibly upset upon returning from his weekly training with the priest. He had denied anything was wrong but disappeared into his room until dinner where he was unusually quiet. Billy's mother also reported that she had doubted Devlin's story of Billy choosing to walk home that day, as it had been drizzling, and Billy knew that his parents had planned to pick him up. Also, several of Billy's friends lived near the church and would likely have seen him walking home if he had done so.

For the fourth night in a row, Billy's death was the topic of conversation over dinner. Emily couldn't get it out of her mind, seeing all the signs that something very wrong had been happening to this innocent young boy long before he died. "I just can't stop thinking about this, Paul. It's all right there in the parents' story. But Devlin can be so convincing to parents. He's a smooth talker when he wants to be. I remember how he would talk to the Huttons after mass and tell them what a great student I was and how he enjoyed working with me. Little did they know what kind of 'work' he meant! I don't know what the police are waiting for. Surely they're going to arrest him soon!"

Paul looked at her solemnly. "So, what are you going to do about this, Emily?"

"What? What do you mean?"

"I mean, you know something about this man that the police don't. And there are more victims out there. As you said, he wouldn't have stopped. Compulsions don't just go away. Your story might be the thing that helps the police put this predator away for the rest of his life."

Emily pulled her hand away from her husband with a look of horror on her face. "Are you saying I should tell the police what he did to me? I couldn't possibly! The very thought gives me the heebie-jeebies!"

"I can't tell you what to do, love, that's a decision only you can make. What I'm saying is that you have a chance to make sure that no more children are victimized by this wretched excuse for a human being. And maybe that will be the means by which you are ultimately healed from the emotional wounds he caused."

"Are you saying I haven't healed? Because I have! You have no idea what kind of a mess I was before you met me."

"That's not what I'm saying. You *have* healed. Both from what you've told me and what I've observed, you have come a long way. But I also see your reaction to this article, the fact that you haven't been able to think about anything else since Sunday, and that Danny has been dropping food on the floor for the last five minutes, and you haven't even noticed."

Emily jumped up. "Oh, for Pete's sake! Why didn't you say something sooner?" She ran to the kitchen sink for a rag and took Danny's plate away from him. A few minutes later, mess cleaned up, she put him in his playpen to amuse himself for a while before it was time to get ready for bed. She returned to the kitchen and stood in the archway, leaning against the frame. "I hear what you're saying, Paul, but I just don't know if I can do it. I'll think about it. Give me time."

"Of course, darling. I know this is terribly upsetting for you. I probably shouldn't have brought it up while you were still so upset about this latest development. I'm sorry. And truly, this is completely up to you. I don't want to pressure you in any way. Okay?"

Emily nodded and walked into his arms. She leaned into him and put her hand on his chest, absorbing the solidity of him. He was her anchor while her past was being stirred up just when she'd thought it was behind her for good.

On Friday, the headline read, 'Altar Boy Died of Asphyxiation.' The coroner's report confirmed that the boy had been murdered and suggested there was evidence of sexual assault. The Clarks had been interviewed again and were reportedly hysterical over this latest information. Mrs. Clark was quoted as saying, "How could he have done such an obscene thing to our son? He just wanted to be an altar boy. He was a good boy! And that man defiled him and then killed him. He ought to be hanged." The detective in charge of the case, Lieutenant Richey, was tight-lipped, saying only that an arrest was imminent.

Emily's hands were shaking as she lowered the paper, imagining the heartbreak of those parents. She thought of how much she loved her little Danny and how it would feel if she were to lose him for any reason, much less murder. Her stomach turned at the idea of anyone putting their hands on him or inflicting anything approaching what she had experienced at Father Devlin's hands. It was more than she could bear just to think of it. She was particularly quiet that evening, and Paul was quick to notice.

"What's going on, darling? You haven't said a word, and you look a thousand miles away."

"It's this poor dead boy, Paul. I can't stop thinking about him, about what was done to him, and what his parents are going through. It's just so awful! He was so young and full of life, just wanting to serve God as an altar boy in the church, and his innocence and vulnerability were taken advantage of by the vilest of men. It's disgusting! Why haven't the police arrested him yet?"

"I don't know. I'm sure they are taking their time, being careful to build an airtight case. I know it's hard to wait though. What was done to that boy is truly is an abomination. And your anger and outrage are compounded by what happened to you. It seems like you want justice for Billy, because it might feel like it would also be justice for you."

Emily thought for a moment. "Yes, I think you're right. I want both. And really, not just for Billy and me, but for all of the other children I'm sure he must have abused along the way."

The next morning, Emily was up first and went out to get the paper from the front porch. The bold headline shouted, 'Priest

Arrested in Altar Boy Murder.' She picked it up and raced back into the bedroom. "Paul! Paul! They got him! They arrested Father Devlin! Thank God. Oh, thank God!"

Half-dressed, Paul rushed over to embrace her. "That's great to hear. I figured it was only a matter of time. The police rarely tell the press what evidence they've got, so as not to show their hand, but they must have enough now to move forward. What else does it say?"

"I didn't read any further than the headline. Let's see. . . something about Devlin's blood type matching blood found under Billy's fingernails and his fingerprints on Billy's belt buckle. And of course, Devlin is denying the whole thing, says he's a scapegoat for the police department's inaction. He claims public outrage put so much pressure on them that they arrested the most convenient suspect to avoid being seen as incompetent. It figures that he would put the blame on someone else."

"Well, he would hardly confess right off the bat, would he? But what matters is that he's in jail, and they are going to work hard to keep him there. Did the paper mention anything about bail?"

"No. He won't be arraigned until later today. Hopefully, they won't let him out."

"I doubt the judge would do that. If he did, there *would* be a public outcry. And now, I'd better finish getting dressed, or I'll be late for work!"

Throughout the day, Emily could think of little else but this latest development. She thought about Billy's parents, about other parents whose children had been molested by predators like Father Devlin. She thought about the way it seemed the diocese had protected Father Devlin from the possible consequences of his actions and turned him loose on other unsuspecting parishes. How many others had he abused? How many more would he harm if he was somehow found innocent? Would a jury think there was enough evidence to convict?

Paul came home bearing the news that the judge had refused bail and remanded Devlin into custody until his trial. Paul had personally been the one to edit the article that would appear in the next day's paper. "Thank God!" Emily exclaimed. "I'm so relieved. It's where he deserves to be, and he can't hurt anyone while he's locked in a cell. And I'm guessing he won't have an easy time of it in there." A tiny, satisfied smile played on her lips.

"I thought you might be pleased with this news. Maybe your anxiety will ease up a bit now."

"Well, about the possibility of running into him, yes. But now there's something else."

Paul looked at her curiously. "What do you mean?"

"Well, I've been thinking all day, and I think you're right. I need to tell the police what he did to me. They need to know this wasn't just a one-time thing. They need to be able to establish a pattern so he can't say he would never harm a child. I need to speak for Billy, because he's not able to. And something you said the other day really stuck with me. Justice for Billy means justice for me as well. By doing this, I will be choosing not to be a victim anymore. I was too young and too vulnerable to fight back when he was abusing me—too afraid of not being believed or of being rejected by the Huttons and sent back into the custody of child services. I was too ashamed, too certain that I must have deserved what he was doing. But I'm none of those things anymore. And I'm so much stronger. I *can* fight back and make sure that he never touches another child again."

"That's my girl! I'm so proud of you. And I will support you in any way I can. I know it will be hard to face him on the witness stand and tell people what happened to you, but I also know you can do it, and I will be right there in the courtroom when you do. And have I mentioned lately how much I love you?"

Emily smiled and threw her arms around his neck, raining kisses on his cheeks. "I love you, too, Mr. Graves."

Emily sat nervously outside Lieutenant Richey's office, waiting for him to get off the phone. She had called him the day before, and he had sounded eager to hear her story. They had scheduled an appointment, and Emily had asked Paul's mother to come and watch Danny for her while she was gone. Finally, the detective poked his head out the door and invited her in. When she was seated, he asked, "Is it okay with you if I record your statement? It just helps me remember what you say and how you say it, your intonation, and that sort of thing. Plus, I'm sure the district attorney is going to want to hear this, and he wasn't able to be here today." Emily nodded her assent, and he pressed a button on the device on his desk. "Now, Mrs. Graves, please just start at the beginning, and if I have questions, I'll chime in."

"Okay. I guess the beginning is when my mom died. My dad had been killed in the war, so it had just been my mom and I for three years until she was killed in a bus accident. My parents were both only children, and my father's folks were dead. My mother was estranged from her parents, so there was no family that could take me. Our landlady took me in for a while until the state could find a suitable foster family. I remember being terrified that I would be sent to an orphanage, so when they did find a family, I was so relieved. They were Catholic and sent me to the Catholic school in their parish. Father Devlin was the parish priest who offered to tutor me in catechism since I was so behind the other kids in my grade. From the beginning, I felt uncomfortable around him. When I was in his office, he would touch me a lot, like stroking my hair or rubbing my arm, stuff like that. And he would sit beside me on his couch and put his arm around me, talking to me about how hard it must be to lose my mother and live with a family I barely knew, not to mention having to change schools and be the new kid.

"My foster mother was an invalid due to a stroke late in pregnancy, and the baby was stillborn. This loss impacted her profoundly. One minute she would be tearful and morose, and the next she was agitated and irritable. She drank a lot and misused the drugs her doctor had prescribed for her nerves. In short, she was not an easy woman to deal with. They had two children at home, and it was my job to care for them after school and to cook and clean. My foster father was a lawyer who put in long hours, so he was rarely around. I'm sorry—this might seem like a lot of detail, but I think it explains how Father Devlin was able to do what he did without too much concern that my foster parents would figure out what was going on."

"Not to worry, Mrs. Graves. The more detail the better at this point. Please continue."

"Okay. In the beginning, Father Devlin was fairly no-nonsense and intimidating, but then he started having me sit on his lap sometimes to talk to me after my lesson. I always felt so awkward about this, because I felt I was too old to be sitting on a grownup's lap. And now that I'm an adult and understand the mechanics of sex, I think he was getting an erection during those times." Emily paused to gather her composure. It was embarrassing to talk about such intimate details, and she knew that she was going to have to be even more graphic before she was through.

Lieutenant Richey spoke. "I know this is hard, Mrs. Graves, but every piece of information you can give me is going to help put this monster away. You're doing great."

Emily took a deep breath and resumed, hands clasped tightly in her lap. "For a while, that's all he did. And then he started touching me like I said before, gradually getting more and more . . . bold, I guess would be the word. Sliding his hand down my back to squeeze my bottom or moving it around to my chest. And then there was confession. I always went last because of where I sat in the classroom, and once he was able recognize my voice, he would wait until the rest of the class had filed out and push aside the curtain between us. He made up so-called games as my penance, like rubbing his, uh, privates. At first, it was just through his clothes, but he would moan, and his eyes would glaze over, which made me feel—gross. Later, he would unzip his pants while I did it, and then eventually, he made me put it in my mouth." She stopped again, feeling nauseous and wishing she had accepted Paul's offer to come with her.

Sensing her discomfort, the detective turned off the recorder and stood. "Let's take a short break. Can I get you some water?"

"Yes, thank you. That would help." He walked down the hall and out of sight. Emily realized that she was shaking. Lord, help me get through this, she prayed. And then a line from the Psalms came to her—"The Lord is my strength and my shield."

She felt the tension gradually ebb from her body as she repeated those words in her head until her breath began to slow and fall into the rhythm of the litany. By the time Lieutenant Richey returned, Emily was calm and ready to continue. She took the water glass he handed her and took a sip.

"Better? Are you ready to continue?" he asked.

Emily nodded and began to speak. Horror by horror, she related the things Father Devlin had done to her—the "lice checks," the endless invasions of her body, the shame he provoked in her, the pretext of a love that others wouldn't understand, the admonitions not to tell, the gradual increase in severity until that final anal ravaging before he was placed on medical leave.

When she finished, the lieutenant turned off the tape recording and sat silently, stunned. He had gone quite pale, and when he lifted a hand to rub his face, it was trembling. "Mrs. Graves . . . Emily. I can't imagine what it took for you to tell me all this. I am truly sorry that you had to endure everything this . . . *fiend* put you through. And I'm incredibly grateful that you were courageous enough to come here today and share your story. But I'm going to ask you another favor. I'm absolutely positive that there are more victims out there, and if they know someone has come forward, they might be brave enough to come forward too. The more victims that testify to his deviant actions, the better chance we have of making sure he never hurts another child. So that means making your statement public. Can you let me do that? Not the gory details, but that he had sexually abused you as a child. It's possible that I can maintain your anonymity for now, but once you testify at trial, I won't be able to keep your identity out of the papers."

"I had already thought of that, Lieutenant. I do work for a newspaper, after all. So yes, I am prepared for what's coming. I'm a private person, but in extraordinary times like these, we are called to step up and do the right thing even at great personal cost. Do what you need to do."

The man shook his head, impressed by her sheer determination. "I can't thank you enough for your cooperation, Mrs. Graves. I will be taking this tape to the district attorney as soon as he's available, and I'm sure he will want to talk to you personally. I'll be in touch." He stood and reached across his desk to shake her hand.

Emily responded with a firm grasp, a commitment sealed, a promise made. There would be no going back.

When Emily got home, Mrs. Graves was rocking Danny and reading a story to him. She looked up and smiled. "I sure do love this little charmer. He's such a good baby."

"He looks quite content for you to hold him. You're reading his favorite story, too. Thank you so much for coming over. I'm probably going to be leaning on you again once the trial starts, so please let me know if it gets to be too much."

"Nonsense! I love getting to spend time with him. I've always loved babies, and they grow up too fast. I think it's why we ended up with four kids. Every time one would reach toddlerhood, I would get the hankering for another baby. That's the great thing about being a grandma. I have four offspring who are keeping me supplied with babies to hold."

Emily laughed. "Well, enjoy this one Mrs. Graves, because it's doubtful we'll be able to contribute any more to the menagerie."

"Why's that, Emily? You don't want more children?"

"Oh, it's not that. I'm not able to bear children. My first husband and I tried for a long time with no success. That's why Danny is such a gift to me, to us."

"I'm sorry to hear that. Not for my own sake, but for yours and Paul's. You are such a good mother to Danny. But speaking of mothers, I've been wanting to talk to you about what to call me. I think our relationship is past the point of you continuing to address me as Mrs. Graves, but I also don't want to dishonor your own mother in any way by asking you to call me Mom. Do you think you could bring yourself to call me Elaine?"

"Oh! I guess I never thought about that. When I was a child, it was ingrained in me to call adults by their formal title. I called every adult I knew by Mr. or Mrs., but I guess I'm an adult now too, aren't I? I'd be happy and honored to call you Elaine—if I can remember! You'll have to nudge me if I forget."

Elaine rose from the rocking chair and gave Emily a one-armed hug before passing the baby over to her. "You call me anytime you need me. There's nothing I'm involved in that's more important than supporting you through this trying time. I hope you know that."

"I'm grateful for your support, Elaine. It means a lot to me."

As predicted, two things happened next. An article appeared in the paper with the headline, 'Local Woman Reports Past Abuse by Murder Suspect.' The article didn't name Emily but related her story with time and location. Lieutenant Richey had told her to expect this, because it broadened the area and time frame for Devlin's possible abusive activity. By doing this, the police hoped to catch the attention of further victims in hopes that they would come forward to testify. And then, she received a call from the district attorney, Sam Waters, inviting her to come to his office. This time, Paul insisted on coming with her after she had shared how difficult the first interview had been.

When they were ushered into the DA's office, Emily was surprised to see Lt. Richey also there. When everyone was seated, Waters spoke. "Thank you for coming in, Mrs. Graves. We appreciate how difficult this must be for you. Hopefully this won't be as traumatic as your interview with Lt. Richey here, but I will need to ask you some questions that will likely be uncomfortable. Please let us know if you need a break at any time." He gestured to a water pitcher and glasses on a side table. "Can I get you some water before we start?"

"Yes. Thank you," Emily replied.

He poured a glass for both Emily and Paul, then resumed. "As you can see, I have a recording machine here. I want to play the tape that was made of your prior statement to Lieutenant Richey. Sometimes, hearing the story reminds you of details you left out or incidents you forgot that might be pertinent to the case. Are you ready?"

Emily nodded, and he pushed the start button. Paul reached out to take her hand. They both listened intently. Once she got past the strange sound of her own voice, Emily tried to listen dispassionately and focus on the facts of her story, things she might have overlooked. After a few minutes, she heard a strangled sound from Paul and turned to look at him. He had turned quite pale, and his eyes were closed in distress. Emily realized this was the first time he had heard the full details of what Devlin had done to her, and he was struggling to maintain his composure. She pushed his water glass closer to him. He opened his eyes and looked at her with deep sadness, then took a drink and dropped his eyes to the floor. He gripped her hand more tightly as if clinging to a life raft. His grip conveyed both strength and sympathy, and it allowed Emily to acknowledge just how much it took to listen to her own voice detailing the atrocities Devlin had committed.

When the tape came to an end, Waters replaced it with another tape, so he could record Emily's responses to his questions. "I know that wasn't easy for either of you, but it was necessary. Now, Emily, did anything new come to you as you listened to the recording?"

Emily paused, steeling herself. "Not much, except when I was listening to the part about him making me do things during confession, I remembered the time I purposely went to the end of the line as my class walked down the hall toward the chapel. When nobody was looking, I ran away and hid in the janitor's closet. But when it came time to be my turn, and he discovered I wasn't there, he came looking for me. Of course, he found me and was absolutely furious. He just came right into the closet with me. And . . . well, he punished me in his own perverted way. He wanted to make sure that I would never hide from him again. He made me perform . . . oral sex, and he was more vigorous than usual, thrusting so hard, and he had his hands around my neck at the same time, so I could hardly breathe. Then he climaxed, and I was choking . . . I thought I was going to die . . . .." Emily's eyes widened. "Oh, dear God! That's what he did to that boy, isn't it?" A choking sound tore out of her throat, and she bent over and put her hand to her mouth to keep herself from vomiting. Her body shuddered uncontrollably.

Paul knelt beside her and took her in his arms. "I'm here,

darling. It's okay; it's okay. He can't hurt you or Billy anymore." He held her and rubbed her back until she began to breathe easier and was able to straighten up.

The two officials looked uncomfortable and repentant, yet they still had a job to do. Once Emily regained control, the DA spoke. "I'm so sorry, Mrs. Graves. I don't think any of us was prepared for the intensity of that memory. Now more than ever, we want nothing more than to keep this monster behind bars and make sure he never sees the light of day again. Do you feel ready to continue?" Emily nodded. "Good. Just a few more questions. First of all, did you ever tell anyone at the time what was happening to you?"

"No. I was too ashamed, too afraid of what might happen to me. My foster mother wasn't a very sympathetic person, as wrapped up as she was in her own grief and ill health, and I feared she would just blame me, then send me away for being too much trouble. My foster father was a good man, but he wasn't someone I would have felt comfortable telling such personal things to. And I didn't think any of the sisters at the school would believe me. After all, he was their priest and their ultimate authority. Plus, he sometimes talked about how pretty my foster sister, Meg, was, which I took to mean that she might be his next victim if I ever told anyone. I just couldn't take that chance."

"Okay. Obviously, your husband knows. Was there anyone else you told later that can corroborate your story?"

"Yes. At one point, my first husband assaulted me in such a way that it brought all my memories of Father Devlin to the forefront, and I had what would probably be called a nervous breakdown. I was overwhelmed with memories throughout the day and had horrifying nightmares when I was actually able to sleep at night. I finally broke down and told my best friend about it, and she urged me to talk to the priest at my local parish. I was very reluctant, but he was completely different than Devlin—warm and sympathetic—and I ended up telling him everything. I eventually told my foster father as well."

"Good. That should shut down any accusations that you're just making this up. We can call those people as witnesses to confirm your story should it become necessary. Now, I have one other question that may be difficult for you but could be of great value to us. Were there any unusual scars, markings, or abnormalities on Devlin's body that wouldn't be visible to people who hadn't see him naked?"

Emily's eyes widened, cringing inwardly at the thought of purposely recalling details of her abuser's private parts. Nonetheless, she lowered her head and concentrated. Paul put his hand on her back to remind her of his presence. After a few moments, she looked up in surprise. "Yes! He did. I can see it plain as day. He had a large port wine birthmark just under and to the right of his belly button. It was about the size of a baseball but with irregular edges. Sometimes I would focus on that, so I didn't have to think about what was happening to me. How could I have forgotten that?"

"Great job, Emily! That's an important detail. I should be able to get a subpoena to photograph this birthmark as evidence. I can't tell you how helpful you've been. We're very grateful. So, I think that's all for now, but if any other questions occur to me, I'll be in touch. And if you remember anything else that might be pertinent, no matter how inconsequential it might seem, please do call me. As soon as we get a trial date, I'll let you know. We'll want to meet again so I can fill you in on how the trial will proceed and so on, plus I'll want to coach you on your testimony and cross-examination. Thanks again, both of you."

Over the next few days, interest in the murder of Billy Clark had waned, news coverage of the crime moving to the inner pages of the papers. Reporters had taken to interviewing friends and neighbors of the Clarks, members of the parish, and anyone who had even the thinnest of connections to the parties involved just to keep the story alive. And then, a new development splashed across the front page, 'More Victims of Priest Disclose Abuse!'

"Look, Paul! It worked! My story prompted other victims to come forward! I knew there had to be more. Obviously, they're not naming names, but there are three from Spokane and two more from the Lynnwood parish."

"I saw that. I'm sure DA Waters is very pleased. Not that other young people suffered, but that this will bolster his case and hopefully ensure a conviction and prevent others from falling prey to Devlin's machinations. I'm really proud of the part you played in this, Emily."

"Yes, but it's not over yet, not by a long shot. I still have to face him in court. I get queasy just thinking about it."

"Emily Graves, you are the epitome of doing hard things. I have absolute faith that you are going to stare that man down as you tell the world what a monster he is." Paul reached across the breakfast table to take her hand. "Your anxiety is understandable, but it doesn't need to stop you from exercising your formidable nerve."

Emily smiled. "How is it that you always know the right thing to say, Paul? I don't know how I could do this without you."

Paul glanced at the clock and slid back his chair. "I've got to run, or I'll be late!" He dropped a kiss on the top of Danny's head as he was smearing oatmeal around on his highchair tray and gave Emily a more lingering kiss on the lips. "You two have fun today. I'll try not to be late." Danny gurgled and slapped his hands on the tray, his own version of goodbye.

"Bye, darling. Have a good day. And thank you for being by my side through all of this. You've truly been my rock." Paul blew her a kiss and left with a smile lingering on his lips.

Within days, the district attorney was on the phone to Emily. "I just wanted to let you know that a trial date has been set for January 15th. The defense attorney asked for more time to prepare his case, and the judge wanted to push it past the holidays so as not to create undue hardship for the jury pool. I know you'd prefer to get this over with sooner rather than later, but I think it will be better in the long run. I'm still interviewing these new witnesses, and then I have to lay out my strategy. I'll be in touch in a few weeks to go over your testimony. In the meantime, enjoy the holiday season, and try not to fret too much about testifying. I'm confident you'll do great."

And so, for the next two months, Emily did just that. She and Paul marveled at Danny's development—the almost daily acquisition of new skills and emerging personality. He entertained them with his smiles, laughter, and funny faces. He never tired of Paul blowing raspberries on his belly, which caused him to squeal with delight. They assiduously recorded each milestone in his baby book—sitting up, crawling, pulling himself up to stand on wobbly legs.

They were also justifiably proud of how well Anna was doing in school, bringing home A's and B's on a regular basis. Biology seemed to be her only real challenge, but Emily reminded Anna that she couldn't be good at everything. She was making friends, too. Sometimes, she would invite one or two girlfriends over to do homework or play with the baby at Paul and Emily's, and it did Emily's heart good to hear Anna giggling like a typical teenager. Even Jack seemed to be thriving. He had gotten a promotion at work to shift supervisor, which helped the siblings with their finances and allowed them to feel less dependent on the good will of Paul and Emily. And being a part of a caring family had smoothed Jack's rough edges and given him hope for a future different from his father's.

For Emily, being part of Paul's family was a blessing she could never have imagined. Their easy camaraderie and gentle teasing gave her a sense of belonging and security that gradually erased the underlying anxiety that had plagued her from the moment her father had died and had increased with each subsequent loss or trauma. She began to trust that there was a safety net she could rely on. But the sheer volume of family gatherings was something she was still adjusting to. She had forgotten what Paul had told her the previous year about their traditional Christmas Eve party to whom everyone they knew was invited, and the reality was exponentially greater than she had expected. The uproar when they walked into the senior Graves' home almost drove her back out the door. But then Elaine appeared out of nowhere to snatch Danny from her arms to show him off to all and sundry, and Paul and Emily were swept into the tide of revelry. Emily stayed by her husband's side as much as possible, but inevitably they were pulled in different directions. She caught Paul's eye for a moment across the room, and his wink assured her that she was going to be just fine. Then Emily turned back to Paul's sister who was telling a funny story about the time Paul had gotten his head stuck in the neighbor's fence. As Emily laughed, she felt the last threads of worry slip away, and she abandoned herself to the joy of family.

Paul was off work the day after New Year, so Emily took advantage of his presence to run some errands while he stayed home with Danny. She lingered for a while, enjoying the freedom of not having to watch the baby every minute to keep him from grabbing things from the shelves. She swore he had an invisible set of arms that he deployed while she was trying to keep track of the original two. When she got home and walked in the front door, Paul and Danny were playing on the floor. "Look, Danny! Mama's home! Let's show her what you can do. Sit on the floor over there, Mama."

Emily dropped her packages on the couch and knelt down a few feet away, wondering what surprise awaited her. Then Paul said, "Go get Mama, Danny. Go get, Mama." He steadied Danny on his feet, then gradually pulled his hands away so the baby was standing on his own. Emily held her arms out, and he took one step, then two. On the third step, he started to sway, and Emily swept him into her waiting arms.

"Mama."

"Paul! Did you hear that? He said 'Mama'—and he walked!"

"I heard! We've been working on his walking all morning. Isn't it fantastic?" He scooted over to her and took them both in his arms. Emily nodded her head, unable to speak through her tears. All her longing for a child, all of the grief believing it could never be, all erased in this moment with a little boy's arms around her neck, his voice repeating the name she never thought she would hear.

Emily sat in Mr. Waters office once again a week before the trial was due to start. He was laying out his strategy and the order in which he wanted to call witnesses. "At this point, Emily, my plan is to call Billy's parents first to get background on Billy—

what kind of kid he was, what activities he enjoyed, et cetera. I
want the jury to know Billy as a person, not just a victim, to see
who he was in life, before Devlin ended it. I also want them to hear
anything he might have said about Father Devlin prior to his
disappearance, what his behavior was like when he came home
from his altar boy training, any changes in personality in the weeks
leading up to his death. Then I'll have the Clarks lay out the events
of the day he disappeared, Devlin's demeanor when they
questioned him about Billy's whereabouts, and so on. After that,
I'll call up the police officers that were part of the investigation,
detailing their efforts and the evidence they found. This will
include pictures of the scratches on Devlin's torso and the
birthmark you told us about. Then the coroner will lay out his
findings, which will lead straight into your testimony.

"I'm going to ask you for the story of your abuse at
Devlin's hand, the gradual grooming he did, the ways he took
advantage of your tentative status in the Hutton household, the
frequency and duration of the abuse, and the various acts he
committed. Then I'm going to ask you to tell me the story of him
finding you in the closet and forcing you to perform fellatio. I want
the jury to hear you talk about how scary that was and especially
your comment that you couldn't breathe and thought you were
going to die. That part is absolutely vital."

Emily nodded. "I understand. I'll do my best."

"I know you will, Emily. Trust me, I know that this won't
be easy for you. And while you may want to try to be stoic and not
fall apart on the stand, the jury needs to see your emotion, needs to
see the impact this has had on your life. The other victims of his
abuse are going to be helpful in bolstering our case, but you are my
key witness. Their stories aren't quite as compelling as yours, so
their testimony just serves to reinforce that this was a pattern of
behavior that had been going on for a long period of time in
several different parishes. Do you understand?"

"Yes, sir, I do. I won't hold back. I want to see justice done
as much as you do."

"Good! Now, let's talk about cross-examination. . .."

After another hour of coaching on the do's and don't of

responding to the defense attorney's questions, how to handle his challenging of her testimony, Waters told her to report on the second day of trial. "I will probably need the entire first day for opening statements, the parents' testimony, and maybe some of the police officers. It's hard to know how long those things will take, depending on how hard the defense attorney goes after those witnesses. On the second day, I'll put the remaining police witnesses on the stand, then the coroner. I want you on the stand immediately after the coroner, because your story will corroborate the evidence he found on Billy's body. So even if I don't get to you on the second day, I want you there. It will be pretty boring for you, because you can't be in the courtroom until you are called. You will have to wait in the corridor outside. Then, after you testify, you can stay and observe the rest of the trial if you want. The other victims will give their testimony, and then it will be the defense's turn. I don't know yet whether they will call Devlin to the stand in his own defense or not. I hope they do. In fact, he may insist on pleading his case. My sense is that his ego is big enough that he believes he can persuade the jury of his innocence, but I think I can push him enough that the façade begins to crumble. I want them to see that he is capable of doing what he did."

Emily looked up suddenly. "Make him mad. He can't stand to be challenged. And his temper is explosive. If you do it right, he will lose control, and the jury will see."

"That's helpful, Emily. I'll see what I can do. Now, do you have any questions? If not, I'll see you in a week. You know where to go, right? If not, check with my secretary in the outer office. Try to stick to your normal routine in the meantime, and don't think about this too much. You're going to be fine. We're going to get this bastard, okay?"

Smiling at the unexpected swear word, Emily replied, "Yes, we are! Justice will be done—for all the children, past and present, who need to know somebody sees them and will fight for them. Thank you for what you do, Mr. Waters. You give me hope."

That night over dinner, Emily picked at her food while she shared with Paul the details she had gleaned from the district attorney and the more practical matters related to her participation in the trial. Elaine had agreed to babysit Danny for the duration, and Paul insisted on being present when Emily testified. "You are going to want a friendly face in the crowd when you tell your story to the whole world while Devlin looks on. I can't imagine how hard that will be."

"Yes, but it must be done. I mean, I'm nervous about it. I've even been feeling kind of queasy lately, but there's a part of me that looks forward to staring him down, saying to his face what he did to me. For a long time, all I felt was helplessness and fear. But so many people have helped me move on from that place—you, Lottie, Father McCaffrey, Reverend Patterson, Anna, Mr. Hutton, even my parents in a way, the memories of them that helped me believe in myself. And I trust that God is with me in ways I might never understand. So, I'm ready to do this, to play a part in putting him away, not just for Billy, but for all of his victims—past, present, and future."

"Spoken like a real trooper, my love. That man isn't going to know what hit him! And even soldiers get scared before battle, but they don't let that stop them from entering the fray. I have faith in you, and I know that my family does, too."

Just then, Danny squealed and threw a handful of peas in Paul's face, and his parents dissolved into laughter. The serious moment passed as they cleaned up the dishes and got their son ready for bed.

As Emily walked up the courthouse steps with Paul the morning she was to appear for the trial, she stopped for a moment to take in the grandeur of this building, the gravitas it conveyed. She thought about the justice that was administered here, the wrongs righted for victims whose lives had been shattered by the worst that humans could perpetrate against the small, the weak and the vulnerable. And she prayed that justice would be done for Billy, for herself, for all the victims Father Devlin had preyed upon. They entered through the imposing doors and looked around the marbled entry, taking in the Ionic columns holding up the arched ceiling. Then, gazing down at the polished floors, Emily saw the words of the prophet Amos etched in the center of the grand foyer, "But let justice roll down like waters, and righteousness like an ever-flowing stream." And she dared to hope.

"The prosecution calls Emily Graves to the stand." The courtroom observers craned their necks to watch as a bailiff opened the rear door and Emily walked down the aisle to the witness stand, placing her hand on the Bible proffered by the clerk of court.

"Do you solemnly swear to tell the truth, the whole truth, and nothing but the truth, so help you God?"

"I do." Emily sat down and focused on the district attorney as he approached.

"Please state your name and address."

She did so, still not looking at the man seated at the defense table.

"Thank you, Mrs. Graves. Now, please tell the court how you know the defendant."

For the first time, Emily looked directly at Father Devlin. He met her glance and glared menacingly, as if warning her not to tell. She was surprised by how much older he looked. It had been twelve years since she had seen him, and his previously salt and pepper hair was now pure white. It seemed that the intervening years had not been kind to him. Steeling herself, she held his gaze as she responded, "He was my priest at the parish I attended in Spokane from 1948 until 1950 when he was placed on medical leave by the diocese. He also tutored me in the catechism to help me get caught up with my classmates."

"And what were the circumstances that led to you to need that extra attention?"

"My mother had just died three years after we lost my father in the war, and I was placed in a foster home. My foster parents were Catholic and sent me to the private Catholic school in their parish."

"And what was your experience of Father Devlin?"

"He made me uncomfortable. He was very strict when he was teaching the whole class, but when we were alone together, he would touch me in ways that weren't normal for other adults I knew. And he would want me to confide in him about the situation at home."

"And what was that situation?"

"My foster mother, Mrs. Hutton, was an invalid, and because of her condition, she was often depressed and irritable. She wasn't exactly motherly, and at times she was very difficult. I was a caregiver and servant more than a daughter to her. And Mr. Hutton worked long hours at the law office and then spent most of the evening with his wife or their children. Father Devlin made a big deal out of my precarious standing in the household. See, I wasn't actually Catholic, but I had lied and said I was, because I was desperate to be placed with a family for fear of ending up in an orphanage."

"Can you be more specific about what Devlin did that was uncomfortable?"

"He would sometimes pull me onto his lap after the lesson was over and rub my back or my thighs as we talked. And he would get what I now know was an erection."

"Objection, your honor!" shouted the defense attorney. "Prejudicial!"

The judge turned to the district attorney. "Where are you going with this, Mr. Waters?"

"Sir, based on opening arguments, Father Devlin's defense is that he has never and would never abuse a child in his care. Mrs. Graves' testimony will prove that claim to be false."

"Objection overruled. Please continue."

"Thank you, your honor. Now, Mrs. Graves, was that all Father Devlin did?"

"No, sir. After he had been tutoring me for a while, he knew my voice well enough that when I entered the confession booth, he knew it was me and pushed aside the curtain. I knew this was a no-no, as confession is supposed to be confidential, but I was too intimidated to say anything about it. Anyway, I confessed to something minor, I don't even remember what, and he said my penance was to play a little game with him. He made me stand between his knees and rub his lap through his clothes. He got this really strange look in his eyes that gave me the creeps, then his body shuddered, and he patted me on the head and sent me back to my classroom."

Waters looked from Emily to the jury, who were looking uncomfortable, then back to Emily. "And did this behavior continue?"

Emily steeled herself, knowing that Waters needed her to be as graphic as possible. "Yes. It gradually got worse. Eventually, he made me unzip his pants and rub his, um, penis, or I would have to pull up my skirt so he could touch me, down there."

"Was the confessional the only place these things happened?

"Oh, no. It happened in his office during my tutoring all the time. Once, we had an outbreak of lice, and he offered to check me for them, since Mrs. Hutton was incapacitated, and Mr. Hutton didn't have time. But he didn't just check my head. He also checked my private parts and . . .." Emily's voice trailed off. She looked up to see Paul looking at her, willing her to stay strong, reminding her that he was with her, encouraging her.

The jury was looking increasingly uneasy, even sickened. Emily took a deep breath and looked at Mr. Waters. "I know this is difficult, Mrs. Graves." he said. "Do you need a short recess?"

She squared her shoulders and shook her head. "No sir, I can continue."

"Okay. Please tell the jury the full extent of the nightmare that the defendant put you through."

Emily went on, telling about the gradual descent into the worst of Devlin's depravity—the touching, the acts he forced her to perform on him, the first time he pushed himself inside her, the anal rape after she started her period. By the time she was done, both Paul and the jury were pale and shaking. Some of the women were crying. Devlin was glaring at her with fury in his eyes.

"Now, Mrs. Graves, was there a time when you tried to escape from Devlin?"

"Yes. It was time for confession, and I was dreading it as usual. I hung back to the end of the line as my class walked toward the chapel, and when no one was looking, I snuck away and hid in the janitor's closet. I waited and waited until I heard the other kids walking back to class. Then I waited some more. When I thought the coast was clear, I slowly opened the closet door, and there he was, standing there waiting for me. I could see he was angry. He forced me back into the closet and unzipped his pants. He pushed me onto my knees and thrust his penis into my mouth. His hands were around my neck, squeezing as he held my head still . . .." Emily faltered again, her hand on her throat as though she could feel those hands even now.

"Take your time, Mrs. Graves. Take your time."

She took a deep breath, closed her eyes for a moment, lips moving as if in prayer. *Once more into the breach . . ..* Then she lifted her head and nodded to the prosecutor.

"What were you thinking as Father Devlin was doing this, Emily?"

"I was terrified! I was choking and desperate for air. I thought I was going to die."

Waters let the stunned silence grow, let the implications of those words sink in as jurors and observers remembered the coroner's testimony regarding how Billy Hutton had died.

"Thank you. I know this was extremely difficult for you, and we're almost done. Can you tell us if there were any identifying marks on Father Devlin's body that wouldn't have been visible to others when he was fully clothed?"

Nodding, Emily replied, "Yes, there was a large port wine birthmark on his belly below the waist. Sometimes I would focus on that during . . . well, you know."

Mr. Waters walked over to the prosecution table and picked up a large photo. "Let me call the court's attention to Exhibit D already entered into evidence during the coroner's testimony." He walked over and showed it to Emily. It was a picture of someone's lower abdomen, showing a navel, several scratches, and a dark red birthmark. "Does this look like what you observed on the accused's body?"

Emily studied the photo carefully, trying to set aside the sickening realization that the scratches must have been made during Billy's frantic attempts to escape Devlin's clutches. "Yes, that's the birthmark I saw. It was seared into my memory. Even now, it makes me cringe."

"Thank you for your courage in being here today. I know it wasn't easy. I have nothing further for this witness, your honor."

The judge looked at the clock. "I see that it's 4:30 now. Let's adjourn for the day and save cross-examination for tomorrow, shall we? Nine AM sharp. Court is adjourned."

The next morning found Emily seated once more on the witness stand, the judge reminding her that she was still under oath. Her gaze swept the courtroom, settling on Paul to ground herself before what she expected to be a difficult cross-examination. Then she shifted her glance to the defense table and Father Devlin to remind herself why she was here, what was at stake. She saw Billy's parents sitting behind the prosecutor, leaning into each other for support, grief written on the faces. Finally, she locked eyes on the defense attorney, Mr. Oliver, and lifted her chin. She was ready.

He rose and approached the bench. "Mrs. Graves, you told us quite a story yesterday. Unfortunately, there's no way we can ascertain the truth of it, is there? There doesn't seem to be anyone in this courtroom that had any knowledge of what you claim Father Devlin allegedly did to you. Your foster parents aren't here, nor any of your teachers or fellow students. Which begs the question, did you tell *anyone* at the time, what you described in your testimony yesterday?"

"No, sir, I didn't."

"And why would that be? It seems to me that if someone were causing me such grievous harm, I would be shouting it to the world."

"I was ashamed. He always made me feel that it was my fault somehow, even when he was professing his love for me. And he threatened me with the horrible things that would happen if I told, that I would probably be removed from the Hutton's home and put in a children's home, or that he would start doing things to my foster sister."

"You were afraid your parents would put you in an orphanage?"

"Yes. What you need to understand is that my foster mother was a very rigid woman. She didn't tolerate even the smallest mistake or misdeed. As I said before, she was a bed-ridden invalid and a drunk. They had really only fostered me because they needed someone who could help care for their younger children after she fell ill, but that also made her resent me for being the one they ran to when they needed something or had a bad dream or a scraped knee. And my foster father worked long hours and tended to his wife in the evenings so I could do my homework. He was often mentally absent even when he was at home. All of this made me feel very tentative with them. If I failed to meet their expectations in any way, I felt that they could easily send me back into the system. Besides, they were devout Catholics who would never believe that their priest could be capable of such heinous acts."

"But what about your teachers? Couldn't you have told one of them?"

"Again, I didn't think anyone would believe me. And I thought I deserved what he was doing to me, that I was just a bad person who deserved all of the bad things that had happened in my life—my father's death in the war, my mother's accident, the abuse—all of it!"

"Why would you think it was your fault? Did you ever instigate this sexual contact?"

"No! It was always Father Devil—I mean, Devlin, who approached me."

Mr. Oliver roared, "Move to strike, your honor! Prejudicial!"

The judge nodded. "Sustained. Jury will disregard." He turned to Emily. "Please refrain from using that term again, Mrs. Graves."

"Yes, your honor, I'm so sorry. Force of habit, I guess. All the kids used to call him that. Nobody really liked him."

Oliver started to protest again, but the judge interrupted him. "Save your breath, Counselor. Again, the jury will disregard. Recorder, please strike the witness's last statement from the record."

The defense attorney paused for a moment, considering. "So, what was Father Devlin like as a priest, setting aside what you claim he did?"

Emily shrugged. "He was stiff, stern. None of the students liked him much." The entire room waited for Oliver to object again, but he did not. Emily looked at the judge, but he nodded for her to continue. "He was a strict disciplinarian, and he berated the kids who failed to provide correct answers when he was teaching catechism. One time I witnessed him twisting the ear of a student he was standing right next to when the kid got something wrong. He would even yell at the teachers in front of their students."

Mr. Oliver rubbed his jaw as if in deep thought. "So, would it be fair to say that, even without the alleged abuse, you didn't like Father Devlin very much."

"I guess you could say that."

"Isn't it possible then, that all of this is just an elaborate lie to get even with him for the fact that he punished you harshly, and you didn't like him?"

"No! I am not lying."

"But you hate him."

Emily's voice rose to a shout, "I hate him, because he violated and *raped* me, over and over and over! Can you even imagine what that was like? Can you?"

The defense attorney tried for several more minutes to shake Emily's story before realizing that he was just digging himself a deeper hole. He said, "I have nothing further for this witness, your honor," and sat down.

Waters stood for re-direct. "Emily, you've testified that you didn't tell anyone what was happening to you at the time. Have you *ever* told anyone about this prior to sharing it with the police and me?"

"Yes. I told my best friend a couple years ago, as well as my priest in Spokane at the time, and eventually my foster father, Mr. Hutton. I've also told my husband and the minister who married us."

"So, there are at least five people who can corroborate that you told them of your abuse prior to the murder of Billy Clark."

"Yes, sir."

"Your honor, I'd like to enter into evidence these affidavits from the five named witnesses to Mrs. Graves revelations of abuse, signed and notarized." He handed the statements to the judge before thanking Emily for her testimony. Emily rose on shaky legs and walked back to where Paul was sitting. When she sat, he put his arm around her and pulled her to him. She let out a deep breath and leaned into her husband with relief.

After the lunch break, Waters called Devlin's other victims to the stand, with repeated objections from the defense. Waters continued to assert that their testimony was intended to establish a pattern of abuse, not only in the pervasiveness and types of acts, but also in the repeated singling out of children who were troubled or unpopular or otherwise vulnerable to the special attentions of their abuser. The judge overruled each objection, and at the end of the day, the district attorney had rested his case.

That evening over dinner, Emily reflected back on her two days of testimony. "I feel strangely at peace. I mean, it was hard to share such intimate details in front of a room full of strangers, but it's like something has been exorcised for me. And it was so validating to see how the jurors reacted, the repugnance on their faces over what he did to me. I could see Devlin fuming over the fact that I dared to tell. Even now, I think he would try to punish me if he got the chance. He looked like he wanted to jump right out of his chair and strangle me. In a way, it's freeing, like I've been released. But I'm also glad it's over."

"I'm sure you are, darling. I'm so proud of you! You handled yourself so well up there, even when the defense attorney and the judge reprimanded you. And even though Oliver tried to turn your own words against you, I think it backfired on him in the end. I actually wanted to stand up and cheer! Now, are you still planning to go back tomorrow? And are you sure you don't want me to come with you?"

"Yes, and yes. I'll be fine, Paul. I feel like I need to follow this all the way through to the end, however it turns out. And now that I'm done testifying, the rest of it should be a piece of cake. I'm just grateful that your mom is willing to come and babysit our busy boy for us. Now that he's walking, he's really keeping her on her toes!"

"He is definitely doing that. Mom looked a little frazzled last night when she left."

"Well, hopefully it will only be a couple more days, and all this will be over."

When they went to bed that night, Emily reached for Paul, needing the joy of their lovemaking to erase the final vestiges of her testimony from her mind. Afterwards, they lay tangled together, skin to skin, breath co-mingling as they dropped into a deep and dreamless sleep.

Seated on a bench in the courtroom, still slightly nauseous even though her part in the drama was over, Emily watched Mr. Oliver begin his defense of Father Devlin. He brought up a parade of character witnesses, former church youth and altar boys who spoke on his behalf, stating categorically that the priest had never once made any kind of sexual advance toward them. Waters objected, but the judge overruled him. "You had your turn to bring in a slew of witnesses with no knowledge of the case at hand. Now the defense gets the same privilege." The district attorney accepted this ruling, but with each new witness, he asked if they were loners, had problems at home, or had any kind of disability that would have made them different, unpopular, ignored or lonely, anything that would make them vulnerable to the predations of a molester. For each witness, the answer was no.

Finally, Oliver called Father Devlin himself to the stand. The judge frowned. "Are you sure you want to do that, Counselor?"

"Yes, your honor. The accused is adamant that he have the opportunity to speak in his own defense."

"So be it. Come on forward and be sworn in, Father."

Oliver took Devlin through the events of the day Billy disappeared, emphasizing that Billy had left the church at 3:00 intending to walk home, and that the priest hadn't become concerned until 4:00 when the Clarks arrived to pick him up. He stayed at the church while Billy's parents searched the neighborhood in case Billy returned there for some reason. He was still there in his office when the police arrived to use the church as a staging area for a door-to-door search. The priest had even joined in, having become more and more concerned.

"Now, the prosecution has made quite a fuss over the scratches that were found on your body when the police questioned you after Billy's body was found. Can you explain how you got those scratches?"

"Yes, of course," Devlin answered in a superior tone. "I had been doing some yard work on the parish grounds that morning, pruning trees and such. I lost my balance at one point and fell into a pile of broken branches that scratched me up pretty badly. That's all. A simple tangle with the shrubbery. Happens to everyone, right?"

"Now, Father, I have to ask. Did you kill Billy Clark?"

"No, I did not."

"Did you put his body in the sacristy closet?"

"I absolutely did not."

"Did you sexually assault him or touch him inappropriately in any way?"

"I have never and would never do any such thing to any of the children under my tutelage. The suggestion that I did is outrageous and patently false."

Mr. Oliver turned to the district attorney. "The witness is yours, Counselor."

Waters stood, buttoning his suit jacket and walking slowly toward the witness stand. "About this pile of branches—what were you wearing when you got entangled in them?"

Devlin looked superior and smug. "The same thing I'm wearing now, slacks and my cassock."

"And it looks like this cassock is somewhat heavier than one you would wear in the summer. Is it wool?"

"Yes, what difference does that make?"

"I'm just trying to wrap my mind around this. Are you asking the jury to believe that a few branches would be able to pierce through a heavy robe *and* a pair of slacks in order to cause the numerous deep scratches that are seen on the photograph of your lower abdomen? Because, by my calculation, you would have had to be *naked* in order to receive such wounds!"

Oliver jumped to his feet. "Objection, your honor!"

The judge nodded. "Sustained. Strike that last statement. But the witness still must answer the question that preceded it."

Devlin nodded. "Yes, that's what I'm asking you to believe, because that's what happened."

Unfazed, Waters kept digging. "Then how do you explain the fact that Billy was found to have skin and blood under his fingernails and that the blood type was the same as yours, AB negative, which is the rarest blood type in the world?"

The priest shrugged. "It's a big city. I'm sure I'm not the only person with that type. It's just my bad luck that the killer was also AB negative."

Waters walked to the prosecution table and picked up a piece of paper. "I'd like to enter into evidence this church calendar for the week that Billy was killed." The judge nodded, and Waters then handed it to Father Devlin. "Please read for the court the activities that are listed for Thursday, October 13th."

Devlin rolled his eyes in contempt. "It says here that there was a women's sewing circle at 10 AM and an altar boy training at 3 PM. So?"

"Well, if the altar boy trainees were meeting on Thursday, why was Billy at the church with you on a Saturday? Alone."

There was a fleeting look of anxiety in the priest's eyes before he spoke. "Well, Billy was having a little trouble with the curriculum, and I felt he needed some extra help. And some of the other boys had been teasing him about not being very athletic like they were. In short, they were calling him a wimp."

"Interesting. Are you sure you didn't single Billy out for special help so that you could molest him?"

"Of course not! I've told you I never molested any of the children I worked with."

"Right, you did. Now, you no doubt heard the Clarks testify that when Billy would come home from meeting with you, he was not his normal cheerful self and would retreat to his room to avoid their questions. How would you explain that?"

"How should I know? He was a typical, moody eleven-year-old boy."

"Yet his parents stated that this was highly unusual behavior for their son."

"Who knows! Maybe he had a fight with his friends or something."

Waters paused, thinking, then continued. "How long would you say you normally spend in tutoring your altar boys?"

"Oh, usually about two hours."

"But you've stated that your meeting with Billy began at 2 PM, and he left at 3 PM. Why was that?"

"Uh . . . well, he said he wasn't feeling well and wanted to go home. So I excused him."

"Just like that? You seem like a man who is a stickler for following your agenda, paying strict attention to the requirements."

Devlin was beginning to appear impatient, frustrated, even angry at this line of questioning. "What's your point? He said he was sick, and I let him go. I certainly didn't want him vomiting in my sacristy!"

"No, I can see that. Instead, he died there."

"You're twisting my words! I did nothing wrong!"

"Okay, so you're suggesting that Billy left the church at 3 PM, that someone in the neighborhood molested and killed him, that you were at the church the entire time until joining the search party at around 6 PM, and somehow, during that time, the killer snuck Billy's body back into the church and hid it in the sacristy closet . . . without you seeing or hearing a thing."

"That's the only possible explanation. I don't know how it was done, but that's what happened. When I'm in my office, I can't always hear everything that's going on elsewhere in the building."

"But don't you think someone in the neighborhood would have seen Billy walking by on his way home?"

Devlin shrugged. "I guess it was just bad luck for me that no one was looking out their window during that time."

"Isn't it more likely that you were taking advantage of Billy's youth and innocence, abusing his trust by sexually assaulting him, that you went too far, strangled and killed him, hid his body in the closet until it was dark enough to take him somewhere else, feigned ignorance when his parents came, and joined the search party to throw the police off, hoping they wouldn't think to look inside the church?"

"No! That is *not* what happened! How many times do I have to tell you?" The priest's demeanor was becoming increasingly anxious and angry at the same time.

"And *if* it happened in the way you hypothesize, why on earth would the killer have chosen to hide Billy's body in the church? Since that was the last place Billy was seen, it would certainly be the first place the police would look. If I were a murderer, I would want to prevent the police from finding the body for a long time, wouldn't you?"

"Since I'm not a murderer, I wouldn't know. Maybe he wanted to pin it on me. Maybe he has something against the Catholic church."

"But there's another problem with the evidence. As you heard, the coroner put Billy's time of death between three and four PM. He also testified that the lividity evidence means that Billy was put into that closet almost immediately after death. He could not possibly have been killed elsewhere and then moved at a later time. How do you explain that?"

Devlin glowered at Waters. "I told you, I don't know! I have no idea how Billy ended up in the closet without me knowing. I just know that I didn't do it."

Waters paused as if planning his next move, then spoke, "Okay, let's move on. The Clarks testified to the fact that Billy had asthma, and his doctor stated that it was quite severe and would have been triggered by any severe stress. Did you know that Billy had asthma?"

"No, I did not."

"Really? I'm surprised by that, because his parents said Billy took his inhaler with him everywhere he went and usually had to use it several times a day. Are you saying that you never saw Billy use his inhaler or even on his person, that you didn't know *why* he couldn't play sports like the other boys?"

"That's what I'm saying." Devlin seemed to be fraying

now, ever more anxious and defensive.

"Do you know what might happen to an asthmatic who has a large object blocking his airway while someone is clutching at his throat? When there is semen choking him? When he is frantically clutching at those hands in an all-out attempt to breathe? When his vagal nerve is compressed for even a moment too long?"

The priest surged to his feet. "NO! NO! Stop saying that! I didn't know! I didn't know! God help me, I didn't know! I didn't know he could die. I wouldn't have done it if I'd known. It was an accident! An accident!" And he slumped back into his chair and broke down in sobs.

"No further questions, your honor."

The courthouse erupted, and the judge rapped his gavel repeatedly until the furor subsided. "Counselor, do you have any further witnesses?"

A subdued Oliver replied, "No, your honor."

"Okay, then. Let's call it a day. Perhaps you should consider having a conversation with the district attorney. Otherwise, we'll hear closing arguments in the morning."

Astonished by this turn of events, Emily pushed through the tide of people leaving the courtroom until she was standing in front of DA Waters. "What does this mean?"

"The judge just suggested that the defense try to make a plea deal to keep Devlin off death row. I need to speak to the Clarks before I agree to that, but how do you feel about it?"

"I actually think that would be better. Prison would be worse for him. He would be stripped of his collar, his respectability, and his power over others. And God only knows what would happen to him in there. But I want to talk to him. I need to speak to him face to face. Can you arrange that?"

"I don't know, Emily. Are you sure that's wise?"

Emily nodded. "I know it sounds ridiculous, but I feel like it would be the final step in my healing."

"Well, I can try. But it's up to him and his attorney. I see Oliver gesturing at me now. Stick around for a bit, and I'll let you know."

"Thank you! Thank you for pursuing justice so doggedly.

I'm sure it means a lot to the Clarks, and I know it means a lot to me."

He smiled and squeezed her arm before grabbing his briefcase and walking away. Emily plopped down on the nearest bench, overwhelmed by what had just happened. She watched as the two attorneys talked and Devlin sat forlornly at the defense table, broken and afraid. She looked at the Clarks still sitting, stunned, behind the prosecution table. Then she walked slowly out of the courtroom and sat on one of the benches near a window, mind whirling. She was taken aback by her own sudden desire to confront her abuser without a courtroom full of people watching. She hadn't had an inkling of the unconscious need to confront him until the words had come out of her mouth. For the next hour, Emily thought about what she would say to the man who had in many ways defined her life for so many years.

Eventually, Waters emerged from the courtroom with one of the bailiffs. "Devlin has agreed to see you. This officer is going to escort you to his cell downstairs, and he will wait for you right outside. Now, if you'll excuse me, I have some paperwork to complete." Then he winked and smiled before walking away.

Emily followed the guard, suddenly in a panic and wondering why she had thought this was a good idea. She took several deep breaths in order to keep from throwing up on the polished courthouse floors. And then the same words of Scripture that had calmed her in the police station weeks ago came to mind, "The Lord is my strength and shield," and she was steadied.

They went through a door at the end of the hall and found themselves in a dank concrete stairwell, far different from the opulence of the space they had just left. Down a flight of stairs was a heavy metal door, which the guard unlocked and opened, gesturing Emily through. Then he took the lead again, down a plain narrow hallway past a few occupied cells until they reached a room in which there was a bare metal table and two chairs, one of which held a hunched old man. The guard had stopped, and Emily was startled to realize that the man was Father Devlin. He looked like he had aged ten years in the past hour.

The guard unlocked the door, saying, "I'll be right here if

you need me."

Emily slowly sat in the chair opposite the priest. The two stared at each other for long moments, coming to terms with how the world had changed for each of them. Finally, Devlin spoke, "You wanted to see me? To gloat?"

"No, Father. I just—I guess I wanted to confront you at last, explain to you what you did to me, the pain you caused, the ways your abuse impacted my life. I wanted you to know that I didn't just get over it once you left the school."

"I think you made that abundantly clear on the witness stand."

"No! I just told them what you did in cold, clinical detail. I didn't testify about my endless nightmares, my lack of confidence, my constant fears. Because of you, I married the first man who showed any interest in me, and he was just like you—completely uninterested in what I might need or want, focused on his pleasure above all else, rigid and demanding, and ultimately, a sexual deviant like you. And apparently, you rendered me unable to conceive a child, which was the last straw for my husband, who decided that I must have been a prostitute to have all that vaginal scarring, so he raped me! Just like you did after I started my period and suddenly could be impregnated, so you bent me over your desk to take your pleasure as violently as possible."

Emily paused to take a breath as Devlin flinched at her harsh words. "I'm sorry . . . I never meant to cause you harm. I loved you."

"You loved me? Did you love all of them? Did you love Billy when you throttled him to death? Just don't! Your talk of love while you abused me was a mockery of what real love can be. I know that now. And sorry isn't enough! Not for what you did to me, how it affected every part of my life! You stalked me in my dreams for years! You made me feel worthless, like a piece of trash. I believed that I deserved every bad thing that ever happened to me. I carried shame like a heavy weight around my neck, while you got a year off on so-called medical leave and then blithely went on to another parish, more children to ravage and despoil. Until one of them died."

Devlin tried to lift his hands in frustration but was thwarted by the shackles that held them prisoner. "That's not how it was! You just don't understand. I wanted you to know how special you were . . ..

"Special? I certainly didn't feel special. I felt dirty, shameful, defiled. I didn't tell anyone, because I knew they would be disgusted by me."

"No! You were beautiful, and nobody saw that but me. I'm sorry if I hurt you."

"*If? If* you hurt me? Weren't you listening in there? Why do you think I was crying all those times you were using my body for your own pleasure? When I whimpered or cried out in pain?

"I truly didn't know. Why can't you believe me?"

"You didn't know because you have no pity, no compassion. Everything you do is for your own pleasure. Children only exist for you as objects used to fulfill your twisted desires."

"That's not true! I loved you! I thought you felt the same. I thought you wanted it. I'm so sorry, Emily! Please forgive me."

Emily stared at him with cold eyes for a long moment. "And did you think Billy wanted it too? While he was clawing at your belly in an attempt to save his own life? I'd tell you to go to hell, but I can see in your eyes that you're already there. You know that you are going to be locked away, probably for the rest of your life, such as it is, and there will be no children there for you to defile, no tender young flesh for you to violate. In fact, the tables will be turned. You will become the prey instead of the predator, and that will be unbearable for you. No, you're already in hell, and God will have to forgive you if he can, because I am utterly incapable of it. Goodbye, Father. Guard! I'm done here."

Upstairs, Emily sank onto the nearest bench, shaking but triumphant. She was filled with a powerful energy like nothing she had experienced before. She felt as though she could move mountains, and perhaps she had. Then she got up and ran down the corridor toward the front doors, eager to tell Paul what she had done.

Paul was already home when she burst through the door and ran into his arms, face beaming. "I take it there was a guilty verdict," he said.

"Not yet, but wait 'til you hear!" She quickly told him about Devlin's breakdown under cross-examination and added, "but that's not the best part! I actually got to confront the Devil in his cell and tell him off. I feel released!!"

"Whoa, slow down. You did what?"

"I asked to speak to him, and he agreed. I don't know what came over me. I was asking Waters what would happen next, and suddenly I'm saying, 'I want to talk to him.' So, he got permission and had a guard escort me down to where the cells are. Did you know there's a whole jail down there? Anyway, I told him what his abuse had cost me, and he had the gall to ask for my forgiveness. I basically told him to go to hell, and God would have to be the one to forgive him, because I couldn't. And then I left. I can't even begin to describe what this feels like. I'm bursting with—I don't know—a sense of freedom and power, like I could conquer the world. Is that silly?"

"Not at all, my love. I always knew you could accomplish anything you set out to do if you believed in yourself. You just did the bravest thing of all, and I'm thrilled you got that opportunity to face your own personal demon."

He kissed her hard, holding her face in his hands, then looked at her and said, "You've never been so beautiful as you are right now. You're glowing!"

"I feel that! It's incredible."

"Well, I just put Danny down for a nap, so we have time to celebrate properly." He grabbed her hand, and they ran to the bedroom laughing.

Back in her usual seat the next morning, Emily waited eagerly to hear Devlin's fate. She watched as all the key players filed in—Devlin downcast, dressed in his jumpsuit rather than his usual priestly garb, Oliver looking equally grim, and Waters, with a satisfied look. They rose as the judge entered, took his seat, and rapped his gavel. "I understand the two sides have come to an agreement as to a plea deal. Is that correct?"

The district attorney spoke. "Yes, your honor. In acknowledgement of his witness stand confession yesterday afternoon, the defendant has agreed to plead guilty to a lesser charge of second-degree murder and one count of child rape with a sentence of twenty-five years in prison without possibility of parole. The victim's parents are amenable to this agreement."

"Very well. Both parties will meet me in my office to sign the pertinent paperwork. We are adjourned. Jury, thank you for your time and attentiveness to this proceeding. You are free to go." One more rap of his gavel, and it was over.

Emily made her way to the prosecutor's table and gave him an impetuous hug. "Whoa! What's this?" he exclaimed.

"I'm just so grateful. You did something very important here, and all of Devlin's victims are now free from the specter of his abuse. Thank you, for all of us." She then turned and hugged Billy's parents. "I know this doesn't bring Billy back, but at least you know that justice was done. Now you can focus on your grief and begin to heal. I wish you both well." They smiled and nodded, too overwhelmed to speak, but the relief in their eyes spoke volumes.

Emily was home before lunch and sat at the kitchen table with Elaine processing the trial and its outcome. When her mother-in-law left, she called Paul to fill him in on the events of the morning. She peeked in on Danny, who was napping, and then settled on the couch to reflect on the events of the last few months. Thoughts and feelings crowded her head and heart, and eventually there was only one way to express them, through the poetry that had been her lifelong friend.

> My life now an empty page,
> A future yet to be written—
> The past—for good or ill—
> No longer binds me.
> I am free to choose,
> What to claim
> And what to let go.
> I choose life,
> I choose love.
> I choose the road that beckons.

She leaned back and rested her head, falling asleep within minutes. When she awoke, the nausea she'd been experiencing lately was back and worse than ever. Emily raced to the bathroom to vomit. Shaking and pale, she leaned against the bathtub, wondering what on earth might be causing this ongoing stomach distress if it wasn't connected to the trial. Suddenly, her eyes widened.

When Paul walked in the door at the end of the day, she and Danny were waiting, Emily's face beaming.

"What's that smile for? More good news?"

"You could say that. I think I'm pregnant!"

Epilogue

Because I could not stop for Death--
He kindly stopped for me--
The Carriage held but just Ourselves--
And Immortality.

We slowly drove--He knew no haste
And I had put away
My labor and my leisure too,
For his Civility--

—Emily Dickinson

2016

In Memoriam
Emily Snow Graves
Feb. 27, 1937—March 20, 2016

It is with a heavy heart that the Seattle Post-Intelligencer announces the passing of our own Emily Graves, age 79, after a long illness. Emily was a wife, mother, poet, and columnist for the Seattle P-I. Her beloved columns delighted readers for many years with her fresh descriptions of Seattle landmarks, parks, and events. Upon her retirement in 2002, the P-I published a volume of her favorites, the first printing selling out within a month. A book of her poetry entitled *The Salvation of Poetry* was published in 1987.

Emily was born and raised in Spokane, Washington to Daniel and Madeleine Snow. Her father was killed during the D-Day invasion in World War II when Emily was seven. Her mother died in a bus accident three short years later, leaving her an orphan. She spent seven years in foster care. After graduation from high school, Emily worked for the telephone company before marrying her first husband, George Edwards. They separated three years later, and she moved to Seattle where she was hired by the Seattle P-I to work as a switchboard operator. Her skill with words soon came to the attention of Paul Graves, who brought her into his copyediting department. Her first feature column was written after her co-workers insisted she attend the Christmas Ship Parade with them, and Graves asked her to share her experience with the paper's readers. This began her many years of entertaining readers with her vision of our fair city. After her first husband died, she and Graves were married in 1961. They adopted her great-nephew and had a child of their own. In addition, Emily and her husband took in many foster children over the years, fueled by her own experience in foster care. When asked why, her response would always be, "The need is great."

Emily was a bright light to her family and all who knew her. She enjoyed gardening, reading, and writing her beloved poetry. She is survived by husband, Paul Graves, son Daniel Graves, daughter Madeleine (Bill) Dougherty, twelve foster children, seven nieces and nephews, and five grandchildren. Memorial donations can be made to the Fostering Success Foundation to support youth who are aging out of foster care.

ABOUT THE AUTHOR

Sue Magrath is a retired mental health counselor and spiritual director. In her work, she encountered many survivors of child sexual abuse whose spiritual wounds were just as deep as the physical and emotional wounds they bore. This led to her first book, *Healing the Ravaged Soul: Tending the Spiritual Wounds of Child Sexual Abuse.* Seeking to reach a broader audience about the issue of child sexual abuse, she conceived of this novel. She is also the author of *My Burden is Light: A Primer for Clergy Wellness.* A resident of Washington State, she enjoys reading, hiking, kayaking, and playing with her three (soon to be four) grandsons.

ACKNOWLEDGMENTS

The first draft of this book was completed during the early months of the COVID-19 pandemic. Everything got cancelled, creating space and time for me to bang out the ending that had been in my head for five years. This also meant that my husband had to deal with a wife who was often mentally unavailable for large blocks of time. A mere 'thank you' fails utterly at capturing the depth of my gratitude. Tom, your patience and tolerance went above and beyond. To Cathy Warner, who has been my trusted guide through so much of this process, as she has been for two previous books, I am eternally grateful. I am also grateful to the readers who gave me invaluable feedback: Chris Packard, Heidi Thumlert, Pat Rutledge, Denise McGuiness, Eileen Groby, Mary Huycke, And Marcy Yates. Your comments helped shape the final version for the better.

Made in the USA
Columbia, SC
24 August 2021

43599330R00252